KATE AND EMMA

KATE is sixteen, a victim of cruelty, neglect and chronic poverty. We meet her in a London court 'in need of care and protection'. EMMA is a bare two years older, daughter of the presiding magistrate. A girl from a comfortable background, with a mind of her own.

Between these two an enduring, if turbulent, friendship is struck as Emma toils doggedly not only to lift Kate out of the mire, but also to make sense out of her own life and love.

KATE AND EMMA—Monica Dickens' strongest, most poignant novel yet, lit with an understanding of humanity that would have delighted her eminent Victorian ancestor.

'Harrowing, extremely moving ... a book everybody should read.'   *Queen*

'Exhilarating, challenging ... you cannot put it aside.'
                                              Books and Bookmen

'The sincerity of the attack on cruelty to children is unquestionable.'   *The Sunday Times*

KATE AND EMMA

MONICA DICKENS

UNABRIDGED

PAN BOOKS LTD : LONDON

First published 1964 by William Heinemann Ltd.
This edition published 1966 by Pan Books Ltd.,
33 Tothill Street, London, S.W.1

330 20155 7

2nd Printing 1967
3rd Printing 1969

PRINTED AND BOUND IN ENGLAND BY
HAZELL WATSON AND VINEY LTD
AYLESBURY, BUCKS

Kate and Emma

Part One

'SHE FELL DOWN.'

'She seems to be bruised all over.'

'She falls all the time. I never seen a child so clumsy.'

'She ought to see a doctor.'

'I'd have fetched her up to the hospital last week, but my leg played up.'

'I can get the doctor to come and see her.'

'Who told you to come here?'

'That doesn't matter.'

'I can guess anyway. There's some people born to make trouble. Whatever you're thinking, it's a lie. I've treated that child like my own.'

'She's not yours?'

'My daughter's. I bring her up as mine.'

The child sat on the floor, wedged in a corner against the torn and greasy wallpaper, staring, passive, her chill little hands turned palms up, unoccupied.

This is how they sit, the children. They sit and wait. They sit on chairs and beds and collapsed sofas and wait for it to be time to eat, or time to sleep, or time to move away from the fire, because at last it's spring.

Even the babies just sit there like dolls, solemn, unfocusing, wetting on the mattress or the newspaper, or the worn velour of the chair, wherever they have been planted.

The older children don't play or do anything. There is nothing for them to do, except rattle drawer-handles and pull on the mother's clothes, and she slaps at them vaguely, like flies.

Some of the small ones climb on to Mr Jordan's lap when he sits down. He always does sit, if they ask him, although in some of the places he would probably rather stand. So I sit too, self-effacing in the background, and I was so happy when a small crusted girl who turned out to be a boy with long matted curls, climbed up on to me, that I didn't mind the smell and dirt of him.

I even loved him more for being like that. Or was it that I loved myself for my large heart? The sort of facile sentiment with which people exclaim over pictures of starving Asian babies, when they have no intention of doing anything about it.

Most children soon stiffen and wriggle away, like cats that jump on your lap and then off, sneering if they think you like it. This boy just sat and leaned on me, and I felt such a surge of love for him that I bent my head in case Mr Jordan should think I was trying too hard.

I am the daughter of a magistrate in the Children's Court. My father thinks I am too irresponsible and unaware for eighteen, because, in an ungainly attempt to amuse or attract attention, I make jokes about things which are not supposed to be funny. When I said that some of the eleven- and twelve-year-olds who had been assaulted looked as if they had asked for it, he asked Mr Jordan, who is the local Cruelty Man, to show me some of the things that lie behind the children who come to court.

Mr Jordan is a big, burly man, with a pugnacious face that breaks up into a sort of sweet innocent wonder when he smiles. In an unwieldy overcoat like a grey blanket, he looks extra large and healthy in the cramped and cluttered rooms where the cold squats like a spider. I was paralysed before the day was out, holding myself stiffly, so as not to collapse in a rattle of bones and teeth. It was a miracle that all the babies had not perished in that worst brutal month of winter. I think some of them had.

Mr Jordan goes about in a little noseless car which he drives like the Italians, as if it were a toy.

'Don't be afraid,' he said, as we went on two wheels into a grey yard between grey old tenement flats, scattering children like chickens.

'I'm not.' Since I was braced with terror, I didn't go through the windscreen when he stopped.

'It's a bit rough here, but they won't eat you.'

We climbed the kind of stairs that should only lead down into a dungeon, not up to a place where people live, and he knocked on a door that said, PIGS LIVE HERE in pencil at the bottom where the paint had been kicked off. When it was

8

cautiously opened by a boy in men's trousers cut off at the bottom with a blunt saw, he went ahead, saying, 'Can I come in?' as he went, so that he was half-way down the passage before anyone could say, 'No.'

A man's voice called out thickly from behind a closed door, and his wife said he was on the night shift and trying to get some sleep.

'Sounds drunk to me.'

The woman did not seem to think this insolent, although she neither confirmed nor denied it.

Mr Jordan, looking very large and reliable in the tiny defeated room where the family were clustered round a small electric fire standing on an upturned bucket in the fireplace, asked her if he had hit any of the children again and she said, 'Not since last Saturday,' as if she were telling harmless symptoms to a doctor.

She was a shell of a woman, bloodless, lustreless, husked empty by childbearing, yet somehow pregnant again, the swelling grotesque on her scant frame. On her hip was a furious red toddler almost half as big as her. A baby with no hair wheezed on the dresser in a cardboard box and the other children waited numbly, while layers of wet napkins on the fireguard raised acrid steam between them and the bar of warmth.

Next door was a larger room, but it was full of bicycles, boxes, rag piles, broken furniture and things unrelated to domestic living, like a car door and a big drum of what looked like telephone wire. I had glimpsed the bathroom and the kitchen on the way in. The bath was full of empty paint tins and the kitchen was little more than a slot, with old soup cans and broken crocks washing-up against the stove. They had silted themselves into the small room, which was not much bigger than a railway carriage.

Mr Jordan sat down, and one of the barefoot children, who was wandering about with a plastic feeding bottle stuck in its mouth like a lollipop, climbed on to his knee. The mother was pretending to look for the rent book, although I got the impression that she knew where it was, so I sat down too in a corner behind the table, and that was when the little boy crawled up on me and leaned his head on my chest with a sigh, like a dog.

The top of his head was scabby under the tangled hair, and his mouth and nose were surrounded by such painful-looking sores that you could feel them tight on your own face. I loved him more than my sister's children, who have everything and don't need me. This child, who had nothing on but a bigger boy's shirt over torn grey pants and was mottled like a marble Christ-child in that chill, malodorous room, accepted me as his own.

The boy with the sawn-off trousers found the rent book, which showed arrears of almost thirty pounds.

Mr Jordan was angry, since money had been given last week to help the debt, and the woman, whose large weary eyes were still beautiful, admitted that her husband would not mind going to prison to clear it.

'You and the children could be turned out. Where would you go?'

'I don't know. My sister has a farm in Kilkenny, you know. I've always thought . . .'

'Would your sister take you in?'

'I don't know. I've not heard from her for years, but I've always thought . . .' A dream to keep her going through the hopelessness and the disasters. Somehow they had muddled on, but if all failed, there was still My Sister, although the farm was perhaps only a bungalow and a chicken-run, and the sister long gone away.

Mr Jordan put down his child, who was wearing the tatters of a flimsy party dress given away by someone too mean to throw out anything useful, and stood up briskly. Listening time was over. Now it was telling. He told her that he would try to get another grant, and that he would be back tomorrow to talk to her husband, when he was sober.

'*Is* he working?'

She pretended not to hear. The boy said that Dad had left the tannery because it turned him. Mr Jordan looked very stern, but I think it was because he had run out of things to say.

I was depressed when we left. My boy cried when I put him down among the breadcrusts, and I wanted to pick him up again with his poor sore face against my black sweater and take him home and hear my mother talk about people who should be sterilized.

'What if one offered to take a child away and give it the things she can't?' I didn't mean patronizing things like clothes and food and school and a new accent. I meant love, and being noticed, and having your ideas listened to, which I couldn't imagine happening in that railway room with the wet grey smell. 'What would she say?' I asked, as we sped desperately for the narrowing gap between a bus and a petrol tanker. 'Would she be glad?'

'I doubt it.' We just made it through the gap and shot out across the lights like toothpaste from a tube.

'How can she stand it? I can imagine her as a girl, pale-haired and delicate, with those big eyes, dreaming of some marvellous man she'd marry.'

I could see her with a tiny waist, leaning on a rustic bridge over an Irish stream with the other soft-haired girls. I saw them in muslin, like a Rodgers and Hammerstein chorus, which made the vision less real, but more poignant.

'Don't fret, Miss Bullock.'

I hate my name. I wish he wouldn't use it, but he would not call me Emma if I asked him, because my father is a magistrate, and this Jordan is scared stiff of the court. Literally stiff. He stands there like his old Army days, with his jaw square and his feet at forty-five degrees, but I have seen the papers in his hand trembling as he tries to give evidence the way my father likes it.

My father is irritated by policemen and any type of official when they use that kind of courtroom language like: I then proceeded to instruct, instead of: I told. He will make a dry little joke which nobody laughs at except Miss Draper, the sycophant, and so he frightens people like Mr Jordan, which isn't fair, because that is the way they have been taught to speak in front of him.

My father is supposed to be one of the best magistrates in the juvenile courts, and no doubt he is. He is very painstaking, and fair, too, but sometimes when I watch his elaborate patience with some surly teenager who hasn't really tried, I laugh mirthlessly to think how hard it can be to get his attention at home when it is a day when there is too much of me and my hair and my voice and my energy on the stairs. I should have married first and left Alice at home. She keeps out of his way, and would let him grow middle-aged in peace.

'It used to fret me terribly,' Mr Jordan said. 'I used to take it all home with me and rail to my wife against the unfairness of people having to live like that. Then it began to fall into a pattern. I saw some people who'd been through the worst things and fought their way out. But the others – I began to see that half the mess they make themselves. You can help them up to a point, but you can't cure them of the disease.'

'What disease?'

'Poverty. They keep slipping back, like malaria.'

I said nothing, because I didn't agree, and I didn't want to start an argument since it was his day and his job, and he might be shy of arguing, even though he knew more about it than me. I haven't seen much squalor, in spite of my father's work, because he is remote from the real stink of it. But people don't do this to their own lives. Life does things to them, as it has done to that scoured woman with the unseen beast in the bedroom and all those children who happened to her probably without joy, when he was drunk.

I spent the whole day with Mr Jordan. He went imperturbably in and out of one-room flats and basements and the odd little broken-down cottages that still hide in London corners. I tagged along behind him, stumbling with cold, and gave sweets to the sitting children and tried not to look like a social worker.

Why not? I want to help, but I don't want to be labelled. Yet I am labelled already. Emma Bullock. What else could she be but a social worker? I will now call for a few words from our secretary, Miss Emmaline Bullock, whose wonderful work among the unemployed weavers of the Meon Valley is such an inspiration to us all.

Why should I mind? This is probably the only country in the world where the name do-gooder is risible, like vicar. I don't want to do good to people. I want to feel things about them, like my heavy-headed boy. If you start doing, you might have to stop feeling.

One of the places we went to that day, that numbing day,

when I cried afterwards at Charing Cross, with my hands turning from yellow to blue to red in a basin of warm water, was a house with the top floor shut off and a piece of old tent over the hole in the roof, and miles of unworn clean clothes on strings across the kitchen ceiling. Heels sank a good half-inch into the filth on the floor, and it was a marvel that the crawling baby had not died of septicaemia.

One of the boys had stolen some coppers from a wishing-well at an exhibition. How had he got in? By waiting near the ticket office until a simple customer arrived, then asking the price of entrance and looking so crestfallen at the answer that the simpleton paid for him.

'That's how he gets in to the cartoons and newsreels,' his mother said quite proudly.

Three and ninepence he had got, in pennies and halfpennies, and he was due in my father's court next week.

He was such a lovely little liar, all fanned-out lashes and gritty dimples, that I took the day off from the business college where I am taking a course forced on me by my Uncle Mark, who runs the family firm, and went to court with my father.

He was pleased. He wants me to be interested, and he likes me for an audience. He never had my mother, even when he was a rather theatrical junior counsel, because the courts are full of the kind of people she resents, both in the dock and out of it.

In the magistrates' room we waited for Miss Draper, who was on the bench with him today. Miss Draper used to be headmistress of a girls' school, and she is in love with my father, which doesn't stop her being late for his courts. She has been late for everything all her life, including all the fearful joys.

She came crashing into the room in a hat like a Russian delegate's and a coat like buffalo hide.

'Don't tell me I'm late again!'

'I don't have to,' my father said rudely. 'You can read the clock.'

She would have blushed if her skin had been thin enough to transmit colour, and I shook hands with her to make her feel better. My father put on his juvenile-court face, judicial but humane, and started off for the courtroom without asking Miss

Draper if she was ready. She struggled out of the heavy coat and followed him, and I followed her. Everyone stood up when we went in, including a nervous couple sitting with a fat baby in the middle of the room, and a vital hairpin fell out of my head and down inside my collar.

I sat beside the Magistrates' Clerk, at right angles to the long table where my father and Miss Draper sit, and the Honourable R. F. D. Coghill too, when his presence graces the court.

A juvenile court is not like a proper courtroom, apart from managing to be airless and cold at the same time. It is quite a small room with ordinary tables and chairs where the policemen and probation officers and people from the Council sit, and the children stand in front of the Bench which isn't a bench, with their parents sitting behind them. It is supposed to be not frightening for them, but mostly they are terrified, except the hardened cases, who behave as if this were merely a rehearsal for the real thing later on at the Old Bailey.

It transpired that the nervous couple were there to adopt the baby, and would have been taken to the magistrates' room if my father had not hurried in before the Clerk called him because he wanted to make Miss Draper feel that she had been holding him up.

So they both had to go back again. He turned to take his stick off the back of the chair, and I could see that he was annoyed, although he pretended to be forbearing, which was great of him, considering it was his fault.

He looked tired. Now that the skin is loosening into little folds under his eyes, he sometimes looks sad. In other years, when he was a barrister, busy and mobile, making a production out of even his dullest clients, his face did not look as if it could ever slip into sadness. The only time I caught him crying, after my brother was drowned at Poldhu, his face was red and tortured as if tears were too difficult. But now it is folding into a slight melancholy, although, as far as I know, he is content.

He has enough money and enough work in the legal department of a chemical firm to bring him to town most days of the week, and his house and terraced garden have the finest view there is only twenty miles from London. He has come to

14

terms with his leg, and he has come to terms with his marriage, which is to say that what he can't alter he accepts. His elder daughter is married to a man without an accent, and her children have their thumbs growing in the right places. Even I, who nearly killed everyone by getting kidnapped at thirteen, am growing into the semblance of a woman, and I am neither pregnant nor a drug addict nor in love with a married African revolutionary, like some of the girls we know.

The Clerk of the Court, whose wife sends him out smelling of camphor, gave me a case list. The little liar of the wishing-well was about half-way down.

At the top were three or four girls of fifteen and sixteen, listed as Care or Prot., which usually means that they have been found in a coffee bar, or a transport café, or penniless in a railway station.

My father and Miss Draper came back, and the Warrant Officer brought in the first girl. 'Mother is present.'

'Where is the father?' asked mine.

The mother said shrilly, prepared to air all the grievances of her married life, that he had left her two years ago, and my father grunted and nodded, as if he would have done the same. His nod put the woman into a chair, where she sat clutching her handbag like a bomb, challenging the Bench to make one move and she'd throw it, and the girl stood out in front of her, exposed all round and looking sullen. There was plenty to expose. She had been found fifty miles from home with some soldiers, but the experience had taken no weight off her.

She would not talk to my father. She bit her lip and hung her head and clenched her fat fists at the sides of her cracked leather skirt, which was as big from hip to hip as from waist to hem. She might have talked to Miss Draper, who has quite a reassuring way with her, like a slow farm animal, but Miss Draper does not often get a chance to ask questions. She writes things in a ledger, and nods or shakes her head, and pretends to compress a laugh if my father makes a joke, and from time to time he leans over and they consult without moving their lips or looking at each other, like television panellists.

'Come forward, Mother,' my father said. He calls the

women Mother because he can't remember their names, and he thinks it is insulting to stop and look for it on the case notes, although I think it is more insulting to call them all Mother, as if they were in a labour ward.

The mother talked, a dirge of complaints, and the girl did not look at her. Parents and children hardly ever look at each other in the juvenile court. It is as if each were equally ashamed of the other, although the parents usually do their best for the children, however much they may have threatened them with the Law beforehand. When it actually strikes, they are always 'So surprised' at the theft, or 'Can't understand' why he cheated the railway, since he has always been a good boy and had only to ask at home if he was short.

When my father asked the fat girl whether she wanted to go home, she shook her shaggy head.

'You'd rather live somewhere else, Arleena?' He pronounced it carefully, as seriously as if it were Joan. A few years in the juvenile court, and you can tackle any name.

Although the mother had said nothing in favour of her daughter, she now took a step forward, as if she were going to lob the bomb into my father's lap, and cried, 'You can't put her away!'

'We're not going to "put her away",' he said, putting irritable quotes round it, although he has heard the phrase so often that it should not bother him any more. 'Holly Lodge is a hostel, not a prison.' He explained the Order that he was going to make, talking to the girl, not the mother, which he always does, even with the morose ones, so they won't feel that things are going on over their heads.

'If her dad had stayed to his duty, this wouldn't have happened,' the mother said, chewing on her spite. 'Ask me if I've had a penny from him since. Just ask me that, if you don't mind!'

'I do mind,' my father said, with the kind of shocking urbanity he shouldn't use here.

'They don't care,' the woman said to no one, and followed her daughter out of the court, feeling worse than when she went in.

Children came and went, frightened, rebellious, unbalanced,

16

shifty. Parents trooped in and out – gangs of them sometimes, if several boys were involved together. The women had bags like week-end luggage, and red hands from waiting in the cold hall. The fathers had belted overcoats like tubs, and were flawless patriarchs who had always upheld the difference between right and wrong.

A boy had stolen a motorbike because he was bored. A girl had stayed out all night because she was fed up. Another had been lodging with the Indian lodger. A ten-year-old in heels and stockings more ladders than nylon had been to school four times in seventy days. A whiskered Zen Buddhist had picked a pocket. A boy with acne like leprosy had broken probation for the sake of a packet of cigarettes. It was a normal morning.

My wishing-well boy, scrubbed up a bit and wearing some of the clean clothes so jealously hoarded on the ceiling strings, lied freely and sweetly, while his mother sat back and nodded and smiled, as if she believed him.

My father, who has a very beautiful smile, lifting like a bird's wing, his eyes very deeply blue, played along with him, liking him for his sparkle and cheek. He and the boy threw charm at each other for a while, until my father suddenly tired of it, and rapped at the boy that he would send him away to be disciplined.

The boy backed away as if he had touched fire. My father has done this at home. As children, the excitement of a wild game with him was heightened by uncertainty, and I have seen him romp with a dog and then suddenly slap it hard on the jaw; but I didn't think he would do it in court, and I was afraid of what would happen.

Nothing. Smoothly he had substituted Probation even before the Children's Officer had finished clearing his throat for a polite protest, and I saw that the others in the room only thought he was acting, to teach the boy a lesson. I was the only one who knew it was a flash of cruelty. And the boy knew.

I didn't want to stay any longer. I caught my father's eye and tilted my head at the door, and he raised an eyebrow which meant would I lunch with him, and I put my hand on my waist which meant I wasn't eating today, and I was just getting up to slide out of the door behind him when the girl came in.

17

The Warrant Officer had her by the arm, as if she had tried to run for it outside. She shook him off, with a quick sideways look of pride on her small blunt face, and went to stand in front of my father with the toes of her thin shoes exactly in line, as if she had been there before.

I was half out of my chair, but I sat down again. She was another Care or Prot., a little younger than me, short, with a childish figure, and not very clean. Her lips were almost as pale as her skin, her wary eyes were ludicrously pencilled, and her chopped saffron hair had been roughly back-combed into an attempt at a good shape. Her legs were bare, the light hair on them standing out with cold, and her clothes looked as if she had snatched them off a younger sister.

She stood staring through my father and biting her nails, although there was nothing left to bite.

'I saw you two weeks ago, didn't I?' My father had his hands clasped on the table and his head slightly tilted, trying to put her at her ease, because she was rigid with antagonism.

'Yes.'

The children never call my father Sir, although most of the parents do, either from fright or ingratiation.

'And you've been at Pinkney House. Let's see what they say about you. "Fairly co-operative as long as everything goes her way . . . poor attention to work, either daydreaming or sulking . . . slightly aggressive." Yes, well.' My father laid down the Remand Home report and looked at the girl over the top of his glasses before he took them off. 'Not very good, is it?'

She shook her head, keeping the immature chin tilted up.

'You were remanded to Pinkney because your parents weren't here last time. Why weren't you here, Father?'

The man had a stubble of greying hair like the top of a barrister's wig, and flat, elliptical eyes too close together above a brutalized nose. He licked his lips and put his hands on his knees truculently, with the thumbs outside. 'I couldn't get off work.'

'Stand up.' The Warrant Officer nudged him, and he stood up reluctantly, folding his short arms for comfort, which made him look more uncomfortable.

'Did you ask?'

'I'm on the vans, see.'

My father raised one eyebrow, and decided not to pursue it. 'And the mother – where is she?'

'She couldn't come. Look, she's got the kids, and the shop too. How could she come with Kate not there to see to it?'

'If Katherine were at home, there would be no need for anyone to come here,' my father said mildly, and the man's belligerence bounced back at him unused, and reddened the folds of bristled skin above his shrunken collar.

Katherine. Kate. She attracted me. Why? She was under-nourished and grubby and childish, and a policewoman had found her with a much older man in a place known as a Club, for want of any other label. It was not sudden attraction, not something jumping out excitedly from yourself like a flying-fish at the unspoken call of a stranger. It stayed within myself. There was no discovery. I seemed to know her quite well. When the other girls had stood there, with the same kind of story, I could watch, listen, try to imagine what it was like to be them and to have had their kind of life. With her, it was oddly as if I knew.

This has never happened to me before, with women or men. I have fallen in love in a flash, committing myself utterly to devotion. I have liked girls instantly, if they looked at me with pleasure instead of appraisal. With Kate, it was different. She looked at me without moving her head while her father was telling mine what a bad girl she was. Her eyes were pale blue, unsuited to the Cleopatra make-up. She looked at me for a second as if I were the only familiar thing in that courtroom, then slid her eyes back and shut them, the lashes flickering.

She stood with her head up and her hands clenched white as her father told a one-sided story which sounded good to him, but to no one else. She would not speak, even to my father, and I wondered if he realized that the tilt of her head was not aggressiveness – favourite Remand Home word – but plain hydrology, to keep the tears from spilling over.

Why didn't they leave her alone? She had set her mind on silence. If she spoke, she would cry, and she had set her mind against the defeat of tears.

'Why did you run away?' my father asked her again, and

Miss Draper's stomach rumbled sharply, like a school lunch bell. 'Don't you like it at home?'

Leave her alone! She pressed her pale lips together, and the tears glistened along the absurdly blackened lashes.

'Never *comes* home.' Her father began to whine through the battered nose, seeing his last chance to get a hearing. 'We can't do nothing with her. She never comes home, and that's the truth. Eleven, twelve at night —'

And she suddenly cried out, as if it was being wrung from her by torture, 'What is there to come home for!'

I WON'T cry. I won't. They're not going to win that way and think I'm sorry.

I'm not sorry. I'll do it again, if they make me go home. It was all right with Bob, though two nights in that cellar was enough. With Douglas, it was the first time I felt grown up, when he talked to me about the sheep, and the pavement burning your feet.

All the time I had to stand there – and the Spanish Inquisition had nothing on it, believe me – they thought I was listening to what was being said, and the report from Stinkney and that. But all I was thinking of was holding on and not crying. They would have loved me to cry, don't doubt it, sobbing all over the court like a sinner at a Billy Graham rally, so I wasn't going to give them that pleasure, with their eyes looking pity at me, and the careful kindness, and that woman bogey with her jolly manner. It's no wonder she chose the Force. What else could you do with those legs?

All but that one girl. I didn't know who she was, and I wasn't that interested, but she didn't seem to belong there in that yellow coat, and her hair was coming down in a heavy brown loop at the back and she didn't want me to cry.

I could see her not wanting it. She was on my side. Well, the others were too, of course, in their way, but it's a different way from hers and mine. Theirs is organizing people. Ours is just wanting to be let alone and see what comes next.

Why ours? I knew as soon as I came into that room, among

the solemn, kindly stares, that she was my sort. She isn't as pretty as me, unless you like that big-boned squaw type. But she looked at me, not with that case-worker look they all get – understanding, but watch your step – but truthfully, as if she was showing me herself.

I'll never see her again, I daresay, but it helped, her being there. It helped me not to let go and give them a reformed delinquent. It helped me not to cry, and so I stood there and held on to that while Dad bellyached on, and the beak tried to be fatherly, and my mind floated off away like it does if you concentrate on something physical, like beating your hand with a hairbrush and whirling it round till little points of blood start up all over it. Bob and I do it sometimes to see who can bleed most.

I should have held on longer though, and not broken out like that and yelled at them. I didn't mean to. I wasn't going to say a word, just let them do whatever they wanted with me and not give them the satisfaction of knowing whether or not I minded, though if they had sent me back to Stinkney, I'd have gone in with Lynn and her lot and really showed them. But while I was standing there holding the damn tears and floating off down that road that curves away round a corner I never get to, I could hear Dad steaming up to that self-righteous bit about all they've done for me, and I suddenly came back to it all in a rush. The hopeless ugliness and the way we all fight round and round like animals in a cage and the voices and the shop door buzzing and the mouse droppings and the milk sour and the damn baby wetting in my bed, and I had to yell.

It shocked them. The noise suddenly in the small room. Not what I said. That was no news. A woman in a suit she'd knitted herself got up later and told how she had been to our home and what it was like. It was a bit much, hearing her say words like filth and slovenly – after all, it was our home – but Dad said never a word, and the old piece who is one of the magistrates but not allowed to talk kept sneaking looks at the clock. It was getting on for one. That's the time they go for their dinner, you've got to consider that. So they wrapped the thing up.

After I'd yelled out like that and shocked the plaster off the walls, I did cry, but only for a moment. Tears came gushing out like when the kids get the fire hydrant open, but I knew that if I just let them fall without putting up a hand to rub at them, they'd stop. They did, and I felt better, like letting a bit of gas out of your stomach to relieve the pressure.

I'd given them their answer, and I had stopped being afraid of crying, so I could take some interest in things, and look at the girl in the yellow coat again, but she was leaving. She was going out a door at the back and I thought well, you ruddy sod, deserting me, though I was nothing to her, nor she to me.

But it just shows you. So I felt dead rotten then, and I let myself listen to what they said, and answered Yes, which surprised them, since I'd been labelled uncooperative, and we all parted friends, and Dad went out the door we came in.

I'd never looked at that door, not once the whole time, although I still thought, even at the end, that my mother would come. She didn't. Why should she? Miss Reid took me out the other door, which didn't lead into the hall, but it didn't matter. I knew she wasn't out there.

I SPENT the afternoon in a cinema, and found that my father had gone home on an earlier train, because the car was not at the station. Our house is not far from the railway – it's not far from anywhere, for that matter: you can hear the neighbours breathing on a quiet night – so I would just as soon walk, although it is mostly on a main road, between two Medway towns.

As soon as you step up on our black drive, you can see the view dropping away beyond the hedge. The fields and the little common where the gorse is blocked in like a schoolroom print in the spring cannot be built over. Only the Ministry could despoil the wood beyond and the single, perfectly shaped chestnut-tree in the middle of the empty meadow.

It is absolutely pretty and I dislike it absolutely. A pose? All right, but when the hundredth visitor has stood on the terrace, dutifully exclaiming and wondering where the drinks are, the view begins to purr and simper. The Green Belt, for God's sake. A narrow green girdle of Socialist niceties, a feeble attempt to disguise what they have let London do to the Weald and the Thames Valley and the spurs of the Chilterns.

Only twenty miles from London, the visitors exclaim, and all this country! A cheat. If you rode a horse into the valley and up the meadow on the other side, you would be into the washing lines of the Estate before you were really galloping.

My parents were lucky. They bought this house long ago, when people were more relaxed about the Green Belt, and this was not exclusively the best view twenty miles, etc., etc. Prices all along our road are very high now, and my father could get twice what he gave, and he might have, five or six years ago, and escaped. But he is losing initiative. He is losing the dream with which he beguiled me. Or perhaps he never truly had it.

Our neighbours are mostly richer than we are. It is quite social, with the same people at all the parties, and a proportion of adultery, like a pale imitation of O'Hara suburbia, because the gin is weaker.

The teenage parties are as dull as the grown-up ones, for different reasons. The host parents are conscientious about Being There, which means they go upstairs and hang over the banisters trying to hear something lewd, like the mother in *Peyton Place*.

When I went into the house and draped my yellow coat over the acorn end of the banister, my mother was in the little room off the hall, drinking sherry out of a glass she couldn't get her nose into and reading a novel by the fire.

The drawing-room is hard to heat, so we sit in the little room when we are alone. Not that we sit together very much. After dinner, my father, who often brings work home, goes to his room upstairs whether he has work or not, and my mother reads with her dark sculpted eyebrows up, making little noises like a sleeping pony. I sometimes try to watch television, and when she begins to ask: How can you bear to watch that trash? I go up and read in the bath with my hair draped over my breasts like wet seaweed.

When I have finished training and have a proper job with Uncle Mark, I shall have a flat in London. She doesn't know

23

yet, and we'll let that battle keep. Often I think I can't wait so long, but until I'm earning, the only alternative is marriage. Who with? None of the people I have loved so far have loved me. Some of them didn't even know me.

'This is a ghastly book,' my mother said.

I used to say: Why read it? I don't any more.

'All the people are so worthless. Why must one read about worthless people?' Since books nowadays aren't written about the kind of people she considers worthwhile, it's hard for her.

She said that I could have some sherry — if she knew what Derek and I put away when we go out — and I invented a few clean and poignant things about the morning, because the truth makes her talk about bringing back the birch, and then my father came in, which was what I'd been waiting for since I fumbled out of the courtroom with my hair coming down.

'Why did you rush out like that, Emma?'

'I had to meet someone for lunch. It was late.'

'I thought you weren't going to have lunch.'

'I didn't. We had coffee.'

'Oh. I thought you were upset by that girl screaming. Poor child. They don't have much of a chance.'

I had thought I would tell him, but, with my mother there, I couldn't. I couldn't say that I was torn with pain for Kate, and that when she cried and bent her head, and I saw the strawberry birthmark staining the back of her vulnerable neck, it was suddenly too much.

Perhaps I would tell him later. Perhaps not. Confidences saved up can misfire. It might sound like hysteria. Actually, it had been more like being hit.

'You saw the boy you were interested in, didn't you? Attractive little devil, he was trying to fool me.'

'Why were you cruel to him?'

'I wasn't.'

'You were. You teased him along, and then lashed out. It was deliberately cruel.'

My mother passed her sherry glass from the table to her lips without looking up from her book. She knows that he and I can fight on the same level, without hurting each other. Alice tells me: Don't speak to him like that! But he can take things

24

from me that he never would from her, because she is afraid, and he knows it.

'Listen, Emma.' My father has hair the colour of a pigeon's wing which he wears conceitedly, brushed back long at the sides. He is not very tall, so he often stands up when other people are sitting. He puts an arm on the mantelpiece and the foot of his bad leg on the fender and looks down at you with that lifting smile, and I sometimes want to yell at my mother: Look – look at him. Look properly at him!

She is still in love with him, but she doesn't let it show. She has a childish, rather anxious face, and beautiful thick black hair which she wears in a square doll cut. It swings and bounces prettily, and he sometimes plunges his hand in it, but not often. He is kind to her, but too polite. That must be galling, when you're over forty, because he can't have been, when they were young and passionate.

He demands things of her, but they are not, alas, the things that love demands. Meals must be on time. His friends must come before hers. She must never keep him waiting. Anything that goes wrong with the cars, the drains, the dogs is her fault, since the garage, the plumber, the vet are her affair.

She demands almost nothing of him. Too little, much too little. I don't know whose idea the twin beds were, but if it was hers, she's an even bigger fool than he thinks.

'Listen, Emma. I wouldn't keep my job long if I were a sadist. All right, I lost my temper with that boy. Why him, when there are so many more repulsive? He was enjoying himself too much. I saw him coming back and back to court, something a little worse each time. Not caring. Mum would pay the fine. Stupid woman, you can tell by looking at them they aren't going to take it out of the pocket money.'

'I don't think he has any. You didn't see the place where he lives. I did.'

'I hope you washed your hair,' my mother said.

'I wash it every night.' It's a temporary obsession, but for the moment I am like the boy's mother with all that compulsive laundry. 'It was disgusting with dirt and smells. The other children look like maggots. If a boy can come out of a place like that still thinking life is fun, you shouldn't crush him. You should give him the earth.'

'Whose earth? The taxpayers'? He'll take it anyway, what little bits he can knock off,' my father said. 'He's headed for delinquency. I've learned to spot it.'

'The parents should be put in gaol,' my mother said automatically. This is one of her things, like taking away the vote from anyone who can't pass an intelligence test, and sterilizing them.

'The father is there already, and I'd hate to tell you what for. Delinquency is a defeatist word,' I told my father. 'That's not what Mr Jordan said about that little boy.'

'Jordan is an optimist. You have to be, in his job, or shoot yourself.'

'He is a realist.'

'It's possible to be both.' He smiled. Someone else might have added: Though not at eighteen, pretending they know what we are like.

We had dinner then, something I loved, red, juicy meat like tigers' food, but I ate too quickly, hardly noticing, because I had hedged and sparred with him and put off asking about Kate. She'd die at home, and die in an institution. What can happen to her?

The girl who works for us at the moment is from Yorkshire, and everything she cooks tastes meaty, even cakes. My mother gets pregnant girls through a society, like getting paper bags for vacuum cleaners. When they get too big, they plod off somewhere and she gets another. It is her social work. We used to have Spanish or French or Italian girls, but this is less responsibility, since they are pregnant already.

The one we have now is called Dorothy and she is quite unhappy. Why wouldn't she be? Bad enough to have her luck without having to cook and clean for someone else as well. Her mother is dead and her stepmother kicked her out, glad of the excuse, Dotty says. She and I play cards at night, and drink flagon burgundy, which I buy to keep her healthy, and we make up fantastic stories about the unlikely people who will adopt her baby.

My parents and I have dinner in the dining-room, quite

26

formally. Dotty, or whoever happens to be bumping round in the kitchen, pushes the food and plates through the little window over the sideboard, and I pass things round, and we have candles and good china and sit too far away from each other.

The dining-room is cheerless, like a Wimpole Street dining-room used for waiting patients. Do the specialists and their thin discreet wives eat breakfast and dinner there? It never smells of bacon or gravy.

Our oblong table has been taken good care of, no painting or cutting out ever, and the mean-seated chairs have always looked repelling, even as long as I have known them. The leaves of the plants are sprayed to make them shiny, and they look like plastic. Golf and tennis cups and a small trophy I won at dancing school and Alice's last school photograph when she was head girl, in the middle with her hair up, are spaced exactly over the fireplace, which has an electric log fire that we all despise, but need. There is nothing of Peter's on the mantelpiece. Everything is put away.

We should knock down the wall to the drawing-room and make it one huge sunny room with two window-seats and a fireplace at each end. Then we could get rid of the Dorothys and buy some scarred oak furniture and redesign the kitchen and have our meals in there, with the stove and mess out in the pantry with the sink.

I don't press for change any more. It's their house. They are only forty-five and fifty, not paupers, and healthy. The T.B. germ that lamed my father's leg is not likely to recur. They could go and live almost anywhere in the world, but they stay with the dining-room and the cheating view and the aubrietia and the pregnant girls.

Once, the year before Poldhu, when we were at that fishing inn at Raglan, wet all the time from the river or the rain, and we all suddenly got to know each other very well, and wanted the same things, my father said, 'Why can't we always live like this, Emmie?'

'We could,' I said, but he never did anything about it.

I ate my dinner quickly, and asked if I could go. They were going to stay and drink brandy and make a little talk. When I am married, my husband and I will *read* at meals if we want to.

As I pushed back my chair, Dorothy broke something in the kitchen into a thousand pieces. No one looks up any more or exclaims, because dropping things goes with it. Dorothy slid open the window and looked in, with that one wild tooth on her lip. 'Somebody say something?'

'It's all right, dear.' My mother did not even give her the satisfaction of asking what was broken, and Dorothy slid back the window like a disgruntled booking clerk, and I went to the door.

Hanging on both knobs, with my feet against the edge, I asked casually: 'What happened to that girl – you know, the one with the pock-marked father, just before I left?'

'The girl who shouted? A lot came out after you'd gone. A probation officer had visited the home. A little back-street shop, two up, two down behind for the family, all very squalid, and neither the father nor the mother seemed to want the girl back except to help with the shop and the children.'

'You took her away.' I swung on the door, and my mother told me not to, gently. She reads articles about teenagers which tell her not to nag at them.

'You can't take them away unless they're in danger. They don't belong to the State. You can ask them if they want to leave and if they say Yes, the parents usually agree. Half shame, half pride. If that's the way she feels, the hell with her, sort of thing.'

'If I yelled in court that I didn't want to go home, would you let me go?'

'If it was as bad as that, I'd have let you go long before. We'd let you go,' he corrected, smiling at my mother, for she is allowed to think she makes some of the big decisions, as a sop to having to make the small irritating ones. 'There's some possibility of a job for the girl, if I remember. I didn't want to send her to a hostel. There was some more from the Remand Home I didn't read out because it would have pleased her to know she'd made such an impression. We thought better a foster-home, and old Draper came up with a good idea, her first all morning. Mrs Arthur. That mad woman who's always clamouring for more foster-children, though she's got about six of her own already.'

28

My mother started to talk about birth control then, and I left the room and went up to wash my hair.

Dorothy came up with the hot-water bottles and sat listlessly on the edge of the bath and dabbled her hand in the water as if she were boating. I had been thinking of Kate thawing out, softening in the mad woman's home full of warmth and love and milky babies.

'You were in a foster-home for a bit, weren't you, after your mother died?'

'Yeah.' Dorothy patted her stomach, then got up and put out her tongue at the glass in the medicine cupboard before she opened it and started to hunt for the Alka-Seltzer.

'What was it like?'

'Bloody awful. They only do it for the money, everyone knows that.'

I T W A S tough at first and there were times when I felt like taking off and heading for home, only I was afraid they wouldn't take me in.

Of course I'll not go back, I mean that, but you can be homesick even when you hate your home. I found that out at Stinkney House. All those bells and polished floors – and you know who polishes them. I had to dream I was somewhere else, and Butt Street was the only place there was.

Now there's this place and is it something. I never knew people lived like this, but there's a lot I didn't know. I found that out with Douglas quick enough. I knew about living in a mess, because that's the only way I did know, but I never knew you could live in a mess and yet it not be a mess, with everyone on top of each other but nobody hating each other.

When Molly asked me about the end of the first week how I liked it, I said it was like a lot of puppies in a box, able to be tumbling all over each other without fighting and cursing. 'Didn't you know that was possible?' Molly asked. I didn't answer. No one's going to sermonize over me. Not that she would, but she's not going to get the chance.

Molly let me alone the first two days, and I didn't even have to eat or speak if I didn't want to. I stayed in bed most of the time, because it was the first time I had ever had my own room. There's only space in it for the bed really, but it's mine and I wouldn't let the kids in then, although now there is always someone climbing over the high iron rail at the bottom and taking a dive on to me.

I came down when I was hungry and took the food back to bed. Like a squirrel, I heard someone whisper, when they were pretending they didn't know I was in the larder. No one minded. Mr Molly is up north on business, which sounds grander than it is, because he is only an insurance assessor, and I heard Michael, the oldest boy, asking loud and clear: 'What will Dad say when he comes back and finds we've got another one and it's a great girl?'

'He'll say Good,' Molly said, raising her voice for me to hear that too.

About the third day, when it was either come down or grow into the mattress, I came down and sat by the fire in the room where everything was going on: piano, homework, fretsaw, doll's-house, babies sleeping, eating, crawling, clockwork trains, dogs, ironing. There was a big basket of washing on the floor with the cats in it. Better nobody ask me to fold it, that's all. They just better not ask. I wasn't going to lift a finger. If they thought they'd got me here to work, they'd another think coming. I'd had that.

Mollyarthur, they call her, all one word, like Pollyanna. She was ironing away, lifting the baby away from the cord with her foot, and a cup of tea with a bun soaking in the saucer at easy reach.

She's always eating: biscuits, bits of cake, strained baby food the little ones leave. But she's thin because she works it off. She eats the peel from baked potatoes if someone's fussy, and toast crusts, ends of the loaf, anything but the dog food. 'I balk at that,' she says.

She has very white, even teeth. Mine have little brown ridges on them, which the school dentist said came from measles, which I don't remember having unless it was that time when my mother was in the hospital having Stewart and Dad sprayed me with flea powder. Molly's teeth are like the people in the toothpaste pictures. 'My one beauty,' she'll say, gnashing them at you. But really, she's not bad-looking – if she knew anything about hair and make-up. Bright red lipstick and pin curls. I ask you. She's going to let me make her over when she's got time. She's putting it off because I mean to pluck her eyebrows, and she is scared.

It was very cold this first day when I came down and sat, and I needed the fire. It's a tall old house, sort of a brown brick mansion gone to seed, which used to be part of an estate before the Park went municipal, with swings and benches and a frozen wading pool. Molly keeps the fire big. She got extra coal because of the children. My mother couldn't get any extra. She couldn't even get delivery, and we had to take the pram and get a bag.

It isn't fair, but Moll is in with everyone, that's what does it. Mollyarthur, they all say round here, and then laugh, but not in spite.

I am going to take Ralph's red wagon and fetch some coal round to my home, but I haven't done it yet. Perhaps the weather will let up.

There are fires in the downstairs rooms, but the bedrooms are as cold as bedrooms always are, only worse here, because you don't sleep so many in a room and everyone has their own bed. We all go to bed in socks and jerseys. I was nervous when I first came because I don't have hardly any clothes (Lynn or one of her lot nicked that good blouse I had), but Molly has whole piles of them in drawers, all sizes jumbled up and anyone who's cold or naked can go and help themselves. She found me a red sweater with a high turtleneck. Why have I never had one before? It comes right up to my hair at the back and I think it is why I am happy.

I sat by the fire all that day, floating off a bit at times, with the curved road running away from my eyes. She brought me a sandwich and some tea, and in the afternoon, one of the little ones, Tina, that's one of hers, came up on my lap and I didn't push her off.

I had a little bit of a cry, because of Loretta at home saying: Where Katty? It was nice, the salt trickling into my mouth, and no one bothering me. In this house, if anyone wants to cry, he can and no one yells: Shut up that bloody row! If they make too much noise, or it's temper, they have to go away or do it in another room.

But I cried quietly, and Molly gave me a banana when I'd done. So I bathed two of the kids because no one asked me, and because I'd never bathed kids in a real bath before, and it's much more fun than in the sink with the dirty dishes.

So then I bathed everybody, the whole outfit, except the Chinese baby who was asleep. There's ten of them all told, six of hers and four fosters. Michael, the eldest, is nine, and the Chink baby is five months and would have a better chance if he was a refugee, but since he was born here, nobody wants him.

Molly didn't make a big thing about it. She said, 'Thanks, Kate,' and let it pass, so I may do it again.

I shall have to watch my step though. I am *happy*. I've been happy before and it's always been taken away. I'm not going to let go. I'm not going to let them think they've got me – and then they'll do me in. I once told my mother I loved her and look where it got me.

Look where it got poor Bob. If he hadn't gone soft on me, I wouldn't have left him like that, smack in the middle of Charing Cross Road. His face! I saw it from the top of the bus. He'll have got home all right, simple as he is.

There's books in this house. There's two bookcases. Mr Mollyarthur made them and they have books in them and magazines and gramophone records. She says I need glasses, but I'm eating the book, that's why I'm holding it close.

Six kids and four fosters, that's what she's got. When HE came home and tried to be nice, he said, prompted by her, no doubt, 'Oh good, another foster-child,' and I ran up to my room. It's marvellous having somewhere to run to. At home there was only the street.

I am not a foster-child. Get that into your head, mister. I am not a child, and anyway, I have a mother and I can go home any time I please. I am staying here because I don't choose to go home, and I have no money, and the State is obliged to support me. When I start the job at the nursing home next week, and save some money, I'll be out of here and take a room, don't kid yourself.

32

He had been told by Molly to say, 'Oh good.' I know that. I know him. I know that kind. Plaid socks, shirts clean, very proper. He shines his shoes every day. Every *day*! Get alone with him in a dark corner and you'd soon see. I can't lock my door at night, so I push the foot of the bed against it. In the morning the little ones come up and scratch like dogs, and I move the bed back and let them in, and the dogs as well sometimes.

A friend of Molly's who was here the other day said it, but so would anyone, 'Doesn't Jim mind all these children, and another one every time he turns his back?'

All right, lady. I know who you mean, but I stayed in the room.

Molly laughed, with all her teeth on show. 'The more you have of your own, the less trouble the extra ones are.' She smiled at me, but I went on eating cornflakes.

'It's always people like you,' the friend said, 'who do more for others than anyone who has much less to do.'

They were going together to visit some old duck in hospital, and I was going to baby-sit and start the tea when Mike and Ralph and Donna got back from school. For money of course.

'I'm a baby farmer,' Molly said, picking up Ziggy, who is half black and half white, and not too bright either.

'Hardly,' the friend said. 'You can't make money out of what they pay you.'

'How much do they pay?' I asked, flinging it out, prepared to add something rude if they said: None of your business.

But Molly told me, just as if I had said: What's the time? and honestly, it isn't much. You couldn't make a penny on it, not and feed us like she does. Don't ask me why she does it, because I do not know.

Mollyarthur, they say, and laugh. I'm not surprised.

MY GRANDFATHER was a grocer, like his father before him. Don't picture him with a long stiff apron and a mouthful of raisins. He had started like that, said my grandmother, but my cousins' parents and mine neither remembered nor believed it. When his cautious father retired, he had swiftly become a tycoon, in his small way, with three Bernard Bullock shops in London, then six, and twelve when he died, not counting the one in Camden Town, which the Germans burned down in a redolent inferno of roast coffee and melting brown sugar.

The small empire went to his boys. Uncle Mark had done his war in the Catering Corps, with crossed knives and forks on his cap badge, and was a true son of his father. David, my father, had gone back to the Law when the Army let him out, and since the grocery outlook was bleak, with the Food Ministry apparently a permanent fixture, he sold out his share to Uncle Mark, glad to be rid of it. His heart had never been in cheese and sausages. He says my grandfather always smelled of Stilton, but I think he has made that up to fit the general aura of grocery in which he was brought up.

We felt sorry for Uncle Mark, stuck with the old-fashioned business with the name in black and gold glass over the stores, and the old clientele of particular ladies who cared how their coffee was ground fast dying out. We had been clever, taking the money and investing it in businesses which were someone else's worry. Money is better than margarine. One of my father's phrases from my childhood which has stuck.

Things looked bad for Uncle Mark. Groceries were going modern. They were beginning to wash vegetables, freeze food, seal up meat in packets, dabble in self-service. The story was out that my uncle, with his lines of square biscuit tins aslant along the front of the counter, was tottering, was even going to take Derek away from Harrow, Derek told me excitedly, the Christmas after the summer when he and I had said the Black Mass for the English master.

And then he did it. He went self-service, and in five years he had got rid of the shops in bad situations and turned all the good ones into supermarkets, and was building more.

Other expanding grocery chains took foody-sounding names. He stuck to my grandfather's. B.B., with the big red letters high over the roof, and Derek had to finish his time at Harrow and then go to Pitman's to learn how to add before he went into the firm.

When I decided to leave school and not go to college, because I was at that stage when you think that the only education that matters begins after you stop being educated, my Uncle Mark offered to take me in.

He put it that someone from our side should be in B.B. (they had planned it for Peter), but I felt that it was more grudging than that, as if I were a poor relation. We are not poor, but I am not my uncle's type. He likes them quick and obvious, in sports cars. Serves him right to have a daughter who is even less like that than I am. He would never employ Nell in the business. She isn't even very clean.

I am taking this business course in a college with green walls and curved stone wainscots, like a hospital, and every Saturday morning I go to one of the B.B. supermarkets to do field work. I am a nuisance to everybody, because my stacks of soup tins totter and the paper bags I pack too full burst before the customer had got to the door, and she's spread-legged there, trying to catch the rolling stock and hang on to what's left. They chant that everyone has to learn, because I am M.B.'s niece and they are stuck with me, but I daresay each manager hopes on a Saturday that it's not my turn for his store.

About a month after I last went to court with my father, I had to go to the B.B. market which is in the neighbourhood of the turreted old grey school which is now the courthouse. The manager there is one of the classless young men my uncle so cleverly picks, with a flat grammar-school accent and a sharp, conversant mind.

His name is Mr Burdick, and it will be just my luck to start off in his office before I pass on to headquarters. He is brisk with everybody, as if the world was due to end in half an hour, and he spins briskly on the ball of his foot when he turns. He is especially brisk with me, to show that he doesn't give a fish finger for the Bullock family. He rushed me down, still in my fur boots, to the jam section, and threw me at a solid man in a white coat with the red B.B. on the pocket, who was stamping prices on the jar lids.

'See how you get on with *that*!' said Mr Burdick challengingly, as if it were a formidable task, and left us.

The solid man's name was William Fender. It is B.B.'s latest conceit to have the assistants labelled. It's supposed to make the shoppers feel at home, but actually it may daunt them, because anyone with his name pinned over his heart in a plastic case might be too grand to be asked where the soap-flakes are.

'You haven't a coat,' said William Fender, and looked down at my black boots with the white fur cuffs.

'He didn't give me time to change.'

'*I* know.' He smiled, and we were colleagues, bonded indissolubly against the boss. He showed me where to go, and I weaved through the Saturday morning crowds of women and husbands and children shouting: 'Get that!' at cereal packets with spaceship models on the back, went through the butchery, where grim women in hairnets were wrapping uniform shapes of meat, and found a shelf of coats at the back of the storeroom. The one that was the right size said Marjorie Beale on the pocket so I turned the card round and wrote Gladys Heifer on it and pinned it back on.

'I thought you were Miss Bullock,' William Fender said, stamping Bee Bee brand blackberry jelly with practised speed and grace. 'Excuse me, madam,' as a woman with her head swivelled backwards ran her cart into him.

She pulled the cart back, rounded his bulk and moved on in the coma that falls on women in places like this. In ordinary shops, they spy and peer and pick things over, sharp-eyed. Here among the aisles of abundance that would feed half Asia, they wander like zombies, hypnotically taking things from the shelves, which is why my uncle is rich.

'When your cousin was here,' Mr Fender went on, 'we had quite a time. Found him smoking back of some cauliflower crates in the storeroom in the end. His dad was wild.'

'How did he know?' As if it wouldn't be just like Burdick to tell.

'He was here that day, and spotting through the one-way in the office, and missed him on the floor.'

The manager's office in the gallery above the cash registers in each market has a window you can see out of, but not into. It is supposed to be for catching shoplifters, but is more often used for spying on the staff.

After we had done the jams, and cleaned up a jar of honey

which a woman swept from the shelf with a Superman cape, we moved on, our heavy rubber stamps weighing down the pockets of our coats, and attacked a monstrous tower of condensed milk cartons, waiting to be shelved and priced. Mr Fender showed me how to alter the set of the stamp without getting ink on my fingers, which was the only useful thing I learned that morning, opened one of the cases for me and went away.

It was very boring. The milk was our own brand, Bee Bee. Quality is Our Busy-ness, and a picture of two excited bees about to fight, or worse.

The huge clock hands on the wall above the freezer that jerked round the letters B E E B E E B E E B E E (it would be the end of all if you forgot what store you were in) moved grudgingly for me, but I was quite pleased to find myself clock-watching already. It made me feel I belonged.

I imagined that I was a woman doomed all her working life to wear a white coat that said Gladys Heifer (she never married because of her mother), and to stamp prices on tins and stack them on shelves for other people to take down.

'Leave them alone!' I yelled silently, as time and again people took down cans of milk and made gaps in my phalanx. It was clear that before G.H. had been at this game very long, she would have lost all sense of the purpose of the job.

I liked it best when customers asked me things. 'Could I exchange this tin of meat for a tin of salmon?' Even if the salmon had not cost more, the meat had not come from one of our shops. What did she take us for? 'We can exchange, but not substitute,' I told her hard-eyed.

'It says two for two-and-nine. How much is that each?'

'Have you seen a little boy in a pink woollen hat?'

'Where are the toiletries?'

Where is/are the tea, the matches, the baby pants, the lemon squash, the soup, the soap, the *drying powder* – what the hell was that?

Labelled or not, no one was in awe of Heifer, with her rope of brown hair over one shoulder secured by a rubber band. She knew the answers – had not she spent two Saturday mornings learning the geography before Mr Burdick allowed her within smelling distance of a price stamp? – and was glad to oblige,

37

even if the question was: 'Where is the condensed milk?' when it was staring them in the face.

Roll on my one o'clock. I bent to prise open (death to the nails) what should have been the last carton if there were mercy, straightened up for the stamp, and there was Kate.

Pushing a cart with a half-caste baby in it, another child hanging on her skirt, her yellow hair cleaner, though still back-combed like a thorn bush, a red polo-necked sweater doing good things for her shape, mascara not so glue-pot – smiling! Having a joke with a small boy who had stolen a packet of jelly and opened it to chew on the squares.

'Katherine?' I could not help myself. If you think about doing something like this, you don't do it.

She blinked and screwed up her eyes as if she were short-sighted, although her eyes did not have the soft lustre that goes with that.

'Hullo,' she said uncertainly.

'I'm sorry. I was in the court when you – well, I was there. I remembered you.'

'I remember you, I suppose,' she said rather slowly. Her accent was not as thick as her father's, the moderation of the cockney natural not refined. 'I didn't recognize you with your hair like that. What are you doing here?'

'You may well ask,' I said. 'Or you can ask what I was doing in court.'

She shrugged to show me that she'd ask if she wanted to, so I said: 'My father is the magistrate and my uncle owns the B.B. supermarkets.'

It was an ungainly thing to have to say, but for some reason it embarrassed neither of us. I didn't feel I had to make a rotten joke to cover the fact that she had been given too little and I too much.

She stood and stared at me for a moment with her foot in a cracked sloppy shoe on the rail of the cart, like a mother gossiping over the prams. When a tall woman with short curly hair and a pleased round face came round the custard corner carrying an oriental baby, she said, 'Look, Moll. This girl was in court when I was there. She's the beak's daughter, and her uncle owns this thieving crib.'

'Never.' Moll was Mrs Arthur, the mad woman with six children, unaware victim of my mother's plan for forced contraception. Mollyarthur, Kate introduced her, all in one word, like Moriarty. 'It's very exciting. I've seen your father. Not spoken to him, of course, but sometimes one of my children is there for a Fit Person order or something, so I go to court. I admire him very much.'

'So do I.' I felt bad about the Gladys Heifer label, and wondered if I could palm it away without her noticing.

'I've seen worse,' Kate conceded.

The change in her was remarkable. In court, she had been a defiant little tramp, grubby, buffeted, alone. Here in the market, like any Saturday shopper, cleaned up, fed, the mob of assorted children bumping round her, she could almost have been Mollyarthur's daughter.

She was on the way up, away from whatever hell or haunting had brought her before my father. It had been much more than pity I had felt. Now there was no need for pity, and the rest remained.

She liked me too, God knows why, for I must have been hard to place, labouring among the condensed milk and talking familiarly of magistrates. Whose side was I on? Perhaps, instead of the plastic Heifer label, she saw my heart pinned on the white coat, for she jerked out suddenly: 'I like your hair,' with such unintentional sincerity that she had to qualify it quickly with: 'You've got a nerve to wear it like that.'

Mrs Arthur did most of the talking. She talks all the time like a hilarious budgerigar, and Kate and I stood and smiled at each other like idiots, while the children kept running back from forays and throwing things into the cart, until the negroid baby was half-submerged in tins and bottles.

Just as I remembered the one-way window and started stamping prices again like a demented passport officer, Kate said, rather belligerently: 'Why can't we ask her to my party?'

She said it as if Mollyarthur had already said she couldn't, as if things were only of value if they were forbidden.

'Why not?' Mrs Arthur's smile spread to a grin round her clean white teeth. 'It's Kate's birthday. She's asked some of her friends and the girl she works with at the nursing home.

Will you come, Gl —' She looked at the card on my front. 'But your name is Bullock.'

'I put this on.'

'She's ashamed of working here,' Kate said.

'Oh no,' I said, too quickly. 'Of my name.'

That wasn't what I meant. Not what I meant at all. I meant – oh hell, they should have known what I meant. I shuttered my face into redskin reticence and they collected the children and went away hating me. They wished they hadn't asked me to their rotten party. I wouldn't go anyway, even if they had told me where they lived.

Molly sent the postcard to my father at the court, not knowing where I lived. Short, crimped writing, like the baby's hair, not a pronoun in sight. 'Forgot say where live. Grove Lodge edge park. Friday evening. Bring gram recs. M.A.' On the other side was a glazed picture of two kittens in an upturned hat. 'Anyone I know?' He gave it to me when I came home. My mother, who is honest about all the wrong things, never reads other people's postcards, but my father and I do.

'It's the – it's a girl I know at the college. Shan't go bring gram recs.'

'Don't blame,' he said, taking the card back to look at the kittens again.

Sometimes when I come home at night, he kisses and hugs me as if I were a small child again, galloping in with pigtails and a gym tunic. Sometimes he doesn't and, if he doesn't want it, you can't start it, as my mother must have found out at cost, some time ago.

Standing by his desk, looking down at the narrow grey head which at times you can see as a skull, I again almost told him about Kate, and again I couldn't. Why not? He is not a snob. Perhaps I was afraid that he would think I had inherited her through him. Taking over where he left off. Trying to help.

Good for you, he would say. Someone her own age can do more for her than anyone. Then it would get to my mother, and she would want to discuss it, picking it to pieces like a dandelion clock, until there was nothing left. She had done this with school friendships, ambitions I revealed, love affairs.

I tell her now mostly surface things that sound like my life, and keep quiet about what matters.

There is only one park in that neighbourhood, a bleak stretch of bitter grass with chained swings, a shuttered kiosk humped against the winter, and a few men hurrying along the walks head down to get home.

I walked half-way round it and found Grove Lodge, a monstrous brown brick villa with a motorbike with cowboy trappings in the garden and a lot of windows in unsymmetrical places. Music poured out of the ground floor, and smoke poured out of the fat chimneys, as if the house were half-way across the Atlantic, with the ship's band swinging.

The bell did not work and there was no knocker, so I thumped. After a while, some of the squeals and feet inside channelled into a clattering run to the front door, and I was in, with two small boys hurtling past me down the chocolate-cake steps and into the bushes.

'Come back in here!' a woman's voice called from somewhere, as if she had something in her mouth. They didn't come, and she didn't come to see why, so I shut the front door, put my coat on top of a pile of magazines on a chair, plugged in a hairpin and pretended that I wasn't afraid of Kate's motorcycle friends, and of Kate herself in this new environment.

The doors off the hall were shut. The music came deafeningly from the room on the right. I opened the door and went in.

A girl with a nose turned up square at the end like a pig's was dancing on the linoleum with a boy like a knife blade, his lemon-coloured hair in sidewhiskers, one side longer than the other. Grimly apart, they were dancing in a manner slightly reminiscent of the parties along our road, but more respectable.

A thick girl, the same shape all the way down, was sitting on the floor in front of the fire, her legs stretched out in front of her like deadwood. A pallid boy with a forelock of soft black hair sat smiling in a rocking-chair, legs crossed very high, one thick rubber sole pushing him gently back and forth.

He and the thick girl looked at me. The couple went on

dancing, both so concave that you wondered about their guts. Kate stood by the gramophone with her back to the door and pretended not to know that I had come in.

There was nothing for it but to cross the room and say, 'Hullo, Kate.'

She turned slowly, as if it didn't matter. 'What?'

'Hullo!' I shouted. The noise was fierce, a crescendo of the battering sounds my generation is supposed to need, which is driving us all a little askew.

The noise died away suddenly to a whimper, the needle slid across the record and Kate said rather sourly: 'I thought you weren't coming.'

'Am I late? I didn't know what time.'

'Oh well. You bring any records?'

'A few. But I don't know if they're the right kind.' They were piano, the only ones I have, people like Garner and Peter Nero playing old stuff in a way Cole Porter never expected.

'Ta.' Kate took them and put them down without looking at them. It was clear they wouldn't be played. I should have borrowed some from next door.

We were all just looking at each other, like dogs, or street gangs sizing up for a fight. Nothing happened. I seemed to have paralysed whatever initiative had before made it possible to put on a record, to start dancing. The boy in the chair had stopped rocking. Pig girl and sideburns stood on the torn linoleum with their little fingers twined. Kate, who is meagrely shaped, looked almost heavy with inertia. To have introduced anybody would have cost her as great an effort as to lift feet nailed to the floor, which they seemed to be.

If I had said, into the silence: I'm Emma Bullock, it would sound like an indecency, and so would their names, if I forced them to divulge.

At least she had minded because I was late and she thought I wasn't coming. I would have turned with an incoherent excuse and run away if it wasn't for that, and if I hadn't been dressed right. Kate had put on all her eye paint, and a short tight black skirt, with red tights and the red polo-necked sweater. The log by the fire was in a string-coloured sloppy with what might prove to be a skating skirt when she got up.

Pig wore a long barrel sweater, home-knitted and cast on too tight round the hips. I had the black chunky number which makes me look very Aztec, and I had wound my hair round and round my head like knitting wool, and the thick girl had built hers, apparently days ago, into a tottering ginger beehive.

Give the teenagers a chance, Mollyarthur had obviously said, shut herself in the kitchen, and forbidden the little ones the room on pain of death. So there we were in the square bare room with the chairs pushed against the walls, like strange children shoved into a nursery and told: Play.

I cleared my throat. 'Shall we —' I began desperately. I don't know whether I would have said Have another record, or Tell our names, or Play Sardines, but suddenly, as if I had pressed a button, Kate dropped the needle back on the record, the boy with the lemon hair leaped into the air crying, 'Hit it!' and was away with pig, Kate pulled the other boy out of the chair and galvanized him into loose-jointed action, and I was so invigorated by the relief from paralysis that I almost bent over the log girl with my hand in my waist and said: Shall we dance?

Instead, I sat down beside her, and she told me behind her hand, which is the way she said everything, with little digs of the elbow that her name was Joan, dig, and she worked with Kate at the nursing home – what on earth did they *do* among the old ladies being starved to death for their annuities? – that the rocking-chair boy was called Bob, sniff, and the other two were Kevin and Sonia, old friends of Kate's, dig dig, well, it takes all kinds.

No one asked me to dance. No one talked to me, although I tried. Even Joan had nothing more to convey behind her hand. Between records, the boys were completely silent, with clodding feet in prehistoric shoes, and Kate was featureless in her Queen of the Nile make-up, wishing she had not asked me, for she couldn't be friendly with the others there, and with me there, she couldn't let go with them.

Would it hurt her more if I stayed or left? Who cared anyway? Thank God I hadn't said anything at home about coming here, so I wouldn't have to face: Well, how did it go?

IT WAS awful. The worst party I've ever been at. Not that I've been at any except those brawls at the Teen Club, with McDonovan blowing his whistle.

Because I've never had a birthday party, nor even a birthday – but Molly knew because of the date on my papers – she was bound I should have one.

I said O.K. When Molly's got an idea, you may as well go along with it. Who to ask? Don't lose touch, she said, so I asked Sonia, that I used to go with at school, and since you can't ask her without Kev, I asked him too.

I didn't know Molly knew about Bob, but of course she'll have read the reports and things where it tells about me and him going off – my whole life laid bare for the world to see – so she was bound I should ask him. The funny thing about her is this. Everyone else thinks it was bad that I ran away with him. Old Moll thinks the bad thing is that I ran away *from* him, in Charing Cross Road. I sometimes wonder why they let her be a foster-mother. She doesn't think like any mother I know. If she's trying to buy me by never criticizing, even when Matron came in person to complain about my work, she's wasting her time. I belong to no one.

Never did to Bob. He knew that, so he bears no malice. He told me he saw the Horse Guards after I'd gone, and spent all day in Hyde Park waiting to see them come back, before he went home.

Joan had never liked me ever since I first set foot in the nursing-home kitchen and caught her at the shortbread, but she had asked me to Sunday dinner with her people – boiled mutton, never again – so Molly said I had to ask her.

Not much of a party, but there it was. I'd never had one, and if I hadn't been all steamed up about it, I'd never have invited the Bullock girl.

She is a bit queer, mind you, because there's no need for her to work in that market, though she told Molly she likes it, but she is – different. Different to what? To everyone. I've never met anybody like her. She has all this bunch of hair, and at the shop it was hanging like a rope, so thick the kids could have swung on it, and she's the kind you don't waste a month getting to know each other, like I and Bob when we used to stand

44

on the iron bridge and watch the roofs of the trains because we couldn't think of anything to do.

With her, you like know her at once. I felt that in court, though I thought that was part of the dream, because the whole lot was hazy. Doug was like that too. As soon as he said: 'You going anywhere, or coming somewhere with me?' in that crazy Aussie voice, I felt all right with him.

I must have been daft to ask her like that, but I never thought she'd come anyway, not after the way she looked when we left. It hadn't been right to ask her. I'd been wrong thinking she isn't the same as all the rest. She is. She couldn't possibly be friendly with someone like me, with Butt Street written all over them, too thick for Grove Lodge to ever wipe off.

Molly said she'd come. I knew she wouldn't. When it was an hour after the others had got there, then I *knew* she wouldn't.

For a moment when she did, I wanted to rush across the room and grab her, but I've never done that to anyone in my life, and it wasn't the time to start, with Joan sitting there like the Beast from Outerspace, and Sonia looking at everyone as if they were something the cat did.

So I kept my back turned, because she was late on purpose to make me think she wasn't coming. She came over, and she had these corny records, nothing anyone ever heard of, and she looked smashing, I mean that. She's ugly really, feature by feature, but that hair like yards of thick toasted silk is really something, and so is that square black sweater. My beloved red was suddenly all wrong. I've got to get a loose black turtleneck, and I've got to let my hair grow.

And then suddenly the party was all wrong too, and I wished she hadn't come. Why had she? To make fun of us? To show us up? The others just stared at her, and we were all dumb like our own funeral.

It hadn't been what you might call gay before, but whatever it was, she had ruined it, and I hated her for that, although it was my fault for asking her. Molly's fault for letting me. Kev's and Sonia's fault for being so, I don't know. Poor Bob's fault for sitting there with that silly smile, and falling all over me when I made him dance. Joan's fault for whispering things about me to Emma.

Emma. Whoever heard of a name like that? I ask you. Emma's fault for being there.

If that's a birthday party, I'd not missed a thing. I was ready to throw the whole thing up, when all at once there was a shrieking and yelling and the door burst open and some of the kids crashed in in their pyjamas and shouted we'd all to come into the room.

The room is the one at the back of the house looking over the Park where we do everything, and there's no space in there for five more people, that's why Molly had shoved us in the play-room. The room is the centre of this house, the only place I've ever felt really safe in, but I didn't want Emma to see all the laundry and the babies and the animals and that awful moulting bird and the come and go at the round table – there's always someone eating, day and night – and the walls chalked over any time anyone feels artistic, because that can't be the way she lives, and I want to be her equal.

But the kids rushed us down the hall, and Kev was shriek-ing: 'Hit it!' and jumping at the ceiling, and Ralph had a hold of me and tugging, and Donna pushing from behind, and when we got past the stairs and to the door, someone flung it open from inside, and there it was. My birthday.

The room was half-dark, just the fire, and the nightlights. It was all decorated with coloured paper like Christmas, and bells and silvery things and the birdcage all hung with leaves and little bright shiny balls. All the toys and clothes and carpentry and stuff were in the shadows, even the ironing-board had gone, and on the round table in the middle of the room, in-stead of the sauce bottles and the last person's dirty mug, there was this huge great cake with seventeen candles on it.

Someone pushed me and I went up to the table. All the kids stood in an arc behind it with the candle flames like pinpoints in their eyes, and Tina had on that long nightdress and her voice all filling up her mouth like cake, and the boys not shov-ing and giggling, singing dead earnest.

Happy birthday, dear Katie, they sang. Happy birthday to you, and my heart came right up through my chest as if I was going to cough blood.

THE BIRTHDAY party was the beginning of the real friendship between Kate and me. After Molly had broken her down with the cunning staging of the cake and those heart-breaking children in the candlelight, she dropped the shield and dagger she'd been carrying round like a Roman Legionary, and risked enjoyment.

She had to wash her face after the emotion of the singing. When she came out of the kitchen scrubbing at her face with a dish-towel, Sonia said, 'You'll have to do up your eyes again,' but Kate said, 'Who for?' and stood on her head up the wall beside one of the small boys who was relaxing there, with his pyjama jacket fallen over his face.

Mollyarthur's husband is the hale, shock-headed kind, like a man in an advertisement for pipe tobacco. He has a loud slow voice with a few West Country vowels, and a laugh out of all proportion to the joke. Ha, ha, ha, he goes, ho, ho, at almost anything I say, and makes me feel I have a rare wit. Kate walks wide round him as if he were going to rape her, but he is as mild as bread, and accepts all the extra children stoically, as if it were a disease that Molly had.

There was a cottage piano in the corner shadows, with panels of painted swains and ladies, and its hammers and wires exposed. After the food, he played, nodding rhythmically over his square pelted hands, and we sang old easy songs with the children. Sonia and Kevin told each other it was corny, and soon roared away on the cow-punching motorbike, and when the children had straggled off to bed like the Lost Boys going up the tree-trunks, we sat on the floor and told ghost stories.

I was afraid to go home after the one Kate told about the Claw – she has seen every horror film ever made – so Bob walked me to the station, for what that was worth. He is like a great amiable child, with his shambling walk and his gullible grin, and if he really ran away with Kate, as I seem to remember someone saying in court, they must have been like Hansel and Gretel.

'Well, how did it go?' my mother asked me next morning, and I forgot where I was supposed to have been, so I said I liked it, which was the truth, and that I had made a new friend, which was also the truth.

47

'Let's hope this one lasts longer than Hugh.' Docketing her ideas as she does, my mother expects girls of my age to be exclusively concerned with the opposite sex.

'She's training to be a nurse,' I said, although I knew by now, because Kate and Joan had let go profanely about the nursing home, that they were only unwilling drudges who washed and scrubbed and swabbed and soaked and rinsed all day long in the unending battle against senile incontinence.

I go to Mollyarthur's quite often after work. I am not in love just now, and the girls I know are away at college with utterly liberated morals, or married to television actors, or engrossed in some much more interesting job than mine. No one is training for retail grocery, and they have never been very real friends anyway.

At Grove Lodge, which looks better as the winter begins to loose its hold, Donna left when her mother came out of prison, but the twins have come to take her place, sad balding three-year-olds who have never had enough of anything, food or sleep or fresh air or love. If Kate and I will put the children to bed, Molly will give us kippers or chops for supper. If not, it is all the left-overs thrown in a frying-pan with eggs broken in the middle, which isn't bad either.

I am her sixth foster-child, since Kate refuses the title, and Mr Arthur, whose name is Jim, groaned and said it was getting worse than a Remand Home.

'Don't hurt Emma's feelings,' Molly said. 'If you had been taught to shoplift by a stepmother who chained you to the bed at night, you'd be delinquent too.'

He laughed ho, ho, because it is his nature, but he only plays card games with us, not this game. One of the things we do is inventing gruesome backgrounds for this sixth foster-child. It doesn't bother Kate; in fact it was she who started it, and she who keeps throwing in macabre details like burnings and starvings and babies abandoned in sewers, which have a faint smell of truth under the Gothic exaggeration.

One of Molly's friends who heard us at it, told Molly that it was in bad taste, in view of . . . and made a mouth.

'You mean me?' Kate called from the kitchen, where she

48

and I were doing Michael's arithmetic for him while we discussed my youth under the white slavers.

'Oh no,' the friend said quickly, and Molly said: 'We weren't talking to you anyway. You run your life, I'll run mine,' which always makes us shriek with laughter, very childish. But we are childish, romancing and dramatizing and making up exotic things which might have happened at the supermarkets or the nursing home, and crimes the nurses have committed (Kate detests them all), and marvellous things that are going to happen to us when we are famous and adored, and impossibly marvellous men who are going to come charging into our lives: always older, lean, sardonic yet tender, the kind who don't exist.

The only thing that comes charging is Bob, who wanders across the Park from time to time and sits in a chair and eats raisins until he is told to go home. He seldom talks, unless you get him on to soldiers, which are his dream. He still thinks that one day he will be in the Army. He has been rejected already, but he does not understand why. He thinks it was because of his feet, and he wears supports inside the cumbersome rubber-tyred shoes and does push-ups on his toes when he is standing, which is only when there is nowhere to sit down.

When Kate and I are off on a saga, he will sit and listen peacefully, throwing raisins into his smile and occasionally asking a question about people who don't exist, as if they were real. Kate treats him like a child, and calls him Molly's seventh baby, since there are enough fosters, but I never see her touch him or look at him as if there were anything between them or has ever been.

We are getting so that we can say anything to each other. We talk about everything that is in our heads, without pausing to think if it's safe, as you do with people who are friends of circumstance, or friends of convenience, not friends of choice. The only things we cannot talk about are the purplish-red mark she carries like a yoke on her neck, and we never talk about her home, and the misery that drove her away and that keeps her from going back.

'Moll is stuck with me,' she says, and Molly says Good, and starts to plan how we'll arrange the furniture for the wedding and whether Jim shall take Kate to church in a hired car or the old brown Ford with ribbon streamers.

I think that may be why Kate started to concoct all the horrors about me, to foil discovery of any of her own, like a child babbling about dragons in the shrubbery so that no one will look at the trampled flowerbed.

I am leading a somewhat secret life, almost like a furtive love affair, because I cannot describe Grove Lodge at home without my mother thinking that I am slumming, although she would make an effort to be pleased at what she called bravely my 'unusual choice of friends' when I brought the Nigerian home from the college.

And my father? I am going to take him to Molly's soon and show them to him, and show him off to them.

I find myself wanting to include him more in myself. Although I have this secret life, which is making me happy and is exciting, because Kate and I discover things about each other all the time, and I am watching her grow towards what she might have been if her life had been different, I want him too. I want to do things with him, grab him, keep him. He slipped away from my mother years ago, but I am not going to let him slip away from me.

When I was a child, our closest times together were out of doors. I wore out one shoulder carrying his golf clubs, and later he taught me to use them. He taught me to ride, and tennis he taught me, although I was always too slow. I was a lumbering child. People called to me: 'Straighten your knees!' but it didn't help. He was not expert at anything, but he could do everything fairly well. He taught us all, including himself, to sail, and he taught Alice and Peter and me to swim, and we soon swam much better than he did, which was why he hadn't been able to get to Peter when he was going out in the Poldhu current.

My mother, with her lack of grace, which she has passed on to me, was hopeless at anything athletic, except fishing, which she was brought up to. Apart from those two times when we went to Raglan and she was the expert, she was always the one who had to watch and applaud, and come in the car with blankets when the sailing dinghy capsized, and sit knitting on a backless bench outside the riding ring while we went endlessly round and round.

My father and I used to ride together. Once when Alice was ill, we selfishly went to the New Forest for a long week-end and rode ponies all day along the spongy cathedral aisles. I have never forgotten the magic of that. We rode all day among the great greenwood trees, and he read *Wuthering Heights* to me at night, and brushed my hair carefully before I went to bed. It was so good that I think I may have imagined it, but he says that it did happen, although he remembers it raining all the time, which I don't, and his riding-boot splitting, and a raconteur who used to spoil his times in the bar after he had put me to bed.

Golf and tennis are out for him now because of his leg, and so are the walks we used to take, with one of the succession of hysterical terriers my mother has always had. There is no reason, however, why he shouldn't ride, except that he hasn't for years, and my mother is always telling him that he is just the age for a lightning heart attack.

I know a boy called Alan, who comes from Shropshire and can't go long without a horse. He says it like that, as another man would say it about a woman. He is a laboratory student and he lives in a nasty room in Fulham and he has no money, so I take him to the stables near us sometimes when I can afford it. When they started to let us take the horses out on our own, instead of in jostling groups of rumpy blue jeans and grimly expert infants on white ponies, it was so lovely that I made my father come too.

He didn't want to, but I forced him. This one thing he was going to do with me, this last relic of the childhood things we had shared.

His boot hurt his leg. When I went to his room to see if he was ready, I found him sitting on the fat leather stool with his leg stuck out in front of him as if it was wooden.

'I'm not coming.'

Ignoring his strained face and the little twitch of his mouth, I pulled him up and handed him his stick. Once he was on the horse, he would be all right. Alan, who was a bit sceptical about the whole project, for he is one of these Peter Pan fools who discount everybody over thirty, would be amazed when he saw how well he could ride.

The first trauma was that he couldn't get on. I tried to give him a leg up, but the trashy horse the stable had given him would not stand still. Alan, who is the kind of boy who orders first for himself in restaurants, even when you're paying, and will go off anywhere without looking to see who's following, was already up and half-way to the yard gate.

When I called him, he dismounted with a visible sigh and got my father on the horse, then rode ahead all the way and never looked back to see how well my father handled the horrid poky horse. If he had been looking back when my father fell off, he would have seen that the horse shuffled its foot into a hole and stumbled. I explained this, but I could see he didn't believe it. My father sat on the ground rubbing his leg and lighting a cigarette, and Alan kept circling round on his tall restless horse saying, 'Are you all right, sir?' and I said, 'He won't be if you step on him.'

Alan had to get off and help my father up again. Jumbled up together in the narrow path between the trees, the horses began to kick and bite, and Alan had the nerve to tell me, 'Better not bring him next time.'

'There won't be a next time,' I said, and pulled my horse back and rode with my father, who smoked cigarettes all the way home and rode with his bad leg stuck straight out like a cow-hand.

A few days later, when we were all at a cocktail party in London, he introduced me to a woman of about thirty-five with coppery hair and marvellous amused eyes. He told her, 'This is the girl who's trying unsuccessfully to keep me young,' and she said, 'You keep on doing that, whatever he says.' But he refuses to come riding again.

He will come to Grove Lodge though. He is getting lazy, but I shall tell him that it's part of his job.

If he remembers Kate, and to him, after all, she is only one in a process of rebellious waifs, he will be amazed at the change in her. It is not just that she is growing her pale hair and has caught the shampooing mania from me, but she is happy, and in court it seemed she never could be.

It is partly due to him (we'll forget that it was Miss Draper's idea), partly to Mollyarthur, and partly to Kate, who has turned her stubbornness into survival. When he has seen her, and understood that I love her, then I will ask him for a loan which I'll repay when I am earning. A birthmark can be removed by plastic surgery, but it costs money.

I was surprised when Mr Jordan, the Cruelty Man, telephoned me one evening and asked me if I had time to go out with him again.

'I thought I was a nuisance.'

'No, you were a help.'

'How could I be? I was just there.'

'It helps, discussing things in the car between visits. Trying to explain to you what's gone wrong with someone, it helps me to get my own thoughts straight about them.'

'I'd like to go.' Not from curiosity, not because I could help, but because I have to see. In my life, I may never be selfless enough to lessen by one grain the world's misery, but it's worse not even to know it's there.

'I'd like you to come.'

He could say that over the telephone. When we met, he was once more rather shy and formal, although he rocked the little snub car just as recklessly round the streets and courtyards, hazarding infants and slow grandfathers.

When I thanked him for asking me again, he said: 'Your father thinks that you should see more of this work, since it's really part of his,' which wasn't at all what he had said on the telephone.

I like him, though, and admire him. He has the physique of a man who tears telephone books in two and keeps a punchball in the cellar, but he has no conceit or violence. He used to be a sergeant-major, but I can't imagine his voice ever terrorizing anyone into step. Perhaps he broke it, there on the barrack square, and that's why it murmurs now, unmilitary. His hair grows like a boy's from a point on the back of his head, and his smile makes nonsense of his soldierly jaw. He is often silent, not necessarily in thought, but because he has nothing to say, and he is absolutely marvellous with the people he takes care of.

Although he is the Cruelty Man, and some people think he goes round in a paddy wagon carting sadistic parents off to gaol, Taking Care is the right description for what he does.

We took some shoes to brothers who had been going to school on alternate days because they only had one pair between them, and we went to the Assistance Office to try to get more money for a widow with a mongol baby, and we went to see about a father's debt, and a holiday for a child with asthma. Although I had done little more than play with the children and listen to the bailiff's sinister Dickensian jokes, I felt that I had done more good in one morning than in my whole life.

As we drive round this ugly, grey and teeming neighbourhood where Mr Jordan has worked for five years, grown-ups call out and wave to him, and urchins bang on the little tin car at red lights and cry: 'Gis a ride, Mr Jordin!' He is not the avenging angel, but a familiar and welcome figure, like the ice-cream man.

We slowed down in a back street beside a monstrous beery woman shoving a child in a rickety pram, and her violent face split like a dropped tomato with pleasure at seeing him. She chatted like an old friend, droning easily away about the discomforts of her new flat and the low class of people who surrounded her.

When we drove away, he laughed: 'You should have seen the place I got her out of,' and wrinkled his nose. 'And she's doing her best to make the new one as bad. She and her husband have both been up for neglect. She's got two kids in Care and I'm watching the others, but she's always glad to see me.'

When he said that his wife had told him to bring me home for lunch, 'if you care to, Miss Bullock,' I said: 'Oh yes, but please call me Emma.'

His neck got a bit red, and after that he didn't call me anything, not even Miss Bullock.

His wife called me Emma though, right away, and said that she had seen me in the B.B. supermarket, and that I shouldn't let them sell sardine tins without an opener.

She is a lovely woman, just right for him, soft-haired and squashy in front, with pink cheeks and strong arms. The go-

anywhere, do-anything kind, who would look right fraterniz-
ing with the neighbours in Army married quarters or feeding
chickens at a farmhouse door, or living on a lighthouse or
answering the telephone and typing out his case notes.

They live in a small terrace house with a gable and a bay
window and a sign on the door, so that people can come and
complain about their neighbours, or leave unwanted children
on the step. He has just painted the wood of the house, and
repapered the hall with violent bouquets that clash with the
carpet. In the kitchen where we had lunch, he has painted all
the doors and cupboards yellow, with Austrian stencilling,
and converted the old coal-range alcove into a cottage fireplace with carved inglenook seats.

'He works all the time,' his wife said, 'but it's always for
other people. It took me six months to get him to do any of
this for me.'

She is very proud of him, her pride no less affectionate for
being expressed in terms of complaint. He is comfortable with
her, stowing away great forkfuls of meat and potato in proportion to his build, the peace of his home strengthening the
tolerance he shows outside. We had been to two places this
morning where I had been with him before, and I felt the
defeat of it, because the women had made no progress, hadn't
taken his advice, hadn't kept the rent money safe, had still
not cleaned out the back room or taken the child to the dentist.

It's so disheartening, but he doesn't give up. 'Just have to
keep going back and back,' he said. 'Takes half a dozen trips
sometimes to get the floor scrubbed or a mattress burned, but
you have to keep on.'

'Or burn the mattress yourself,' his wife said. 'He's been
known to do that too. And get in there after the dirt. Remember the time we cleaned out those two top rooms in Ely Street?
Fifteen bathfuls of it, the Council took away, and the neighbours all went out because of the smell.'

She laughed, as if she might add: Those were the days. 'He
gets all the gravy, running round in that little car and everyone
knowing him and waving, but it's me he gets to do his dirty
work.'

'Half the time,' he said, 'when I come home, there's a child in my bed or a baby being changed on the kitchen table. Comes a bang on the front door and there's a kid crying or a bundle in a kitbag, sometimes just while they go off for a visit, sometimes for ever. If I'm not here, Jean will take them in. They know that.'

They have one child, a girl of about ten, who came home from school before we left. She is soft and capable, like her mother, and unflurried, like her father. His name is John. Johnny, his wife calls him. Johnny Jordan. 'I've only one more family to see,' he said, 'and it's a bit of a distance. Would you rather I leave you at the station now?'

I almost said Yes, because I was full of food, and tea was swilling in me. Although it was not nearly so cold as the last time when I all but perished, it had been raining for days, and I was afraid to surrender the warmth of Jean's kitchen to the chilly damp of the homes of Mr Jordan's customers.

Courage. What is this? I thought you wanted to see and know. One doesn't crusade so well on a full stomach, but when I said I'd come, Johnny Jordan, who had eaten twice what I had, drove off with me as eagerly as a fasting monk.

'It's one of those cases,' he told me in the car, 'you find them quite often, where only one child is abused. You'd think that if parents were capable of ill-treating one child, they'd do the same with the others.'

'But with dogs,' I said, 'there's sometimes one puppy which gets pushed away from the milk, or the mother rolls on it.'

'Yes, or the father picks it up and takes it away. We had a collie once did that, in our camp, I mean, where I was stationed in Germany. He put it under a hut, that dog did. We reared it with milk on our thumbs, but it was wasted time. When it was grown, we gave it to the Colonel's wife, and it tore the heart out of a sofa and bit one of her children.'

'Perhaps the father was right.'

'Perhaps. With kids, Miss Bullock —'

'Emma.'

'Yes. With kids, when they pick on just one, it's as if there was something about that child they couldn't stand. I was called out once in the middle of the night to a woman who had beaten her child to death. She provokes me, was all she

56

said, both then and in court. She gets on my box. She kept talking about her as if she was alive and she'd do it all over again. Her other kids were fine though.'

Most people are less talkative after food. He was more so, or perhaps it was because I had been to his house, and his wife and I had liked each other. He wasn't so shy with me.

'Perhaps you thought you were going to see horrors like that, coming out with me?'

I didn't answer, because naturally the beast in me had, but the non-beast had hoped not. So he went on, talking to the car ahead – he doesn't, at least, turn his head from the road to look at you when he speaks – 'It's not anything remarkable, where we're going. The girl all the trouble was about, she's gone, but, after what came out in court, I was asked to keep an eye on the rest of the family for a while. Your father's court, as a matter of fact.'

'Why was she there?'

'She ran away when she was about sixteen. Found with a man, the usual story.'

'I know. My father says he sees them in a recurring pattern, like wallpaper.'

'I wish I had your father's tongue.'

'He wishes he had your ideals.' That wasn't exactly what my father had meant when he had called Johnny Jordan an optimist, but near enough, and it delighted him, although he pretended not to hear, for want of a reply.

As we turned a corner into one of the nastiest streets in this peculiarly nasty district, he still had the pleased smile on his face. The sign on the dirty brick of the end house said Butt Street. The car stopped with a crunch of broken glass in the gutter half-way down the flat sick terrace outside a house whose front room had been converted badly, long ago, into a little shop. A sweetshop, I suppose. Or not. Rat poison and firewood in the cluttered window. A cardboard ice-cream cornet. Steamed jars of peppermint and fruit balls.

I got out and followed Johnny Jordan in, like his dog, sapped of initiative. Would I have asked him to leave me at the station if I had known? I should have known. When he talked, in the car, I should have known where we would end. I could stay in the car now, say I was tired, bored, anything. I was spying on Kate, ransacking the secret drawers of her life, but I could not stop myself. I had to know. I followed him into the shop.

When he opened the door, a small buzzer sounded, sourly. There was no one in the tiny shop, and we could have stolen a bar of chocolate, or a plastic bucket and spade with the colour bleaching out, or a card of pins from the wall.

There was an ice-cream freezer in one corner, the chipped enamel spotted with black fingermarks. When I opened the lid to look inside, the door beyond the counter opened instantly, as if the woman who came through had been watching us behind the curtained glass.

'Oh hullo,' she said to Mr Jordan. 'It's you,' although she might have been watching us for a good two minutes as we waited there, he stamping his feet discreetly among the little wads of grey gum on the floor to attract attention, since he was in one of his silent spells where he couldn't call out.

'Just dropped in to see how everything is going.'

'Not too bad.' Either from habit, or for security, she had moved to stand behind the narrow counter while she talked to us, hands on the broken linoleum top, flanked by the glass cases of toy soldiers and cigarettes and chocolate bars.

I nodded when Johnny Jordan identified me, and stood against the sticky ice-cream freezer, wishing I was older, so that I could look properly at new people without myself getting in the way. I am like a mother with an awkward child, wondering what they will think. The woman stared at me while she talked listlessly to Mr Jordan. Who's that girl leaning clumsily on my choc bars and lollies? Her ankles are too bony for tights. Why doesn't she say something?

I wished that I could see people whole and perceptively, not as a jumble of scattered impressions. Kate's mother. I wasn't seeing much except her slack shape, wrapped round in a faded blue overall with frying stains on the front. Not fat, but so far out of control that you couldn't tell if she was pregnant or not.

Kate's mother. She had never talked about her, not once, and I had not asked. She had talked of her father a little, making a face and using some crude epithet, but of her mother

58

nothing, so that I had once asked Mollyarthur whether I had missed something in court, and the mother was dead.

Molly had said No, and then, 'You saw the father. I think her mother must be worse.'

So I had imagined a vulgar and violent woman, coarser even than the pock-marked van driver with the misbegotten nose. I had imagined a gross caricature of a woman, like the beerbarrel we had met that morning with the pram.

Kate's mother, standing with her tired hands on the counter, the wedding ring deep in the swollen flesh, was not a monster. She was just a woman in a back-street shop with her faded yellow hair tied back with a bow of frayed tape, the only girlish thing about her. A woman who might once have been nice-looking if anyone could remember.

A baby had been crying all the time in the back room, and she muttered impatiently and went through, telling Mr Jordan he could see Loretta, she supposed. I followed, although I wanted to go away, because I didn't know how to feel. I had thought I would feel hatred, as Kate had when she was here. *Had* she been here? I tried to imagine her traipsing sullenly into the shop at the flat summons of the buzzer, deterring customers with her lower lip, slopping the sherbet powder messily into the penny bags, waiting for the something wonderful that never came in from that despondent street.

What kind of woman had made Kate into what she was when I first saw her? I didn't understand. This was only a woman with no joy of life, muttering back and forth between the buzzer and the baby, picking the baby up and rocking it with uncaring, unfocused eyes.

The father was out, which was a good thing. 'He doesn't like you coming here,' she told Mr Jordan. 'I told him you was helping me with Loretta, trying to get her into the special school and that, but he'll not have it that she needs help.'

Loretta was about five, perched on the arm of the collapsing sofa, her mouth open, dribbling a little. When she held up her arms to me, raising them together, like a doll, I picked her up and she clung and giggled and made strange words.

She was rather lovable, but then she wasn't mine. How lovable would she be day after day when you were poor and

59

tired and had a baby and two boys with running noses and graveyard coughs whining and fighting in the few crowded rooms that crouched round the dud little shop? She was wet, she had torn out her hair round the edges, she couldn't talk properly, her dull eyes and dropped jaw made her look what she was. Why, if this man and woman were going to ill-treat a child, why not this poor idiot, their failure, instead of Kate who was quick and clever and full of an unused love which she had never dared to express, even as yet to me?

Kate's mother did not ask us to sit down, and there was nowhere to sit anyway that wasn't piled with rubbish; so we stood while Johnny Jordan patiently tried to persuade the woman to let him take Loretta for examination himself, since she obviously wasn't going to.

The buzzer sounded and she cursed and went out, putting the baby down on the floor, where it began to scream and crawl under the sofa, butting its head against the sagging springs. When she came back, she said: 'Bloody nerve. Two sticks of gum.' She was really angry. It must be a brave neighbourhood child who would trade his pennies there. Why didn't she sell the shop? Who would buy?

The room we were in was no more tempting, with its broken furniture and the oilcloth on the table covered with the remains of several meals. The ugly, coughing boys played in the foul yard outside, throwing pebbles at the railway wall. When they had begun to fight in the slot of kitchen where a soup of underclothes broke grey scum bubbles in a saucepan, she had turned them out, suddenly tense with irritation, as if she couldn't stand much more.

At times she drifted vaguely off, incapable of moving her body or mind. Standing biting at the quicks of her stubbed nails, she fumed at the baby, who was now half under the sofa, roaring into the dust, but did not move to pull him out. She would neither agree to let Mr Jordan take Loretta to the

. clinic, nor promise to take her herself. Her eyes dreamed dully, then sprang alight with rage at the buzzer or the rowdy boys. She looked like a woman who might suddenly scream and run out, leaving the whole mess. Why not? She should never have got into it.

When Johnny Jordan finally gave up, and nodded to me that we should go, she said sharply: 'You'd best not come here again. I don't want you coming here no more.'

'Because of your husband?'

'Because of me! I don't want you snooping here, with your staring girl, whoever she is. Going to make her living off other people's bad luck.'

'And Loretta?' Mr Jordan stood his ground, rocking back and forth in his well-cleaned shoes, as he does when he is under fire.

'She's our business. You let her be.' She took her from me roughly, but the smell stayed with me, and the dribble on my jacket. The child was soaking, and she made a face and put her down on a peeling leather stool, and Loretta climbed down, crowing angrily, leaving a dark patch.

'Someone else will come, if I don't. She'll have to —'

'Why don't they let us alone? I've got four good kids and we've never had no trouble. Let us alone, can't you?' Loretta and the baby matched her rising voice, and the two boys pressed noses white against the window to see what was up. 'If you don't get out, he'll catch you,' she shouted, throwing her voice wildly at the walls, 'and I'll not answer for what he does.'

Mr Jordan put on his cap, which he had been holding behind him, as he rocked imperturbably from heel to toe. 'I thought he'd be on the road,' he said, with his hand on the door knob.

'He lost his job, if you want to know. I don't know where he is, except he's not out looking for another.'

As we went through the shop, a woman came in from the street with a plaid shopping-bag. She stared at us, and then looked out of the window over the dusty packets and went out again quickly, to tell a neighbour perhaps that something was up.

No, it was because she had seen Kate's father coming. We met in the doorway. From behind, I could see Johnny Jordan's broad shoulders tensing for a fight, but the man was so drunk that he just pushed past us and into the back room, kicking open the door. A hand slammed it shut and, as we left, we heard the voices rising and the baby screaming and Loretta wailing like an animal.

Neither of us said anything. We drove out of the street, the woman with the plaid bag staring after us, and a small boy pitched a stone. Mr Jordan hummed without a tune, frowning. He didn't speak until he was stopping the car by the station. 'Sorry you came with me?'

I didn't answer, and he looked at me and his eyes opened in surprise as he saw the tears in mine. 'What's the matter?'

If only one could cry inside oneself, silently letting go without trace. Not with your face swelling up hot and your nose filling up like a blocked drain and your mouth pulling down. I wasn't going to bawl in his ear and look disgusting and have to go into the station like that.

I wanted to cry, but since I couldn't let myself cry, I let myself tell him. 'I know the girl who ran away from there,' I said. 'She's my friend now.'

'And now you've seen what she ran from?'

I shook my head. 'Not that. I had to see that. I – oh Johnny —' If he had been my father, I would have flung myself all over him, sobbing, wanting his arms round me, his murmur. 'Her mother never said her name. She never mentioned her. I've got four kids, she said. We've never had no trouble. It's as if Kate had never been.'

My voice cracked, so I didn't say any more. I wondered if he would tell his wife I was hysterical. When I fumbled my way out of the car and managed to thank him, he said: 'Thank *you*,' and called me Emma.

WELL, I know now. That magazine article, it all matches up. Check with your doctor, it said. What do I need with a doctor? I'm seventeen.

The thing is, I don't know whether to tell Bob or not. He's such a kid himself, it hardly seems fair. You're supposed to be bitter against the man. Don't feel bitter, the magazine said. But I don't. I feel sorry for him, really, because he won't know what to do. I don't know what to do either, so I'll wait and see. I'll ask Sonia, though I doubt she'll talk to me after the party. I could ask Noreen if she's out of the Remand Home. She'd know if anyone would.

I can't tell Molly. I'll never tell her. People who are married are so bloody righteous. They can do it every night and good luck to them. Me and Bob – just that one night, and bad luck to us.

If it hadn't been that I was baby-sitting, it wouldn't be so bad, but that she'd not forgive, with the kids all over the house and Michael not even asleep, I don't think. And I disobeyed her. She'd mind that even more.

She's got this thing about trusting people. I don't make rules for you, she said, that second week after I began to talk to her. I just tell you how I'd like you to behave, and then I trust you. That's why I didn't bolt again, I suppose, although I still had it in my head to go back and look for Doug. He was well known round those parts where he took me.

She trusted me not to have Bob come when she and his Lordship were out, so I can't tell her. She knows about when I ran away, because she's read the reports and that monster at Stinkney would be sure and put in his bit, you can bet on that. In any case, when a boy and a girl shove off, it's obvious what for, and I don't suppose anyone would believe that when I ran to Bob that night and chucked stones at his window so old Marbles wouldn't hear the bell, I never thought of that.

Nor he. After all, if that was it between us, we'd had plenty of chances last summer, on the common and that. He came with me so sweet, never stopped to ask why, just came.

I summon thee to heaven or to hell, and he came.

I was still shivering then, and sick at my stomach, but when he came down grinning like a loony in his socks, and put his arms round me with his shoes in his hands in that cat cemetery she calls a front garden, it was better. I forgot then, for a time. We were two lovers eloping and old Marbles was the wicked stepmother. She's after us! We kept hollering all down the street. All is lost – run for your lives! When we were in the Underground, we were secret agents. We picked out who was spies and who wasn't. The man in the bowler, he was an agent too, from the C.I.D., so of course he knew us, though he never moved a muscle, so well trained. He couldn't acknowledge us because of that Commie woman who was pretending to read, but watching us all the time. She was a man dressed as a woman really. Her legs had all hair on them.

When we found the cellar under that old bank they were knocking down – they'd taken the money out long ago – we played it was our house. I was a bride and I made Bob carry me in over the pile of bottles, though he didn't understand why, because he doesn't read stories. But if I tell him it is so and this is what they do, he does it. He's as good to play with as Tony used to be before he got old enough not to do what I said.

We divided it all up into rooms, laying out stones, and where the workbench was, that was the kitchen and we ate the meat pies in there and shared the bottle of Coke. Bob wedged up the broken chair with a bit of wood, and that was our sitting-room, and he sat back with his foot wagging and his cigarette on his lip while I knocked the picture out of the frame, and that was the TV.

I stuck my face through it and sang for him and joked a bit, but I was running out of fun and I knew I'd sob and howl pretty soon, because it was all coming back over me, cold and sick, and I knew that even if we played games for the rest of our lives, it would always be there. I couldn't shut it out, so I sang the God Save for him and made a face like the Queen sitting on that horse and went into the corner we'd said was our bedroom and laid down on the sacks.

Bob came and stood over me and said: 'Why are you shivering, Katie?' and I said it was because I was cold, because I couldn't tell him. So he laid down too, close to me, and after a while it really was cold. We'd been daft not to bring more clothes, but there wasn't time.

I was shivering when he put his arms round me, and I don't know whether it was the cold or the despair, but anyway there it was, and with a boy like Bob, so sweet and childish, no one is going to tell me there is anything wrong to it.

They didn't at the Home, I'll say that for them, but then they thought it was Douglas, and not my fault. It was still cold afterwards. More so, and we both cried. Then I told him

64

stories till he went to sleep, and I did too, in the middle of Sir Lancelot, and we only got out just in time before the workmen started on the upstairs.

The next night it was better, because we had the blanket, but that was almost the end of the money, after we'd had some food. We didn't think much about what we'd do. If Bob didn't go back to the factory Monday, they might not take him back at all, but he'd get something else, for he's clever with his hands, you'd never think it. We played House again, and we'd been married for years, and all the kids asleep – I made them out of bits of rags wrapped round stones – and then when we were laying down again, I got a giggling fit and said: 'If we go on like this, it could be a real one, not stones.' But it didn't seem to matter then, so of course it wasn't. So of course then after, in my room at Molly's when I never thought about it at all, then it was.

But magazines don't know everything. How can they know about me?

In the morning, it was Sunday, so we stayed in bed and talked about who would go downstairs and make the tea and bring it up. That made us want the tea, so we had to get up and walk miles till we found a place that was open.

Bob wanted to go on playing we were mother and father taking the children to church (he was brought up rather nicely), but I felt pretty rotten then, and tired and cold and hungry, and he said: 'Your strawberry's gone all blue.'

I've never minded him talking about it, for some reason, though if anyone else dares – even one of Molly's kids, her own or the rejects – they'd get their teeth kicked in. Moll never would. Nor Em. Last thing Em would ever do. We've never talked about it, though God knows we've talked about everything else in the world and out of it. I've never had a friend like her.

It may be that she doesn't see it. Has never seen it. Perhaps it isn't there. I can't feel it, and if I don't use two mirrors, I can't see it. If I can't see it, it isn't there.

I don't mind about Bob, because he's such a child and when he says things that would hurt from anyone else, they don't hurt, because he doesn't mean them to.

He took my hand and squeezed it, which hurt because I was cold. 'I love you, Katie,' he said, and it sounded so queer, coming from him, that I laughed. He thought it would make me feel better, I suppose, but it didn't.

When he said after breakfast: 'I'm getting a bit sick of this,' he wasn't running out on me, he was just saying what he thought. But I'd been thinking ever since the start of that Sunday morning that I'd have to push off on my own. Bob is all right, but you can take just so much of him. He wasn't young Lochinvar, and I didn't fancy any more nights in the cellar, so when he said that, tripping over the kerb in Charing Cross Road, I said: 'So am I,' and ran for that bus that was just starting up, and he stood rooted. I never will forget his face.

I wouldn't do that to him again. I see now that it was mean, although at the time I just did it without a second thought. That was the Before-Molly me. I'm nicer now, God help me, for I can't let the poor good woman think her efforts have been in vain. She never gives up on anybody. That's why I can't tell her. And I can't tell Em, because I never had a friend like her, and I never shall again, if she leaves me.

They don't know, and if I don't say anything, it will go away. Like when I used to see the Hood at night in the attic. If you pull the covers over your head and don't call out (who'd come anyway?), it will go away.

SPRING EXAMINATIONS were coming up at the college, and I was in a mild panic that I would fail and disgrace our bit of the family, and put Uncle Mark to the test of whether he was employing me for myself or for the clan.

I took no days off and no more long lunch hours. I took books home, those terrible books written by people with made-up Christian names who have never seen a supermarket, let alone a live customer. I studied some nights, and on the others I was busy being in love.

It didn't last very long, but while it did, it was incandescent. He was German (one more I couldn't bring home to my mother), with the romantic name of Gerhart.

66

He was a student too and we met every lunch-time and after work, and walked dreamily about and kissed on benches and in doorways. When you see someone else doing it, it's repellent. When you're doing it yourself, it's All the World Loves a Lover.

Gerhart took up all my free time and all my thoughts, including when I was supposed to be working. The only picture I had of him was creased and torn at the corners from too much handling. I showed it to my father and said: 'I am in love.' I can say that to him when I have had some wine and must talk or burst, and he will take it equably and not refer to it again if I don't want to. If I said it to my mother, she would either get in too deep and start worrying it like a rat, or say: That's all very well, but how will you feel about him five years from now? With someone like Gerhart, you are not even sure you'll know him five *days* from now.

While it lasts, however, it is consuming, and there is nothing else. Love is supposed to make you sweeter, kinder, a more 'fully realized person'. Actually, it makes you terribly self-centred. The Gerhart kind of love does anyway. When I got Mollyarthur's postcard, I realized with a shock of guilt that I hadn't been near Grove Lodge for almost a month, and had hardly thought about my friends there. I had written to Kate when the exam scare started, and then I met Gerhart in a banjo cellar where I had lost my cousin Derek in the noise and smoke, and that was it.

The postcard and the death of Gerhart came at the same time. We suddenly realized we had nothing to say to each other, having gabbled our life stories too exhaustively too soon, and the girl with the glaucoma eyes who had been warming herself at the outskirts of our fire came into her own.

When I got to the station that night, I telephoned home to ask someone to fetch me. My father came, although he was working, because of the sound of my voice. In his presence, I tore the photograph up into little pieces and dropped them with gracefully fastidious fingertips out of the window of his car.

'Now dust off your hands,' he said, so I did, and I felt very empty, not specifically for Gerhart because I didn't want him now, but for what he had supplied. At home, my father poured me a whisky, and my mother said, 'At her age, David,' but I am almost nineteen, for God's sake – nineteen! and handed me the postcard, picture up, to show she hadn't read it.

It wouldn't have mattered if she had, since it was incomprehensible to all but initiates. There were bluebirds on the front, carrying eggs in one of those things that are all handle and no basket. The message on the back said: 'What do? Need talk. All miss.'

I went to Grove Lodge the next evening. Kate wasn't home from work, but Molly and the children gave me such a welcome that I wondered how I could have stayed away so long. Molly was painting one of the upstairs rooms, with a table on its side across the doorway to keep the younger children from the paint pot. I sat on the upturned table edge and nursed the coloured baby, and Molly said: 'Tell me about it.'

She was the kind of woman who would never say: Where have you been? or: We thought you'd forgotten all about us, stressing your absence rather than your presence, so that you wished you never had come back.

'About what?' Ziggy rubbed his astrakhan head under my chin, sensuous as a cat. She went on painting, slapping on the wall colour like a craftsman, sure of me.

'Exams,' I said. 'I've had to work.'

'Not that hard. Not my Emma.'

'I've been in love, Moll. That's why I haven't come.'

'Tell me.'

'Well, there's this place they call the Banjo Room —' I started to tell her, sounding like one of the children recounting the story of a film. Kate came up the stairs, pale and dragging her feet, her eyes shadowed, but not with make-up, still wearing the red and white striped dress from the nursing home, and I related to them both the tale of Gerhart. Kate sat on the table edge with me and looked at her grubby little hands with the nails worn down square, and I was disappointed to find her monosyllabic, less interested than I wanted.

To spark her, I elaborated, made it more romantic than the doorway and cinema and coffee-bar stuff it had been; but even when I had Gerhart betrothed to an heiress in the Fatherland

and our renunciation a tragedy instead of a quiet fizzle, she only said: 'Is that right?' although Molly was enthralled.

I thought that Kate was annoyed because I had stayed away so long, and that made me angry too. If she was going to be stupid and cheap like that, why should I bother? I'd stay away longer next time. She might need me, but I didn't need her.

I thought all this resentfully, as I was putting Ziggy and Madeleine to bed in drawers in the linen cupboard because it was their room that was being painted, but I knew it wasn't true. I did need Kate in a way that was just as unexplainable and inescapable as our being so alike when all the outward circumstance of our lives was so different.

But I could need her and hate her at the same time, and love her and hate her too. We had a fight at supper because I said I liked her hair that length, and she said it looked awful and she supposed I thought she was growing it to be like me.

'Aren't you?' I asked, and she retorted that she was only growing it to spite the matron at the nursing home, who wanted her to cut it off, so not to flatter myself.

'Girls, girls,' said Mr Arthur mildly, putting chunks of cheese on his bread like a French roadmender. Kate told him to mind his own bloody business, so Molly sent her out of the room, and I stayed behind, uncomfortable, as if I had won some worthless battle by cheating.

'I like it when she punishes Kate,' George said, helping me to take out plates. 'She's too soft on her, because she's had a worse time than what we done, but she don't know the half of it, Mum don't.'

All Mollyarthur's foster-children call her Mum, except the temporaries, who call her Auntiemoll in one word like animal, and Kate who calls her Moll.

'The half of what, Georgie?' He is a bright child, with red hair flopping over the scars of the car crash that robbed him of his parents.

'Nothing much,' he said, fixing me with his eye to see how much he should tell. 'She hits the littleuns though. You should see.'

'You're making it up.' Georgie had once said he was on the

bottom of the sea for three days with an octopus, to cap one of our inventions.

'Am I then? Ask Maddy how she got them bruises then, only she can't talk. Mum thinks she fell out of bed.'

'Why don't you tell her?'

'Kate said she'd do us too if we told.'

'Told what?' But he burst suddenly into song and ran from me.

Just as well. If he was lying, I shouldn't encourage him. If it was true, I didn't want to know. It could be true and yet not true. A slap isn't cruelty. Madeleine might be an easy bruiser, as well as a mewling child, born to annoy. Who in this world could swear that they never laid a finger on any child, ever? I once struck out in exasperation at my sister's boy, and went in terror that I had made him an idiot. I've seen even Molly smack a child a bit too hard for trying to drive her up the wall. She's not a saint. Well, she is, but the earthy kind, with all the natural instincts.

Molly came into the kitchen and shut the door in case Kate was going to come back.

'I've got to tell you what I think,' Molly said. It isn't often her face falls out of its smile, but this was one of the times.

She told me, and I said quickly: 'She's put on weight with your cooking, that's all.'

'But you see how she is. She was so happy. She isn't any more.'

'I thought she was upset because I stayed away too long.'

'Kate's not that dependent,' Molly said. 'She's had too many things taken away from her in her life to show she minds. If you died, she'd be destroyed, but she'd not let it show.'

'Why don't you ask her?'

'I can't, if she doesn't tell me.'

'You want me to ask her. Is that why you sent the postcard?'

'Oh no, Emma.' Molly put her hand on my arm, shocked. 'I just wanted to talk to you, because I don't know what to do.' I had never heard her say that. 'I'm supposed to report it to the Council, anything like this, but she'd have to be examined.

Perhaps forcibly. That's what happened at the Remand Home. They had to tie her down. Not good.'

I went up to Kate's room at the top of the house. It is just a little slit of space wide enough for the bed, and I leaned over the knobbed brass rail at the foot and looked at Kate lying there pretending to read her magazine. She didn't look like any of the girls have looked who have come to work for my mother, but then they don't look like anything special except themselves, dark or fair or black or white, and a bit bulkier.

I thought Molly was imagining, seeing pregnancy everywhere, like my mother since she took up her good work among the fallen. Anyway, you don't go into your friend's room and ask her if she's going to have a baby. You wait for her to tell you.

'Please come downstairs, Kate,' I said. 'I've brought you a record.' She grunted, moving her eyes moronically back and forth along the lines of the moronic movie magazine.

'Georgie told me you hit Madeleine,' I said, to make her look up.

'Georgie's a dirty little liar.' She sat upright and pressed the magazine down on her knees so fiercely that it tore. 'He tries to get me in trouble. He's jealous because Molly likes me the best.'

'He hasn't told Molly.'

Her tight little face relaxed. 'She wouldn't believe it anyway. Only people like you would believe it.'

I would have hit her if the high end of the bed hadn't been in the way. I took my chest off it and tried to calm down. 'Why are you so vile?'

'I don't feel well. I'm tired.' She began to whine, sticking out her lip. 'The work's too hard, and Matron is a bloody slave-driver. The nurses make me sick, starching around and leaving all the dirty work to me. Joan too, that lazy sow. All she does is tell tales on me.'

'If you're going to be miserable,' I said, 'I'm off. I wish I hadn't come.'

Kate suddenly plunged on her knees to the foot of the bed and grabbed my hand. 'I'm glad you came,' she said. 'I missed you, Em. Don't leave me.'

'Never,' I said. It was all over, the trouble, whatever it had been.

'Get my hairbrush.'

It was a hard one, with plastic bristles set in rubber. Kate banged it on the back of my hand and then on hers and we both had to whirl our hands round and round until the blood started in tiny points where the bristles had hit. Taking my hand, she pressed the back of it against the back of hers and mingled our slippery blood.

'Blood comrades,' she said, and her eyes were flat and staring, like a sleepwalker.

I felt a bit dizzy and the back of my hand was like a nutmeg grater, but Kate was content. She came downstairs with me then and we played the new record, and Jim Arthur gave us each a glass of warm beer and we sat on the floor in the room while he and Molly played draughts, and started to kid each other along over the beer until we were back into one of our old games again.

I was once more Mollyarthur's foster-child, a baby abandoned under a church pew in a cricket bag – that was from Jim, who joined in with a great Ho ho, from relief at Kate's change of mood.

I was a gipsies' child, brought up to beg and steal. I was the bastard of one of the royal family, a Cinderella drilling through my fingernails with a sweatshop sewing-machine, unable to read or write, I was a drudge, a slave, my parents had sold me to a wicked step-uncle who ran a supermarket with cheap labour and at night I bedded down in a dark cellar among the rabbit corpses with their heads in the bloody buckets. We were working each other up wildly, as if we'd had six beers instead of one, and suddenly Kate's voice went up hysterically on a laugh that turned into a sob and she screamed: 'No!'

She stood up, tense, her hands in quivering fists. Molly and Jim sat with their heads turned, Jim's hand frozen half-way across the board, and I sat staring on the floor unable to move as a torrent of shouted, incomprehensible words began to pour from her like a haemorrhage.

No! No! It wasn't like that. Where I slept in the cellar, it wasn't dark because the street lamp shone in all night through the railing in the pavement and I could see the bottom of the people's filthy shoes going over it so I couldn't sleep, and I laid there sweating, because of Miss Fern and wanting to be clever.

It's never dark in town. It's in that mucky country where the village kids thought my mother was a witch because of where we lived, and the attic was black, and the Hood used to come down at the end by the trapdoor. Nights when there was moon, it was all right. Nights when they stayed home, I could hear them banging about downstairs. Mostly it was him yelling. Once one of them fell down so hard the whole house shook, and my bed moved. They were in the dark downstairs too because there weren't any more candles. I bathed myself in the moon. I sung to it. But it always got little again.

That time they went to the seaside, I stayed awake all night with the moon, but they never come back. No, it was the street lamp. Lord's Lane, that must have been, because I sat by that window all the time behind the curtain so no one would see. None of their bloody business. Mrs Elia, she used to give me biscuits on the street. I buried them in the backyard in case they went off again, and then they did, and I couldn't find Mrs Elia's biscuits.

I used to bury sweets too, and ha'pennies, things people give me. They'll find it all one day, like history. I had threepence, but the door was locked and I couldn't get out. It was always night-time. Once I jumped out of bed and ran in to her to wake her up, and she held me. He wasn't there. Once after he hit her, she come and woke me up, all crying, with her hair all over and her dress torn, and laid down with me and we told stories and I was her mother and made her feel better.

Lay down, I said the next night, lay down with me, but she flicked me on the face and called me a dirty name.

Cold. Coming home from school, it was always cold, empty. Last one to go, Miss Fern said. If you like school so much, why don't you come more often? She give me a book about King Arthur, mystic, wonderful. You can sell books for tuppence down the Lane. He took the other ones too she give me. Where's your mum? the truant man said. At work. The nursery won't take the baby no more, because of his head. He was all wool, lovely little bootees she'd made, with bows. At school, we had hot dinners. The lady give me some shoes because mine were too small. Where'd you get them? I wasn't afraid of him. I used to spit, to show that. Get your hands off her. She'd have six pair like that if it wasn't for you. She was standing up in the middle of the room, holding the baby. She'd washed her hair in Lux and it was soft with the light all round it, saintly.

When I was a kid, she told him, I wanted for nothing, and she was so beautiful, remembering, I put my arms round her legs, but she was staring out the window at the flats and didn't notice.

All right – she was beautiful! I told her. That was when we were in the shop and she was crying because all the money had gone buying it and it was all broken stuff where the boys had got in while it was empty, and none but me and her to clear up. The little kids were crying from the journey and we gave them cornflakes from the shelves and a can of milk and there was still some chocolate the boys hadn't taken. She was crying after, when we went into the shop and started to kick the boxes and rubbish into a corner. Let's take the kids and go before he comes back, somewhere he'll never find us.

You don't understand, you don't understand. She was still crying and she looked so ugly and awful I had to tell her. You're beautiful. I run out then into the street, because I – because I – I —

M O L L Y A N D Jim and I all moved together. I got to her first and put my arms round her. She was sobbing dryly as if she had been running.

'We love you, Kate,' I said. 'Don't cry, it's all right. I love you.'

I L O V E you, Kate.

I love you, I said to her in the shop when she was crying and ugly. I was running. I waited behind that bit of wood fence, but she didn't call me back.

Get your hands off me – let me go! I hate you! There was a black hole in her face and the words coming out of it and beating on my hands over my ears where he put his cigarette on me to burn me. We don't want you and my hand was on fire when I put it to my mouth. We don't want you and he laughed and I was screaming rot in hell —

A B O U T A week after that hellish night when Kate hit out at me and fell on the floor screaming and Jim dashed a glass of beer on her because it was the first thing to hand, I came out of the subterranean college cloakroom and found Molly waiting for me at the top of the steps. No babies in sight, and no smile either.

I was going to ride to the station on the back of Sean's scooter, but when I saw Molly, childless, unsmiling, I took the scarf off my head and told him: 'Don't wait. I'm not coming.'

'Why not?'

'I want to talk to a friend.'

'Oh.' He assessed Molly rudely from under his hair, taking in the neat agreeable look of her: good legs, bright colours, no style, and walked away without responding to her friendly smile.

'Have I spoiled something?'

'He saves me bus fare. What's up?'

She took my arm and walked me away from a crowd of people coming up the steps. 'Have you seen Kate?'

'Not since I came back to your house to see if she was all right, and she pretended not to remember what happened.'

'She didn't come home last night. She's gone.'

'Where?'

'I don't know.' We were standing by the pillar-box, whispering for some reason, although no one was listening on the hurrying street. 'Yes, I do though, Emma. I think she's gone home.'

'To her mother and father? After what she —?'

'Listen.' Molly stepped aside for a girl with a bundle of

letters, and drew me close to her. 'Quite a long time ago, she took some coal. She put it in a potato sack and hid it in the toolshed. Ralph told me. It was there for weeks and now it's gone. I'm not going to tell the probation officer, but I wanted to see you before I went to her home.'

'Let me go.' Molly didn't know I'd been to Butt Street. No one did except Johnny Jordan.

'No, I'll go. I can stop in and see poor old Mr Bluett in the council flats over there.' It was typical of Molly that even in a crisis, she could plan to kill two birds with one stone.

'I'll come with you.'

'Not a deputation. We might scare them if she's not there.'

'Suppose she's with Bob again?'

'I thought of that. I could find him. I know where he lives.'

'Let me. Let me do it all, Moll.' I am shorter than her, and will never have her sense if I live to be a hundred, but for the moment I felt taller, wiser, in charge. 'I'll go to Bob and then I'll go to her home.' I was scared, but I would go.

Bob lived on the top floor of a house like Mr Jordan's: bow-windowed, with a little Swiss porch over the door and a few laths laid into the stucco for timbering, the roof part of a gabled pattern all down the street. Here the pattern was in steps, each identical house a few yards above the other, parallel up the steep hill.

Most of the miles and miles of boarding-houses in London were never meant for more than one family, but the tall, pillared terraces seem to take to it naturally. These decorated villas seem more violated by the occupying army of multi-coloured lodgers. When I rang Bob's bell, panting from the climb, it should have been his family home, and a warm round mother like a scone should have opened the door in a floury apron and asked me in.

But his mother was in Belfast and no one ever said anything about his father, so here he was, and the woman who opened the door with a jerk, as if she were at war with the stuck hinges, didn't smell of baking, and she shut the door half-way when she saw me, to keep me outside.

This must be the famous Mrs Marbles with her passion for

offal, who fed Bob on stewed heart and blood pudding. When I asked for him, she said: 'He's not here,' and I thought Oh God, he and Kate have gone, and now there'll be trouble.

'Not home, you mean,' I asked nervously, 'or not living here any more?'

'If I answered every meddlesome question put to me,' Mrs Marbles said, sighting down her thin red nose as if I were a rabbit, 'I'd have time for nothing else. There was a girl here only yesterday with a whole impertinent list. Why should I tell her what brand of washing powder I use? If you're one of those, you're wasting your time, for I'll not disclose the secrets of my sink.'

'Oh, I'm not. I'm a friend of Bob's.'

'A good friend?'

'Yes.'

'Well then, you should know where he is,' said Mrs Marbles triumphantly and shut the door.

It was clear that Bob had gone, and she was covering, not for him, but because she wasn't going to be caught not knowing. Or had she been bought off with the bag of coal to foil pursuers? If Kate was with Bob, she wasn't at Butt Street, but I had told Molly that I would go there, so I must. I would ask loudly for something in the little shop, and if Kate was there, by some freak, she would hear my voice and come out.

I was striking off again down the hill into the western sun that was pinkening the villas and the faces of the children in the street, when a voice hooted, 'Em!' at me, and there was Bob.

He hurried across from the other side of the road without looking at the traffic, and grinned and waved at a car which squealed to a stop.

'Hullo, dear,' Bob said, standing in front of me with his hands hanging and his head on one side. 'Fancy meeting you here. This is my street.'

Bob always uses the possessive adjective, like a child. My street, instead of Where I live. I read it in my paper. What's for my supper?

'I know,' I said. 'I've been to the house. She told me you weren't there, and I was afraid – I thought —'

'Meeting at my works,' Bob said, in his bustling, trade union voice. 'Very important. You come to get me? Are we going to the pictures then?' He and Kate and I have been to the cinema a few times, which he adores, sitting between us, with his eyes bulging at the screen and his mouth full of nuts and chocolate. 'Where's Katie then? Didn't she come with you?'

Thank God. He wasn't capable of having her hidden away somewhere without giving it away.

'Bob, where can we talk?' The pavement was full of running children and home-going men pressing up from the station, and the street was full of old cars and puny vans struggling up the hill in low gear.

'What do you mean?' Bob almost never talked. He listened.

'Can we go up to your room?' At the idea of trying to sneak past Mrs Marbles, watchdog at the secret sink, we both laughed. So we walked for a bit and I told him Kate was gone, breaking it with a gentle tact, which was quite wasted since he didn't even show distress.

I tried to find out if he knew anything, but all I could get from him were a few irrelevant things about Kate, and something vague about the Australian, which I could not get him to remember. In the end we got on a bus and rode to a place behind a tiled public house where the buses end by running into different concrete slots for each route number. I told him that if I didn't find Kate, she would fetch up in court again and so would he if he knew anything about it.

I thought he was listening to me, but he was watching the buses come in to the terminus, and when I said: 'Tell me the truth, Bob,' he said: 'Isn't it a marvel how each bus knows which hole to go into?'

He had taken a little tin soldier from his pocket as we sat in the empty bus, and his hands were never still, turning the toy over and over, stroking it, tapping it with a black nail, following its outline with the tip of a wondering finger as if it were a lover's face. He was tired of me because we were not going to the pictures after all. He either did not take it in about Kate, or else in the world he has always known to be missing is not a crisis.

When I left him, I said: 'I'll let you know,' and he said: 'About what?'

Big dreaming idiot. Why couldn't he have known where Kate was? Now I had to go on. The walk with Bob, the ride on one of the homing-pigeon buses, the frustrating conversation had all been to put off having to do what I had known all along was inevitable.

It was getting dark. It was getting late. Now I would have to go back to Butt Street.

THE DAMN buzzer went like a bluebottle just as we were having supper. Dad swore and Tony copied him and my mother said: 'Shut up that, you little bastard,' so I said something worse and he and she both turned on me.

It was just like old times, and I wondered how long I could stand it this trip. I'd thought it would all be different. Shows what stupid ideas you get, from a distance. I'd thought I'd come back and say: 'I'm going to have a baby,' and she'd take me in and say: Don't worry, and understand why I had to come home.

Instead she spoke first, before I could get a word in. 'Why have you come back?'

I said: 'I got fed up,' because I knew then I couldn't say: I'm going to have a baby and if Molly finds out she'll have me put away.

I've heard about those places they send girls. No thanks.

Loretta was the only one who was really pleased to see me. The boys don't care, and Dad and Mother – well, they didn't exactly throw me out, but they made it clear this was no place for me. They wanted to send me right back, but I said: 'Let me stay a couple of days and get my breath.'

They're afraid they'll get into trouble, since I'm on probation. Ever since the court, she said, there's been people snooping, bothering, fussing about Loretta. She's afraid the Cruelty Man will come back, although she fed his ear for good last time, him and some girl who was with him. She had a long hank of hair, my mother said (that stuck in her throat because

79

although she wears hers down, which she shouldn't at her age, it never grows past her shoulder blades). A bloody great long hank of hair, she said, and it made me think of Em. I'd die before I'd let her see any of this. I felt queer because I don't know where I belong any more.

It's stupid to keep the shop open so late, but it's the time for cigarettes, after the men get home and find the old woman's smoked the lot, so they send one of the kids out for that, or for something she's forgotten, and they have to come to us because everywhere else is closed. Nice way to do business. You only get the customers when they're desperate.

We were having supper, so in the end, because I was nearest the door, it was me got up to go into the shop when the buzzer rang.

As soon as I saw her, I knew. It had been her came with the man. She knows him. I should have guessed when my mother said that about the hair, only I was seeing her too clearly at Molly's then. Not here. Spying on me, sneaking in. How dare she?

'Hullo, Kate,' she said.

'Hullo yourself.'

S H E   W A S going to turn back into the room behind, but I grabbed her. 'No, Kate. Talk to me a minute.'

She looked over her shoulder, then shut the door on the grumbling hubbub within and stepped behind the counter, just like her mother had done.

'I'll talk to you,' she said, leaning forward on her fingertips. 'I'll talk to you about spying here behind my back.'

'I didn't know we were coming here,' I said, my mouth dry and my stomach contracted in the alarm of being found out. 'I mean, when we came, I didn't know it was your family. Don't you believe me?'

'No.' Kate was too practised with lies not to recognize mine. 'Well, you saw, didn't you? You saw what you wanted. What did you have to come back for?'

'To find you.'

'What made you think I'd be here?'

'It's your home.'

She made a face. 'I haven't got a home.'

'Molly's worried,' I said, 'and I was too. Come back with me, Kate. There'll be trouble with the court if you don't.'

She didn't say anything. She leaned on the counter and stared at me, but she was still Kate, still my friend, so I went forward and put my hand over hers, the child's hand with the bitten finger-nails, and asked her if she was going to have a baby.

I have never seen Kate spit. She spat then, and it hit my hand. Then she called me a bloody social worker and went into the back room.

Kate had to go back to Molly's of course, since the court had placed her there. Her parents didn't want her anyway. She had to go back to work too, and I wished, as I had many times before, that I could get her out of that unlovely dead-end job and into something worthwhile.

Mollyarthur was ill. 'I'm never ill, I haven't time.' She fought it for long enough to make herself worse, and finally collapsed on the bed and into a sleep which had been owing to her for years.

I went every afternoon to help. I'd do anything for Molly. Anyone would. I was there one day, mopping the kitchen floor, with three of the children sloshing about barefoot in the soapy water. The knocker on the front door thudded like doomsday and I paddled down the hall in my bare feet, the children trailing after me like a brood of ducklings.

The woman on the doorstep had a pug nose and a bulldog jaw and a yapping terrier voice, dog all over. She asked for Molly and when I said she was ill, she stepped into the hall without being asked and said: 'Then you can give her a message for me. Are you the maid?'

I said: Yes, although with a brief child's apron that said Mother's Little Helper and my hair screwed up on my head in a lopsided ball with two knitting-needles which Carol had thrust through it, I didn't look like a maid anyone would ever employ.

81

'You can tell her it's about Katherine,' the dog woman said, humping her large brown plastic bag higher under her arm, as if the children were pickpockets.

'Nothing wrong I hope?' A relation of one of the patients? A back-room girl from the Children's Department?

'Merely that I cannot employ her any longer.'

'Oh, you're the Matron.' It figured. Kate had described her as being without any recognizable human feature, either of body or soul. 'I'm sorry you're not satisfied. Katherine has worked so hard to please you.' I bared my teeth in what she could take as a smile if she chose.

'If so, which I doubt, then she has failed. It's no business of yours, but I cannot have that kind of girl in my Rest Home.'

Some rest. The way Kate described it, the old people incarcerated therein would get no rest until the final one.

'There's nothing wrong with Kate,' I said angrily. 'What's wrong with her?'

'If you don't know,' said the Matron, 'which is unlikely, since you seem to be very familiar in this house, then I shall tell you.' She glanced at the barefoot, open-mouthed children, saw that they were too young to understand, and said: 'The girl is pregnant.'

'That's a lie. How dare you say that? It's libellous.' I wouldn't have been so angry, I suppose, if I hadn't known at the back of my heart, ever since Molly suggested it, that it was true. The truer it was, the less I wanted to hear it, especially from this woman.

'Don't shout at me!' Matron shouted in a nurse-lashing tone which must once have woken all the sleepers in the ward. 'If you're trying to tell me I don't know pregnancy when I see it, you've come to the wrong shop.'

'What's going on?' Molly appeared at the top of the stairs in her blue woollen dressing-gown with her hair on end. 'What's the matter, Emma? Oh, it's you, Matron. Is there something I can do for you?'

'You can explain to the Council why I can't employ Katherine any more.'

'Yes, I see. Well, she couldn't have stayed much longer anyway.'

A lot of the wind went out of Matron's sails when she found that she couldn't shock Molly as she had shocked me. 'What are you going to do about it?' she asked. 'The girl is in your care.'

Molly weaved a little on the top step, but put her hand on the banister post and answered with dignity: 'It's perfectly all right. Kate is going to be married.'

Matron yapped a bit more about social duty and ingratitude and learning her lesson, and when she had gone, Molly sat down on the top step and laid her head against the wall.

'If you send me there when I am old,' she said, as I went up to her, 'I'll hang myself with the sheets.'

I WAS knitting something. I'll never finish it, but Moll had cast it on for me, and she likes to see me knit. I'd nicked some toy soldiers from my mother's shop while I was there, and Bob was on the floor with them, making them drill round the leg of a stool.

'Molly thinks we ought to get married, Bob,' I said.

He smiled up at me, his soft black hair over his eye, game for anything, then went back to his soldiers, pushing out his lips in little band sounds as he marched them.

'I couldn't marry you, Bob. It would be like marrying a child.'

'Yes, that's right,' he agreed.

SHE CAN'T marry Bob. She can't. Molly says that she should but Molly, though liberal in many ways, is surprisingly stuffy about this. Not angry with Kate, just stuffy. She'll help her, but on her own terms, and her terms don't include fatherless babies. She has had enough of them as fosters, Lord knows, but perhaps that's why.

Things like this set up barriers between generations. It's like talking about the war to someone who is old enough to have been grown up then. It has never quite left them, and it shuts you out.

Molly is thirty-four. I am nineteen. We are the same age in outlook, until something like this comes up. She is rigid. A baby means marriage.

But marriage is the purpose, not the expedient. I argue with her all over the house. 'To chuck away your life for an unborn baby who will never thank you anyway. Who ever thanks their mother for giving birth to them, let alone making a sacrifice of it? Suppose you make her marry Bob, and the baby is born dead. What then?'

She was cleaning windows, standing on a stool to reach the top panes in one of the high Victorian rooms. I did not offer to help, because I was angry with her. 'She'll still have Bob.'

'That's the trouble.'

'Bob's all right. He's not as simple as he looks. He earns a good enough wage and he's reliable.'

'So is a chair leg.'

'He's worse with Kate because she orders him about and makes him more childish.'

'She doesn't want to marry him.'

'How do you know? She hasn't said she won't.'

'She hasn't said she will.'

Kate won't make any decisions. She sits about looking slightly bloated, eating chocolate and reading in a pair of glasses with plain lenses because she wants to look intellectual. If you try to make her plan, she says: Plenty of time, as if the baby wasn't coming for twenty-four months, instead of six.

I could kill her for letting this happen, just for the sake of a few minutes' dubious fun in that ridiculous high iron bed wedged so tightly into her room under the roof that you have to climb in over the end of it. She told me where, although she hasn't told Molly, because she was supposed to be baby-sitting.

She has messed up everything, just when she had the chance of a life with something better in it than the poverty and dirt and fighting squalor she ran away from. I even find myself wishing she had the sense to get rid of the thing. She won't, I know, and I feel guilty when the wish passes through my mind unbidden. But thoughts are not crimes, I suppose, unless you grab at them as they go by.

Now I have an idea. It is the idea to end all ideas, and I

shall carry it through in the gnashing teeth of all opposition. Here at last is something I can do for somebody. I am selfish. I am an inflated egotist. I feel no urge to help the whole of suffering humanity, but I could help just this one small unit, since it would be for myself too.

Don't leave me, Kate said, and I said: Never. I could show her now that I meant it. It could be our baby. Mine too. We could bring it up together. I could get her a job in one of the B.B. markets, if Uncle Mark doesn't fire me. We could share the flat I am going to have next year. People could think it was my baby if they liked. I wouldn't care. No harm in being thought an unmarried mother if you're not. We could call it Kathaline, from both our names. Paint its room yellow. Get a kitten for it. A rocking-horse. A tricycle. Take it to the sea.

Kate caught fire on the details. She said at first: 'Oh, can it,' then gradually woke from lethargy to enthusiasm, until we were throwing ideas back and forth like ping-pong balls.

'We'll do the cot up in roses, have one of those rugs with all pictures, wheel out a pram and have everyone turn and stare after us because we are so young and pretty.'

'On Sundays. It will have to go in a nursery while we're at work and we can take turns fetching it and baffle everyone.'

'Should we have our hair down or up? We'd want to make a good impression.'

'Mature, mysterious, enriched by motherhood. Let's do the flat all white, with blood-coloured curtains.'

'Oh, Em. We could have steak and hot chocolate every night and never go to bed. We could have real parties, with me in coloured waistcoats and give them spaghetti and wine, like they do. Oh, Em —' She looked at me with a strange shining simplicity, all her defences down. 'I could be like you.'

I am terribly happy. Life has suddenly a huge and brilliant purpose, which makes me see that before there were only negative purposes: things I didn't want to do, people I didn't want to get mixed up with, the kind of person I didn't want to be. How could I, even fleetingly, have wished the baby dead? Now that it is partly mine, I begin to feel the same ache for it as for that wretched scabrous child I nursed in the cold railway-carriage room I went to with Mr Jordan, where they threw the tin-cans into the empty grate.

Frustrated motherhood? Why not? I am nineteen. Some of my friends are married, none of them to anyone I'd be seen dead with, let alone conceive by. Now I can have the baby without a husband.

'You're mad,' Alice said. 'People will say you're queer. The next thing we know, you'll be breeding cairns and live in Essex.'

She had come for the week-end with her husband and children. It was like dropping into a warm bath of the past. Marriage has matured her outwardly, but she can still shriek with laughter like we used to, scattering small rugs all over the house. She lives too far away. I always forget how much I like her until I see her again.

I had come home excited, crashing into the house in a rude sort of glow, and found her coming down into the front hall with that knock-kneed Alice waddle, and spilled it all out to her on the stair carpet.

'They'll hear you.' She looked at the drawing-room door. Alice is a secret person, afraid of trouble. My father used to be rather brutal with her at times, because she was fat and un-lucky, with a nervous compulsion to say the wrong thing. She is still plump now, but attractive, I think, because I admire women who don't show their bones like I do. She is the wife of a Birmingham gynaecologist, ten years older, whose patients fall morbidly in love with him, to no avail. This has given her some poise, but she has never lost her fear of being caught out. If Gordon complains, she jumps to make excuses or to do something she has forgotten, nervously, as if she were afraid of him. He is not frightening. He is large and golden like a well-washed retriever, with a voice that is balm to women in their hour of need.

'Don't talk so loud.' The finger to the lip was a familiar gesture.

'I'm going to tell them anyway.'

'Not tonight. Don't spoil the evening. There's lobster, and everyone is happy. Don't upset them.'

I knew who she meant. Nobody bothers much about upsetting my mother, because her outlook is so defeated already that one more disillusionment won't hurt. I have given up trying to hoist her into life on my shoulders. She has always slipped back, missing the fun, the new experiences, the stunts. Alice has never been afraid of her, but she has always tried too hard to placate my father, and it doesn't work with him as it does with Gordon, who absorbs it blandly, like a sponge. If my father shouts, it's better to shout back.

I got him out of the drawing-room on a pretext, and told him alone, in the little room across the hall. It isn't fair to lump him as an audience with my mother, because he can understand, and she has to have it spelled out. What do you mean? is her first reaction to startling news, and it slows things up.

'You remember that girl in court when I was there, the one who ran away from home?'

'I remember a thousand girls in court who've run away from home.'

'The one who screamed out at her father, and he stood there like a brutal ox, as if he didn't care.'

He remembered. 'Rather an appealing child, under the dirt and fury. I sent her to that insatiable woman with all the children. I wonder what happened to her. I never know unless it's the worst, and they come back to court.'

'She's changed,' I said. 'It's wonderful. There was so much in her that had been crushed and smothered by that ghastly home. If you had sent her back there, she'd have killed someone, or herself. Now she's my friend. I've been going to Molly-arthur's, and we have become best friends.'

I sounded like my past self telling him about some school-girl crush. She's my best friend. She's moved her desk next to mine. I could almost feel the serge of my gym tunic.

'Why haven't you told me about her?' He was leaning on the mantelpiece in his charmer pose, his head slightly tilted and the foot of his bad leg on the fender. He wasn't trying to charm me. He just looked charming.

'I thought you'd disapprove. Or laugh.'

'Have I ever?'

I wanted to say Yes, but I said: 'No.'

87

'I'd like to meet her. Why don't you bring her home?'

He should know why. 'I had been going to ask you if you'd come to Molly's house. I wanted to show them to you and you to them. But then I thought that it might come between Kate and me, because you're not like anybody she's ever known. No, it wasn't really that. It was – oh hell, Daddy, I'm such a coward. I'm afraid to risk an idea in case it doesn't work, and I will have lost even the idea.'

'You usually jump in with both feet, all the same.'

'I'm going to now. You'll meet her now. I've had this superb idea, and I'm going through with it whatever anybody says, because it's what I want and it's what she wants.'

Too belligerently, expecting him to protest at any moment, I told him about the flat, and getting Kate a job, and that when her probation was over next year he must free her to go where she liked. Then I stopped and looked at him because his face was giving nothing away, and I didn't know how he was taking it.

'Go on, please,' he said, as if I were a hesitant witness.

My throat was tight, but I got it out. 'She's going to have a baby. She can't marry the boy. He's not very bright, and she – she's really intelligent, in spite of her family, like a swan in a cuckoo's nest. She and I are going to bring the baby up between us. It will be ours. Mine if people want to think that. I shan't care what anyone thinks, and you mustn't either, because this is the one thing I want more than anything in a whole lifetime of wanting.'

He didn't say anything for a little while, just stood and looked down at me where I was sitting on the stool with my hands round my knees, clutching them white. He is so damn attractive. Not only to me. I see the way other women look at him, with speculation. The lines are deepening in his face, but his eyes will never fade and grow dull, even if he becomes a helpless old man, bullied by some matron like Kate's dog woman. If the iridescent grey of his hair flattens to white, his eyes will still be deeply, dramatically blue.

'You've made up your mind,' he said at last, not as a question.

I nodded, rocking backwards with my feet off the floor, hanging on to my knobbly knees.

'You can't expect me to like it.'

'You will, when you know Kate, when you see how well it works out.'

'Suppose I don't give you a chance to let it work out?'

'You can't stop me. I'll be earning. I'll be independent. You can't make me a ward of court for wanting to share a flat with a girl friend.'

'And a baby.'

'The baby's incidental. It goes with the girl friend.'

'If the father is not very bright, the child might not be either. Have you thought of that?'

'I've thought. All the more reason to help.'

'I like you, Emma,' he said. 'I like the way you set your heart on things. Your mother has never wanted anything really badly in her life.'

'Except you.'

'That was easy. She didn't have to fight for it. Her family liked me in their grudging, noncommittal way.'

'If I was asking you to let me marry someone horrible, what would you say?'

'The same, I suppose.'

'The same as what? You haven't said anything.'

'It's your life, Emma, that's all. It's your life, not mine. God knows what people are going to think, but if you don't care, I'll try not to either. The older I get, the less I care what people say, and I wish I hadn't wasted so much time caring in the past. I'm glad you don't. I like you, girl.'

'I like you, Bullock.' I got up and kissed him. 'Will you back me with —' I jerked my head towards the hall, where I heard my mother's voice, and her terrier's nails headed for the kitchen on the polished floor.

'She won't like it.'

'I don't care. Is that cruel? I'm just telling you. I don't care.'

'At least pretend. To me as well, if you want me on your side.'

'Tell her for me.'

'Tell her yourself.'

'I can't. She'll offer to take Kate into the kitchen. It's the only way she knows to deal with pregnancy.'

He laughed. I can always make him laugh, and I stretched my arms high up above my head and felt absolutely wonderful and he saw it, and I said: 'This will be the first good thing I have ever done in my life.'

'You're always doing good things.'

'Name one.'

He couldn't, so I asked him then about the money, and if he would lend me enough later on to add to the sixty pounds I had already saved for plastic surgery for Kate.

I had not meant to ask him yet, but he was going to the South of France for a holiday, and I was afraid to wait until he came back, in case his mood had changed.

'Don't you mind him going without you?' one of us asked my mother when she came into my bedroom to tell Alice that one of her children looked flushed.

'What do you mean, mind?' she asked, a little flushed herself.

'Whose idea was it – his or yours?'

Alice was in my bed, bosomy in an expensive nightgown, and I was sitting on the side, pounding my hair with a brush, letting it fall sideways in a spread curtain through which I saw my mother fiddling with things on the dressing-table, talking to her own face, not to us.

'I didn't want to go, Emma. I've told you that.' She stared at the mirror, her face dramatically lit from below, full of strange glows and shadows because she was standing higher than the lamp. 'They're his friends. I've hardly even met them, and it was obvious they only asked me because it would have looked odd otherwise.'

Alice gave an impatient exclamation. 'Don't fish.'

'They're too rich, I couldn't have stood it. And they're intellectual. They play clever games after dinner. I got into that once. Your father was in his element, of course, but I felt an idiot.'

I could imagine her suffering glumly, unable to go home because he would not take pity on her for not trying.

'In any case,' she said firmly to the mirror, 'it does us good to get away from each other now and again. People must lead their own lives, you know, even when they've been married for more than twenty-five years. My hair has kept its colour well though, I'll say that,' she added, as if marriage were a greying ordeal.

She stayed talking with us for a while about past things, indulging herself in the illusion of the three of us together at bedtime, as we used to be before Alice married, before I grew up. She said no more about the south of France holiday, and nor did we, because Alice and I were both aware of her futile pretence of thinking that by not bothering him, she could preserve a relationship already disintegrated.

When she had gone to her room with its familiar smell of dog on the bed and her innocuous scent, Alice said abruptly: 'Do you think he's got a woman?'

'Oh my God, no. He'd *never*.' I thought she was pretty filthy even to think of it, but she has never known him as well as I do. He has always liked me best, and she knows it. But that gives her even less right to lie in my bed with her round chin on her nightdress ribbons and say that. If anything is going to be said, I'll say it.

He had told me that he would find out the name of a surgeon who might do the operation on Kate's neck, but then he went away without remembering.

'Oh Lord, I forgot,' he said at the airport. I said it didn't matter, because it could not be done until after the baby, but I had wanted to tell Kate that it was all fixed.

At the last moment, I said to him: 'Let me come with you!'

Did I really think he would say: Come on? He said, 'You haven't got any luggage.' He is getting very staid and middle-aged.

His flight was called, and I kissed him and left. As I went out through the main hall, a woman was coming through the doors from a car with all the bustle of an attractive woman arriving late, breathless, getting attention without demanding it.

I looked at her, because she was what I would never be at

that or any age, colourful, exciting, none of her ripeness lost, and saw that I knew her. It was the woman at the cocktail party who had told me to keep my father young after he had fallen off the horse.

As she went by me in her own little dramatic bustle of porters and airline officials and expensive luggage, she saw that she knew me, and said: 'Oh, hullo, how are you?' without knowing who I was.

Alice would have said that she was travelling with my father. It's surprising the mind she has under the nervous respectability. But that was impossible, since he had supposed that my mother would go with him, until last week when she said she wouldn't. I thought how middle-aged he had been when I said goodbye, and how short and British he had looked limping away down the passage to the passport desk with his stick and his raincoat, and I thought perhaps I ought to wish it possible, for his sake. But I will never allow him that.

I got through my examinations at the college and am going to be at the head office in the autumn, in something called Merchandising, where my cousin Derek works.

Derek and I either take or leave each other according to circumstance and the changing state of our glands. When we were small, we fought. When I was about twelve and he fourteen, we were in love, experimentally. Then we lost interest, then came together again in an unpassionate liaison because we both had spots and could attract no other intimates, but veered away again as the surplus grease cleared from our skins and scalps and new worlds opened. Now we go out together from choice, not necessity, and use each other for confidences or boastful sublimations of adventures that are not quite so gaudy as the telling. We fight at times because we know each other too well, then suddenly come together in a moment's passion in a lull when no other is on tap.

Uncle Mark is afraid that we might eventually marry, which is perhaps why we are to be in the same department, because Derek at work is forgetful and cynical and at his worst. My mother knows that cousins who marry never have normal children. Query: Would she want to have Derek and me sterilized?

Until I go to the head office, I am sojourning, with pay, thank God, in the several B.B. supermarkets in various parts of London to see how the layout of the store affects the buying habits of the customers. It is very interesting. The traffic pattern varies, with the floor plan, from store to store, and even from district to district. In Edgware, for instance, the housewives head for the meat like jungle beasts, while south of Putney Bridge they must get their hands on a loaf of bread before they can look at anything else.

In Fulham, my Uncle Mark came to the store while I was there, and took a turn round the aisles as he often does, padding with his knees slightly bent and his hands behind his back, like a bearded undertaker. He wears the beard to cover a rifle wound, a brindle, crew-cut beard, which, although he has had it as long as I can remember, still looks as if it were hooked on behind his ears.

I don't often see him, since our two families don't mix very much, so I plucked up my courage to ask him about a job for Kate next winter. He is short-sighted, and at first he didn't recognize me in the white jacket with my hair braided round my head like an Austrian lieder singer. I have my own plastic label now that I am on the pay roll. Emmaline Bullock. Behind the meat counter, I look like part of the display.

He asked me what I was doing, and I told him that I was observing the effect on the customer of scaling dog-food prices from left to right in relation to the direction of their approach. Thank God I knew. He said: 'Good girl, Emma,' and I stepped in front of him as he was about to pad on, and asked him about Kate.

He said something about it probably being all right, but not to bother him now, and I saw it through his eyes. So unimportant as to be almost non-existent. One more girl among hundreds to stamp prices on tins, to weigh grapes and wrap them in cellophane, to erect Today's Bargain, tottering in an irresistible pyramid. Faceless to him they came and went. One left, there was always another to take her place.

SHE HAS asked her uncle about a job for me later, and he has as good as said Yes. I don't know what to do. I don't know how to tell her. I couldn't find the words. I can laugh and joke and make up silly stories, but I don't have the words to say the truth, not when it's too good, or too bad.

We have fun playing the game, planning all about the baby, and how we'll do up the flat, and the people we'll know and the parties we'll have and the fine new life that will come pouring into our laps day after day.

I could be like her. Different. I could be a girl who had never known Butt Street, never known that room in the attic, nights when there was no moon, nor no one else. I could do it too, I know I could. I talk different now, and I look better. With my hair in a long bell like this, and clean all the time, I look like anybody.

Em is so excited, like a child. She knows a lot of things I never will – there wouldn't be time in a whole life to learn all the things I don't know – but sometimes she's childish and I am years older. You need to live, cock, I tell her. But I'm glad she hasn't. Not my way.

She's like a bull when she gets an idea. I haven't the heart to say I can't go through with it. Or can I? I am at what they call a crossroads of my life. This is a crossroads of your life, one of the cows at Stinkney said. What are you going to choose?

As if there was any choice. Back to the court and they'll label you and send you off like a parcel. Thank God Em's father had the sense to ship me to Moll.

I stand at the crossroads and look at all the roads. When I've been with Em, I believe that it really can happen, and forget that it can't. She's steamed up to the lid on this one. The baby will be ours, and the hell with the rest of the world. But she can't say the hell with the world. I've got nothing to lose, but she . . . How can I do this to her?

I met Sonia at the library. Funny place to meet her, but she was waiting for the fellow she goes with now she's broken with Kev. They sit and talk there where it's nice and quiet, and the librarian, who is a real crackpot, thinks it's better than getting up to something on the streets.

She saw at once. Trust her. She didn't say anything about it, just asked if I wanted an address.

'Who?' I asked. We were by the fiction, DEL to HARM.

'One of the Indians. They'll fix you up if you've got the money.'

I gave her a pencil and she wrote the address on a corner torn off a newspaper and I put it in my pocket. This is it then. This will be the first good thing I have ever done in my life.

'YOU GOT any money saved, Em?'

'A little.'

'Fifty quid?'

'Yes.'

'Lend it to me.'

'What for?'

'It's to help someone.'

'Can they pay it back?'

'I don't know. Later maybe.'

'No, Kate, I can't.'

'You must. It's a matter of life or death.'

'It can't be as important as what I want it for.'

'What's that?'

'I wasn't going to tell you. I've been saving it to pay for a – for plastic surgery for you.'

'Then it's already mine, like.'

'In a way, but —'

'Please give it me. Cash, Em. You've got to give it me.'

'I'll get it tomorrow.'

BOB WAS ill in bed with the flu, and I went to Butt Street to get some more toy soldiers for him.

It's easy. What I do, I'm with them in the back room, and when the damn buzzer goes, I say: I'll go, very helpful, and as soon as the customer is gone, I nick the box of soldiers into the big pocket of my skirt, and there you are.

With Em's money burning a hole in my bag so hot you can almost see smoke coming out, I could buy him a whole army, but I'll need it all, Sonia says, and also it's more fun to steal from home.

When I went, my mother was hanging out clothes in the back yard, with her arms raised and her long back stretched, the way I used to see her in the country – the best times, when it was daylight – with the wind tearing the sheets away from her.

I had picked up Loretta on my way through, and she was crowing and playing with my hair, her silly face all grins.

'Hullo, Mum.' I thought I made a nice picture in the little bit of sun that slid between the wall and the bakery chimneys, one any mother would be glad to see.

'Why have you come here?' she said. 'You're not to come here no more.'

'Why not?' I tried to carry it off, very cool, very casual.

She was going to say: Because we don't want you, but she changed it to, 'Because of the court order.'

She picked up the rotten fruit basket she uses for the wash and turned to go indoors. I followed her and sat down by the table with Loretta on my knee and began to dab at the crumbs with a wet finger and eat them, which is the only way the tablecloth gets cleared.

'Just come to see how you were all getting along,' I said chattily. I had to stay long enough to get into the shop and knock off the soldiers.

'A lot you care,' my mother said. 'What's the matter with you? Your skin is all chalky.'

It flushed red. She had noticed something about me. Why should I care? I didn't. Not any more. I shifted Loretta a bit to cover my front, not that anything shows yet unless you know me well, and God knows my mother hardly knows what I look like by now.

Thank God I didn't tell them about the baby. Molly has been threatening to do it herself if I don't, but I've been putting it off. None of their business. I've heard them talk about other girls, without mercy. I'm not going to have them talk about me that way.

But now I won't have to tell. Now they'll never know. No one will. Em and me will start on our beautiful new life together, and no one will ever know.

The damn buzzer went. My mother was putting the washing-basket up on top of the leaning tower of cupboard, and I jumped up and dumped Loretta on the settee and went quickly through to the shop.

Foiled, curse it Jasper. It was Dad, home from a long run north by the looks of him, for his eyes were swollen and red from the driving and his mouth wet and loose from what he'd taken to wash away the taste of the road.

'What the bloody hell are you doing here?'

All right, all right, we've been through that. No sense everyone saying the same thing.

'It's my home.'

'Not no more.'

'Who says so?' I squared up to him very cocky, with my jaw stuck out and my head on one side. I like to do that because it makes him roaring mad. He took a swipe at me and I slipped through into the back room, and he followed me, roaring like the Zoo at feeding time.

'I thought you weren't due in till tomorrow,' my mother said, in charming welcome. The baby had woke up at the noise of him and was crying like all our babies have always done, Tony, Stewart, Loretta, as soon as they wake up and find it's true.

She picked him up off the pile of old stuff where he was wedged in the corner and held him, swaying and patting his back without knowing she was doing it.

'So that's it then,' he said. He put his little cracked suitcase down in the middle of the room, and when he stands like that, with his head forward and his hands hanging, he is more like a gorilla than he should admit to. 'You have her here when I'm gone, is that it? I thought I told you she wasn't to come here no more.'

'Think you can stop me?' I laughed at him, and that did it. He went for me and fell over the suitcase, reeled against the wall, catching himself with his hand flung out, then spun round and took a smash at my mother.

She turned just in time, or the baby would have got it, and took his hand on the back of her shoulder.

Loretta began to scream like a cockatoo. 'Don't you hit her!' I shouted, and even as I added my own noise to the menagerie, I saw very clear, like on a screen, the red and white flat and me and Em joking back and forth between the rooms as we got ready for a party, and felt sick and excited at how different it was going to be.

I've always sided with my mother against him, no thanks for it, but she expects it, and now she began to whine, thinking that I was back of her. She put the baby down, moaning to him what a bloody awful dad he had, and he hit her again and knocked her on the floor and she sat there, with her hair come out of the ribbon and hanging over her eye.

'Get the police, Kate,' she wailed. 'You saw what he done. Get the police, I can't stand no more.'

As I stood there in the stink and filth and hate of their living, a great sickness and weariness come over me, and I said: 'It's not my mess. Don't drag me into it any more. I got out. I'm free.'

'Help me, Kate.' She was pretending to be hurt, her hand on her empty breast.

'Why should I? It's your own bloody fault for marrying him.'

'I married him because of *you*!' She spat it at me from the floor. 'I tried to get rid of you, don't think I didn't, but I didn't do it right, and when it didn't work, I had to marry him. I hate you for it.'

'Didn't you know?' Dad said. He was leaning up against the broken mantelshelf, paring his nails with the knife she uses for vegetables. 'Didn't you know who put that mark on your neck? There's your proof that she tried to kill you before you was born.'

'I wish to *God* I had,' my mother said.

Now there is only Bob left. The dreams are all gone.

I went to his house, where he lives, and rang the bell. Mrs Marbles opened the door after a while and looked at me, and her thin eyebrows went up like whips because I was shivering and shuffling my feet.

When I asked if I could see Bob, she said No, with her mouth tight, and was going to shut the door, but I took a pull at myself and said, very grand: 'It's perfectly all right. We're going to be married.'

'And about time too,' she said, practically delivering the baby with her eyes.

Bob was in bed, lying quite flat, with his eyes shut and his chin over the patchwork counterpane, rimmed black with beard.

'You brought the soldiers?' he asked as soon as I came in the door, walking cautiously in case he was asleep. I shook my head and he was quite depressed. He began to pick at the counterpane, but when I sat down on it and took his hand to still it, and said: 'Let's get married,' he cheered up at once.

'Then the baby can be mine too?' He sat up, excited, with his hair in black points. I hadn't known he cared that much, but he cried, he was so happy.

I held him tight and said: 'It's all right, it's all right. I'll look after you. We'll have a little cottage,' I told him, 'with all hollyhocks and birds in the thatch and have currant loaves for our tea.'

He clutched me and purred, like he does, and it was like that time in the cellar, when we played house. 'You got any money, Katie?'

'Fifty quid. I'll buy you a suit to be married in. I'll buy you a fort, Bobby, and a big box of Life Guards, with silver-plumed helmets and black horses with long black tails with waves in them like a lady's hair.'

I was crying too, with my cheek laid on his poor hot head, and it was funny, because his tears were for finding a dream, and mine were for losing one.

Part Two

K A T E A N D Bob were married in a small grey church crushed between new towering flats like a child in a crowd. Bob's father was dead and his mother disinterested in Northern Ireland, and so there was nobody in church but me, Jim, Molly, Michael, Ralph, Susan, Carol, Tina, George, Madeleine, Ziggy and the twins.

Kate's mother and father must have known about the wedding, because they would have to give their consent. I risked asking her if they would come, and her face closed up, blank as an effigy, blind and deaf.

Sitting in the dark little church, trying to quiet the fretful twins, I was afraid that they might come after all, blundering in with drink on his breath and a trail of dirty children in hard banging boots. Afraid, yet almost hoping, for I could not imagine being married without one's parents. I could see myself even loving my mother in the prodigal benevolence of the day.

But the service was quickly over without them. I was the only one who twisted round expectantly when an old woman in a muffin hat creaked open the church door. Whatever had happened between them, they were dead for Kate, and she was dead for them.

They are living in Bob's room for the time being and have been promised a Council flat when the baby comes. 'Which if you get it,' Mrs Marbles says, 'will be entirely due to graft and influence and a crying scandal to the Lord, with so many waiting in vain.'

It would be hard to find anyone less likely to exercise graft or influence than these two babies, Mr and Mrs Robert Thomas, playing at house in a top-floor front with black and white chequered linoleum on which they play draughts with bottle tops. But Mrs Marbles has seen Mollyarthur, and recognized her with fury as the type who has an In with the Council.

I don't go often enough to see Kate and Bob. I tell myself that it is because there is no time, and it's true that I am all over London at the B.B. markets, here this morning and there this afternoon and the other side of the river tomorrow, like a debt collector. But actually it is because I have been hurt. Hurt and jealous. Empty and cheated.

I let fly with it all at Molly one day. The sickening let-down, like dropping out of a plane into nothingness. Holding at one moment the exciting promise of being able to do something real and vital, and the next empty-handed, our plans and dreams suddenly not there.

Molly said: 'Do you think it could have worked out, how you were planning to live?'

'I know it could. We both knew it.'

'Somehow I don't believe Kate ever really meant to go through with it.'

'Then why pretend? Why cheat me?'

'Look, Em,' Molly said, 'people brought up the way Kate was learn to live for themselves, to survive. They don't have the same ideas of loyalty.'

'She does. Don't make excuses for her. She's ruined everything.'

I don't discuss it at home. I told them briefly that, when I found a flat, I was going to advertise for someone to share it, if I couldn't afford it alone.

My mother sighed and turned her eyes up under her black fringe, like a drunk man I once saw passing out. 'Thank heaven you have come to your senses. My prayers have been answered,' she said with a touch of surprise. She prays away like mad, but never really expects to hear from God because she thinks that prayers are answered with exactly what you pray for, like: Oh God, please give me a bicycle, and here it comes descending from the roof of the church.

My father said: 'You haven't let this girl down, have you?'

'She's let me down,' I said, in a dark and bitter voice.

'Be happy, Emmie,' he said, rather abstractedly. 'I want you to be happy.'

When I am with Kate now, she treats me the same as usual, and we are almost the same together as we were before, except that I no longer feel that I can say absolutely anything to her that comes into my mind.

I don't quite trust her. Perhaps Molly is right, and she can't entirely escape her past. I don't believe it. I believe that the deep sources of the spirit of people can't ever be touched. You can change at the edges, but where it all comes from, the core, is inviolate.

That's why, although I thought that I was through with Kate, I have found that I still love her, and in some odd way still need her.

She needs me too, God knows. Bob is at the coachworks all day, beating panels, and she has few people to talk to except Joan who occasionally stumps her thick legs up the stairs when she's off duty to complain about the nursing home, and the woman in the top back floor, who wears tasselled boots with heroin concealed in the heels.

Kate is getting huge. It sticks out in front of her as if it belonged to somebody else, because her frame is so small. Mrs Marbles shuts her downstairs door ostentatiously loudly when Kate comes through the hall, because she has a rooted distaste for pregnant women, even when married. She will turn them out, of course, even if they don't get the Council flat. This will be her way of getting back at Kate, for Bob, over the three or four years he has been there, has become a sublimation of the son that Mrs Marbles was too genteel to have.

Kate and I don't believe she was ever married, actually. We went through her sitting-room once when she had gone out and untypically forgotten to lock the door that leads to the back part of the house where she lives. No pictures of any male Marbles there or in the vestal bedroom, where the photographs are all of women looking like aunts or grandmothers. The ones who are dead have a black *moiré* bow tacked to a corner of the frame. Most of them are dead, and high time too, from the looks of them.

There is a snapshot of Bob stuck into the kidney-shaped mirror over the gas fire in the sitting-room. Bob at a holiday camp, snapped by the crowded pool, looking rather deprived in a pair of striped bathing-trunks, with not even the sense to push back the wet black hair plastered over his forehead when he saw that he was going to be photographed.

She still tries to feed him titbits, luring him into the kitchen with offers of chicken liver and pig's fry when he comes home from work. But Bob is loyal to Kate and always takes the plate upstairs, and they share it with the cat that came in from the roof one day and stayed.

Kate is hungry all the time. She can cook well enough, but she can't do much with the little hot-plate, so they eat things like meat pies and sausage rolls and cold shop-made rissoles.

One day at home, when we were between pregnant girls and my mother and I were doing the cooking, I made mounds and mounds of macaroni cheese for some reason. It was good, but we could not possibly eat it all, so I took some in a pie-dish to Kate.

When I rang three times, which is their signal, I heard Mrs Marbles' door open and then Kate's feet running heavily on the stairs. She is always delighted to see me. She never has anything much to do, and she throws her arms round me as close as she can get to me, and I forget that I am supposed to be still disappointed with her.

Bob was home, and we would all have macaroni cheese for supper, if she could warm it up. 'Oh, Mrs Marbles —'

The door beyond the stairs, which had been ajar, closed softly as she spoke.

Kate stuck her tongue out, went down the hall and knocked. The door opened at once, revealing the five foot two of printed-cotton disapproval that was Mrs Marbles in her lounging wear.

'Could I use your oven for a few minutes?'

'The pressure's been very low all evening,' Mrs Marbles said guardedly.

'I only want to heat something up. It's for Bob.'

'All by himself he's going to eat that?' Mrs Marbles eyed the big dish which Kate was resting on top of the baby, and then sighted past her down the hall at me.

'It's only Emma.' I seldom heard Kate so polite and wheedling. 'You've seen Em before.'

'Yes indeed. She tried to take my census. I told her. I told her straight out.'

'She's got a new job now,' Kate said soothingly, for we have never been able to eradicate the first impression of me as a field worker for market research. 'She takes care of people who are dying from cancer of the lung, and she's been on duty all day without a meal. So may I?'

'That's different then.' Mrs Marbles stepped aside and let Kate in with the pie-dish. She is dead keen on lung cancer. She once reported a man who merely took out a cigarette and looked at it wistfully in a non-smoker, and Bob has to smoke sitting on the window ledge with his head out into the street, because she can smell tobacco through the keyhole, even though they never let her into their room.

I have a vast handbag, which I bought last year when we flew to Spain, to cheat that girl in the fore-and-aft hat who weighs the luggage, and I had it this evening with beer bottles in the bottom, wrapped in newspaper. It is absurd to be so afraid of Mrs Marbles, because she can't put them out until the baby comes, and probably not even then if they sit tight, but the landlady trauma is part of the game that Kate still plays with life. If you live in lodgings, there is always an ogre downstairs, so Mrs Marbles has to be it.

She is only playing at being married to Bob. She treats him like a pet, giving him caresses or orders according to whim, and talking about him when he's there as if he could not understand more than a tone of voice. If he makes a sensible remark, which he does at times because he has taken to reading other bits of the newspaper besides the sports page and the comic strips, now that he is a man of status, she either turns it into a joke, or repeats it with amused wonder, like a mother with a bright baby.

He doesn't seem to mind. He is happy to have Kate there all the time and I don't think he knows what marriage means. Does she? Do they know it is for life? Up there in the chequer-board room under the gables with the bed made into a couch and all the coloured cushions that Molly gave them to brighten the place up thrown on the floor for a seat under the window, they are not the Babes in the Wood, but Peter and Wendy in the tree house, and when the curtain comes down, all the children will clap and go home to tea.

When Kate went downstairs to get the macaroni cheese out of the oven, Bob was a little gay on beer. It doesn't take much with him. I had not been alone with him since that abortive conversation on the bus when I was looking for Kate, and I had no idea what we should say. He was sitting on the window-sill, blotting out the violet evening with his round sweatered shoulders, drumming his fingers on his knees and looking at me with his head one side and his thick black eyebrows up, as if he were waiting for me to go into a dance.

'Kate looks well,' I said, for want of anything else.

'Kate's too big,' he said, and laughed. 'She'll look better when she's had my baby.'

'That's a bit unfair,' I said, and he agreed, 'Yes.' Unable to sit opposite his tilted grin, I got up and went to fix my hair at the mirror on the wall. To my helpless surprise and undying horror, he attacked me from behind like a man-eating gorilla and bore me down with him on to the bed.

It was just about the most horrible thing that has happened to me so far in my life, although there may be more as my acquaintance widens, and to make it worse, Kate came puffing in while I was still struggling to get him off me.

He was her husband after all, but she walked to the table, put down the hot dish, licked her fingers and said without even turning round: 'Oh, come on, Bob. Stop acting up and get your supper while it's hot.'

He got up with his hair all over his face and shambled over to the table like a tame bear.

'He went for me,' I said, sitting up and looking for hairpins. 'That filthy beast, he went for me. Do something. Scream at him. Hit him. Kill him.'

'Oh, let the poor thing alone.' Kate began to ladle out great sticky spoonfuls of my macaroni. 'It's hard for a man,' she said with the complacent pursed mouth of years of experience. 'He can't get near me now, poor soul.'

'You're just as disgusting as he is.'

'All in good fun, Em.'

I looked at her, and saw with loathing the face of the Kate

of my father's court, common, cheap, uncivilized, come back to taunt me for my crazy attachment. God! I pinned up my hair roughly and lunged for the door, leaving them sitting on either side of the low table like brother and sister playing tea parties.

'You've forgotten my empties,' Bob said.

I slammed out of the front door, collided with the drug runner at the garden gate and felt the gun concealed at her hip, and pounded off down the hill, jarring the joints of my knees. Like a fool, I looked back and saw Kate under the gable waving at me, a white face in the window like an imprisoned child.

EM HAS never said anything about the money. I was afraid she might, that time when she ran off in a rage. I was afraid that Bob and I had messed it up for good and proper, and all I would know of her would be a demand note for fifty quid. But of course, being Em and me, we came together again like the bits of mercury when I used to break the thermometers at the nursing home and nothing said.

I had meant to keep it, well, some of it anyway, and pay it back, but somehow it all got spent. An operation, she said. I didn't know they could. New skin. But that was in that other life, back when anything was possible. When I could still even go to Butt Street to steal toy soldiers. Even think about – about them there without having to go down to the toilet and heave.

I heaved because of Sammy. It was all his fault. I heaved all the time I was carrying him, and everyone says that's not right, and one day I'll ask him: How would you like to have someone inside you pushing your guts up into your throat with those fat rubber fingers?

When he was being born, he tried to kill me, but of course they didn't let him at the hospital. That's what they're for. A surprisingly easy time with that small pelvis, the doctor said. The strange young one who wasn't anything like my Doctor Watts, who calls me Childie.

'Where's Doctor Watts?'

'He's on another case. Bear down, dear.'

Bear down your bloody self. A nice easy time, he said, with the spectacles catching the light so you couldn't see his give-away know-nothing eyes, and he didn't even flinch when I told him what he could do with it, so I never knew if I'd said it, or only in the dream that took me away round the corner of the road.

When I saw Sammy, he looked so funny that I only felt surprised. I didn't think I'd like him, but I do quite. He is so helpless. If it wasn't for me, he'd die. Have you thought of that? Animals get on their feet and get out and hunt for food, but a baby would just quietly starve to death while you sat and looked at him, if sat was all you did. Not quietly. Sammy yells louder than Loretta used, when she was tiny, and Bob or I come hastening with the bottle, his willing slaves.

He is king all right. Samuel Dean Thomas, after Bob's father. No harm, he's got to be called something. Bob's mother has written she may come over, and she'd better have her return fare, that's all, but I envy her, I really do, what she will see. The proud boy-father, working overtime to get more of the good things of this world for his son. The radiant young mother, scarce more than a child herself, with her ash-blond hair falling softly on the shoulders of the loose blue gown (Joan gave me that, you'd never credit her with the taste) as she bends tenderly over the tiny morsel in the gaily painted cot.

Em gave me the cot. She has her own flat now, the one we would have shared, but I have mine, two rooms, kitchen and bath on the fifth floor. I have never lived so high, and Bob loves it. He has made a bird feeder outside the bedroom win-dow, very ingenious. He only likes the little birds, so it's on a spring, and when the pigeons and crows perch on it, the lid shuts down on the food. But the sparrows and starlings sit there and peck away and the big ones sit on the ledge with their feathers ruffled up, like people who can't get into heaven.

Old Marbles cried when we left. She *cried.* I felt like Prin-cess Margaret and them with the baby in a shawl, and we had a taxi, and one of Bob's mates from work brought our stuff round in his van. There isn't much. What Bob had, and a few old bits that Moll gave me, but Bob's getting a raise and I'm going out to work soon and we'll save to get more. This old cow two doors along the balcony, she watched our stuff going in – and her face! She is a spy from the Council, put there to see you don't grow cucumbers in the bath. She looks at me as if I was dirt, so anything that's gone bad, I sneak along and put it in her bin.

THE GIRL in my flat is not at all like Kate, and living with her is not anything like it would have been with Kate and the baby. Time has dulled the worst of the hurt, but I still feel bereft, as if something had been taken away from me forcibly, like Alice felt after her miscarriage.

The miscarriage of my too-eager girlish plans has left me somewhat less girlish, I hope, though no less eager to find something that will appease the hunger of living only for yourself. Perhaps I shall take up good works after all, and be Miss Emmaline Bullock, whose wonderful work among, etc., etc., is such an inspiration to, etc., etc.

Meanwhile I have Lisa. She is large and soft with squashy upper arms and fine silky hair hanging like curtains on either side of her untroubled face. She is not the kind who follows you about all over the flat and waits outside the bathroom like a dog, talking about herself through the door, but she is the kind who goes for group fun, rather than couples, and she is always bothering me to be a group.

When Lisa goes out, I would rather enjoy having the flat to myself, eating smoked fish and things she doesn't like, washing my hair and trailing about with it spread on my shoulders to dry like hemp, touching and feeling the backs and arms of furniture and rejoicing: You are mine. Temporarily mine, but when it is your first own place, a furnished flat seems completely yours, down to the last incredible vase, the last stainless steel teaspoon of a pattern no sane person would choose, or even be able to find.

But Lisa says: 'Colin and I are going to the new Italian film. How about getting someone and making it a four?' As if she were going to play golf or bridge instead of fiddle around a little in the cinema, and have a bit of a go in the back or front of the car, depending on who is driving. To her, the other couple are not superfluous, but in some way necessary. I have figured out that it is because she doesn't really enjoy it as much as she thinks she ought, and so she has to convince an audience that she does, like near-impotent men who talk about it all the time.

If I have been out by myself and I come back and find her on the slippery red sofa with Colin or the Hairless Mexican or the Frenchman with the jodhpur boots, she says: 'Don't go away,' when I back out. 'Stay and talk.'

I don't. I don't go much to the kind of parties that Lisa haunts in her quest to prove something or other to herself. They are slightly more advanced versions of the teenage romps I used to go to along our road, with the voyeurist mothers. Nothing to do but fall over bodies unless you are one yourself.

There are disadvantages to Lisa, but it could be worse. My parents like her because her father has been made a baronet for completing some Government defence job without being accused of homosexuality, so there are no arguments at home and no atmosphere when my mother comes to the flat. She comes sometimes 'on her way home from shopping', although Fulham is by no imaginable route on the way from Knightsbridge to Charing Cross.

Lately she has been coming more often. Lisa gets home first because she is a civil servant, and I find my mother drinking sherry with her when I get back. Once my mother came up just to see me. She had not been shopping or having lunch with my father or seeing any friends. 'I just felt I wanted to see you,' she said, and put out her hand and touched me, as if she wanted to make sure that I was real.

There is a sadness about her that I think was always there, but I notice it more clearly now that I am away from her. If her object in coming to the flat is to make me feel bad about leaving home, then she succeeds.

When I have children, I shall be delighted when they become independent. I shall cut loose and travel to weird places and cast off the conventions I stuck to so that they wouldn't be ashamed of me.

I shall begin a new life. But my mother behaves as if hers

were over. Alice in Birmingham. Peter drowned. Me in Fulham. We have all let her down.

Lisa pays fair shares of everything, and does her share of the work. She is an amiable girl with the inherent lovableness of a big ambling dog, so although I usually turn down her pleas for foursomes, I agree just often enough to show goodwill.

I usually bring Derek, since he is as celibate at the moment as I am. We are both in a rather sad patch, and we spend quite a lot of Uncle Mark's time in the office discussing what is wrong with us.

One evening before Easter, it was suddenly as warm as summer, after a belated bitter spell when Kate's baby had been in the hospital with bronchitis because she left him out in the sun and the sun moved, and Lisa and I had to stuff the pillow back in the broken window again.

She knows a boy called Bernie whose parents have a summer cottage on the river, and we would all go there in Derek's car and take food and drink and possibly stay the night, if Bernie thought he could do it without his parents finding out.

'So what if they do?' Derek said scornfully, and I didn't let him down by giving away how puritanical Uncle Mark is. Derek and Nell do more or less what they like, as long as they don't ask him beforehand or tell him afterwards. He does not want to know what goes on in our world, and there are times when I don't blame him.

The cottage is at the end of a rutted muddy lane between flat wet fields, part of an old estate which was once a dairy farm. The original house was burned down, but several little white-washed houses have been made out of the sheds and dairies and cowmen's cottages. Bernie's cottage squats on the sodden ground like a mushroom, with a roof too big for it hanging down all round. It used to be the gate house, although now there are no gates, and the other houses are farther on down the puddled tree-hung lane that used to be the drive.

It was not quite dark when we got there, with a warm strong wind that carried the rank sweetness excitingly into my face when I jumped out of the car on to the squelching grass. The wind was in the high trees, making more noise than movement.

The air was full of a sighing roar, and it was not until we went through the house and straight out the other side to the garden that I realized that it was the river, not the wind.

Beyond the white fence at the bottom of the garden, the water from the weir came rushing, a swirling brown flood of rainwater charging off to London and the sea. It was high up the banks, tumbling over its own shoulders, eddying in slack pockets, streaked smooth in swatches as if a hand was drawing it flat from underneath, turning back on itself in a brief curl where the huge poplar had a root out to catch the scum and twigs and bits of paper that were trying to get away on the flood.

The noise of the weir filled your head completely, muffling thought, leaving only sensation. I stood transfixed by the low fence, watching the river surge past me, my hair whipping across my face to go with it, as if the wind were driving the water.

'We are going to stay, aren't we?' I asked Bernie. We had to shout, as if we were at sea. But he had gone. They had all gone in, and I realized that I was hanging tightly on to the fence, so as not to be swept away.

I let go and went back to the house. They were pouring drinks and I asked if we could sit outside in the shelter of the porch, but Lisa and Derek said they couldn't stand the noise, and Bernie said in a knowledgeable Mr Toad voice: 'The river's high. It's not usually as bad as this.'

Bad. I didn't say what I had felt like, hanging on to the fence out there with my hair blowing like vinegar into my mouth and the water galloping through my head. Bernie would think I was trying to make an impression. Derek is different. If he and I had been alone, I could have made him stay outside, and he would have been able to lose himself in the excitement of the shouting river. But the other two found it tiresome, so he chose to side with them, since his relationship with me, in all its fluxes, has never encompassed blind loyalty.

Lisa and I were cooking in the little kitchen and drinking wine out of empty meat-paste jars which were all we could find, since Bernie's mother had most of the cupboards locked. It was quite dark by now, and we had found the main switch and turned on the lights, and the damp of the stone cottage, unused all winter, was pushed back into the night. Derek and Bernie were droning comfortably away in the other room, and we were getting that feeling of being in a shell, a world complete within a world, when there was a violent bang on the back door.

'Bernie's parents!' Lisa whispered, although, from Bernie's description of them, they would not knock, but would come storming in to catch us in some beastliness.

Because of the river, which filled the house, muffled but insistent, I had not heard a car, or feet approaching. It was a disembodied knock, like the night asking to come in, and I was the aghast old woman in *The Monkey's Paw,* knowing the Thing that clawed and gibbered outside.

'Open it,' Lisa and I said to each other. She was afraid too, with some private horror of her own out there. The door opened on a gust of wind, and a man in a torn shirt put his head in cautiously. Then he laughed, relaxed, and came in. 'I'm sorry,' he said, talking to me, not to Lisa. 'I saw the lights and I thought someone had got in. Kids have been breaking into houses round here all winter.'

'Tom?' Bernie came through from the other room. 'Ullo, me old cock.' That is the way Bernie talks a lot of the time. It's very trying. 'What are you up to down here?'

'*I'm* making bookcases. I've been coming down by myself every night all week. I didn't expect to find you here.'

'I'll buy you a drink if you'll swear not to tell the old folk.'

'Aren't you allowed to come down without them?' The man was about thirty, perhaps more. He didn't look like anyone I had ever imagined falling in love with, which made the shock worse.

'Not with girls.'

'Oh, I see.'

I was still staring at him and he was still looking at me, and had been ever since he came in, even when he was talking to Bernie. It was like a scene in one of those shallowly directed plays where two characters suddenly stand in profile and stare at each other, with distended eyeballs if that is all they know about acting, and nobody else on stage notices – only a few hundred people out in the audience.

But this was life and not a play, so everyone noticed. I didn't care. I didn't care what Derek or Bernie or Lisa thought, nor what they did. I suppose they sort of shared Lisa. I don't know. I can't remember anything about the supper, or what happened when we were in the house. I only know about the shuddering poplar and the dark urgent water, and how my love galloped away rejoicing with the untiring river that filled the night.

E M I S going with a married man. It's a funny thing, but when she told me about it, I was shocked. I'd not have thought I would be, but that's what marriage does for you.

Not that I didn't want to hear about it. I did, although I couldn't help thinking she was on the wrong bus. She told it all to me, as if she really needed to let it out. That's what she came for, I suppose. I've not seen very much of her since Bob and I got married, especially after that macaroni evening at old Marbles'.

I have missed her. In the old days she was round all the time, at Moll's. We both knew everything the other was doing and thinking. It was like being sisters, almost like living together. That's almost two years ago, but I still miss it. I miss Em. I want someone to talk to.

Often I've thought I'd write to her, or go to the phone box on the corner and ring her flat. She gave me the number, that time I was there.

I didn't want to go at first, because I was afraid of seeing her and me in the flat together. In the end she came for me in her father's car, stuck my coat on me as if I was a child and made me go. I didn't want to take Sammy. He was tiny then and a bloody nuisance most of the time because he'd get all this stuff in his throat and threaten to choke on you. I was going to leave him with Barbara, but Emma said he had to come and see the place he nearly lived in, which was really why I didn't want to take him, because remembering any part of that time makes me start seeing and hearing things I don't want to think about, ever again in my life.

There was a woman here not long ago from the Health, taking statistics. When she asked me: Father and mother living? I said No. My voice dropped it in like a stone. Dead.

Emma had her way, as she usually does in the end with me. We wrapped up old Sam in a blanket, and I'll say this for him, he didn't give any trouble all afternoon. The shock of going in a comfortable car instead of that hot-rod of Ron's and Barbie's must have stunned him.

Em's flat is in one of those sad old squares where the bricks used to be red before London got at them, and the garden in the middle used to be green before the kids got at it. It didn't look much, the house, when we stopped outside. The entrance to our flats is smarter, really, and of course Em doesn't have a lift, although her place is on the top floor.

But if she did, it wouldn't stink, that's the thing. I saw the woman who has the ground-floor flat, and I saw another girl going in the house next door with a shopping-basket and a couple of kids in grey school uniform. I thought of the Nelsons on our ground floor, and some of the people you meet on the stairs when the kids have put the lift out of business, and I saw what I knew already.

This is all right. It's shabby and old and a dreary bit of London with the power station breathing down your back, and everything could do with a lick of paint, but it's all right because of the people who live here, and the rent Em has to pay proves it.

That's why she has this other girl living with her, to share the cost. With me, it would have been from choice. With this Lisa, it's from necessity.

Not that there's anything wrong with her. She was rather nice really, and she was quite daft about the baby. Sat and held him all the time with her hair falling over her face and her long clean fingers stroking his cheek. Well, I said, when you get one of your own you'll soon get sick of that.

She laughed. I thought I'd feel awkward with her. I was angry at first when she came home, and thought Em should have picked a time when she wouldn't, but she was quite easy, and the two of them seem to get on all right, but not like Em and me. They don't have the laughs we used to, I can see that, nor the excitement of letting your brain run away like a bolting horse. When Em and I started kidding about Mary Gold, along the balcony at our flats, the wreck of the Golden Mary, we call her, and how she grows hemp in the window-box and keeps all the coppers supplied with weed, she took it dead seriously and believed every word.

The flat is lovely. Oh my God, is it lovely. A lot of things in it are all the wrong shapes and seen a good bit of use, but they have got some pictures up with colours that make your toes curl, and in the kitchen they've made it like a French café, with all magazine pictures of beautiful food stuck higgledy on the red walls.

We've got a lot of things newer, Bob and I have, that will be paid off some time, never, and he's painted the bedroom and the bath, but somehow it doesn't look like this.

The first thing I did when I got back to our place was to take down the pictures Bob tacked up. I kicked all the junk laying about the kitchen in under the sink where the pipes and sour smells are and cut up that red and white tablecloth and tacked it across. It looked better. At least it did before the tablecloth got all splashed and stained, and the junk began to creep back on to the shelves and draining-board again.

I've seen Em on and off since then, but there have been many times when I've needed her, and I've wanted to write or phone. But there isn't a stamp, or I haven't the money for the phone box. Even when I've had the pennies. I've been afraid to butt in. All the time I was at the Fulham flat, Em never said: I wish it was you here with me, so of course I talked my marriage up, to show I'd got something better.

Suppose that girl answered the phone. She's got one of those soft, superfine voices, like face tissues, not like Em who can bellow as loud as me when she likes. If Lisa answered, I might panic, and she'd say to Em with that peaceful smile: Your queer little friend rang up.

Who does she think she is? I could have been her. My hair is almost the same colour. I could have worn it like that, Lady of the Lake stuff, if that's what you have to do. Barbie is on at me now to cut it, and I may do. The grease is darkening it like it did with Sammy, and it's too much bother to keep washing it, and the colder it gets this winter, the colder the hot water gets.

Modern flats with all utilities. I could tell some tales about peeling plaster and the woman next door's sink water coming up the plughole of my bath. Some of the girls get on to me to go to the tenants' association meetings and speak up, but the wreck of the Golden Mary goes, which makes it bad news.

I had just thrown up that day, in the afternoon it was, a funny time, and I was washing my face when Em rang the bell and hooted through the letter-box, and I went to the door with the towel in my hands, no make-up on nor nothing. I was so glad to see her.

'What's the matter?' Em never says Hullo or the ordinary things that people greet you with, just whatever comes on to her tongue. 'You don't look well.'

'I was washing my face,' I said. 'Come in the bedroom while I do it up, and then you'll know me.'

The dressing-table is one of the things that may have to go back, so I make the most of it while it's here. It is polished wood with an oval mirror, very low, and you sit on the low stool that comes with it and have all your stuff in the little drawers with painted metal bows on them for the handles. I need a tiny pearl-handled revolver in there among the musk-scented handkerchiefs and the oblivion pills in case of capture.

It's new since Em was last here, and she was impressed, but she forgot about it almost at once, and when I sat down low to do my face, she fell flat on the bed with her shoes on my good spread and gave an ecstatic groan and told me about being in love.

I have never known her talk quite like this. He is twelve years older than her, she says, and it's made her a lot older, I mean that. When we've talked about men before, it was fun, but it wasn't like this.

'I want you to be pleased about it, Kate,' she said, and I was, but it still nagged me like a tooth that something had happened to her that I could never have.

When you're married it's all over. You can't pretend about the white charger any more. We went to pick up Sammy to feed him and he was all in a stinking mess, and this is what marriage is, so I said, to bring her down to earth, 'Why don't you marry this Tom then?'

That was when she told me he was married, and I was shocked.

He is in business of some kind, it seems, and his wife has her own hat shop, one of those tiny places you daren't go in because there's only a few hats displayed and you can't say No after they bring out a dozen others, each one farther out than the last. That's what Em says, but she doesn't wear hats anyway.

She went in the shop once just to get a look at the wife, and asked for something they wouldn't have, like a sou'wester, so she could get out quick.

'She's ugly as sin,' I said, staring at Em's new face, the one she's in love in, more vivid, the expressions changing faster. I was beginning to get over the shock, and to enjoy the tale in our old way. I wanted this Tom to be chained to some beast not fit to breathe the air with Emma, but Em made a face and said: 'That's the hell of it. She's beautiful.'

'Beautiful, but cruel.'

'No, She's very kind. He rather likes her as a matter of fact.'

I was shocked again. 'You're trying to have your cake and eat it, Tom boy,' I warned him.

'It's not that. It's just that he won't hurt anyone. But he was never in love with her. She was in love with his friend, and the friend married someone else, so Tom married her because he was sorry for her.'

'That's what they all say.' I wagged my head, very wise, very married.

'It's true. He tells me the truth about everything. He's the first man who has. He was in prison once for knocking someone down when he was drunk. He had his twenty-first birthday in Wormwood Scrubs and one of the warders' wives made him a cake. He told me.'

Sammy was sending back bubbles of apple sauce, which meant he'd had enough, so I took and held him over the sink to wash him off. 'What are you going to do about it?' I said.

'I don't know. We have to be together, that's all. I don't care what happens to her. He doesn't talk about her, not unless

I make him, but he never says anything against her. He's still sorry for her, because she's barren. She would be. Anything to get his pity. I can't go back in the shop again, so I walk past sometimes and look in to remind myself who my enemy is.'

People in love are boring as hell. Did I go on like this about Douglas? He's the nearest I've been to it, though it didn't amount to much. But kid though I was, and a mess – well, two nights in that cellar – it might have come to something if they hadn't caught me. I remember talking about him to Em for quite some time afterwards, and wondering why she wasn't more interested.

Just as she was wondering now why I didn't want to talk about Tom all afternoon. She was obsessed, possessed, her dark Minnehaha eyes looking inwards. But she made an effort to talk about me, so I thought I might as well give her something to make it worth her while.

'I've chucked the job,' I said.

'Oh Kate. I thought you liked it at the shop.'

'It didn't like me.' That's an expression she hates, I know. You shouldn't use stale phrases, she says, if you're bright enough to invent your own. But you try living with Bob and Sammy, and see how bright the conversation is.

'They sacked you?'

'I sacked myself. I got too tired. Well, all right, Em, why not? Other people have babies when they're married. Why not me?'

'You're only eighteen.'

'I'll be nineteen when I have it. There's a girl my age two floors down going to have her third, and her husband's been off work three months with his back.'

'How does she look?'

'Terrible.'

We burst out laughing. We still have that. It isn't funny, if you know Doreen, but Em and I have always had to shriek and sob at all the wrong things. No harm. It's nothing to do with Doreen, or anyone. Just laughing.

Sammy laughed too, crowing like a chicken the way he does, and Em picked him up and hugged him, and crowed with him, then put him down again to crawl. He crawls everywhere, not on all fours, but hitching himself along with one leg tucked under him. If he doesn't stand up and walk soon, I'll go out of my mind.

Bob came in, with a big grin for Emma. He likes her. She doesn't understand that's why he went for her that evening. It's about the only way he knows to show he likes you. That and butting his head against you like a cat to make you stroke the sides of his hair.

Em has got over it. She can joke and tease with Bob again, like she used, but when I went out to the kitchen to put on the potatoes, she came with me, I noticed.

'Is my dinner ready? What time are we going out?' Bob asked. He was on the floor with Sammy, rolling over and over with him, one way to get the dust picked up, it was all over the back of Bob's jacket.

'Not till seven.' We were going to play Bingo at the big place that used to be a cinema. We go there at least once a week. It's keen. I won a ham once, and Bob won that set of queer-shaped dishes we've never used. I meant to ask Em what they're for, but I forgot. Once I won five quid. Five quid! The cards are a shilling each. What can you lose?

'Who takes care of Sammy when you go out?' Em asked. She had picked him up and was saying goodbye to him, telling him she'd be back soon. She credits him with understanding more than he does, like she did with Moll's cats.

'Barbie Johnson. She's a friend of mine across the yard. She'll always take him.'

'Have a good time,' she said, when we were in the narrow passage that goes to the door. They didn't waste any space when they made these flats. Golden Mary will get stuck in her front hall one day and walk out in the street wearing the building.

'We will. It's special prize night, and after we're going up West, the four of us, and see what's doing.'

'Who are you going with?'

'Barbie and Ron. They're fun.'

'I thought she was going to look after Sammy.'

'Oh Em, don't fuss at me. He'll be all right. I'll give him two aspirin to get him to sleep and he'll never know we've gone.'

'Kate, you can't!' You'd think I'd said give him rat poison.

'Why not? It doesn't hurt them. I used to give it to that Chink baby of Moll's when he was teething. He knew no more till morning. What's wrong? You talk about me being young, and that. Well, I am. We've got to have some fun.'

'I'll stay with Sammy.'

'Don't be daft.'

'I'd like to. Please.'

'Your funeral. If it makes you happy —'

'I've got some things to do. I'll be back at seven.'

She kissed me and went off quickly, forgetting to make the sign against the evil eye as she passed Mary's window, like I've told her to do. I shrugged and went back in to put on the dress I got when I started to know about Sammy, but no one else did. I'm into that already. It's disgusting.

I RANG Tom's office and found him still there. 'I can't meet you darling.' He had answered the telephone himself. The switchboard girl had gone home. She's a private eye for Sheila and the League of Moral Decency. If I ring during the day, I am the woman in the barber's shop of the hotel where he gets his hair cut. 'Please understand. It's something I can't help.' I told him about Sammy. 'He was once almost half mine, don't forget. It's the least I can do.'

'Sheila's going to the theatre. I'll come and be with you there,' Tom said.

It is more than eight months since we met by the river, but we still grab every chance to be together. Ten minutes at lunch-time in a drab little bar near the restaurant where he usually takes his clients. Three minutes at the station if I have to catch a train home, Tom running through the crowd at the last moment with his face afraid he's missed me, as if I were going away for ever. Someone is going to see him looking like that one day. Someone who knows Sheila.

'No, you can't,' I said.

'Why not?'

'You can't.' Why did I have to think of Kate sneaking Bob in to Grove Lodge when she was baby-sitting for Molly?

'No risk. I'm hardly likely to see anyone there I know. Give me the address again. I'll get there after they're gone.'

I hurried to get back to the flat before Kate and Bob left. I was afraid they might go off without waiting, and I wouldn't be able to get in. A drop in the ocean, what I was doing, if she was often leaving the baby alone, but my insistence on staying might make her see that it mattered. Mr Jordan would be proud of me. Our own Miss Bullock, one of our most conscientious case workers.

'I still think you're daft,' Kate said, and her friend Barbara, who is very glamorous, with fantastic hair and iridescent eyeshadow, said, 'No, Katie, some people are like that. They devote their lives to the little ones,' as if I were a sublimating spinster.

'She's right though,' Ron put in from behind his teeth, which are too big for his mouth, so that he has difficulty closing his lips round them. 'Kate shouldn't leave the kid alone. I knew a family once, had a paraffin heater —'

'Oh, lay off,' Kate said.

Bob was standing behind her with his big gentle hands on her shoulders, as he often does, as if touching her gave him confidence. 'If Katie says it's all right, it is. She knows what's best for my baby,' he said in a sort of drilled monotone.

From the balcony I watched them away in Ron's car, a souped-up old saloon with a skull and crossbones on it and the orange undercoat showing in patches. No Tom yet, thank God. What would he wear? If he came straight from the office with the black suit and hat and briefcase which disguised him as just another man, Golden Mary would think he was the tax collector.

I gave Sammy a bath in the plastic bowl in the kitchen because the bath was dirty and I didn't see why I should clean that for Kate as well. The things she learned at Molly's seem to be coming unstuck. While I was waiting for Tom, I poked round the flat a bit and put out a dozen souring milk bottles from behind the stained curtain under the sink, and found things in drawers and cupboards that made me shut them again quickly. Other people's mess is their own affair.

If she and the baby had lived with me at the flat, it would have been different. She would have been different, proud of what she had, proud of herself and what she could be. When she came to the flat that day and Lisa was so condescending, although Kate didn't notice it, I wanted to say to her: I wish it was you and me and the baby here. But Kate talked as if she were quite satisfied with what she'd got, so I didn't say it.

I don't wish it now anyway. It wouldn't have worked with Tom in my life.

Sammy was still awake when he came, sneaking past Mary Gold's as I'd told him, in his ski-ing sweater and a pair of tennis shoes, as if he were running messages for the Secret Service. I fed the baby and I cooked ham and eggs that I had brought for us, and we played house in Kate's Council flat which was built in austerity just after the war, so you have to keep your voices low unless you have nothing to hide from the neighbours.

We played that we were married. We used to be able to do that long ago by the river, but soon the people began to come back. Bernie's parents. The film people in the converted dairy. Tom's wife. There were people about all summer in the river cottages, and in the autumn when they left, Sheila let theirs to a friend who was writing a book.

'A boy friend?'

'No, this gruesome woman with the moles and metal earrings.'

She never has a boy friend. She has no children. She has nothing but Tom, and she doesn't even know she hasn't got him. Sometimes when Tom or I get desperate, we say: We've got to do something, but we never do. We don't know what to do, so we let it go on like this.

He left before the time that Kate and Bob might come home, and they came soon after, having found nothing doing up West but a liver and bacon supper and a glass of lager.

I stood at the bus stop with my red coat wrapped round me like a soldier's shroud, smiling secretly to myself to show the couple waiting with me that I didn't need to envy them for having someone to hold them close against the funnel of wind between the flats.

A little blue car streaked down the road, stopped with a rocking squeal beyond the bus stop, and shot back like a clockwork train thrown suddenly in reverse.

Johnny Jordan leaned across and stuck out his head. 'What are you doing on my beat?'

'I've been to see Kate. That girl I told you about. Remember when we went to Butt Street?'

He nodded solemnly. Of course. I had cried. Although so long ago, he would have to remember it solemnly.

'She lives in those flats.'

'Married then. I'm still seeing the mother off and on. She's never told me.'

'She wouldn't.'

He opened the car door and I got in, feeling the envy of the hugging couple, because I had been rescued. 'You can wait all night for the buses here. I'll run you to the station.'

'I don't live at home any more. I have my own flat now, in Fulham.' I should say something which would show that I had not been thrown out or walked out, in case he might think my father had failed as a father, but I let it go.

'Come home then and have a cup of coffee,' he said. 'Jean will be so pleased. We've often talked about the time you came. Then I'll run you home.'

'It's too late. Your wife —'

'She always waits up if I'm called out, in case I come back with a child.'

'Do you often?' I was still living in my secret smile, still half with Tom, but talking easily, very relaxed, like being woken from sleep without having to get up.

'Once in a while. Sometimes she feeds them before I take them to the Home. It was a false alarm tonight. The neighbours were edgy. This woman had reported them a year ago because their baby kept crying, so they turned round and reported her. Her husband had given the boy a hiding, nothing much, but they'd waited a year next door to catch the sound of blows. The woman, she caught me on the way out and played war with me for not taking the kid away. I'm not a kidnapper, ma'am. No, you're a bloody fake, she said. They think you can just walk in and take anyone's child away in the middle of the night, like the Gestapo.'

'Well, dear, I brought you one back!' he called out, as we went into the house, smelling so delightful after the dubious air of Kate's flat. Jean came down the stairs in a dressing-gown wearing a face of welcoming concern for a miserable child, which broke into a broad smile when she saw me.

We sat by the kitchen fire in the inglenook where the old range used to be. We had mugs of coffee with foam on the top, and the last of Jean's Christmas cake. They were nice. Jean, who is still an enthusiastic patron of my Uncle Mark, wanted to hear what went on behind the scenes at B.B., so I told them a few of the funny bits to make them laugh. She laughs out loud, easily. He keeps his mouth shut and laughs inside the smile.

I didn't talk much. I was sleepy, and he wanted to tell her what the mother tonight had said and done when she guessed who had telephoned him, which was much more fascinating. When it was time to go, and Johnny went to get our coats, Jean said: 'I *am* so glad you came. Do come and see us again. We're very fond of you.'

'Wasn't it lucky I saw her?' Johnny came back with my red coat and held it for me. When Tom does that, he keeps his hands there after it's on and slides them round me, just touching my breasts for a second if we are in a place where there are people. But they aren't likely to be people we know. We have to go to other kinds of places.

'I spotted her by her hair,' Johnny said. 'She's the only girl I know who'd dare to wear it all loose down her back like that.'

'It doesn't take much courage,' I said bleakly, because I would kill myself if he knew that my hair had been pinned up when Tom came and we were eating ham and eggs. It was the first time I had felt guilty about Tom, or seen it as a furtive, cheap and dirty thing.

I had a week off. Horrible time to have it, but I was the most junior in our department, so if anyone was going to have a holiday in March, it was me.

Tom and I had made fantasy plans of how he would take

some days off and we would go to Scotland, but of course he couldn't and we didn't. We never can. He has a business and a wife. I am an extra. I recognize that. I don't make demands on him. I did it once, early on, and I learned a lot from that mistake. I shall be twenty-one this summer. I shall tell my grandchildren: I learned everything about men before I was twenty-one.

I went to see Molly, but she had taken all the children to her mother's, with a note on the door for someone called Red, presumably an older Care and Prot. out at work: Gone S'gate. Back 8. Key under u no wot. Start pots heat pie feed all an'ls.

I took Kate some books which I had promised her. Bob has made her a bookshelf, the height of gracious living, wider at one end than the other. Very practical. You put the taller books at one end and the paperbacks at the other.

I had nothing to do. I wasted the days, waiting for the end of the week when Sheila might be going to Paris to see Collections. Please, Sheila. Oh come on, Paris in March is entrancing. I am as dependent on her movements as if it were her I were in love with.

My father telephoned me one evening in the middle of the week. 'Lisa? Oh good, it's you, Emmie. I thought you might be out.'

'I don't go out so much.' I didn't, if I couldn't be with Tom, and there were many, many hundreds of evenings when I couldn't be with Tom. But I kept most of them free, in case. I had lost a lot of friends in the last year, along with a lot of my egotism. If you are still in love with yourself, you aren't in love. That's one of the things Tom taught me.

'This is your week off, isn't it?' my father said, and I thought: Oh God, don't let him be wistful. 'Are you coming home?'

Of course, he wouldn't be wistful. He said it casually, so that I could say: 'I wish I could, but I've got so much to do. I'm spring-cleaning the flat.' Well, I was in a way. I was washing the curtains. 'I'll try to get down for the week-end, but don't count on it. I may have to go to a football match.' Well, I might. Tom and I can go where there are shouting, amorphous crowds.

'How about lunch with me tomorrow? There's a fairly short list at court. We should get through it in the morning.'

'Where will you take me?'

He hesitated, and then said: 'Why don't you give me lunch for a change? Let's have it at the flat.'

Tom telephoned later, from a call box where he was supposed to be posting a letter. It was a frustrating conversation, full of pauses. He had a contract problem with an American firm, which wasn't interesting, but he had fought with it all day and couldn't think of much else. I had done nothing. I had nothing to tell him except the things I couldn't say with Lisa in the room. She knows about Tom, of course. She is not very interested any more – anything that lasts over three months is as dull as a marriage – but whoever I am talking to, she always stops what she's doing and listens. It's a bad habit of hers. I'm going to tell her one day. God, I'm getting crabby. The next thing, Lisa and I will be into a neurotic battle, and the magistrate will say jauntily, hoping to be quoted in the evening paper, when we are up for assault: It's the age-old problem of two women and one cook-stove. Magistrates never know the current names for anything. They talk about motor-cars and wireless sets. Even my father has been known to ask juvenile-court clients: Are you good at your studies?

Frustrated with Tom, and feeling separated from him by vast expanses, although his house is only a mile away across the slate roofs and chimneys from my bedroom window, I welcomed the thought of my father coming tomorrow. I wanted to see him, and I was glad he wanted to see me. The next morning, I went out into a dark drizzle and bought cold roast beef, left it ready with the kind of salad he likes, and went back to the drab district I know so well because Molly is there and Kate is there and the juvenile court is there.

In the outer hall, the usual dispirited bunches of grown-ups and children were waiting on the benches, making little puddles on the stone floor with umbrellas and rubber boots. It is always cold out there. When the mothers come into the court-room, their hands are always red, from cleaning everybody up before they come, and then sitting waiting in the cold.

126

A few older boys were leaning against the walls trying to look as if they didn't care. Some of them didn't. I saw a wild-haired boy I had seen twice in court last year. He had a black eye and a plaster on his cheek, and his father, small and tubercular, looked as if he were afraid of him.

There were still about a dozen cases, by the look of the hall, so I asked the policeman at the door of the court to let me in, and sat at the end of the room opposite the bench, with the policewomen and the students. My father was reading the report on a dejected boy who stood before him, trying to wipe his nose on his sleeve without raising his arm. He looked up when I came in and gave me a smile which should put fresh heart into the dejected boy, if he was afraid of the merciless beak.

Usually, when I come to court, I sit at the side of the Bench with the Clerk of the Court and the probation officers. My father sometimes makes jokes for my benefit, but he can only see me out of the corner of his eye. Now that I was sitting behind the parents and the children, his eyes kept straying beyond them to me, and I wore my inscrutable face so as not to distract him.

It is not easy to stay inscrutable in my father's court, and today was no exception. A desperate boy who couldn't get a job had taken a scooter and fallen off it at the first traffic lights, right under a policeman's nose. A girl had taken her father's savings and no one could make her say what she had spent them on. A fifteen-year-old girl, sullenly bold, admitted that she had tried to get pregnant so the boy would have to marry her. Her mother, swollen with her eleventh child (Get the lady a chair, the cry goes up, as soon as the shape is seen), lodged a long keening complaint with my father, not for what the girl had done, but for what she hadn't, which was to stay at home and look after the younger children.

A girl of twelve had been taken to the Child Care centre because she had been assaulted by the lodger, who was 'just like one of the family'. A mother at the end of her rope stood tight-lipped and trembling before the Bench, and asked for her boy to be taken into Care to stop him roaming. The boy seemed not unwilling, but when my father agreed, he shrieked like a mandrake and the mother weaved about like a reed in the wind, collapsed moaning and legless and was dragged out with her heels thumping the floor.

Children's courts are more emotionally crippling than adult courts, where people are under better control, and what has happened is usually their fault. On the Bench, it is not apparent that my father is a little bruised by the conflicts and the suffering and the blunders that rage under his nose once or twice a week, but when he comes out he often looks drained, and he doesn't bother to try not to limp.

I drove his car to the flat and poured him a large gin right away and sat him in the only comfortable chair. It had no cover on, because I am washing that too, and the strange old tapestried upholstery is the colour of the fungus on jam.

I sat opposite him on the stool whose colour is explained when you see the original chair, desiccating my shins in front of the gas fire, and we talked about the court and the woman who had been dragged out, and then he said, out of the blue, 'What's this I hear about you being mixed up with a married man?'

He knew. I sat perfectly still on the tapestry stool with my shoes off, still looking down. My hands hadn't tensed, but under my shirt I could see my heart battering like an organism separate from my body. He knew. We had been so careful, so agonizingly discreet, but he knew. Who else did?

'How do you know?' I said. There was no sense saying anything else.

'A man at the club, youngish chap, I don't know him very well, cornered me in the bar and said: Do you know that your daughter is having an affair with my sister's husband? It seemed rather a crude thing to say, but people are like that these days.'

'How does he know?' This must be Eric, whom Tom plays golf with. Eric, whose car I was once in when Tom's was at the garage. Eric, who is supposed to think the sun rises and sets on Tom, and gets his whisky for him wholesale. 'How does he *know*, Daddy?' His face was twisted up, as if he would have liked to try and smile, but could only get to it with one side of his mouth.

'It seems quite a few people do. Including his sister.'

'She doesn't.'

'Yes, Emmie, she does. Didn't this – what's his name?'

'Tom.'

'Didn't this Tom tell you that she knows?'

'He doesn't know it either.'

'Oh yes he does. They've had it all out. She doesn't want to divorce him. She is very unhappy.'

'You seem to know more about it than I do.'

'Yes.' He looked at his hands, stroking the loose skin over the knuckles, trying to pull it tight. 'It seems awfully irrelevant, but do you suppose we could have some lunch?'

'Oh yes. I'm sorry. It's all ready.'

I brought the tray and he sat at the table by the window. I didn't want anything. I stood up at first while he was eating, but he said: 'Sit down, you're not a waitress.'

'Here at the table?'

'Why not? I can talk better if I look at you.'

'There's nothing to say.'

'Yes there is. I want to know what you are going to do.' He put down his knife and fork and leaned back with his hands on the table and his chin down a little, studying me patiently, as he does when he is waiting for an unwilling delinquent to speak.

'Nothing. There's nothing to be done. Tom and I are in love. I'm going on with it and so will he. I can't help how Sheila feels. She's lost him anyway.'

'You haven't done much thinking, have you? You've just gone ahead. You didn't know what to do, so you let it go on?'

I nodded.

'Start thinking, Emmie,' he said, 'before it's too late.' He got up. 'I'd better go. I thought I would want to sit here all afternoon and battle it out with you, but I find I don't. I don't want to talk about it any more.'

We didn't kiss or touch each other when we said goodbye, and I didn't go down with him to the car. It was dark outside at half past two. The end of the world that London springs a few times during the winter to justify the bearded old men in

Regent Street with their sandwich-boards that announce the Day of Judgement.

After he had gone, I turned out the lights, and instead of thinking, I fell asleep on the red convex sofa. The telephone woke me at a quarter to five.

'Miss Weir?' We had chosen this name for the woman at the barber shop, because of the background music of our first meeting. 'I'm going to leave the office a little early. Can you fit me in at five thirty?'

'Yes, sir. Very well.' Was it Tom's breathing I could hear, or the switchboard girl? Was she the one who had told the world? 'We'll be waiting for you then.'

If I said: We'll see you here, it meant Come to the flat. We'll be waiting for you meant that I would meet him at our particular entrance of the Tottenham Court Road tube station, opposite the Lyons, where all the perverts in the world go up and down the stairs.

He never gives me much time to get anywhere, But I usually manage it. He asks me to be there, so I am. I waited underground at the exit to the stairs, and he came hurrying, as he always does, to meet me. He always thinks one day I won't be there, but I always am, and the little shock of pleasure when I see his face anxious and searching, then suddenly alight because he has seen me, never gets less. We come together without speaking, and move off without touching to be part of the crowd.

He went to the ticket machines.

'Where are we going?'

'The house. Don't you remember?'

Of course. He had said last night that Sheila might leave for Paris today. I had known it this morning. I had forgotten it some time while I was with my father.

'I don't want to go to your house,' I said, but he was off down the escalator and didn't hear. Partly because we can't be seen together, and partly because he moves so quickly, he is always slightly ahead, with me tailing behind like a short-legged child. One day he will look back and I shan't be there. Yes I will. I dare not lose him.

Tom's house is narrow, in a white terrace with empty

window-boxes and skeletons of almond trees along the pavement and all the front doors painted a different colour. The colour of Tom's front door is lilac. That's Sheila. Everyone else has a primary colour, so hers has to be lilac.

I hate going to her house. I have only been there twice before. Once when Tom stopped to fetch something, and I sat in the car with my head down, pretending to read a magazine and thinking each tap of heels along the pavement was her. The second time she was in Ireland, and I was in the house, using her stove, her sink, her salt and pepper, discovering that she didn't clean the saucepans properly.

I didn't like it, but Tom wanted it. He said that he could only bear to go on living in the house if I had been in it.

There is no danger about going to the house. It is near the end of the terrace, and there is a mews entrance just round the corner. Tom shares one of the mews garages with the people in the flat above and there is a door at the back of the garage which leads to his square of paved garden.

We separate before we get to his street. He goes home, goes through to the garage and unlocks the little door within the big one. It is next to the door which leads up to the flat, so when I wander casually into the mews and go in, I could be going into the flat, if anyone is looking.

There is the danger of meeting someone from the flat, but otherwise it is quite easy. It should be exciting, but it isn't. When I told Kate about doing it the first time, she was stirred, in spite of her surprising disapproval, to say that it was like the runaway nun, with the bloodhounds after her. But, to be exciting, an adventure has to seem imperative. If you were going to commit a crime, you would have to want to do it, or you would get only the fear without the thrill.

Tom thinks it is exciting. We ran across the dark little garden with the white wrought-iron chairs and the empty urns that Sheila brought back from Italy and into the unlit kitchen, and he flung his arms round me exultantly.

'I had to have you here. You should be here all the time. I've wanted you so much all day. You were so far away last night.'

'You were miles away from me.'

'The telephone is useless. Have you ever made a transatlantic call? They sound as if they were in the next room. It costs a pound a minute and then you can't think of anything to say.'

We drew the curtains all over the house before we turned on any lights.

'Won't people think that odd?' If Lisa and I pulled all the curtains, the neighbours would think we were going to gas ourselves.

'No, she always – oh well, it's all right.' He never wants to talk about her, will hardly mention her name, as if that lessened the disloyalty. In the house, he ignores the many signs of her and behaves as if it were just for him and me, but as far as I'm concerned, everything is hers. The house shrieks of her. Her colour schemes. Her carpets. Her cupboards and drawers, all neatly closed, but the clothes and shoes inside are clamouring like the tell-tale heart.

We sat in the narrow room on the first floor which is her drawing-room, and Tom put on Benjamin Britten, whom he has rediscovered through discovering him to me, and expected me to listen quietly, but how could I? Her candlesticks. Her flower pictures. Her cigarettes. Her Mexican brush to sweep the grate. Her photograph on the walnut table by the window, beautiful, assured in columnar-necked black, a face that would surely never betray itself with anything so vulnerable as unhappiness. Eric's sister. Had she sobbed to him? Had *she* asked Eric to tackle my father in the bar of his club? If so, she was a coward. Why didn't she tackle me?

I sat on her white curly rug and, when the record was finished and Tom got up to turn it, I said so abruptly that it sounded childish: 'Why didn't you tell me that Sheila knew?'

'She doesn't.' He had his back to me, bending over the machine. I didn't think he would ever lie to me. Now I knew that he could. Why not? Almost everyone lies instinctively if they are suddenly caught out, like hackles going up. Honesty takes a little more time, a moment or two to let the flash defence of the adrenals strengthen into self-respecting courage.

I told him about my father. He turned round and, for the first time, I saw him falter. For the first time, I felt stronger than him, the leader, not always the one who followed.

'Why didn't you tell me? If only you'd told me. Why have we needed to be so frantically careful if she knew anyway, and you knew she knew?'

'She wanted me to say I'd stop seeing you,' he said wretchedly. 'She was so unhappy. What else could I do?'

I remembered when we were at Brighton, which was one of the places we went to last summer, to be safe in a crowd. We had been together all day, freely in the open air, holding hands and doing what everyone else did. The pier, the ghoulish waxworks, the boat, the slog up with the slogging families to the station.

'It could always be like this,' I had said, 'if only we had the courage.'

'I can't tell her. I can't do that to her.'

'You're dodging it,' I said. 'You want to have her and me both, because you're afraid of enemies. We can't go on like this.'

'All right, I am afraid. Can't I be a coward? Do I have to be superhuman because you love me?'

But he is more of a coward than I knew then. He sat on the floor and held me. It was better that way, not having to look at each other.

'My father wants to know what we are going to do,' I said, pulling at the rug as if it were a thick-haired dog who liked to be roughly handled. 'He's trying to give me a chance to do what he wants me to do without being told.'

'Now that you know I lied to you, it should make it easier.'

'Why? If you're a coward, wouldn't it be pretty cowardly of me to love you less? I love you more. There is a fatal weakness in all the Bullock women. They have never loved heroes. My great-grandmother —'

I could feel him relaxing just slightly, wanting me to joke, to make things easy and provisional again, with no grim tomorrows, but I couldn't manage it. I pulled away from him and stood up, and went to lean my forehead against Sheila's blue wall, rolling it from side to side on the cool paint.

'You want to stop,' he said. 'Is that it?'

'I can't.'

'Turn round.'

'I can't.' I was crying now. 'What are we going to do?'

Always before when we have started these agonizing conversations, we have killed them quickly, before we could force each other to face the truth. But that was before my father knew. Or if he guessed at anything, before he laid it down between us.

'I suppose we could try it.' I turned round and looked at him, our eyes aghast as we saw the terrifying nullity, the *dullness* of not having this.

That was it. We were looking at something so dull. The grand drama of renunciation, on which I should have lived proudly for the rest of a stunted life, resolved itself into me standing with my back to the wall, leaning against it because I could not stand upright, not even sobbing properly but snivelling, and Tom saying, as he came to pull me away from the wall because I looked so derelict: 'Let's not be too wholesale. Let's try it for a month. Three weeks. At least we can say we tried.'

I cheated. On the ninth day, I went to Tottenham Court Road station. I really did want to go somewhere on a train, but I let myself walk from the studio in the Strand where the labels for B.B. products were designed, so that I could use this station.

I crossed two roads and passed two entrances to get to the right one. No matter where I was coming from or going to, I have always used these gents-scented steps, even when I wasn't meeting Tom. I imagine I always shall.

He came up the steps quickly, seething behind two women with bundles who were tackling the ascent abreast. He didn't seem to be looking for me, but when he saw me, he didn't look any more surprised than I felt. There was a dreadful inevitability about the meeting, which made a mockery of all the times during my eight days of struggle when I had passed a telephone and resisted physically the desire to lift it.

Tom was on his way to the office after lunch, and I was on my way to Ealing Broadway to discuss Spring Cleaning Sales with a market manager, but we went down the steps together and took shilling tickets and sat side by side in the first train that came along, and watched our dim, mysteriously attractive reflections in the other window. When we slid into a station, we disappeared. Back in the tunnel, our lovers' faces hung once more on the dark wall.

'This is no good,' Tom said. 'I've been in hell.'

My joy that he had suffered as much as me flooded through the emptiness of the last eight days. I sat and stared in silence at the image of my enraptured self and, when an oatmeal woman on her way from somewhere dull to somewhere duller sat down in front of it, I stared at her.

Afternoon people in the Tube are not obviously going to or from work, so they enjoy the independence of nobody knowing what they're up to. They read the early editions of the evening papers and leave long-distance suitcases by the doors and balance briefcases and midwife-sized bags comfortably on their knees because they are able to get a seat.

The ones who are not reading stare like ruminants. The woman opposite had a piece of her lunch embedded somewhere in her back teeth, but she never found it. She stared at me and I stared at her until we got to Tufnell Park, which was as far as we could go for a shilling. Tom and I got out and waited with his arm round me on the corner of an anonymous street of khaki-stucco houses, warted with bow windows, for a bus to take us back to London.

'What happens now?' I said, somewhere in Camden Town, where it was early-closing day, and newspapers blowing against the cigarette machines chained up in doorways. 'Are we supposed to start another three weeks?'

'What's the use? It didn't make me not love you.'

'That wasn't the point. It was supposed to make us find out if we could do without each other.'

'Well, I found out.'

'So did I.'

B O B   H A S been laid off. Half the men have, in his lot, and if you'll tell me how we're supposed to live on almost half what he was getting with overtime, and keep up all our payments, I'll thank you very much.

There's talk of a strike, but there's always been that, ever since Bob's been at the coach works. They bang on the tables in the cafeteria and talk very threatening, but nothing comes of it.

'It's your own bloody fault you got laid off,' I told Bob. 'You could have seen this coming months ago, you and those braying idiots who do all the talking.'

'We were told it was spite,' Bob said, 'when they cut down on the stores men, with Christmas coming. We didn't foresee this. It's a steel shortage, see, up in the north. It's the politicians, they say, causing trouble between our side and this country where they get the raw materials. Raw materials, that's it.' You'd think he'd said something clever.

'What country?'

He didn't know. He repeats what he's told, that's all.

'It's a chain reaction, like,' he said, fond of the phrase. 'A chain reaction.' He sits there smiling over something like that which tickles his fancy, as if it solved everything. 'A chain reaction, they call it.'

'And you're out of work, that's what I call it. The sack.' I sounded like my mother. I could hear her saying it at Dad that time he lost the job with the Council. Only man ever found drunk in charge of a dustcart, that's my Dad.

He'd hit her that time. She was carrying Loretta, and he hit her in the belly, as if he'd take it out on the child as well. I went for him, and he took my arm and held it over the gas. She put butter on it. No, margarine. I remember asking her: Why is it always me? Why don't he go for the boys? Because they were filthy little devils, you couldn't keep them clean, and her saying, with her mouth gone thin and hard, not soft with pity like it was when she first saw what he'd done: You were born to trouble, Kate. I didn't know then what she meant.

Freddie Turner, one of the men who's been laid off with Bob, says they may not take everybody back. Streamlining the operations, he said. He's as bad as Bob for sucking on peppermint words to make the truth taste better. 'Streamlining our department, and there's those will be found redundant.'

'Not our Bob,' I said, for I never let gorillas like Fred see that I know what a baby I've got. 'Bob will be the first to get his job back. They can't run the place without him.'

Freddie made a vulgar sound, because his wife would never say anything like that about him, even for fun.

Emma and I often talk about Bob like that. He loves it. Last time she was here, when there was talk about the chance of a lay-off, we were making all kinds of wonderful plans for him. How he was going to be acclaimed a genius because of the pictures he draws. All soldiers they are, and he colours them with crayons and pins them up round the walls. I took them down and burned them after I first saw Em's flat, and what she had up for pictures, but Bob went ahead and did some more, so I let them be. At least they cover up the marks from the people before. They must have spent their spare time throwing lumps of bacon fat at the wallpaper.

He would have a one-man show, Bob would, and Em and I would wear little jewelled caps on the back of our heads and velvet dresses, the kind everyone looks pregnant in, so it wouldn't matter about me.

He would be walking outside the Knightsbridge barracks one day and a Guards officer would come out and say: You're just the type this country needs, my boy, and have him inside and into uniform without a second glance at his feet.

He would be taken on by a rival coachbuilding firm and push them so far ahead with his brilliance and industry that the man who sacked him would come in rags, on all fours, begging for a job as cleaner, and Bob would let him sweep the floors with his moustache.

'He hasn't got one, Katie.'

'His beard then.'

Emma and I had some laughs that night, like old times, and Bob was dear and chuckly, like I like him.

But now that it's happened, and the dressing-table gone back – it was the first to go, I knew it would be, that Armenian is as hard as nails – it's not so funny. I'm not going to let the TV go. They can kill me first. You try being cooped up here, I'll say, with one baby out and one in and feeling sick all

137

the time, and they'll go Kchr-eechk with the knife and say: That will cure the sickness, madam. Bob likes the Westerns best. He sits in front of the set with a cap pistol and fires it off when they do. It drives Sammy frantic.

I didn't pay the rent last week. Mrs P. was all right about it when I told her what had happened, but she gets a bit less all right every week, I've seen it. So when Bob sat there talking about chain reactions, smiling and nodding as if going down to the labour exchange twice a week was all he need do about getting a job, I had suddenly had it.

'How do you know they'll take you back?' I said.

'You said they would.'

'Oh God, you hopeless idiot —' But if he didn't know when I was fooling, it was a waste of breath to tell him. 'It may be weeks, months. Why don't you *do* something? I'm fed up sick with having you sit about here all day eating caramels.' Every time he puts one in his mouth, he looks in the bag to see how many are left. Every time. 'I can't stand it any longer,' I yelled at him. I'm almost six months gone now, so it's natural to be hysterical.

'What do you want me to do?' He will never quarrel, not when he's sober, and he is never drunk because he gets sick first.

'Get out and do something. Go down to the library again and look at the job columns.'

'All right, Katie.' I watched him put on his raincoat and go out with the collar tucked in at one side, although I thought the public library was closed on a Saturday afternoon.

I wanted very badly to see Em. I would go and see Em and get human again. She might have something for me. Not money. I'd never ask for money, in case she might mention that fifty pounds. I was afraid once it might come between us, but with someone like her, it wouldn't. But she'll give me a blouse sometimes, or a sweater, things she pretends she's sick of. This old tatter, she'll say. If I wear it to work any more, they'll throw me out. It will do for me to mess about in, I say, and go off with that smashing red number that makes Barbie's famous Dior copy look like the rubbish it is.

138

I went to the phone box on the corner and dialled the number of the flat.

'Hullo?' Lisa sounded as if she were in bed, talking through the curtains of hair, like a four-poster.

'This is Kate Thomas, Emma's friend, if you remember. Is Emma there?'

'Oh, *hullo*. Of course I remember. How are you, Kate? Emma's gone home for the week-end. Shall I give her a message from you?'

She sounded so nice, I almost asked if I could come and see her instead. If I had lived with Em, people like Lisa would have been my friends too. I would have invited her to our flat if she wanted, so why couldn't she invite me?

Barbie came round after that and we went to see a film. When I got back, Sammy had fallen off our bed where I'd left him with the bottle propped. No harm. He'd gone to sleep on the floor. Bob had gone off to see old Marbles, when the library closed, and had his tea there (cold baked hearts), and when he came in, I told him the bruise on the baby's arm was what he'd done taking hold of him to throw him to the ceiling.

'You're too rough,' I said.

'I wouldn't hurt a hair of his head.'

But he hasn't got much hair, hasn't Sammy. He pulls a lot of it out, like one of the twins used, I can't remember which. A sign of insecurity, Molly used to say, but Mollyarthur says a lot of things she makes up as she goes along. I remember her saying one day at Marbles, when I was bitching about all the shoving and kicking keeping me awake: You'll love the baby once you have him, she said. You've no idea what's in store.

I H A D not been home for over a month. I had to go eventually, because my mother was getting that moan into her telephone voice with which she can usually exasperate me into doing what she wants. I had not seen my father since he left the flat on that dark Day of Judgement afternoon. I had no answer to his question. If he asked: What are you going to do about it? I would have to say: Nothing.

From a warm and windy week, it dropped suddenly cold and still on Friday and by evening, as the crowded train made its short dashes south between stations, big wads of snow began to drop on it, laughing silently because people had been thinking the winter was over.

My mother met me at the station in the sheepskin coat she had already put away and camphored. 'This will be the end of the primroses,' she said. It wasn't true, but since the snow could not hurt any of the alpines now flowering in her rock garden, it had to be the end of something.

My father was by the door when we got to the house, looking out from the lighted hall through a curtain of gilded snow. He never waits for me like that. I always have to find him. When I kissed him, he put his arms round me quickly, and I realized that he had been as nervous of me as I was of him. We had thought that we would look somehow different after our last meeting. The relief that we did not was very great.

Since I have been in love, it is strange being at home. My room, the feel of the banister, the warm spots and the draughts, the familiar smell of dog and furniture polish and starch in the curtains are part of another self. How can they all be the same when I am so different?

It is only when I am at home that I feel guilty. Escaped, emancipated, special; but a cheat too. In London, it doesn't feel like cheating, except that time when I met Johnny Jordan after Tom and I had been at Kate's flat.

My grandmother was there for the week-end, which was why I had come, as much as to stop my mother moaning. She is quite rich, because of her B.B. shares, and she drives about in a fat black Austin with a chauffeur who used to be an alcoholic and looks as if he could do with a drink now, but otherwise she is the plain grocer's widow she would have us think her, and still smells faintly of buns.

She gets on all right with my mother, on a level of mutual misunderstanding, each trying to compensate for some lack they find in the other. My mother fusses round Gran in a smothering way that would give me claustrophobia if I were an old lady, and Gran listens dutifully to the trivialities of my mother's days, faking interest.

They both try too hard, and it makes a week-end rather exhausting. Why don't they leave each other alone? They don't even like each other any better for trying so hard. My father doesn't try at all with either of them, and they both love him.

When I took in Gran's breakfast tray on Saturday morning, I drew the curtains and showed her that the snow was lying quite thickly on the garden.

'Are you going out to play in it?' Gran asked. I had on a pair of Bermudas and my hair in two pigtails fastened with paper clips, and she does occasionally have these lapses on first waking, when she forgets what decade we're in.

'There's a big drift outside the garage. Daddy and I are going to shovel it, so we can get the car out.'

'I don't want your father to shovel.' My mother came in with something I had left off the tray, which Gran didn't want anyway. 'Every year if it snows, men his age drop like ninepins from heart attacks. I'm always reading about it.' Those are the kind of news items she never misses.

'David is stronger than he looks,' Gran said soothingly. 'How pretty you look in that green, Laura.' It was red, but Gran sees everything in shades of black and white, so she guesses.

'Do I?' My mother was surprised. It was an old jersey thing she's had too long. She must have looked out of the window and seen the snow lying and more in the sky to come, and thought What does it matter? When I am her age, I shall dress more carefully, not less, especially at week-ends. When I am forty-eight, Tom will be sixty.

'She is pretty,' I said, because thinking of me and Tom at forty-eight and sixty mellowed me. I put my arm round her and felt her awkwardness. She can never relax into an embrace.

'You're getting thin, Emma.' She always says that. It shows motherly concern for a daughter away from home. It never was true when she used to say it to Alice, but it is now, about me.

My father and I couldn't talk much while we were shovelling. The snow was wet and it was hard work. Our faces were red and my knees were mottled red and blue between my shorts and woollen socks, and his breath was like steam from a kettle, because he was panting. It was harder for him, because he can't balance properly with his leg. I could have done the job by myself in the same time, but we used to do it together when Peter was too small and Alice too lazy, so we did it together now, and my mother only opened the window twice to call out: 'Don't overdo it!'

'That's the voice she used to call to us: Don't go too far out,' I said.

'The day Peter was drowned,' my father said, 'she'd stayed in the hotel with you, do you remember?'

I have never forgotten the exact discomfort of the wicker chairs we were sitting in when the ambulance man came in through the hotel porch.

' "If I'd been there," she said afterwards, "I would have told him not to go too far out." '

'He wouldn't have taken any notice. None of us did.'

'But the thing was, she had to say that. It was my fault. We all knew that. I was with him. I should have known about the current. She didn't say it for about a month, and I thought she wasn't going to. Perhaps she hoped she wouldn't. In the end she had to.'

'I love you.' He won't let me rage and storm against my mother, so it is all I can say to make up for these ghastly things in his life.

'I'm afraid you may have a father complex. Perhaps that's why —' He stopped and looked at me. The last time my mother came to the window, we had stopped work to foil her before she called and we were in the earthy little toolshed, putting the shovels away. It was warm in there and we had lingered, stamping and banging our hands, while he lit a cigarette.

I sat down on the table where my mother pots things, to shake snow out of my boot.

'I have to ask you again, Emmie,' he said. 'Have you thought about what you're going to do?'

I shook my head. I could feel my face growing stubborn, but I was afraid of letting go. 'We tried not seeing each other. It didn't work.'

'How do you mean, it didn't work?' He had on a thick brown sweater and a torn tweed jacket and baggy old trousers he'd dredged up from what looked like the twenties. The hat that used to collect rain like a gutter when we went fishing was pushed to the back of his head, and the circulation was coming back in claret patches to his bony forehead and nose. My mother would have screamed Heart! but he was just cold, and nervous about having to talk to me like this.

'We can't, that's all. We just can't.'

'That's absurd. You can't. If you know what's the right thing to do, you should have the strength to do it.'

My eyes stung, and I blinked and looked down. I hadn't expected him to be quite so obtuse. 'Damn Eric,' I said. 'I wish you didn't know.'

'I've known for some time,' he said more gently. 'Not what it was, but I knew there was something. How could I not know? You don't crash about so much any more.'

'I'm grown up.'

'Not very. But you've stopped falling over things.'

'You should be glad. It used to annoy you.'

'I know. Funny, when you came into the drawing-room last night with the tray of drinks, with your hair piled up and the black dress, I found myself wishing you'd trip over the rug.'

'You haven't said anything to Mother?' I knew he hadn't. She could not have avoided at least looking at me wretchedly, even if she had not known what to say.

He shook his head. 'No need for her ever to know anything about it.'

'She'll have to know in the end.' We stared at each other mulishly, antagonists. I wish I hadn't come. I wished that I had stayed in London and waited about, watching the dirty snow, on the chance of seeing Tom. But Tom and Sheila had gone to stay with friends. That was the third reason why I had come home. I hoped it had snowed in Buckinghamshire, and spoiled Sheila's golf.

The toolshed had only been warm compared to the snow-heavy air outside. It was cold and damp now, and I wanted to go back to the house, but my father said, 'Wait a minute. Something has got to be said.'

I was standing by the door, looking at the humped bushes and the sheet of lawn my mother's silly dog had spoiled, going mad in circles on the virgin snow. 'There's nothing to say. I'm sorry, Daddy. I'm sorry as hell to hurt you. I don't expect you ever to quite understand, but I wish you'd try.'

He grimaced as if he were in physical pain. 'You'll think I'm lying if I say I do understand. I've got to tell you something, Emma. You're the last person I thought I'd tell, because —' He groaned. 'I always wanted you to think I was perfect.'

'I do,' I said, because I do, even with everything I know about him.

'Come in again and shut the door.'

He took off the fishing hat and flung it on to a shelf of flower-pots, running his mittened hands automatically up the sides of his head, where the hair grows in pigeon wings. 'Listen, Emmie.' We were like children playing secrets, hiding from the grownups. It was absurd. We didn't look at each other. I was ashamed and embarrassed for us both, especially as he didn't tell it well. My father with his relaxed command of words, never garrulous, timing replies just right, apt and easy with the customers in court – he told me this as if I were a headmaster and he a naughty schoolboy, stumbling over his story and stammering, choking on his cigarette, grinding it out underfoot and coughing again as he lit another.

I didn't want to hear. I didn't care what he had done. Just don't tell me! I cried inside myself. Why do I have to know?

It was the woman with the eyes and hair whom I had met two years ago at the cocktail party. Benita was her name.

'I saw her at the airport when you went to France. Was she going with you?'

'You don't have to know the details,' my father said. 'You shouldn't know any of it. It's only that I – I have to tell you now to stop you making this hideous mistake.'

'Why is it a mistake to be in love?'

'It isn't, if you're free.'

'I am.'

'He's not.'

'He doesn't love her.'

'That makes no difference.' Now that he had got his initial confession out, choking on it like a lump of unmasticated steak, he could talk to me more easily. We were looking at each other again. The earthy smell was damp and pungent in my nostrils. I have never liked this log cabin toolshed since the spiders when we were children. I didn't like it now.

'It's classically simple, dearest,' he said. 'You must see that. It's between right and wrong. Someone like you can't possibly make a life out of the wrong.'

'Why can you?'

'I can't. Benita and I are – chucking it. Putting an end to it. Letting go. There isn't an expression that doesn't sound like a musical comedy.'

'Would you have married her?'

'You can't base a life together on someone else's misery.'

'I know.' I did know. I had known all along, I suppose, even when the flooded river swept by, encouraging me: Love him, love him.

My father never said: He's too old for you.

He never said: He should have told you that his wife knew.

He never said: He's a coward. He's thought of himself all along more than of you.

If he had said any of these things, I would have broken from him and gone out, back to my life. I knew them all. I didn't need to hear them from him or anyone else. They made no difference to my love.

But he didn't say them. He said quietly, with his hands in the pockets of the sagging old jacket, which my mother had tried, ineffectually, to patch with leather, 'You have two choices then, if you won't give up. To wreck his marriage, or to wreck your own life.'

'I don't care about conventions. It's been —'

'Do you like this hole-and-corner thing you've got yourself into?' he burst out violently. 'Don't tell me it's exciting. It's not. It's terrible. Exhausting. Wretched. Destroying. A few friends who know – and leer a bit. The rest can't be your friends. All the places you can't go to together. All the contriving, the lies, the – the ghastly *effort* involved just to meet for a drink – Oh God, Emmaline Bullock! I'm fifty-two. Who cares what a mess I make? But you – you're twenty, and the world is throbbing with men for you, and you should be shot for your insanity – your sheer bloody-minded, depraved perversity that makes you steal and cheat and lie, at twenty. *Twenty*. You should be shot.'

'Help me,' I said. 'What am I going to do?'

'Help you – when I can't even help myself. We'll have to help each other.' He grimaced again, jerking the face muscles on one side, as if someone had run a needle into him. 'It's going to be hell for both of us. Do you want to make a pact that we'll stick to it?'

When Kate and I made a pact, we hit the backs of our hands with a hairbrush, whirled them round to make the blood start out, then pressed the backs of our hands together, joining the blood.

I took a stiff brush that my mother uses for scrubbing flower-pots, and we took off our gloves and I showed him how to do it. The blood sprang up out of my hand in tiny jewelled bubbles. The veins of his were nearer the surface, and one of them broke when the bristles hit it. When he began to circle his arm, I saw that the hand was already covered with blood, so I pulled his arm down quickly, and we joined his dark flowing blood with my bright drops.

'Blood comrades,' I said, sealing my disloyalty to Tom. 'I swear.'

'I swear.'

Part Three

S o E m is off to America. Her uncle is sending her to study sales techniques, she says, but I know it is really to get her away from this Tom.

She's broken with him. I asked her flat out. If I don't talk about it, she said, it's all right. Just don't make me talk about it.

I hated to see her go. I wanted her to be here when I have the baby. I wanted her to come to the hospital and see me sitting up in bed with a ribbon in my hair and that sort of purified look, like they get in the movies after they take the pillow out and pretend they've had it.

It's odd, I've always minded so much about how she sees me.

She's seen me every worst way, from the beginning on, when I'd been two weeks in Stinkney without a change of clothes, and all that talcum in my hair to get rid of the filthy oil they hit you with. But I still, when I'm looking sweet, like people do when they've just had a baby, whether they want it or not, I still want Em to see me.

I rolled my hair the other day the way the models do, all over to one side with the ends flicked out, and my first thought was: I must show Em. But Em is three thousand miles away. I may as well cut the whole lot off and go back to polo necks. Or just let my neck show, who cares? Who cares what I look like? If I ask Bob to admire something new about me, his first reaction is to paw. That's men, as my aunt used to say, the only one of my mother's family who still came to see us. Can't hardly wait till one gets out to stuff the next one in.

If I could have Em as a visitor in the hospital, that Sister would give me more than the fag end of her manners. She's still there, because I asked in Out Patients. If Em came to my bedside with her hair swept round her head like a polished bronze turban and that yellow dress she brought to travel in,

147

there'd be no Get up and make your bed, Mrs—er. You young girls are all born lazy.

Only another month to go. With Sammy, I couldn't wait to be rid of him. Little did I know, though that was another thing my aunt used to say, It won't come out as easy as it went in. I am afraid, and I want Em here to tell it to afterwards and lie about how brave I was. It's one thing I've experienced that she hasn't.

If I didn't look so awful, I'd have gone to the station to see her off, I mean that. Why should I care about her family being there? I'm not afraid of them. They almost had me practically one of them, and Em said at the time that they were pleased about her and me and the flat, though I think she made that up.

It's hell being pregnant in the summer, because you can't cover it with a big coat. If Moll hadn't given me that Hawaiian flowered smock, I'd not have been able to go to the party she gave for Em. I took old Sam to Moll's, because Barbie and Ron had gone to the races, and Barbie's getting sick of minding him for me anyway, now that I can't pay her hardly anything. Some friend.

He's really quite all right in the cot alone, but Molly and Em wouldn't think so, so we took him along, and I was quite proud of him, the fuss everyone made. Em gave him the little red suit as a going-away present. All the things she's given me. Lisa must be mad with jealousy because she didn't get the saddle-stitched jacket. I can't wear it yet, but my day will come.

At Moll's we sang Should Auld Acquaintance. It choked my throat. All the kids were singing, even the new ones who hardly know Em, and I thought of my birthday that evening centuries ago, and how far we had all come since then.

When I was seventeen, and beginning to find so much in life, through Moll, I couldn't wait to go ahead, to get on with the next thing. Now I was wishing I could have stayed right there where I was in the red polo neck with my waist twenty-four and my hips nothing, and all the kids only cherubs in the candlelight, and other people's at that.

They have taken back some of the men at the coach works,

but not Bob, although he's been down there twice and seen a man who always said he would look out for him. That's how they are. It's only people like Molly and Em you can rely on. The rest are with you when you're up, and kick you into the gutter when you're down.

I've heard my mother say that when we didn't have much to eat that winter when the baker's man stopped keeping the stale bread and buns for us. When Dad was in work, and before we had to move to that shack in the mud down the end of the lane, he'd been kind. The lower you get, she said, the harder they kick.

But Molly says she is going to get work for Bob. She knows everyone at the Town Hall, and she thinks she can get him something. He still believes he is going in the Army, in spite of what the recruiting sergeant said last time he rolled in there. He went to the clinic again to have his feet seen, and they said: Splendid! Keep on with the exercises. So he does, it drives you frantic, but they are just as flat. Any fool can see that.

'YOU MUST go by boat,' Uncle Mark said. 'Cut loose and have a dizzy time.'

In spite of having Nell and Derek for children, he still hopes that our generation can reproduce the simple pre-war giddiness of his. An ocean liner to him is a fairyland of romance. He flies everywhere now, so he has not seen the Irish priests in sports jackets, the crew-cut Mormon missionaries, the service families whose children stay up later than the grown-ups.

'You don't meet enough people, Emma. Parties and fun, young men – that's what you need.'

Young men. I must have met some in this last year. I haven't noticed. Parties and fun. If I couldn't go with Tom, I didn't go, and there was almost nobody who could invite us together. Lisa. Derek. Tom's friend Alistair who met us in Edinburgh.

I was still numb with loss, sleepwalking blankly from one day to the next, so I did not make the effort to insist that I would rather fly to New York. Uncle Mark was paying the fare, so I went by boat.

Tom and I had both kept our promise. We had not telephoned or written. We had stayed away from any of the places we might meet. Once Bernie asked me to a party at the river house, but I refused. I was not going to let my father down.

He and I had been a little nervous of each other since the blood-stained pact. At first we occasionally asked each other how it was going, until we were hit by the absurdity. Father and daughter each renouncing illicit love – Feel all right, Em? I'll live, how about you? – like people trying to give up smoking.

If he had said: I know how you feel, I'm going through hell, I would have crawled into his arms. But he didn't. He couldn't know. How could he compare my devouring relationship with Tom to his little circus with Benita and her matching luggage? There were times when I felt that he had cheated me. Then I went home and saw how little he had there, and I knew that he had given up a lot, perhaps even more than me, for I had nothing now, but he still had the dull defeatism of my mother.

At least I was free, with the freedom of emptiness. The flatness of nothing stretched before me like a desert, featureless, with no signposts.

Physically, I was going to New York, to work for Uncle Mark's old lend-lease friend, now chairman of a big grocery chain, but myself was going nowhere. I was huddled up inside, tight and uncommunicative, like a cold hibernating squirrel.

The first day on the boat, when the cranes and cabbages of Southampton had disappeared behind the curtain of rain, and I was gone for a year, with no hope now, I sat in the lounge and held on to myself. My face felt like Stonehenge, and I had to cross my arms, because there was an actual ache in my chest. I thought I might be going to have a heart attack, and how disappointing for my mother that she had been so busy predicting it for my father that she had passed up the luxury of anticipating it for me.

I sat there while the unseasoned passengers came and went through the lounge, exploring their floating trap, and composed the cable that would be sent from the ship. The carpenter would knock up a rude coffin. Where would they bury me? Since we had not yet reached Ireland, they might turn round, and people in a hurry would be angry, but have to pretend not to mind, and get up a collection for my family.

After I got to know Martin and Bess, she said: 'When I came into the lounge looking for Martin and saw you hunched into that chair like a hermit in a barrel, I thought you were holding on to your heart to stop it breaking.'

'I was.'

I told her about Tom, and she passed it on to Martin, and he began to stop treating me like a child, and let me have martinis. I told her many things in those five days, even some things I had not been able to tell Tom. It came flooding out of me like tears. I must have been a hideous bore. I even knew I was at the time, but God, the relief. I had to go on with it, like having to be sick when someone is watching.

Bess is very good at listening because she can sit with her hands in her lap, relaxed, and not make redundant comments to prove she is paying attention. She is very good to look at too, which helps when you are vomiting up your soul. Poised and fragrant, with smoky-blue eyes and the delicate bones and features I wish I had in those bad moments when the desires think darkly of plastic surgery.

I even found myself telling her about the time when I was kidnapped. I have told very few people about that, and my parents know only the bare facts. They know what happened, because I had to tell it in court, but they never knew how I felt about it.

They know that my bicycle skidded on wet leaves and buckled its wheel against a tree. They know that instead of walking three miles home in the rain – what kind of a fool did they think I was? – I had thumbed a car, against all my mother's panic-stricken orders, and got into it with the middle-aged man who was driving.

They know that, instead of letting me out at the turning for home, he had driven on with me for miles and miles, until it was dark and I had no idea where I was. They know that I jumped out once, as he slowed at a corner, and tried to run, and that he caught me and tied my hands and put a scarf round my mouth to stop me yelling, though who was to hear me on the lonely marshes of Romney?

They knew that he took me to a little shuttered house near the sea and kept me locked up there for three days, and bungled the business about the ransom, and walked right into the police trap with his long ungainly legs and his sad reflective eyes. They know that he killed himself in prison a few months later, because it was in the papers, and the story about me told over again.

They do not know that I loved Rocky, and I shall never tell them. They could not possibly understand. Even Tom did not perfectly understand. He made a rather crude joke about thirteen-year-old girls and I wished I had not tried to explain to him.

Kate knew. When she told me about the Australian she was only with for a few hours, I told her about Rocky, and how lonely he was, the loneliest man I had ever seen.

'So was Douglas, I think,' Kate said. 'He didn't have anyone to talk to.'

'He was the first person in my life who needed me more than I needed him.'

'He made me feel I mattered', Kate said, and I remember saying, 'Don't tell Molly,' and her saying, 'She'd be shocked.'

A woman of thirty can fall in love with a man of sixty and no one is shocked. When you are thirteen, forty-three looks like a dirty old man and people won't believe that it was only caring and companionship, because that is the kind of minds they have. Even people like Molly. My mother had me examined after Rocky. I shall never forgive her for that.

Bess and Martin live in an ugly industrial town in Massachusetts, because that is where he makes window frames, but they have a summer house on Cape Cod, and when we talked about me staying there and the beach and sailing and their daughters who would make me stand in the sunset shallows and dig for clams, I realized that I looked forward to it. I felt my cheekbones rising up and out, and I pulled them down.

'You've remembered you're not supposed to smile so widely,' Bess said.

'It seems disloyal. If we – well, coming to America was one of the things we were going to do together.'

'Stop acting,' Martin said, suddenly rough, and I saw him, in fright, as a burly stranger made of nothing but jaw and muscle and ruthless common sense.

At first in New York I was still only half myself. I went about alone a lot, as you can in this city, and be anyone you want to be. It is like being in a film. You can sit in the Automat and eat pie and read a paperback and just be a girl in the Automat, feeling the part without living it. When you leave, you are a girl in a black linen dress and new shoes with a big tortoiseshell buckle holding her hair, waiting for the traffic lights to change. When you cross, your legs criss-crossing with fifty others in front of the panting bus, you are an extra in a crowd scene, existing only in that moment on the screen.

I roomed with two girls from the office, but once in a while I would take a hotel room, and stay there for a night or two with the television and the air conditioning and be a girl alone in a hotel, enigmatic in the lobby, mysterious in the elevator, where the men held their thin straw hats to their chests and stared.

If Brenda and Dodie thought I was with a man, they did not say anything. We were friends on the surface, but we let each other alone. Once when I had rung for breakfast and left the door open so the waiter could get in, a man came into my room in the hotel.

At first he looked surprised, and apologized, as if he had really made a mistake. He took a step backwards and then changed his mind and came on towards the bed. He had a sharp nose and a small petulant mouth with a cleft chin, too pretty, but his eyes were ugly, jaundiced. I managed to say, 'Please go away,' and he smiled, and just then the waiter came in and the man turned and went out, giving me a brisk little wave from the door as if he had been paying a social call.

I don't know what the waiter thought. I was stiff with horror. If the man had touched me, it would have been like a tortoise with its shell off. I thought of my father, as I often did, and wondered whether he was less foolish than I, and could stop remembering.

I had my twenty-first birthday in America. I had made some friends by now, as well as Brenda and Dodie, and they wanted to give me a party, but Bess telephoned because she had remembered the date, and I was to come to Cape Cod.

'They won't let me. I'm doing a survey.'

'What of?'

'Traffic flow.'

'Have you switched jobs?'

'Traffic flow. Which way they push the carts round, and why. Mr Vinson will never let me go in the middle of the week.'

'Ask him.'

I did, and was surprised when he said Yes. He is a very formal fat man with a blue jaw which he constantly polishes with an electric razor in his desk, and a liking for words like connotation and eventuality, which are not in the more casual commerce of speech. I had not realized he was human, but he suddenly relaxed and pulled out from among his credit cards a picture of his family: two toothy teenagers and a wife all looking about the same age.

He gave me a cheque for fifty dollars for my birthday, and I bought a white swim suit with it and paid my plane fare to Hyannis, where Bess met me in an English car with three sun-bleached daughters with brown bare feet.

While I was in their house getting ready for the party, there was a telephone call for me. Long distance from England, the middle daughter said, panting up into my room.

I grabbed for my dressing-gown, but she said: 'Come down like that, everyone does,' so I ran down in my slip, and heard the voice of the English operator, a man, because it was almost midnight over there. Another male voice was coming in in the background, and I said, 'Daddy!' more excitedly than I had thought I would, and then I heard Tom laugh.

I was standing on the marble floor of a little lobby off the front room, and my bare feet were like ice, although my hands were sweating, gripping the receiver as if it could hold me up.

'It isn't only your father who thinks of you on your birthday,' Tom said, and the whole damn thing came flooding back, just when I had thought it was beginning to leave me, just when it was beginning to be a conscious effort to remember his face and voice.

It was, as he had once said, like talking to someone in the next room. It was like talking to him across the mile of London rooftops, from my flat to the telephone box where he had written among the obscenities and scrawled numbers: T loves E for ever.

It costs thirty bob a minute, he had said, and then you can't think of anything to say. All I could say was, 'How did you know where I was?'

'I rang your mother, and said I had a bill to send you. She sounded panicky, as if I was a bookie or a blackmailer, so I changed it to a receipt, and she gave me the address.'

'I didn't want you to know where I was.'

'I do now. I may have to come over later this year.'

'Don't.'

'Emma, I —'

If he had said: I want you, come back, I swear I would have gone. With the last remnants of sanity, I interrupted jerkily: 'How did you know I was here?'

'Someone at your New York number told me. Where are you?'

'On Cape Cod.'

'Oh God, darling. Martha's Vineyard was one of the places I was going to take you.'

'Don't, Tom, please don't. I can't stand it.' I stood there bowed over and shivering in my slip, pleading with him from three thousand miles to leave me alone, just as I had once pleaded with him never to leave me.

His voice changed and he said rather stiffly: 'How is everything, all right?'

'Yes, all right. What about you?'

'Pretty good. Been very busy. Usual thing. It's rained all summer.'

'The sun shines here all the time.'

The seconds slipped prodigally past while we discussed the weather back and forth across the Atlantic, and soon the operator would cut in and he would say goodbye and it would be over, and I would have failed him.

'Emma's shivering!' the child called out to Bess when I put down the receiver. 'Get her a drink, quick.'

I had not failed my father. If he did telephone me on my twenty-first birthday, I could speak to him without guilt. I swear, we had said, and I had stuck to it.

He didn't telephone. I knew it was too late, because my mother goes to bed at ten. I even told Bess the call was from him, and the listening child had opened her mouth, but shut it at my look, and shrugged her shoulders on a mystery not worth pursuing.

At the week-end, Martin took me to the Air Force Base to see President Kennedy arrive from Washington in his plane and take off for Hyannisport in his helicopter. We went to the officer's club for a drink because Martin used to be in the Air Force, and that was when I met Joel.

After that, I went up to Cape Cod often at week-ends, and when Bess closed up the summer house in September and the children went back to school, Joel would hop on planes going to the Base at Poughkeepsie, and borrow a car and suddenly arrive at the house in Brooklyn, where Brenda and Dodie and I lived with secret Mrs Patterson who could not talk above a whisper.

I have never told Joel about Tom. He has forced me back into life by not knowing that I was out of it.

I MUST write to Em. I've been saying that for weeks. It's awful, I haven't written since the baby was born, and she wrote back to say it had been on her birthday, so we dropped the name Linda and called her Emily.

Bob is fond of Em, in his way, because she doesn't laugh at him, and she was always nice with him after she got over the fright he gave her that time at Marbles'.

'Stinking idiot,' I told him afterwards, 'doing a thing like that to a girl like her.'

'She's a girl, isn't she?' he said, with that innocent look he gives you under his hair, his eyes all round and wet. 'I thought she'd like it.'

But he doesn't hold it against her that she called him a filthy beast. Emmaline he wouldn't have, because he can't spell it, but Emily he likes, so one of these days we are going to have her christened. Perhaps we'll wait until Em gets back, and she can be godmother.

Sammy was christened in the second week, but I didn't feel so bad after him as I have since Emily. Anaemic they say, and I should be living with old Marbles, because I'm supposed to eat liver, but we can't afford it, not in the quantities she used to dish out. No wonder Bob rang the bell first try.

So I have these iron pills that taste of dust, and I left the top off one day and Sammy got at them. He's into everything now that he can walk, if you can call it walking, that beery stagger from one piece of furniture to the next, like my dad coming home in the dark. Nothing is safe. He was bad enough when he was a baby, but it gets worse as they get older and you can't stick them down somewhere and leave them. I'd only gone down the passage to see Mr Zaharian, but five minutes is all they need, when they're crafty like this one.

He had to go to hospital and have the stomach pump. He might die, they told me, if it's got into the bloodstream, for I'd no idea how many were in the bottle, so we didn't know if he'd had two or twenty.

He might die. That was a queer feeling. I had to sit there on that metal chair in the corridor outside the ward and think about how much I'd mind. I couldn't see it, not beyond the funeral, with the tiny coffin and Bob and me so serious, and talking in hushed voices. I would be holding Emily, and it would be a symbol, like, of the continuity of life unvanquished by death. Make a nice picture, though I'd have nothing to wear.

He might die, they said, and it came into my mind that it might be better for him. Why should I think that? He'll get by, like I have. I've had some fun in life, with all the rest of it, and I'll have some more when we get out of this business. Bob says when he's in the Army, we shall have married quarters made of red brick, somewhere in Surrey where the earth is sand and it's all yellow gorse and little fir-trees.

Emma wants to know all about the baby, and she sent Emily that all-over suit with feet, thank God she did, for it's about the only decent thing she's got to wear, with the state things were in when Sammy was through with them.

Marge Collins who lives downstairs, and has three kids in Care by different fathers and has milked every government agency and charitable institution, says I can get baby clothes just for the asking, but no thanks. Marge has never been in a Remand Home or on probation. I have. They don't stop at baby clothes. They want to rehabilitate you. My life is mine now. I don't want no case workers ferreting out my business.

Em's letters get sent on from the flats, so she doesn't know we've had to move. I must write and tell her. I'll write to her tomorrow. It's so far away. They've taken her away from me, and we'll never be close again, more than sisters, like we were once. When she writes about New York and that place she goes to by the sea, and this pilot she's got now with his boat and his Thunderbird car, it's because she wants me to share it, but all it does is make me see the gap widening. Her world is growing and spreading. Mine is narrowing, even from what it was. It cramps and smothers me, and I want to bust my way out. That's why I threw that shoe. Bob laughed, because he thought it was at him, and missed, but it was at everything really. He'll have to get that window pane fixed before the cold sets in. Newspaper doesn't keep out draughts, as I should know.

When Bob gets a better job, we'll be all right. Get out of this hole and get a decent flat again, and the school can find someone else to clean up their mess, for Bob will be in a chalk-stripe suit or a uniform, and we'll give his overalls to the poor.

If we ever get another Council flat, which I doubt, if they've got a black list, like the Roman Church with their dirty books, I'll put by the rent each week before I even buy cigarettes. I didn't know how well off we were till I found out how much they were asking, other places.

Four quid we have to pay for this one room with the sink

and that miserable gas fire, and lucky to get it, with two kids. Norma upstairs, she pays more for those three cupboards she calls a flat. Poor Mr Zaharian with those Salvation Army trousers he's cut the bottoms off with the pinking shears I won at Bingo, that three-cornered cell where he cries with homesickness is not much bigger than my room at Moll's.

This old house, which used to be a grand dwelling with servants in the days when this part of London was for those with money instead of those without, is like a picture I once saw of Hell, a big tall house all stuffed full of people wailing and wringing their hands out of the windows.

It's all cut up into separate flats and rooms. There's nine families living here, if you count the singles as families, Dino, Mr Zaharian, Dolly – when she's single – and that poor old woman who creeps up and down the stairs in boots, and nobody knows her name or where she goes in the daytime. I think she's a white slaver, and jabs young girls in the arm as they help her across the road, and bundles them into the back of a van.

When Em comes back, we'll have a laugh talking about all the weirdos in this house. We used to tell things about the people in the flats, but most of it was guessing, because they were pretty stuffy, and whatever they did they did behind their front doors. But here the front doors are just the doors of rooms, and people share taps and bathrooms and toilets, and the downstairs people share a kitchen, and everybody knows everybody else's business. What they don't know they make up, and tell it on the half-landing where Dino has his room that used to be a little conservatory, which is where the women gather.

They all knew about Sammy and the iron pills, and I didn't even have to ask anyone to take Emily while I was at the hospital. Both Marge and Dolly came right in and almost fought for the privilege. So there's that to it, but there's cruelty too, in the way they talk, and judge everybody.

Some of them thought it was my fault, and told Bob so. He repeats everything to me, like a child with a lesson, whether it's going to hurt or not. He can't always tell the difference.

When Sammy had that bruise on his face, I didn't take

him out for three days because of the women on the landing, and Mrs O'Hara who sits on that little balcony of hers, with a lap spread wide as a table, so she can see who goes in and out. When she sits, you can't see the chair at all. She'll fall into the area one day, balcony and all, on top of the milk bottles. I hope it's when Em's here.

Come back, Em, oh I wish you'd come back.

If I write to her, perhaps she will. I used to write letters, but Moll always had paper, or those shiny picture postcards she collected, and stamps. I can't even find a pencil most days. Sammy eats them. Tina used to eat coal, and Molly said she'd started doing it when Ziggy came, and she had to stop being the baby. Sammy is jealous of little Em. I know that. He howls to get my attention, and if he can't or I go out and leave him, he does something bad. I remember when I was little and they used to sometimes make me feel I wasn't there, I'd deliberately break something, or wet on the floor, because being hit was better than being ignored.

I HAD not meant to go home so soon, although there were times when I wished I had the money to flip back and forth like an executive.

There were many times when I missed my father, and wanted badly to see his tired, attractive face, and hear his voice, which is completely English without being upper class about it. In America, you get very conscious of the English voice. What sounds all right in Knightsbridge, the loud clear shopping voice that owns the world, can make you squirm in New York. American parodies of the British are not all that grotesque.

I wanted to talk to him. I was in slight danger of marrying Joel. Why danger? He is charming and just right in everything, like a man in a story, but if I could see him with my father, away from his own country and the service environment which invests him with some of the strength and importance of the planes he flies, it would be safer.

I had agreed to stay in America for two years, so when my

mother wrote that she was 'bitterly disappointed', first about Christmas, and then that I wasn't coming back this summer, it was something she had invented to make herself, or me, feel worse. She offered to pay half my fare. When I have children, I shall never make half-gestures. They shall get all or nothing.

In the spring, however, I came home from work and found Mrs Patterson shuffling through the letters on the collapsible shelf in the hall that collapses if you put a parcel on it.

Brenda says she steams open all the letters, but I don't think she does theirs, only mine, because she is an agent for the F.B.I. and checks me for security since that day she caught me watching deadpan at the far end of the housewares aisle in her local market to see whether shoppers turned left or right after the instant starch.

When I came in, she held out the blue airmail letter upside down, because she had been trying to decipher the return address on the back, and whispered, 'A letter from England', with her eyebrows stretched like rubber bands, as if it were a novelty. 'From your folks?'

'From my sister.' It was hard not to whisper when you answered her. Talking normally sounded like a shout.

'My sister is in Denver. Everything all right at home, I hope?' she asked anxiously, for, in her world, people wrote letters only for disasters. Other news went on the appropriate kind of greeting card. Birth, Thank You (for the present, the flowers, the party), Secret Pal, Sympathy, Congratulations (on your wedding, your graduation, your recovery, your promotion), Get Well Quick, Enjoy Your Retirement, Bon Voyage, Sorry I Forgot Your Birthday, Let's Hear From You – she spent hours at the revolving racks in the drugstore searching for the exact message. When I was at Cape Cod for a week last summer, she had sent me a card with a picture of a sad fisherman's wife saying, 'Miss you, that's for shore. Hurry home from sea.'

I had started to read the letter, for if I didn't, she would think I had something to hide, so I didn't answer for a moment.

'Everything all right at home?' she whispered again, and I looked at her blankly and said, 'Yes – oh, yes thanks, everything's fine,' and made myself walk upstairs, for her feelings would be hurt if I ran.

'Darling Emma,

I have got to tell you this right away, although I know how it will hurt you. Daddy has left mother. They are going to get a divorce. I think you'd better come home. I will ask Uncle Mark to clear it with the New York people. We'll pay your fare. I feel as if it was the end of the world, though I don't see why. It happens to a lot of people. Theirs is the generation that discovered divorce.

Please come home,
Alice.'

When I said goodbye to Joel, he said, 'I have a feeling you'll never come back,' but I knew that I would. I had nothing left in England now. Even Kate was slipping away from me through her awful marriage that was dragging her slowly back to what she had been dragged away from. She was getting my letters and presents, because they didn't come back, but she never wrote. She had called her baby after me, but she didn't need me.

I flew home, since Uncle Mark was not paying for paper hats and streamers and laughter on the boat deck, and Alice met me at the airport in a new car and a new green suit and a new hair colour, which made me realize how long I had been away. Her round face was not troubled, because it can't be, but she hugged me with all that soft awkward weight of hers, and said, 'Oh *God*, I'm glad you came,' so fervently that I felt like a rat and a coward for letting her take the crisis alone.

Alice is twenty-eight. I am nearly twenty-two, and already we felt the sickening reversal of relationship. Our parents had blundered like children. From now on we would have to be the grown-ups who sorted things out.

My mother was waiting for us with a dog on the lap of an old brown dress, being brave. I really was glad to see her after so long, and I was touched that she cried with pleasure when I came, but the critical demon in me, which has to hold her always remorselessly in judgement, wished that she would be brave in something more inspiring than the tube of seated cinnamon wool that should have gone long ago to worsen the burden of the poor. Her lovely thick black hair, which is her best feature, was oily and lank. She looked, Alice told me disloyally in the kitchen, less like a virtuously wronged wife than a woman you could hardly blame a man for leaving.

'I blame him utterly,' I said, and nearly cut my finger off.

Her plants needed watering. Her voice was flat and drear. She wouldn't have a drink. She didn't want her dinner. She wouldn't take a book to bed, as she has done every night since I can remember.

When I went into her room later, she lay propped there like a corpse at an American funeral, with her arms outside the neat covers and her head in the middle of the smooth pillow, looking through the opposite wallpaper at nothing.

The white candlewick counterpane was squared neatly on the other twin bed, pleated in under the pillow with Mrs Baker's nicety, but the ashtray I had made for him at school was beside it, and the second part of *Henry IV*, and a pencil and pad he used to make notes with. They had sold their double bed some time ago after my father's operation, thank God, or I had a feeling she might have lain rigidly on her side of it with the sheet on his side turned down, like the empty chair and filled wineglass at the dead man's table.

'She accepts too much,' I said in Alice's room.

'She has always accepted the way he treated her.'

'But she behaves as if she were mourning him, when she should be sick with anger. Do you suppose she knew?'

'I don't know.' Alice turned round in her nightdress on the dressing-table stool, and I saw that she was pregnant. 'I didn't, but then I never know anything that goes on. If Gordon was involved with one of his gynies, I'd be the last to find out. He never said anything to you?'

I shook my head. I would never talk about the toolshed. I would never think about it. I had decided that, going up Mrs Patterson's stairs in Brooklyn, as soon as I had read Alice's letter. My father was dead for me, and all that had gone between us.

'Why didn't you tell me about that?' I nodded at her stomach.

'I was just going to when this happened. In fact, I'd started a letter to you. Then I threw it away and wrote the other and forgot to put in about the baby. That's how agitated I was. Gordon gave me sedatives,' Alice said with interest, because she is not the type who gets dope prescribed for her.

'How did you hear?' How could he tell her without telling me? That hurt almost as much as what he had done.

'Mother telephoned. He should have told us himself. It was cowardly. What do you suppose she's like, this trull? He's going to marry her, you know.'

'I saw her at the airport, that time he went to France.'

'You should have told me.'

'Not after what you'd said. I didn't want you thinking that about him.'

'What's she like?' Alice asked, her eyes quick with unavoidable interest.

I told her about Benita and her slow, amused voice, and the blaze of excitement that went with her.

Alice groaned. 'Poor mother. What is she on her own? She doesn't seem to have any position, any slot in life without him. Count her friends. Most of them were more his than hers. She's going to be awfully lonely.'

'Perhaps I'll stay at home with her,' I said drearily. Gladys Heifer among the condensed milk, who never married because of her mother.

Alice had to go back to Birmingham after two days, two days in which my mother tried to make us behave like a bereaved family without strength or honesty to mention the departed. If Alice or I spoke about my father, or the practicalities of the divorce, she skated sadly away from it, saying, 'I wish you girls wouldn't *dwell*.'

'What else is there to talk about?' Alice said.

'Oh – the garden, the birds coming back,' she said stupidly. I wouldn't be her solicitor for anything.

It was only when Alice had driven off, as guilty at going as I had felt at not being here (my mother engenders guilt feelings in people very easily), that she relaxed a little.

'I didn't want to upset Alice just now,' she said. 'The early months are so important. Millicent lost a child that way, you know, before Derek, because Mark was missing after an air raid.'

'You told me.' She had, many times, with reflections on the doctor. 'But you've upset Alice far more by being so defeatist. Why do you take it so – so humbly?' I was missing Alice already, more than I had expected. Alone with my mother in this over-polished, overrated house, I felt claustrophobia beginning to set in. 'Why can't you get angry? Why don't you burn his notebooks, smash up his pictures, melt down his golf cups? I would. It's an unbearable thing to happen to a woman, especially someone like you, who – well, you never stopped loving him, did you?'

She looked away, but I moved round and made her look at me. She smiled sadly, with that same infuriating meekness, and shook her head. 'What's the use of being angry?' she said. 'Millicent says I shouldn't agree to a divorce, but what use would that be? It would only make a scandal. If it is all done sensibly and discreetly, the solicitor says, there will be no risk of jeopardizing his position.'

She was so bloody humble that I shouted at her. 'What do you care about his position? He should lose it! Sitting there playing God and telling wretched, unhappy people they should patch up their marriage difficulties for the sake of the children – he shouldn't be allowed to put a foot in court again. He's a liar and a cheat and a phoney. I hate him, and you should too.'

She put a finger to her mouth and glanced towards the kitchen automatically, although pregnant girls are temporarily out of stock and there is no one there after Mrs Baker goes home. 'He's still your father, Emma. You mustn't talk like that. He's still the finest magistrate they have,' she said, with a pitiful, inappropriate pride. 'That doesn't change.'

'If my husband did this to me,' I said, pouring myself a huge drink of my father's whisky, 'I'd get a gun and go after him. Or after the woman.'

She shook her head again in that same submissive way, gently stroking the smelly dog, which had a wart on its lip and disgusting dried blood in its torn ear.

'I know how you feel,' she said, although she couldn't possibly, if she lived to be a thousand, even if she was reborn as me. 'He was so close to you. In some ways, you had more of him than I did. I was always a little —' she puffed through her nose in a brave little mirthless laugh – 'a little shut out. This isn't the first time I've been lonely, you know.'

I should have put my arms round her, but I missed my cue. I couldn't bear her masochism. 'It wasn't *my* fault,' I said gruffly. 'There was room for you too.'

'You were too young, of course,' she said, her eyes musing back, 'to know about the others, and, later on, still too devoted to guess. A girl doesn't want to believe that her own father is less than perfect. Funny how she does, with her mother,' she added with surprising shrewdness.

'Since how long?' I said bluntly, standing with my legs apart, clutching the whisky, looking down at her.

'Oh – years.'

'I don't believe it.'

'Yes. In many ways, poor Emma, this final thing is worse for you than for me. I knew what he was like, you see. You didn't.'

I did not want to see my father. My mother said that I must, but I refused. He telephoned, and I would not speak to him. When he telephoned again, I answered, and slammed down the receiver when I heard his voice. The bell began to ring again almost immediately.

'Telephone, Emma!' my mother called from the kitchen, as if I was deaf, and I let it ring, staring at it, then picked it up limply and listened, and when he said, 'I want you to come and see me,' I said, 'All right.'

'Who was that?' My mother came out of the kitchen, putting her rings back on her wet hands. When she is at the sink, she still makes a great thing of taking off her engagement ring and the sapphire he gave her, laying them in the tiny dish he brought her back from France, and putting them carefully on again when she is done. If I was her, I'd flush the whole lot down the drain, Limoges dish and all.

'Lisa. She wants me to see her tomorrow evening.'

'For dinner? We were going to have the steak.'

That was the kind of thing that had driven my father mad.

The people for the meals, instead of the meals for the people.

'What time, dear? I shall have to —'

'I'll cook.' I clenched my teeth. Good intentions or not, Gladys Heifer was never going to be able to stay the course.

My father had taken a service flat. Strange furniture, unlikely curtains, indifferent carpet stained with other people's drinks. He was like a man in a hotel room, transient, unpossessed. The familiar things, his typewriter, law books on the card table he was using as a desk, bits of clothing, his stick hooked over the back of an alien chair, only increased the strangeness.

Walking down the hall past the scarred red prison doors of so many lonely people was the hardest thing I had ever done. I was afraid of him.

When he opened his identical door and took a step back, instead of forward to kiss me, I saw that he was afraid of me.

So I kissed him, to make it easier, and he looked at me intently and said: 'Thank God you haven't cut your hair.'

'Why should I?'

'I don't know. I had a terrible feeling that you would cut it off.'

'Like a nun? My life isn't that blighted,' I said lightly, as if I were just barely flicking him with a whip.

We had gone through from the absurd bucket of hall into the cramped tea-chest of living-room. A bedroom led off it, so small that you could see all three walls through the doorway, and on the other side was an alcove kitchen no bigger than the noxious nook where Kate's mother stewed the clothes in Butt Street.

'Sit down.'

'No thank you.'

'All right. Like a drink?'

'All right.'

He gave me a drink and a cigarette, and lit it for me. I stood in the middle of the room and held them.

'You've grown up,' he said. 'More sophisticated.'

'It's the cigarette. I don't – I don't smoke, Daddy.'

Looking round for somewhere to put it, I felt myself sag for a moment, and took a deep breath. I wasn't going to give way over a thing like him forgetting that he had promised me fifty pounds if I didn't smoke till I was twenty-five.

In silence, he handed me an ashtray and watched me put the cigarette out. 'Do you want to talk?'

'No.'

'I didn't think you would. I just had to see you before you went back to New York. Are you going back?'

'I may. I have my mother to think of now, you know,' I said insufferably.

'Sit down and have your drink and don't be so damn righteous,' he said harshly.

Because I had expected him to be apologetic, or at least placating, I was surprised into sitting on the hard square arm of a hard cube chair. Where did Benita sit when she came? One of the things I had been afraid of was a smell of her, a comb, an apron. In films, women scatter tell-tale lipsticks or compacts about like chaff. In life, they only leave small parcels, or pamphlets that have been thrust into their hand in the street. There was no sign of her.

Having no mantelpiece to lean on, since there was no fireplace, and no fender for his foot, my father stood on the insulting carpet and looked down at me with his hands in his pockets, resting the hip of his bad leg like a horse.

'They say at the court,' he said at last, 'that I take too long over cases and make people miss trains. Why? Because you have got to understand why things are done before you can judge whether they are right or wrong. I don't think you can understand what I am doing, so don't try to judge.'

I looked up at him quickly. That was almost what I had once said to him about Tom. But he went on talking as if he were unaware of that, as if the lunch at the flat, the agonizing talk in the toolshed, had never happened, and this was new, the first time anyone had ever been caught in the egotism of love and thought themselves justified in whatever they did.

I almost laughed. I could have said: Why tell me this? I knew it before you did. *I swear,* I had said, and he had said: *I swear.* I looked at him and he was a stranger, trying to make a stranger out of me. I got up to go and, when he took his hands out of his pockets, I saw that on the back of the right one was the mark of a broken vein, never properly healed.

I thought I would be all right. I went home and cooked the steak for my mother, and found her a tablet for the indigestion she knew it would give her because it was so late, and saw her and the dog into bed, and even slept myself, with the voices in my head.

But in the morning I went into the toolshed where he had talked to me of right and wrong, and took the stiff scrubbing-brush and whacked it blindly at the flower-pots. I broke dozens of them and left the pieces on the damp earth floor. I told my mother the cat from next door had done it, and she said that she had always believed there should be a tax on cats and bicycles.

I had to see Kate, even if she didn't have to see me.

My mother had kept me with her every day, inventing errands, trips to make, people to visit. She is being very brave about seeing people, but I think she enjoys their embarrassed sympathy more than their disinterested acceptance of her when she was with my father. Discretion is still the word, and those who do not know are not told, even if they say: Where's David? or: Bring David round for bridge next week. Roger wants to see him.

She will temporize and invent, rather than say: He's left me. My demon won't let me concede this to her as pride, because I know it is cowardice.

My grandmother came for two nights, and the chauffeur slept in the room where Dotty and I used to have our cards and wine sessions. Foiled of alcohol, he is now trying to smoke himself to death, and his strangling cough and sodden sinuses were even worse than my mother and grandmother trying to rally each other with games of backgammon and racing demon, and brightly not talking about my father.

My Aunt Millicent came one day with Derek, and brought a bottle of brandy, which was a good thing, because my mother won't take anything from the cellar; but the day was like a wake. My father should have been stretched out upstairs with candles head and foot, to match the hushed, consoling voices.

'How can you stand it?' Derek said, when we went outside to take a glum look at the small gem of view, self-conscious in its primary greens and fresh-turned earth.

'I can't.'

'You've got to get out.'

'I owe her *something*.'

'Anyone can give birth. I'll tell my father to order you back to the States. Then it won't be your fault. Count on me.' He squeezed my hand and we rubbed cheeks. He is turning into the kind of man who will always be there at every crisis, every wedding and funeral, blandly ushering, putting a hand under the elbows of doddering unknown relations, just sexless enough for comfort.

It was almost two weeks before I could get away to town by myself. I took my mother's car. He had left her his, but she refused to use it, and it stood cold in the garage, like the rider-less charger with stirrups reversed.

I drove through the familiar streets, sick with the great grey sickness that lies on all this part of London, to the blocks of brown and grey stone, ringed round with iron balconies that look on nothing.

All the narrow green doors on Kate's level were newly painted. Things were looking up. On her door, the paint was already scarred again on the bottom corner where it had to be kicked to get it open. Things were not looking up far enough to have the door rehung.

It was opened by a woman in a pair of tight shiny pants of that painful colour the Americans call aqua. The baby-sitter? She was sitting without her teeth, if so.

'Is Kate there?'

She shook her head and winked, as if I had asked for a prostitute. 'Wrong flat, dear.'

'Do you know where she is?'

'I don't know who she is, let alone where.'

'She used to live here. I thought perhaps you —'

'Whoever lived here,' the woman said, smacking her empty gums, 'should have their nose rubbed in it. Took me six weeks to get the smell out.'

'Doesn't the Council —?'

'The Council.' She laughed mirthlessly and swung the door at me, kicking it from inside to make it shut.

Turning to go, I became aware of an agitation at a window two flats along the balcony. It was Mary Gold, the wreck of the Golden Mary, signalling at me with the curtain. She was beckoning, so I went to her door, found it ajar, and went in.

I have been to places with Johnny Jordan where you take a deep breath of real air before you go in, and try just to move your diaphragm in and out, like poetry recitals, until you come out. I have been to places where even he looked uncomfortable. The woman with all the cats. The baby with the wad of wet newspaper steaming in the bottom of his pram.

Mary Gold's flat was the worst yet, and I doubt if even Johnny would have got through into the farthest room. You couldn't. The smell was fetid, relentless, the invisible wall of science fiction. Mice and meals and drains and feet gone bad like cabbage stalks, impenetrable as the brambles round the Sleeping Beauty, and, beyond it, Mary Gold sat in her parlour and called to me.

'Looking for Bob and Katie?'

She was grinning and nodding her big grizzled head so benevolently that I stood in the hall and stared. To Kate and me, she had always been a witch, a strangler, a succuba who raped men in their sleep. I had never thought of her as a nice smelly old lady in an armchair with the seat dropped to the floor, watching a tot's programme on the television.

'Looking for Kate?' she asked again. 'It's a long time since I've seen you go by, dear. I should have thought you'd know.'

'Know what?' What horrible thing had happened to Kate, and me not there, who had sworn to stick by her?

'The usual. They'll let you go so long, you know, and owe just so much, and then it's —' Golden Mary licked her spatulate thumb and flicked it over her shoulder. 'Mrs P. isn't Job, you know.'

She pronounced it like a job of work, and fixed me with an eye, so I said: 'I didn't think she was. I knew Bob was out of work, but he was sure they'd take him on again.'

'They took on some of the men, but not im. The wonder is

why they took im in the first place. When she had the second child I said to her, I said: "Now you've got three babies to look after." '

She laughed, and her eyes strayed back to the television, and her thick white hand strayed out to a box of biscuits at her side. 'Have a ginger nut?'

'No thanks.' She still had me stuck in the hall behind the barrier of smell, and there were ants countermarching in the biscuits, but she was no monster. Why had Kate hated her so extravagantly? It was odd that she had never told me that they were at least on speaking terms. She always had to have an enemy. Even at Molly's where she was happiest, she'd had Joan and Matron to hate.

'Where did they go?'

'There was some talk of her and the kids going to a ostel, but I think e got a job in the end. Been drawing is unemployment benefit, but of course they'd spent it as it come. Like kids. I bought a iron off her. Then the man come to repossess it after. You could take her to court for that, he said. Ha! With my family, you stay clear of the courts.'

A little animated wooden man came on to the screen with a barrow. 'Woody Woodman!' Her eyes were glazed and fixed. It was time for me to go.

—

WHEN I OPENED the door and there she was, with her hair piled smooth and high at the back and tumbling forward over her square bony forehead, I could have died.

I was in pyjamas, the torn ones – well, all right, the only ones. I hadn't felt like getting dressed. After I came out of the bathroom and found Dino waiting outside in that mono-grammed dressing-gown he says some woman gave him, and rushed back to the room because I didn't want him to see my face, though he must have heard, Sammy had tipped over a jug of milk, so I clouted him and went back to bed, like a mouse going back to its hole.

When I got up in the end to feed the baby, I wished I hadn't. It turned out to be one of those days when every time

I started to do something, Emily would yell, or Sammy would pull the curtains down on him, or knock something over, or crawl somewhere and get stuck. One of those days? Show me a day that isn't like that.

Two days ago, he fell down the stairs. Bump, bump, bump, all the way down to the half-landing, I heard him. Dino came out in his black trousers with black hair all over his chest – he was dressing to go to work – and picked him up and brought him back and scolded me.

They all scold me, Marge and Norma and them, but they should have my lot. Dino scolds me just for fun. When he saw Bob wasn't in the room, he said: Can I come in?

I told him what he could do with it, but one day he will get in, and you can trust Sammy to tell Bob. He can't talk much, not above a few words strung together all wrong, but he'll manage. The day I bit him because he bit Emily, he told him, clear as a bell: She bit me. How could you, Katie, a little baby? Bob said, and I didn't bother to explain to him that you can only discipline kids with an eye for an eye and a tooth for a tooth. He can't always understand the theory of things, but he's dead jealous, and he'd have no trouble understanding about Dino.

I was in pyjamas with a pair of Bob's jazzy socks on my feet and not a hair of my head combed. When Em saw me, she took in everything at once, the room, the mess, the bed unmade, the puddle of milk on the floor, the wreck of about three meals on the table, the kids in their night things, both wet and filthy, me looking as bad as I felt, and all she said was: 'Oh, Kate, you've cut off your hair!' As if that was all that had happened to me since the days when she and I were equals, sisters, blood comrades.

'How did you know where I was?' was all I could say.

'Molly told me.'

'She went away.' Everyone went away, everyone but me and Bob.

'I know. I wrote to her in York, and she told me where you were.'

'It's no palace,' I said, but she pretended that she didn't see the room, except as a place where I was. She kissed me, and hugged. She smelled so good, I could have stood there hugging her for ever.

Sammy came to her. He looks like one of the seven dwarfs in that trailing old nightgown. She picked him up and said that he was beautiful, and of course he was all wet, trust our Sam, so there was no need for her to ask why he hadn't any pants on. He's always wet, that's why.

I picked up Emily for her. 'We named her after you.'

'She's better-looking than me.' And she is too, I don't mind saying it. If Sammy had her curls and round face and fruity skin he wouldn't be such a gnome.

'You want to be godmother, Em?'

'*Do* I?' and off we went, planning for the christening, what we'd wear, and whether we'd have the baby in short or long, 'my old family lace' – it would have to be one of the curtains – and what we'd eat and drink afterwards, for the party.

With Em and me, we can fall right back into it. I felt she'd never been away, even though she looked a bit different, and I knew I looked a lot different.

'I'll grow my hair again,' I said. 'I promise. I'll get this place cleaned up. I was going to start tomorrow. You've just caught me. I was just going to start.'

She laughed, not believing, and sat down on the bed, and I didn't bother to say that I was going to change the sheets to-day. She wouldn't believe that either. She took Sammy up, and he tipped over the saucer that was beside the bed, and ashes and cigarette stubs went everywhere. I took a swipe at the little bastard, and Em said quickly, 'Bob never used to smoke so much.'

'We both do now. Smoke all the time. Everybody we know does. Got to have some pleasures in life. Mr Zaharian can put a cigarette in his nose and make the smoke come out of his ears.'

'Zaran! Zaran!' Sammy loves him, because of it.

'Why didn't you write?' Emma asked, when I had stopped the child running about like a mad toy and got him on my knee to get some clothes on him.

'I did.'

'Not since Emily. That was almost a year ago.'

'Don't nag me, Em. I did mean to, but there's never any — well, you see how we are here. This is a house of hell. I'm paying for something I did in one of those other lives. Remember about the Roman slaves, and that time we were the cavewomen? This was all we could get at the time. We had to get in somewhere. I had a spell at the centre with the kids, as it was. Never again, no thanks. I felt like Mrs Micawber. Even Bob was a welcome sight to me. Even this room. We'll get out of it. We still owe a bit.'

'How much?'

'Not much.' I looked away. Em was studying me too closely.

'We'll pick up soon. Bob's after a better job. Moll got him in as cleaner at a school, but he couldn't stand it. Those big cans of garbage, it turned his stomach. He's in a shop now.'

'What does he sell?'

'Nothing exactly. He couldn't manage the change. No, he — he cleans up, and that. It's a butcher's shop.'

'That sounds worse than the school.'

'Well, he won't stick it much longer,' I said, and he won't. He could never stand the sight of blood. If he cuts himself, he cries.

'Kate,' Emma said, 'why don't you put the children in a nursery and get a job yourself? Get yourself —' she was going to say out of this hole, but then being Em — I know her so well — she thought: they're only here because it was the best they could do, so she changed it to, 'get yourself some new clothes, and make-up.'

I fished about on the mantelpiece and found a lipstick stuck in a packet half-full of cigarettes where I'd put it to keep it away from Sammy. He eats lipsticks. Soap too.

'That better?' I turned round and grinned at her.

'Much. Now, the job.'

'I can't. I don't feel well enough.'

She stood up. She was actually angry, and I rushed across the room to her. 'Oh Em, don't be cross. I can't help it. It's just one of those things that happen.'

'Not every year. Not to people with any sense. You can't afford to keep two children as it is, and you're worn out with it. At twenty. You're getting used up.'

'I can't help it, I tell you!' I was angry too. What was the use of telling me what I knew already? 'Bob won't do anything. I've asked him – even bought him things, but he won't. He just laughs. There's nothing you can do with him.'

'He should be sterilized.'

'Oh shut up, Em, that's dirty.' I couldn't help giggling though, because it was funny, the way she came out with it, as if he were a mongrel.

She didn't laugh. She asked me what was the matter with me, that I didn't do something about it, and I told her, 'I'm not going to the clinic.'

'Why not?'

'They fit you. They can kill me first. At Stinkney they almost did. They had to tie me down. Not that again.'

'But when you're pregnant, the doctor —'

'That's different. It's the baby he's after, not me. Shut up now, will you?' I couldn't stand this indecent prying into my life. 'What business is it of yours?'

'Can I give Emily a bath?' Emma said, having looked carefully at me and seen that there was no more to be said.

'Help yourself.'

'Where —?'

'In the sink, where did you expect?'

I scooped the potato peelings and tea leaves out of it while Em boiled up a kettle, and we talked about the times at Moll's when we bathed the kids and Moll would give us chops for supper if we did them all. We'd once done eight in fifteen minutes, our record, but of course there was a bathtub and lots of hot water, the way Jim used to stoke that boiler. All of a sudden, I could smell those babies. I'd forgotten children could smell like that.

While she had the baby in the sink, with Sammy sitting on the draining-board, watching her with his round dark eyes that are like Bob's but more secret, not spilling over like a spaniel, she said, with her back to me, 'Would you like some money?'

'No,' I said. Just like that. No. I could have shot myself, but having said it, I couldn't go back on it, and I was so angry with myself that I had to try and make her feel she'd insulted me by offering.

I felt I was red in the face, and went and bent over the bed and started straightening it out, feeling my legs trembling and tense. I get stiff with anger sometimes, and wonder what's happening to me. But it's nothing new. It's just that I've got more to be angry about now. I remember when I had to stand up in the courtroom, the first day I ever met Em, and she was in that yellow coat, and my dad was stood there telling lies about me and I still thought my mother would come, though I knew she wouldn't, I was stiff then. Rigid with fury. That's why I yelled out at them, and Em's father frowned as if he was in pain. I yell now, sometimes. Bob puts his fingers in his ears and so does Sammy, copying him. It's rather sweet.

'Where are your books?' Em asked me.

'I sold them.'

'I'll get you some more. You can't live here without anything to read.'

'I'd sell them.'

'You wouldn't.'

'If I didn't, Bob would.'

'He used to be so proud of what you read. When he made you the bookcase at the flat, he said, "Katie's going to show me how to read them." '

'He can read all right.' I didn't want to think of cosier days when I used to read to Bob sometimes, and he'd sit with his eyes on my face like a child, marvelling at the story. 'Books are a luxury.'

'They're not.'

'You wouldn't understand.'

I'd never said that to Em, but if it hurt, she didn't show it. She got the baby dressed and washed off Sammy's face, and then she wanted me to get dressed and she'd take us all out for a meal.

'Emily can't eat a meal,' I said.

'Don't be stupid. Give her a bottle first, or whatever she has.'

She's getting very bossy, is Em. I don't know who she thinks she is, coming into my flat and ordering me about as if I was a case history and she was one of those hens Marge Collins has in her place all the time, shoving her around and telling her how to budget. Just because she's got everything and I've got nothing, she wants to patronize. There's no difference between her and me except my rotten bad luck. You wait, Emmaline Bullock. It could happen to you. Then you'll know why they call it getting caught.

IT IS quite awful. Worse than I expected. Much worse. It was bad enough when she was at the Council flat and had started to let go of all the things that had begun to mean something to her. But this – a house of hell, she said, and though I hadn't expected to find her in Belgravia, I hadn't expected it to be as bad as this.

I remember, ages ago, the first time I went out with Johnny Jordan, after we had been to see that scoured-out woman with all the children, and the little boy who had leaned his scabby head on my chest. He said then that poverty was a disease. They keep slipping back, he said, like malaria, and I thought he was wrong, but now I am not so sure. There is something about that dreadful room where Kate and Bob and the two children try to live, something that reminds me, most sickeningly, of Butt Street.

It is in a different part of town from her old haunts, but no better. Somewhat worse, if anything, for this is a neighbourhood where immigrants of all nations have come precariously to roost, bringing with them their less savoury habits from home.

Kate's street is a long, tall terrace, marked out for slum clearance if there is any sanity in the Ministry of Housing, but still inhabited to the hilt. It was a sodden, sunless day, standard for London, but the Africans and West Indians looked as if they could never get used to it. They looked miserable, the women did, their strong faces already as pinched and shrewish as cockneys'. Besides the shrill swarms of children, most of the houses had overflows of people on the steps or leaning against the railings. Kate's house on the corner had a monstrous jelly-fish woman squatting on the ground-floor balcony, like a doll over a telephone. She turned to say something disparaging to someone inside, and I went up the steps under her eye, giving her my enigmatic profile, the jaw slightly out.

There had been bells once, but now only rusted sockets. No buttons, and the cards alongside washed anonymous by the weather. One of the peeling double doors, tall and narrow as a coffin lid, was ajar, so I went inside and stood uncertain in the sour, turnip-greens hall. Molly had only given me the house number. She had said it was a flat, but it looked as if it was going to be even less of a flat than that honeymoon eerie on the top floor of Marbles'.

I knocked at the first door off the hall, which still had an embossed brass hand-plate and had probably led to the dining-room in the good old days. A child with what looked like chicken-pox opened the door, and a voice came from over the back of a large leather sofa, 'If that's the Prisoners' Wives' Aid, come on in.'

'I'm looking for Mrs Thomas.'

'Why look here? Upstairs,' said the prisoner's wife. 'First door on the left.'

At the bend of the staircase was a small alcove, where two women were talking outside a frosted-glass door, with someone whistling behind it. The women stopped talking to watch me come up, and moved their heads round and upwards as I passed and climbed on, like chickens mesmerized in front of a white wall.

First door on the left. A passage led away on either side of the staircase. It would depend which side you were coming from. A door at one end was open on a roomful of steam. I thought it must be the bathroom, but when I got closer, it was a three-cornered bedroom, with a kettle boiling away like mad on a gas ring on the floor. In the doorway of this Turkish bath appeared a short dark man with very wide trousers, raggedly cut off, a shirt without a collar, not the same thing as a collarless shirt, and huge brown melancholy eyes the shape of teardrops, drawn in close to a beaked nose.

'I'm making tea,' he said. 'You want some?'

'No thank you.' Our Miss Bullock, field worker, should not be afraid to go anywhere, but he looked desperate enough to dismember me and steam me like salt beef. 'Mrs Thomas?'

'Katie.' He smiled widely, and of course he was not a slaughterer, but Kate's good neighbour, who gave her cups of tea when she was low. He took me to her door, knocked for me, bowed and slipped away in his grey gym shoes before she opened the door.

The last time I saw Kate, her pale hair had hung to her shoulders, brushed and cared for, for she had always been vain, even in the worst times. With her hair cut, and tousled as if she had just got out of bed, she looked unnervingly like the Kate I had first seen, the hapless urchin of my father's court. She wore boy's striped pyjamas, stained at the cuffs and ankles and gone at some of the seams, with a crumpled mauve chiffon scarf tucked into the neck.

I had forgotten how small she is. When I put my arms round her, it was like holding a child. She is bonier, and her face is thinner and drained of colour, like a ghost of Kate.

The baby is as plump and healthy as if it had stolen her strength and blood. The little boy, Sammy, used to be square, but he has elongated, and his legs are like props for a bird. When she took off the preposterous nightdress and I saw his ribs and swollen stomach, I asked her if he had been ill. She said casually that he was always ill, on and off, and the doctor said he was the type who never put on weight.

He has big black round eyes that stare at you without blinking, and his hair, which is downy, like a new growth, is all on the top of his broad skull, which makes him look like a dwarf tribal Indian. He is naughty. Even at two and a half, you can see him being naughty on purpose, watching her to see how much she'll stand. When I took him on the bed and he upset the ashtray, he ducked, even before she swung her arm at him. The duck came with the mishap, instinctively, and I am trying not to think about what I saw in his eyes.

Some of them keep slipping back, Johnny Jordan said. You can only help them so far. She has slipped back. She is still my Kate. She always will be, till death, but she is slipping back, like someone sinking in a bog, and I can't pull her out. She won't even hold out her hand for me to try. She wouldn't take money, or even a meal. I tried to talk to her about the babies, but she made me feel like a prying spinster, looking for a vicarious thrill out of someone else's sex life, so I shut up.

For a while we were close, almost like we used to be, but then we were miles apart, and she tried to make it seem as if I were the one who was aloof, when it was really her shoving me away.

When she asked me, just before I left, why I had come home now when I had said I would be gone two years, I didn't feel like telling her. I had thought I would. One of the things I had thought about, riding here on a bus filling up as it approached with increasingly squalid people, was that I would be able to tell her about my father and that she would understand what he had done to me.

I had only had Alice for those few days, and Derek briefly on the terrace before Aunt Millicent fussed him inside to provide a forgotten date for Gran. I had no one to talk to, no one to say they were sorry for me, because they were too busy being sorry for my mother. I was sorry for her too, and I tried to show it, although she kills demonstrativeness stone dead in its tracks; but at the bottom truth of my soul, I was sorrier for myself.

'What's the matter?' Kate asked, when I made an evasive answer, because she knows me too well.

So I told her. If I was looking for sympathy, she had none to give. She hardly seemed to listen, and then she shrugged her shoulders and said: 'Been a good thing if my dad had done that years ago. We was always better off when he wasn't home. Safer too. The day I run off with Bob, you know, he burned me with his cigarette. Deliberate.'

'God, Kate, you never told me.'

'I've never told anyone. I'll never tell anyone what she did to me either. Never anyone but God the day I die, so they'll be sure and chuck her into hell if she's sneaked into heaven past the guards.'

'What did she do?' Kate has never talked about her black childhood. It is the only thing we have not shared.

'None of your business, ducky,' she said, suddenly flippant. She leaned forward to the baby and, as her frail neck came out of the scarf, the dark red stain was like a punishing hand laid on her.

I didn't know what to do. There was only one thing I wanted to do, so I did it. Outside a public house, I went into a telephone box that smelled of every bad thing the human race purveys, and dialled the number of Tom's office.

'Who wants him, please?' A new voice. Sheila's private eye must have been fired when I left the scene.

'Miss Weir.'

'I'm sorry, he's not in this afternoon.' Why the *hell* can't they tell you that right away instead of building you up with Who wants him? 'Can I take a message?'

'No thank you. No message. Don't bother to tell him I called. It's not important.'

Time was, when I was in a bad way, that I used to go to my father. Sometimes he understood and sometimes he didn't. Sometimes he would give the time to listen properly and sometimes he wouldn't. But he was there. He was someone I could go to.

When you have no one to go to, where do you go? When children have no one who wants them, they turn up on Johnny Jordan's doorstep. I turned up there that evening, just as supper was coming to the table, and was absorbed easily into the meal with no fuss or surprise.

No one asked me why I had come. They were glad that I had. I was home from America, and so I had come to see them. They were having roast beef, and Nancy had made her first apple turnovers so it was a good day for me to be there.

The girl has two long brown pigtails like I had at her age. They come forward into the food, and she keeps flipping them to the back of her shoulders, as I remember doing. Sometimes when she is thinking, she puts the end of one of them into her mouth. I used to do that, and my father used to cry out sometimes that if I didn't stop eating my hair, he would cut it off. Once, when I forgot just after he had shouted, and he thought

I did it on purpose, he came at me with the huge pair of scissors from his desk. Not in fun. I believe he would have chopped the pigtails off then, if I hadn't run away.

Nancy's father doesn't shout. He says patiently: Don't suck your hair, and she says: I didn't know I was.

I know just how it tastes at that age. I still suck the ends of mine occasionally, but it doesn't taste as good when you are grown up.

Nancy and her mother both have round country faces with high colouring, and big easy laughs. When they laugh, they look at each other, like a duet. Johnny is much quieter.

'He's shy,' Jean says. 'You wouldn't believe this man was so shy, some of the places he goes to. Remember those people, Johnny, who lived in that old bus behind the railway yards, and no one ever knew she had a child? Like a little savage, it was, when you brought it home. It bit me.

'No one but this stupid idiot would have gone in there,' she told me, with her affectionate mixture of pride and abuse. 'The man had a knife out, but never mind that, our boy goes right in, like a Jap.'

'Doesn't sound very shy,' I said, for it is all right in this house to talk about and around Johnny. He sits with the sweet smile softening his square boxer's jaw, turning his eyes thoughtfully from one to the other, as you speak.

'Just as long as the customers don't find it out,' Jean said. 'They're scared of him.'

'They're not,' Nancy said, bringing cups of coffee from the stove. 'When I took that box of shoes to Mrs Richardson, and told her I thought the boys had ringworm, she said: "You send your father next time, miss. He don't notice these little details."'

When Jean went upstairs to wash Nancy's hair, I knew that I should go, and not burden the contented household with the things that had gone wrong for me. But my legs would not push me out of the chair, and my voice would not say the words of leaving. I sat on at the table in the yellow and white kitchen, and Johnny made me another cup of coffee and sat down again to consider me.

'You've changed,' he said. 'A bit.'

People say that when you come back from America. They say it without admiration, to stop you telling of transatlantic joys and marvels they don't want to hear. They tell you that you have an American accent, helpfully, as if it were a smut on your nose.

Johnny was not thinking about America, however. He said, 'Last time we saw you, that night I found you at the bus stop with your hair blowing round your face in that cold wind, you were – how shall I say it? – restless. Keyed up. Nervous, I thought. As if you —' he laughed without opening his mouth – 'had been up to something.'

He is more perceptive than you would think, Johnny Jordan. That's why he has this job.

'Baby-sitting for my friend Kate, that's all,' I said lightly. He is the sort of man it's hard to lie to. Not because he is righteous. He might lie like a demon to get himself out of a jam, or avoid a scene. You can't be in the Army as long as he has and not learn that. But because he makes you feel you do it badly.

So I dropped that, and asked what I had been wanting to all evening, only Kate was something between him and me and I didn't want to bring Jean into it. 'Are you still seeing Kate's mother, the woman who keeps that shop in Butt Street?'

'Not any more. I had rather good luck with her, as a matter of fact.'

He never says that he was successful, or has got people to do what he wants. When he achieves marvels with the lost and the hopeless, it's always a fluke, a bit of luck that just happened to come his way.

'The man got a job with a moving company. I happened to know someone in the firm I could send him to, and I got the little girl into the special school in the end. It was stubbornness really that the mother wouldn't see she needed help. She wouldn't admit to herself there was anything wrong. So I had to be a bit brutal. I forced her to see it and, in the end, she was glad to have the decision made for her. It's often like that. They're at the end of their rope, some of these women. They've had too much, and they're in a state that they can't let go. They won't let you help, and then suddenly they break, and they let you have it all. The thing is to know when to give it back to them. She'll be all right now, I think. She has some strength. She made her mistake years ago, marrying that chap. She could have been a different kind of woman, I thought.'

'What did she do to Kate?'

'I don't know. She never talked about her.'

'Kate hates her. And him. Did you know he deliberately burned her? That was the final thing that made her run away.'

'I knew there had been some ill-treatment. That was in the case notes. But the girl hadn't said much, and it was vague. It was the other kids I was checking on anyway, and she seems to be quite decent to them. It's often just the one, like that. Sometimes it goes back to the same kind of treatment in the mother's childhood. Almost as if they tried to get their own back in some unreasonable, useless way.'

I did not say anything. Kate is not on his beat now, and even if she were, I would not tell him. She has been persecuted enough. I would have to get up the nerve myself to talk to her about Sammy. Our Miss Bullock, so conscientious in her field work. But our Miss Bullock can't forget that she saw terror flash into a child's eyes.

I got up to go, and Johnny said that he would call Jean down to say goodbye. For something to say, he asked me what I was going to do, and when I said I thought I was going back to America, he said, 'Was this a holiday for you then, coming back now?'

I hesitated, standing in the narrow hall with the red and blue patterned carpet and the bright infested wallpaper. I hung on to the flat swirl of polished ginger wood where the banister ended, and tried to stop myself telling him about my father.

It was a stale squib of news. It shattered no one. Joel had said, 'He would do it just when I'm hoping to get leave.' Kate had shrugged and hardly heard, and started to talk about herself.

Jean came down the stairs in an apron, smiling, and I looked up at her, and then I looked back at Johnny Jordan, too big and muscular for his little over-decorated hall, frowning at me because I had opened my mouth to say something and no words came out.

'What is it, Emma?'

I told them. Suddenly they break, he had said, and let you have it all. I broke. I let them have it, weeping as hysterically as any of his unbalanced women, living too near the edge.

He put his arm round me, not like my father, because he is much taller and more secure, and I yelled stupidly into his shirt, 'He cheated me, he let me down!'

Jean put me to bed, telephoned my mother, and said that the car had broken down and I was staying with friends. I slept until the next midday. When I woke and dressed, Johnny and Jean were both out. Nancy was home from school, getting her own lunch, and I realized that I had spent the night in her bed.

'Where did you sleep?'

'On the sofa, I often have. We had two pairs of twins once in my bed, the night the Buildings burned.'

I knew that I should stay with my mother, if I was the right kind of daughter, but I was the wrong kind, and I couldn't stay with her.

My father was letting her have the house. 'You can't say he's not been generous, Emma,' she said, because her sickening line now is to try to change my attitude towards him.

She is always dropping in a good word, in the special soft voice she uses for talking about him. If he goes on talking about him like this, as if he were dead, what will she have left to say when he really does die? Perhaps she will die first, of boredom and lack of purpose, and he will live on into his nineties, the old goat, in the health and bloom of sin.

Ninety. That will make Benita about seventy-six, if she stays the course. Well preserved, she'll be, like plums in brandy, and spend too much on clothes. I shall be a raw-boned and leathery colonel's wife of fifty-seven, with Joel at the Pentagon, giving buffet suppers at my split-level in Arlington and pretending I have a maid.

My mother is going to sell the house. It was when she told me, that I realized absolutely that I can't stay with her. I realized then how much the house inevitably means, reeking as it is with the lives of all of us. All the things I detest about it – the pathetically disguised suburbanness, the fake country view, the glass and the tidiness and the things replaced or re-covered or re-painted as soon as they began to get shabby – even these are part of the essence of the house, my home. They could even, if the house were to be loved, be loved along with it, as you can absorb a beloved person's bow legs or taste in clothes.

With the house gone, and my mother's unsubtle taste in decorating transferred to a flat in Hampstead near Aunt Milli-cent, I knew I couldn't make it. If it was claustrophobia in the house, it would be padded cells in a flat.

Uncle Mark took me out to the kind of lunch he has every day, which is why he has to stay late at the office and loses a secretary every few months, and asked me what I wanted to do.

I told him the truth. I can, these days. It is surprising how, as you grow up, your most impersonal relations become human. He said that he would get me off the hook, and ordered a heavy claret and talked business for the rest of lunch, since we had exhausted the subject of my mother over the prawn cocktails.

He has plans for me in the firm. He is going to spread out into Canada, with a B.B. supermarket in a Toronto suburb, as a guinea-pig to see how he can compete. The Canadians are very American in their shopping habits, although they would kill you if you said so, because they see the Great Lakes as a barrier wider than the Atlantic; so if Uncle Mark goes on getting good accounts of me from friend Ralph in New York, he may send me up there to work on the layout.

'She can't fiddle about, Laura,' he told my mother. 'I sent her to America for at least two years – at her request, inciden-tally, and David's – and she'll stay there as long as I want her to. She's beginning to be useful to me at last.'

Words a mother should be proud to hear.

'She's all I've got now.' If you put long felt ears on my mother, she could look like a bloodhound.

'She's working for me. Just because David chooses to make a fool of himself, she's not going to mess about with her career – or my business.'

Although I had already told my mother that I would not be with her in the new flat, she pretended dismay. 'Then I'll have to reconsider all my plans,' she said. 'I had so much in mind for her room. Off-white rug – Emma's much more careful these days. The dressing-table in sprigged muslin. I saw it at Peter Jones'.'

'Buy it,' Uncle Mark said, as crisply as he can say anything through his beard, which muffles and softens the edges of words a little, after they leave his hedged lips. 'I'm not sending her to Siberia. She'll need her room with you. I'll see that she gets plenty of leave, and help with the fare too.' He is trying to make up to her for his brother, but it is hard going. 'She'll be home with you a lot. Everything will work out splendidly, don't you think?'

'I shall be very lonely,' my mother said, in the flat voice that puts an end to all jollying. 'I may have to buy a pekinese.'

EM CAME back to say goodbye, and Mr Zaharian, who keeps his door open to watch out for all comers, greeted her like an old friend. He is always pleased to see anyone coming up the stairs, even Norma, who laughs at him and won't say anything, just laughs and keeps on walking, and Phyll Conroy who won't let her boys go in his room for sweets, but they go anyway.

We heard the racket of him crying: 'Aha! and how are you, lady?' and Bob said: 'Who the hell is that?' He was blocking in a picture of hussars in a colouring book. I had bought him some new crayons that morning. He's easy to keep amused, I'll say that, but the kids are going to have it rough keeping him away from their toys as they get older. He bought Sam some tin paratroops, Christmas, but guess who plays with them.

Mr Zaharian knocked on our door with his bloodstone ring that Sammy likes to suck. I yelled, 'Come on in!' because I was doing the wash, and he flung open the door with a grin and cried: 'You girl friend!' – when I'm rich I'll have him in a turban and red sash, announcing guests at my receptions

– and there was Em grinning too, with her arms full of parcels and flowers.

'Hullo, Em,' said Bob, and his grin was the widest of the lot.

'Get up, you slob,' I said, and he did, and ambled over to put his arms round Em like a tame bear. Everybody loves Em. It's easy to be loved when you arrive in a pink and white suit like marzipan with crocodile shoes and a present for everyone. Don't be bitter, Kate. When she could disentangle Sammy, clamouring like a raving lunatic, she threw the parcels on the bed (thank God I'd made it), and came quickly to the sink and kissed me, and I took my arms out of the suds and put them round her all wet and scummy. I've never seen harder water anywhere, never. It's something in the tank. Rotting bones I shouldn't wonder.

Although I miss her all the time behind the back curtain of my mind, and often at the front of it, thinking of the old days when we were silly giggling girls with Moll to do the worrying, it's when I actually see her that I realize how much I need her.

She is going away again, so all right, I can't have her. I got over crying for what I couldn't have years and years ago. If you could remember being a baby, I'd probably remember screaming myself blue because I was cold or hungry or wet, with results nil.

She had brought toys for the children, a cake, a blouse for me and nylons. Nylons! I haven't even got a suspender belt. I'll have to roll them. Cigarettes for Bob, and a bottle of port. Then she saw Mr Zaharian still standing in the doorway beaming with silly joy over the Lady Bountiful scene, and she was quick-witted enough to give him the box of biscuits and pretend they were for him. He shut the door softly and went away crooning to himself high in his nose.

'Look, Em, you shouldn't —' I began, for we don't need charity from her, or anyone, but she passed it off as going-away presents, and started to talk to Bob, to shut me up.

'Katie's going to have another baby,' Bob said.

'I know.'

'It's good, isn't it? I've always wanted lots of kids. Lots and lots of 'em. I knew a chap at work once, had a whole football team. Soccer, mind. Eight boys and three girls, and they put the baby in goal. When I go in the Army, that should be next year, if they don't call me sooner, I'm going to get Sammy a little soldier suit, with a drum.'

Never a dry eye. He's sopping wet about the boy, Bob is. He's taught him to salute, and they do what he calls drill together.

'Go on, show Em how you salute.' He did, and when we laughed because his hand come up so quick and comic, he fired up red and ran behind Bob's legs, catching at his trousers.

'He's your boy,' Em said. 'Most children run behind their mother's skirt when they're shy.'

I looked at her, sharp. She was getting at something. That's why she came. She's always been critical of me, ever since the days at the Council flat when I used to leave Sammy alone, and she fussed at me. If she thinks I'm too rough on him, she should just have him, that's all. She should just have him for only one day even, and she'd see. There's only one thing that kid understands, I mean that.

He went to play with the car she had brought, and I went over to him and sat down on the floor, so gentle and tender, and showed him how to wind it up. He didn't want to come on my knee, but I pulled him on to me and sat there smiling and talking to him, the very picture of motherhood.

OUR MISS Bullock never did get the chance to say anything to Kate. When I went to say goodbye, she was much better with the boy, and Bob obviously adores the children, so I suppose it will be all right.

I hope it will be all right. Surely an unhappy childhood would make you want to give your own child something better? Johnny Jordan has his theories, but if you work mostly with failures, you see defeat for everybody. Doctors think the whole world is sick, and undertakers see potential death in a newborn baby.

As soon as I was on the plane, even before it took off, I stopped worrying about Kate, and about my mother's poor harmless face, still babyish about the mouth, and puzzled, when she kissed me, brave and tearless, and said: 'Come back soon, Emmie.'

The gush of real love and pity I felt for her should have come much earlier. It should have come when I arrived, not when I was safely leaving.

Mrs Patterson has eminent domain. She made it sound like a skin disease, but it means that a new elevated intersection is going to scoop off the top of her house. Dodie and Brenda have already gone, and since Mr Vinson has raised my pay, or as he put it, upgraded my salary bracket, I am sharing an apartment across the river in New Jersey with a mad Danish girl called Toni. We are planning a new store for a giant housing project on what was once a desolate marsh, and Toni is one of the draughtsmen the engineers are using for the layout, and I'm afraid using may be the right word, for when she works late, she doesn't usually come back to the flat.

Joel delayed his leave, and he spent it all in New York with me after I came back. He is being sent to a weapons school in Texas, where wives are not allowed to go. Next year, he expects to get a posting abroad, and then we think we will be married.

Part Four

WE WOULD have had to leave that room in the house of hell anyway, because there was not enough room with Susannah.

It's a pretty name. My mother was thinking of it once for Loretta, but I picked the wrong time to say I thought it was beautiful, and they said: What the hell business is it of yours? and called her Loretta.

Sometimes I think I will take the baby round there and say: Look, I've got a Susannah. Sometimes I think of going and I pretend that it would be laughter and people jumping up and crying: Look who's here! and I'm afraid I might go. When I'm tired, which is all the time, chronic, like piles, I go off on this road to nowhere like I used to when I was little and alone, and I'm afraid I might get round that corner one day and find it led to Butt Street.

Marge took Emily, and Bob turned in his job and took care of Sammy while I was in the hospital. If they'd only let you stay there a month, it would be worth having a baby every year, for the rest. But they kick you out in a few days with some brisk, kindly words about getting plenty of the right food. Smile.

Bob brought home a great piece of steak that evening. It cost a pound, and we had the bottle of wine Dino gave me for home-coming, and sat at the table and threw bits of steak to the kids on the floor and they ate it like dogs. Emily can't chew, but if you give her red meat, she sucks it white, like a vampire. Then they curled up where they were on the rug and went to sleep, so we left the gas fire on all night, and Bob was like a mad thing, because the doctor had dared him to go after me before, the last couple of months.

But the next day, there it was all back on top of me, and no shillings for the meter, and the baby into the bargain.

We've got to get a bigger place, I'd keep telling Bob, and he'd smile and say: That's right, like he does when he doesn't intend to do a thing about it.

He did get another job though, I'll say that for him. It's something in a warehouse. I'm not sure what he does, but he says they move pianos fifty yards one day and then move them back the next, to give them something to do, but it's better paid than the butcher's shop, and it's muscling him up. You wouldn't know him for the limp and sloppy boy he used to be. He looks quite a man – till you try to start a sensible conversation with him.

He's lazy still. Oh God, you could set his chair on fire before he'll move, but in the end he had to go out and look for a new place for us to live, because of Dino.

When I got my figure back again after Susannah, or as near back as it will ever be, with the punishment it's been getting, Dino got his interest back. He's a waiter, that's the trouble. He's at work when the men are at home, and vice versa, which is to say that he's at home when the men are out at work.

Even Mr Zaharian, who is doing something now for the Salvation Army, who have given him another pair of trousers that fit this time, was out of the house the day Dino came into my room and shut the door behind him.

What to do? When you live in a house like that, you don't scream. You don't advertise your problems.

Sammy told Bob, of course. Trust our Sam. Bob is a dreadful coward. He hit me and called me a terrible name, which Sammy will store up to come out with, but when I said, 'Why don't you go and fight it out with Dino?' Bob said, 'He's gone to work,' as if that let him out.

Three days later, we moved out, with Mr Zaharian waving us down the stairs with his lower lip in a trembling little pout, as if he wanted to come too, and Mrs O'Hara, who is an under-cover agent for the landlord, watching from behind that piece of gunny she calls a curtain, to see we didn't steal the light fixtures.

We are now in a basement flat, and although there's more room to move about, and at least we can call the taps and drains our own, there are times when our old room seems better than it did when we were there.

At least that house had once been something, in the days when maids carried hot water up and down the stairs. I must have seen an illustration in a book, for I could always see them, with streamers on their caps and those brass jugs. That was all they seemed to do. The drawing-room, our room must have been, with the high ceiling and the raised design round the top of the walls. In the summer, when the sun was high enough to stand over the high houses opposite, it came flooding into us through the tall windows, and there was always plenty of light.

Where we are now, there is always plenty of dark. We call it the Tunnel, Thomas's Tunnel, and that's about what it is. This house is in the same district, but it has always been a house of the poor, wretchedly built and full of sodden bugs and sadness. The ground floor and top floor are empty now, because of the roof, and it's a marvel that the basement is still classed fit for habitation, let alone rentable at five pounds ten a week, which is what we are fools enough to pay.

But there's nowhere else. When you are in a hurry to move, there is nowhere but these odds and ends of dwellings, and bloody few of them, thanks to the Spades.

We moved in here at the tail end of last winter, and before we'd really begun to feel the Tunnel's damp soul, down here among the gnomes and mushrooms, the spring came, and then the summer, and it wasn't so bad, and we'll find something else before next winter.

There are two rooms, and a sort of humpy shed at the back where Bob keeps his bicycle alongside the toilet, and a passage between the front and back room with a broken stone floor where the sink and cookstove are. They call it open-plan living.

The back room doesn't have a proper window, just a grated opening high up in the wall, which will have to be stuffed with newspaper if we don't get out before the cold weather, or the kids will freeze to the mattress. They say it's going to be the hardest winter for fifty years.

The front room isn't bad, if you like a nice view of people's feet and ankles going by. Sam and Emily play out in the little space there, and at first I tried to stop Sammy going up the stone steps and into the street, but he's three and a half now, and there are a lot of kids out there for him to play with. He almost got run over once, and the woman in the car asked him where he lived and brought him home. Before I could begin to thank her, she started in preaching to me that he shouldn't be on the street alone. In the old days, I would have told her what she could do with it. Now I can't be bothered. I just said: Yeah, and leaned on the doorframe patiently, until she shrugged her shoulders and went away.

This house is between street lamps, and when the night comes down, our basement is very dark if you don't have the lights on, which often we don't because we are playing Tunnel games.

One we play is that we are doomed miners, trapped by a fall of coal. We have just the one box of matches and a bottle of Coke between us, Bob and I sit on the floor in the passage and sing hymns and tap on the wall in code and talk about our wives who are waiting for us in those shawls, at the pithead.

We do it usually when the kids are in bed, because this one isn't any fun for them. They like the gnomes and rats one better. Sometimes we are men with beards and khaki shorts, exploring an ancient pyramid. We take turns to be the Curse of the Pharaohs, the walking mummy that comes looming out of the shed with a towel round its face, greedy for human flesh. Sometimes we are people in an air-raid shelter, waiting for the dust to settle after the Bomb so we can get out and see who's left, and we plan what we will do with London if there's no one else.

The Tunnel has its points, if you can find them, but then I get to thinking of Moll, and of Em, and Em's flat. It seems I can't get it out of my head, the flat, with that marvellous colour in the pictures they had up, and the smell of clean hair and cooking.

It is all gone. The flat. Em. Molly. Me, the real Kate. There are times when I actually hate Bob. I hate him like red fire, and I would hurt him, kill him I expect, if I was bigger and he wasn't so strong. If I go for him, he can get hold of my two wrists in one of his huge clumsy hams and hold me yelling while he hits me with the other.

Violetta, the big coloured woman a few doors down, who I

am friends with because she has a TV, says, when I get in a temper: Take it easy, or you kill yourself, child.

Well, I will die, and they'll all be sorry for what they've done to me. What have they done? Violetta asks. She makes me ill, she is so stupidly contented. What has she got to be contented about? Her husband has a piece of his jaw eaten away by cancer because he wouldn't go to the hospital soon enough. When she tried to make him, he would laugh and say: You the one who's sick, not me. So now he has to have his food mashed up, and use a plastic glass because his teeth chatter.

Violetta never hits her children, but I think she dopes them, the babies, hers and the ones she minds for women out at work. They sit on chairs or beds quite still, with those eyes like cream sandwich biscuits. No trouble, she says. It's one of her great expressions. Nothing bothers her. She is huge all round like a barrel, with all the grease she eats coming out on her skin and through her blouse.

No trouble. She takes babies for nothing sometimes. She should have Sammy if she wants to see trouble. He does everything he can against me. Why can't you be like your sisters? I ask him, and he just looks at me with those ancient eyes and goes off and breaks something, or gets himself in a mess because I'm changing the baby and he's jealous.

I have dreams about him sometimes. Bad ones, always. I don't understand why a mother would dream about her child like that. He is dark, like Bob, but he hasn't got Bob's big moon face. His cheeks and chin are made of small, angled bones, like mine. He looks like you, people say, but if I had looked at my mother with that haunted stare, she would have put me in the canal.

Bob is fond of Sammy. He likes him better than the girls. But then Bob likes being married to me. That's the difference.

The day Bob got fed up with the job at the warehouse, he brought home a dog. A dog, of all things, a great big collie with a self-conscious smile like a woman trying on hats, and a brand-new collar.

'Where did you get him?' I asked.

'I bought him.'

'The collar, perhaps, but that's a class dog. They don't give them away.'

You don't get them on the hire-purchase either, like the radiogram, and the big blue pram with the white-wall tyres he got me for Susannah, and I knew how much cash he had, or hadn't, unless he'd had a lucky horse at last.

'A chap gave him to me,' he said with his head down, talking from under his hair like he does when he's lying.

'Very nice,' I said crisply. 'Just what we need.' I was preparing to turn the animal out, when Bob said in his soft way, like a kid bringing you a fistful of dandelions, 'I got him for you, Katie. I thought he'd be company.'

'What do I need company for?' I said, but softening a bit, 'in this madhouse of retarded children?'

'Protection then,' he said, 'when I'm at work.'

'I thought you said you'd chucked it.'

'I'm getting something else. A fellow I know is going to get me in to the small-parts shop where he works, back of the coal yards. You're so pretty, Katie. I'm always afraid someone's going to get in after you when I'm out.'

There are times when I wish someone would. Even Dino with his hearthrug chest would make a refreshing change. But I know how to treat Bob – I should after four years, for he's about as subtle as my big toe – so I kissed him then, and thanked him for the dog, and he's been Bob's dog ever since.

Bruce is his name. He barks if anyone moves fast, and lifts his leg on the legs of furniture and even on people, if he's in the mood, but otherwise he's all right.

Bob buys his food and gets his dinner ready, while Bruce lays on the cushion on the chair watching him, like a prince.

You're daft over that dog, I tell Bob, and he says: The dog is daft about me, but he likes Sammy best, actually. He lets the child take pieces out of his dish, even. I think that's very nice, in a dog.

I still think Bob may have stolen him, but I've said no more, for if he did, I don't want to know.

I think he does knock off a bit now and again, but if I ask him, he goes dreamy, or turns a silly joke about it, so I let it go.

He is very dreamy at times. Those weeks he was out of work — for the small-parts shop was part of the dream, it seems — he'd take a chair and sit out in the passage with his arm along the draining-board, flicking ash in the sink, and looking at nothing by the hour. It's one of his favourite places, especially now that Bruce is always in the good chair. We fall over him, but he sits there, chain-smoking and dreaming.

He used to sit like that sometimes in the room at hell house. I can see him that Christmas, when the Salvation Army woman came to see Mr Zaharian, and she looked in on us with some oranges and a little stocking for Sammy.

Sudden kindness always dissolves Bob — he cried, even, when Dolly brought us up that plaid blanket — and I remember him saying, sitting there by the sink with his feet round the rungs of the chair and his hair all over his eyes, 'If I had a bit extra money,' he said, 'I'd give it to you people.'

I thought that was a nice thing to say, but the woman said, very sharply, 'If you had a bit extra, you should do something for your family,' and went out the door and left us looking at each other. I hope she didn't hear us laughing.

When Bob's at home, he plays with Sammy, or takes him out sometimes, and that helps. He takes him up West to see the Life Guards, and they hang about all day watching the sentries at the Palace, or going to a newsreel — God knows what they get up to.

The warehouse wasn't riches, but it was better than the unemployment money, and we were already behind on the rent as it was. I was getting up my nerve to go down to the National Assistance office, although I hate the woman there, and it would be sure to be her day. She is a werewolf. She prowls at night, devouring teenagers. One day she'll forget to change back at dawn, and she'll come in behind the counter in that booth with the dirty remarks scrawled on the partitions, and the bell that you could die ringing before anyone would come, and all the patient, humiliated, desperate people on the benches will look up and see her fangs and red eyes.

She said I was rude to her, and I was, but only to stop her being rude first.

Just in time to save me from the dripping jaws, the Labour

Exchange came up with something for Bob on the roads. He doesn't like working outdoors, but he had to take it, and they advanced something for the rent too.

Sammy had got used to having Bob home, and he played me up. He took Susannah one day – he can just carry her – and I found him trying to put her down the toilet. Another time, he turned on the gas tap on the stove. I lit it then, and put his finger in the flame, to show him.

Bob took off at me about that, but I said: 'What do you want him to do? Gas us all? Pull a pan of boiling water over on Emily?' For he is always at the stove, that child, fiddling, always fiddling and messing where he's no right to be.

I caught him in the bedroom smearing lipstick all over his face. He looked funny, I suppose, like a painted savage, but I didn't see it that way. It was a new refill, Pyramid Pink, and the girl in the advertisement looked like I used to when my hair was long and I had that sweater dress. I was so angry I didn't even know I'd hit the child until I saw his face after, and where I'd cut his lip with my ring.

When Bob came home, he didn't even ask what had happened. He picked up a piece of wood and hit me flat in the stomach. It hurt terribly and I ran off and laid on the bed and screamed, and after a bit I went to sleep. When I woke, I still hurt, and I thought, well, maybe it's a good thing. If I am pregnant again, which I think I am, though I'm afraid to go to the doctor and hear him say it, this may fix it up.

For the first time for ages, I thought about my mother, and let myself wonder what it was she'd done to try and get rid of me. Funny joke, maybe I should ask her some time. And have the kid born with its hands coming out of its shoulders, like Mrs Olson's across the street that she won't have put away.

Yeah.

TRUE TO his word, when I got my holiday the next summer, Uncle Mark paid half my fare to come home.

I should have wanted to come home, but I didn't. Bess had invited me to Cape Cod, and I would rather have spent the three weeks there, with Joel. We need to be together more. There is too much for us on the surface. Not enough of the stuff that turns your guts. If we quarrel, it means nothing. If Tom and I ever fought, we used to be physically sick, both of us. I remember doing it once at his house, in separate basins, one up, one down.

So we try to be together, when the Air Force doesn't foil us. By the time they sent Joel back to the Base on Cape Cod, Uncle Mark had sent me to Toronto to work with the Canadian engineers and architects who are designing the first B.B. market there.

When that's rolling, I am to come back to England for good. Uncle Mark, who my mother accuses of being power mad, but who really only wants to make more money, is going to lay siege to the housewife in the north of England, and my American experience is needed for the wooing. *My* experience. *Me*! Hell, it is getting so they can hardly start a supermarket without me. It's exciting, finding that you are useful after all, not just a dross. The first really important fight with Joel is going to be when he wants me to give it up.

Just before I left for home, Joel heard that he would be going to a base in Scotland. He will be going there about the time I come back to Toronto but, when I am in England again for good, he will still be there too.

So when I got home and was settled into the flat, and had said I liked the off-white rug, and wouldn't have wanted anything for my first dinner but what my mother cooked for me, and had heard the beginning of the disaster saga, from sour waste-pipes to the woman in the flat above with Army boots – there was more to come – I told my mother about Joel.

I thought she would be pleased. Anyone would think that a mother – even my mother – would be pleased to hear that her twenty-three-year-old daughter was thinking of marrying a decent-looking man of her own age with a job and a family who had nothing to hide, or if they did, they hid it skilfully, in Santa Barbara.

Her first words – I shall never forget them – were, 'When you told me you were coming back for good next winter, I counted on you living here with me.'

Useless to remind her that we had all known that I would be working in Yorkshire, Joel or no Joel. She decided then and there, in pique, that she would ask a widowed friend to come and live with her.

'Not Connie! I thought you hated each other.'

'She is my friend,' my mother said, in a tone that implied that everyone else had betrayed her.

'She's depressing.'

'So am I.' When my mother says things like that, you want to run for cover. What is her special gift that makes you feel you said it first? 'She's lonely, Emma. You try being a widow in Criccieth. At least, if I can't have happiness, I can try to bring it to someone else.'

Did she really say that? 'I may have made that bit up afterwards,' I told Alice when I went up to Birmingham, 'but it's helping me to decide about Joel. I begin to see why you married Gordon. Anything to get away.'

Gordon laughed softly on a level note, crinkling his gold-lashed eyes as if I were a private hysterectomy with expensive injections to follow. He is not always sure whether I am joking or not.

I didn't go to see my father. My mother wanted me to, saying that he would be hurt, but I think it was because she wanted me to get a look at the nest he has built with Benita, and report back.

'You can tell him about Joel, if you want,' I said. 'Give you a good excuse to get past the guards.'

'I don't want to see him,' she said, truthfully. It was Benita she would like to see.

'You'll have to see him at the wedding.'

'Would – would she come?'

'Hardly.' Though if she did, and Joel's mother and father each brought their second mates, it would be quite a party.

'He will be hurt if you don't tell him yourself.'

'I want to hurt him. Had you forgotten that? It's none of his business now anyway whether I get married or go to a nunnery.'

'You weren't thinking of that?' She would dislike that too,

combining as she does the true Church of England ragout of ritual church-going and a horror of the cloister.

I will go to see my father when I can take Joel with me too. When I can show him I don't need him. Show him that I have found someone completely different from him in every way. Someone who will never let me down.

I can't find Kate. She has disappeared, and I must go back to Canada without seeing her.

When I went to the tall scabrous house in the yelling street, the jelly-fish concierge had gone. On her balcony, a row of coloured children were perched on the railing like black snow birds, like targets at a fun fair, inviting you to topple them into the area.

Half of the front door is always open, since none of the bells work and the knocker went long ago, probably for a weapon. I went up the stairs without seeing anybody, and knocked on Kate's door. There was no one there, and I was looking for a piece of paper to push under the door with the telephone number of the flat, when I saw that the strip of stamp-paper gummed to the wall said O'Connor.

She had promised me. She had promised, last time I was here, that she would not move again without telling me. She had my mother's address in London. She had the address in New Jersey, and the one in Toronto, if my letters had reached her somewhere and not disappeared into the sad silt of the GPO.

The more she needed me, the more she rejected me. Why? I was afraid for her, and I wanted badly to see Sammy. I had seen his tight gnome face many times in my conscience in the last year, this sickly child who once was almost mine.

Defeated, I turned to go and saw Mr Zaharian standing silently a few feet away. He greeted me soberly but with warmth, and wrung my hand in his calloused one that was not the right shape for work. Nobody knew what he used to be, nor where he came from or why. He never told. If you asked, Kate said, he looked blank, and she thought he did not know any more himself.

'Where's Kate?' I asked, while he was still crooning with gentle pleasure and stroking the back of my hand he held.

'Gone away.' He shook his head. 'This people —' he pushed his soft wet lips at the O'Connors' door – 'drinking and fighting, we don't got no fun no more.'

'Don't you know where she is?'

He shook his head again, so fast that his near-set eyes merged for a moment into one. 'Sorry,' he said, rolling it like a cat purr. 'So sorry.'

When I asked him if he knew why Kate and Bob had left, he told me, 'They was trouble with a man.'

'You?'

'Me?' He exploded into giggles. 'Me?' The idea was too absurd for him to bear. He doubled up, holding the top of his trousers, which were tied round with the cracked belt of a mackintosh. He was delighted. I had pleased him more than anyone had pleased him for years.

BOB WAS sitting at his old pitch by the sink one evening in late October, listening to this little transistor radio he's bought.

Bought? I don't know. I won it, he'll say sometimes when I question some little item he brings home. I won it. And I am supposed to conjure up a vision of Bob and his mates sitting round among the picks and shovels in the dinner hour, playing cards on an upturned barrow.

He sets the radio on a little shelf behind the draining-board where I keep the bits of soap, and listens to it with his head on one side like the dog and one eye closed against the cigarette, playing very soft, like a private world.

The kids were in bed, and I thought they were asleep, but Sammy started to cry, and then he called out, 'I'm cold, Mumma.'

'I'll give you cold.' For he had two jerseys on, and his socks.

'Go in to him, Kate.'

'Go in yourself.' But it would take more than a crying child to move him out of a chair. I went in, and Emily had got most of the blanket wrapped round her, so I pulled some away and tucked it round Sammy, and dared him not to go to sleep.

'I'm cold, Mumma.' That's what he calls me, though a boy his age should say Mum. Even Emily does. But with Sammy it's Mumma, like a baby.

All of a sudden, Bob jumped up and shouted, scaring all the kids awake and the dog barking round his feet in a frenzy, pulling at his laces.

I swore at him, but he said, 'Shut it, Katie. I've got an idea.'

That in itself was rare enough, so me and the kids watched him without interfering, to see what he would do.

He's always been clever with his hands, has Bob, the one thing really you must give him credit for, no matter what you think about the inside of his head. We had been behind with the gas bill for some time, and they were threatening to cut us off, though I don't really think they would do that, they never have yet. They had been saying again on the wireless what a bad winter it was going to be, the worst within living memory, unless you were older than you ought to be. They keep on about it, nagging away about coal shortages and power cuts and what about the old folk – as if old people were the only ones who had to live in the kind of igloos they call houses in this rotten sunless town – and so Bob bought me a huge pair of fur gloves, like a bear's paw. They cost five pounds, which was one reason why we hadn't paid the gas bill, but much more fun.

I didn't know he'd been worrying about the gas – Bob sometimes goes for weeks without saying much that makes sense – but it seems he had, for when they started croaking about the winter again, he jumped up and went into the kids' room where the meter is and fiddled about a bit, and then went back and hunted in the shed among the tools and stuff he's brought home from time to time according to what job he was in, until he found what he wanted.

The meter man with the foxy eyes, who used to look at me very speculative before I had to struggle back into Moll's old Hawaiian smock again, wasn't due for another two months, and before that Bob would fix all back to normal so that there would be enough registered to fool him.

'To allay suspicion.' Bob likes a good round phrase when he's serious about something. 'Being one jump ahead, that's what does it, Kate girl. If it's going to come down like ice, like they say, I shall be the man who saved my family's lives.'

He was as pleased with himself as if he'd invented the Bomb, but he was bloody nearly the man who lost his family's lives, for all that.

Bob and I had gone out that night. It was Bingo at the Moderne, and they were offering double cash prizes, so we had to go, although I look like a beer barrel, Bob says, in that brown coat.

'Get me another then.'

'Have the baby first. Then I will.'

After Sammy was born, he bought me a fur for my neck. He promised me a present before Emily and Susannah, but then when they were girls, he forgot.

I wore the fur gloves. They make a strong hollow sound when you smack your hands together, and you'd think that dog would go out of his mind. Take care of the kids, Bruce, Bob always says when we go out, very solemn as if the dog could understand him, but if anyone did get in, he'd do no more than lift his leg on them, if that.

It was cold already, not half-way into November, and we had stuffed up the grating in the back room with newspaper and rags. Susannah had a cold, which wasn't unusual, her nose is like a tap, and Sammy was still coughing, but he'll not lose that until the spring. Smoking too much, I tell him, and he barks away like a sea-lion.

So Bob wanted to leave the gas on in their room, but there had been a little girl burned alive in the next street when her nightdress caught fire, and so being a good careful mother, I made him turn it off.

If I hadn't, there'd have been no house left, I daresay, let alone no kids.

When we come back from the Bingo, a pound the poorer since the game was rigged and the woman who won most of the cash was related to the manager by marriage, there were no kids, it's true, but it could have been worse.

Though not much. There were two cars outside our house and three policemen sitting in the passage as if they were waiting to see the dentist, and they jumped on Bob as if he was a wildcat and took him away in handcuffs. Handcuffs for Bob, I ask you. He was crying when he left, poor soul, and trying to get his wrist up to wipe his nose. I hope he wiped it on the copper's cuff instead.

The third policeman, who was a plain-clothes man, much more respectable, took me up to the hospital, and I stayed there the rest of the night in a bed in a side room, and they let me bring the little ones home next morning, though they kept Sammy in a bit longer, because they weren't sure of his chest. When I went later to fetch him home, the Sister, who didn't look old enough to be telling anybody anything and would never get a man and children of her own with that boss eye, told me that he was undernourished, so I said he was under a doctor, thank you, for chronic diarrhoea, which was being taken care of.

She said, and you couldn't tell which eye was looking at you, that it was funny there had been no diarrhoea in the hospital, and I said, well, wasn't she clever, she must have cured him, and took him away. He didn't want to come with me at first. He's like that sometimes in public, very embarrassing, so I carry some toffees in my pocket. He'll come for them.

It was Violetta who had found them, and I wish it had been anyone else, because her fat pink tongue is hung as loose in her mouth as a rotting tooth, and there was enough people knew about it anyway, without her filling in all the overblown details to all comers. Not that I care. I'm getting out. I've had it.

She means to be kind, Violetta. It was her overdeveloped sense of kindness that took her to the Tunnel that night in the first place. When Bob and I were on our way out, we met her in the street coming back from the off licence with a few bottles concealed under the tent that is neither a coat nor a jacket, but comes half-way between, where her hips should be.

'Going out, children?' she asked, as we came up the stone steps from the underworld. 'I look in on the babies for you, if you like.'

'It's locked up,' I said, for I'm not such a fool as to tell even Violetta, who wouldn't steal a threepenny bus ride if the conductor was on top, that Bob had not got round to fixing the lock yet.

She went anyway, to see if she could get in, for her husband has a ringful of keys the size of a grapefruit. It was as well she did, for as soon as she opened the door, she smelled the gas, and if she hadn't pulled all three of them outside, that would have been it.

She saved their lives really, although you couldn't thank her. 'No trouble, my dear, no trouble,' she said. 'Glad to help.' As if she had done no more than iron a couple of shirts for me, and when I tried to give her a present, she gave the money back and said, 'You need it more.'

Too true.

When Bob had his flash of inspiration, he had disconnected the gaspipe and fitted a rubber tube on in some way so that it went round the meter without registering.

Very simple, like all works of pure genius. What wasn't so pure was that one end of the old rubber tube slipped half-way off while we were out, so there I was that night with my kids in the hospital and my husband in gaol.

He got six months, which was hard, I thought, but he was scared dumb in the court, and the magistrate thought he was being obstinate. He won't see his child until it's about three months old, but if it's a boy, I shall take it up and show it him, and the warder who stays there with you will look tenderly on the affecting scene and reflect on the courage of the Women who Wait.

The prison welfare officer, they call her, and she was very nice, I must say it, although normally I can't stand her type of woman.

Mollyarthur now, she was different. She took other people into her own crowded life, but these women with folders and little cars, their own lives aren't up and down enough, so they get this craving to go out and live in someone else's.

Look at all the help they give, Marge Collins used to say, as she counted out the loot she'd milked out of one more Council committee, yet another charity outfit, all mad to outdo the others, fighting like jackals over the bodies of the poor.

'Most of them get paid for it,' I said. 'It's just a job, like any other.'

But there was something about the woman from the prison, something bold and honest, with an undercover laugh twitching at her lips to get out, that made me think of what Em might be like when she hit forty, still not caring what she said. When I told this woman that I didn't want her coming bothering me, which I didn't, because the place was in the worst state it's ever been and I didn't want any of the germ maniacs after me to clean up, she said, 'Don't worry, I didn't want to come either,' and we laughed, recognizing something crude in each other.

She was standing in the stone passage with her collar turned up and all the litter of cans and newspaper round her feet and the string of wet grey washing slapping her in the face, since she's much taller than me. Sammy had gone off somewhere with her bag, and I had a flash of insight as I saw her standing beleaguered there with that crooked smile, that although it was bad to be the property of all the do-gooders in the welfare state, it was worse for her to have the burden of people like me and Bob.

But I didn't give in. It might be her today, but next time it would be My Colleague, with a nose like a tapir and a plan for reorganizing my life, so I said that I was quite all right with what I was getting now from the National Assistance, and that the kids and I were moving into a better place.

Both half-truths. The money's enough to keep alive on, that's about it, and the new place isn't better than Thomas's Tunnel, but it's different.

You can say that again.

Violetta couldn't understand why I had to move. 'Six months,' she said. 'No trouble at all. He'll be out before you can turn round.'

'I'm not going to stay here with all the street knowing where he is.'

'Why do you care, child? It happens to the best people.'

But I do care. She thinks it is because I am ashamed of the neighbours knowing, but it isn't that. It's because I don't want them to be sorry for me.

The day poor Bob went to court and never come out again, Mrs Olson came over with a chocolate cake. That's what they do. Any trouble, they bake away like mad, like people send flowers to a corpse to make themselves feel better for not having done anything for it when it was alive. When Pearl Richmond's husband was in the crash with his petrol tanker, someone who'd never spoken to her before because she's a Jap, baked her a fruit cake the size of a tombstone and she was still cutting at it when he came out of hospital two months later.

The chocolate cake was all right though. The kids and I ate half and then Bruce got at the rest.

For some time back, I'd been having nostalgia for my old haunts. This part of London is all right in some ways, but I much prefer the old familiar neighbourhood where Bob and I were for the first two years, and where Moll was at Grove Lodge, and I used to fight with Joan in the kitchen of that nursing home that backed on the Common.

I took the kids over there one day and wandered about and passed the end of Butt Street and made a face down it, and found this flat on a card outside a tobacconist along with all the tarts, now heavily disguised as anything and everything, even Woman to do General Work. They are not allowed to call themselves Models any more, but you can always tell. Barbie showed me how.

If you could pick up this flat and transfer it to Spain or somewhere warm, it wouldn't be so bad. Even if you could just swivel it round on its base so that at least one of the windows got the sun when there was any. After the Tunnel, I don't mind so much it being dark, but it's those bloody great windows that let in nothing but the cold, and when the first snow came last week, it sat on the window-ledge outside the big room, blown half-way up the glass and frozen there like a hand trying to push its way in.

What it is, it used to be the servants' quarters of a big house on the side of a hill, in the days when what you saw down the hill wasn't a million tiny houses with women telling terrible things about their husbands from one back door to another.

When you have lived in this flat for a bit, you begin to see what they thought of servants. Or perhaps it wasn't so damp in those days. Everything is running, the walls, and if you hang the wash outside on a nice day, it stops being dry after you bring it indoors. It probably looked better too, with furniture in, and when the big room was the kitchen, with a fine coal range under the chimney where my crabby little grate is now and a huge table in the middle, scrubbed white, with people kneading dough and chopping onions and shaping sausage rolls on it.

Most of our stuff has been sold, for one reason and another, or gone back where it came from, because of the payments, and the place looks like a barracks after the troops have moved out.

I kept the mattress though, when I sold the kids' bed. The bed that was Bob's and mine, that we got at the auction, I got rid of that because the people who used to live here left behind one of those chairs that pull out to sleep.

'What will you do when your husband comes home?' asks Mrs Martin, who lives in part of the upstairs, very pushing, and is going to have to be told soon to keep her fat red nose out of my business.

She has a great gift for asking the wrong kind of question, a gift which she exercises at every chance, to keep her hand in.

'If he's got such a good job up north, why didn't you go with him?'

'Oh, you poor thing,' she said, the first time she saw me from the back. 'Did you burn yourself?'

'I was born with it,' I said, and turned my collar all the way down, so she could see better, and she said, 'How shocking.'

How shocking. So I don't wear scarves round the house now, so that she'll have to see.

'I heard the boy shrieking. Has he hurt himself?' She stands at the top of the back stairs and yells down at me with her teeth out and legs like cider bottles and the toes of her dirty angora slippers over the edge of the top step.

I don't really like her at all. Her husband, who is a postman

I wouldn't trust with a Christmas card, let alone valuables in the mail, is for ever hammering and drilling. They are wiring the insides of the walls so that when Bob comes back, they can listen in to what we say.

But everything will be all right when Bob comes home. He'll get a good job, though he's sunk himself with the Army now, I fear, and we'll have some money again and get another bed, king size if we want it, with a headboard done up in all brocade. Red.

Because the house is on a hill, part of the flat is half underground. That's the sunny side, needless to say, and it's underneath the front steps that rise up over what used to be the coal cellars, only they're nailed up now, with bodies inside of people who've died of pneumonia down here.

Ours is called the garden flat. Where do you live? Oh – at the top of the hill. The garden flat, you know. And you can see me out there with one of those big flowered umbrellas, serving Earl Grey tea to the vicar.

He came, incidentally, looking for Ruth Sullivan – waste of time, with a name like that, I told him – a great starved man with a face full of horror at what he'd found in the church, and scared the life out of me, asking me if I wouldn't come and find it too.

The garden outside our flat is a junk heap, which was paradise for the kids at first, but it's too cold now to play out there, and everything is covered with snow and frost. I picked up an old cast-iron frying-pan to see if I could use it, and it nearly burned my fingers off. Even the dog barks to come back in as soon as I put him out.

At the bottom of the garden, lopsided a little from the hill, is an old chicken shed where Sammy goes to play some of the time. I'd just as soon he was out of the house. He whines all the time, and cries for his dad. It's sickening.

If it wasn't for you, I tell him, your dad wouldn't be locked up. Coughing, complaining of the cold. He did it for you, I tell him, and the least you can do is shut up grizzling.

He doesn't grizzle when he's up with the Sullivans. He's sly, that's where it is. He knows how to get round them for treats. And he knows how to drive me even farther round the bend than I am already, with the three of them, and the dread of the next.

> **BABY GIRL FOUND ON CONVENT DOORSTEP**
> *When Sister Mary of the Angels opened the back door to take in the milk, she thought she heard a kitten mewing. Then she saw a baby girl, apparently only a few days old, wrapped in newspaper in a canvas toolbag.*

The Sullivans live in the big top flat, and like all women with a lot of children of her own, Ruth never minds a few more. She is going to take mine when I have to go to the hospital. Sam and Emily are up there half the time as it is, thank God. She gives them jelly squares and biscuits, and she has given me a few baby clothes because she says she's finished, but I don't think she is. She's the kind of woman who suddenly produces another at forty-eight and gets photographed with it in the maternity ward, looking surprised.

Ruth Sullivan is not like Molly, with thousands of kids, but still managing to let her husband feel there's room for him.

As if I didn't have enough on my hands, she tells him, without you coming home demanding, though all the poor thing has done is come home from the lumber yard in a perfectly normal way and ask what's for supper.

I like Ruth, because she's kind, in a domineering way, and when you're as tired as I am, you don't mind so much being ordered about, but he's the better of the two, though doomed to go through life unnoticed, because she makes so much noise being a wonderful mother and everybody's friend.

She's quite well known in the district. People say: Oh, you live in the same house as Ruth Sullivan. Isn't she wonderful? but nobody seems to know Smiler.

His name is Ronnie, but she calls him Smiler, because he has a sad, rejected face, like a dog pressed against a locked door on a cold night. He is a big man, slow in his movements – he gets terribly in the way in their crowded flat – and with his shoulders hunched forward as if he was looking for something.

The first time I saw him, coming up the hill one evening while I was pushing the pram up from the other side, full of kids and firewood, my heart turned, because I thought it was Douglas.

I have never seen him since the day they separated us, like runaway lovers, in the coffee bar, but I have never forgotten him. A few steps nearer and I saw that Smiler wasn't like him at all, because Doug's face was stronger and more secret. It didn't have his history written on it. But the stooping walk was the same, that's what fooled me, and when Smiler saw the smile that had begun on my face, he smiled too, as if he had found what he was looking for.

I had stopped by the side path which leads round to my door, and he said, 'Are you the little girl who moved into the downstairs? Hooray.'

I don't know why anyone should hooray over me, with a shape like a sperm whale and three croupy kids, but Smiler and I have been friends from that time on. Ruth doesn't mind. It gets him out of the way when he comes down to see me. He brings half a pint of milk that he's lifted from the kitchen behind her back, and I make hot chocolate and we talk to each other. I haven't had anyone to talk to for ages, not since Em. He can't talk to his wife, because she's never still or silent long enough. So it's someone to talk to, for both of us.

I thought at first that I would be able to talk to their eldest girl, who is about sixteen, and in some ways puts me in mind of me at that age.

Some people are in love with the world. Linda is in hate with the world, like I was for a time, only she's got no reason. Her mother spoils her and her father daren't cross her, because of it. She stays out half the night, with a gang of girls who all do their hair alike and wear the kind of sham-leather clothes I used to think were the ultimate before I changed my ideas, and when she's at home she either sulks, or yells that it's suffocating her and she's being cheated.

What of? She's got nothing to offer that I can see. But she's young, and I wanted to be friends with her because I'm young too. I'm only twenty-two, but I'm old, old, old, and I don't want to forget what it felt like to be sixteen and not give a damn.

But Linda's got no time for me. I'm grown up. I've been caught by marriage and kids, so I'm one of Them, who's done something or other to stop her getting whatever it is she thinks the world owes her for taking up air space.

I CAME home from Canada in late December, and I hope my mother appreciated – No. If she knew it was a sacrifice to stay in London to have Christmas with her and Connie instead of going to Scotland to have it with Joel, it wouldn't be worth making.

Why doesn't he come down here? they asked, especially Connie, because she is a ravaged, sex-hungry woman with the scalp showing through her hair, although she's only been a widow a few years.

I pretended that Joel couldn't get leave. It was not fair to initiate him into the family gathering at Uncle Mark's, with Nell breast-feeding her baby in the room where you put your coat (she's gone from weirdo to peasant since marrying a scientist), and poor Gran not quite with it, and the stray relations who come out from under stones to have a good feed at Uncle Mark's expense.

It was my first Christmas in England since I went to America. In other years, my father had been there to make it human. This year, no one mentioned him. When Uncle Mark gave the toast to Absent Friends, my mother looked hopeful, because she is still rather dedicated, like a general's relict, and Connie cleared her throat threateningly, but Uncle Mark shoved his glass into his beard, and that was that.

Derek and I got a little drunk and went for a walk on the Heath, and kissed each other with dispassionate passion, which did us both good, I thought, so it was just as well that Joel wasn't there.

The next day, Connie told me that I would ruin my skin if I drank too much. I didn't tell her that she had ruined Uncle Mark's party by refusing to drink his beautiful wine and leaving selections of her food in a ring round the edge of her plate. It wasn't true. The party was ruined by my father not being there.

Connie is not as bad as she ought to be, considering her habits. She makes rugs all the time, which is peaceful, and she and my mother enjoy quite a lot of rapport, decrying this and that. They talk of moving to the country and buying a loom.

When Joel came to London, he got on beautifully with both of them, as he always does, because people are meat and drink to his vitality, so never bores. He gave my mother the jollying treatment, and she said afterwards, 'He's not a bit what I expected.'

'What did you expect?'

'Well, an American – I thought I wouldn't know how to talk to him,' she said, and I realized that she had been afraid.

When we are married, she will come to visit us – Connie can stay behind with the loom – and I shall be much nicer to her. It will be easier, with Joel. His tolerance is natural, rather than an attempt to understand. To be what he thinks I am, I have to hide my cruel devil.

He wants me to give up my job. I shall have to in the end, but not yet. I am at the London office, planning the layout of the first of the new B.B. markets in Leeds. I must just see this one through, I tell him. But then there will be another, in Sheffield, and then another. Not much of a marriage, and what happens when Joel gets sent back to the States?

Then I shall be an Air Force wife, planning nothing more challenging than Wives' Club teas, with the bread dyed blue to match the napkins, and high-chested women in hats or hair spray in charge of the ornate teapots from the Chancery Lane silver vaults, whose owners have sat up half the night poking toothpicks into the scrolls and crevices.

I shall be one of the healthily pregnant women disparaging the marvellous cheap clothes and china in the PX, and pushing a cart with a small rude child in it round the commissary. But the drugged look on my face will not be the normal supermarket coma. It will be nostalgia for the days when I was not a customer, but a power behind the scenes who could design you a far better commissary, right from the day the first bull-dozers moved on to the empty land.

Before Joel went back to Scotland, I took him to see my father. He and Benita live near Ham Common. They have a little old brick house in a narrow lane with high garden walls and no proper street lights. My mother, who has driven past it in dark glasses and a hat pulled down like a pre-war spy, says that it doesn't compare to our tiled and timbered house with the view; but it does. It is very small, but it belongs there. Our house never properly belonged on the side of that gentle Kentish hill. It sat on the chalky earth like a townee at a picnic, and the earth resented it.

At the green gate in the walled lane, I hung back, and Joel took my hand and said, 'Don't be afraid. I'm with you.'

'I'm not afraid.' I pulled my hand away to open the gate. How could he not see it? It was because he was with me that I didn't want to go in. It would hurt that I had never come here on my own; only when I had the trophy of Joel to show him.

All right, I had wanted to hurt him. Now I didn't. There was no point.

I like Benita. I knew I would. That is one reason why I haven't been before. She's supposed to be the enemy. I had thought she might daunt me with sophistication, but my youthful memory of her was exaggerated. She looks and smells and sounds good, but not in a way that makes you feel you look and smell and sound terrible yourself.

Joel was very happy and casual, but with his father and mother both divorced and married again, this kind of situation is standard. I was tense. I tried not to try too hard, but I knocked things over, first some books on a little one-legged table, then my drink.

My father said, 'Thank God for that, anyway. I was afraid you wouldn't be like my daughter any more.'

Benita frowned, and he said, 'She told me not to get sentimental.'

'I should have told you not to have three martinis,' she said, with the smile that really knows him, not the tight, tentative smile with which my mother used sometimes to approach him, unsure of her reception.

Connie, and my mother too, secretly, for all her public loyalty, might like to hear that he had gone to seed, drinking too much, ruined by adultery. But he looked very healthy, younger even, and less tired. He had had three drinks because he was afraid of me.

My mother had been afraid of Joel. My father was afraid of me. Joel, with his sociable face that no one would hate and no one would paint, and his animal eagerness to like, Joel was a relief. I could see that. My father was glad for me. Very glad, as if he felt absolved for helping me to break my heart over Tom.

Why can't I be glad for him? He isn't the same man, that's all. Or is it not he who has changed, but my vision of him?

'Oh, by the way,' he said, after we had been in the house for a while, and I was beginning dangerously to relax and let him woo me, 'I forgot to tell you.'

'What?' I was comfortable and warm. I have only been in England a few weeks, but I know already that this winter, if you are warm somewhere, it's all you ask. This winter, some of the subtleties of living have gone overboard in the struggle against the vicious cold that grips this helpless country in an iron hand.

'What?' My eyes were closing, and I blinked across to where he sat in his own blue chair on the other side of the fireplace. My mother made him take the chair, forcing it on him although he said he wanted nothing from the house, and at least Benita has had the taste not to fall on it with a new loose cover devoid of associations.

'That chap Jordan – remember him?'

I nodded.

'You've met him in court. That's right, you went out with him once or twice, didn't you?'

'What about him?' I was going to telephone Jean tomorrow to ask if I could take Joel to see them.

'His wife was killed. A petrol tanker went out of control on a hill. She was crushed against a shop front. About six months ago, it was. Perhaps more. Dreadful business. I meant to write and tell you, but I forgot.'

Forgot! I left Joel with Benita – she wanted to keep him

for dinner and he wanted to stay – and drove dry-mouthed and staring through unfamiliar streets that were somehow in the right direction, to Johnny Jordan's house.

The brass plate was still on the door, for the house belonged to his organization, not to him. I thought perhaps he would be gone, but when I rang the bell, Nancy opened the door.

She has grown a lot since I last saw her, and filled out into a junior version of her mother's shape. She was in her school uniform, but it looked like fancy dress on a grown-up.

She used to call me Miss Bullock politely, but when she opened the door with her mother's instinctive smile for anyone outside before she saw who it was, she said, 'Emma,' and I was able to put my arms round her.

Her father found us standing in the hall like that when he came through from the back of the house to see who it was.

We went into the kitchen. I have never sat in the front room in his house. I don't think they ever do. The kitchen was warm, but empty. Nancy doesn't fill it. The yellow walls looked farther away, and the emptiness sat like a presence on the top of the dresser and the curtains and the chimney shelf, waiting.

'I wish you had written to me,' I said. Thank God I hadn't called him blithely on the telephone and spilled out my news about Joel. Some people are saved by luck from the unspeakable mistakes.

'It's not your sorrow.'

'It is.' But it would sound presumptuous to claim any rights to Jean.

Nancy is fifteen and is taking care of the house, but they want to transfer her father to another town where there is enough work for two people, and they could live with the other man and his wife.

Nancy said, 'I won't go.'

'You'll have to, if they send us.'

'They won't move you about like a pawn, you know that. What about Mrs Allison? What about the Bokers? What about those people squatting in the Army hut? If you want to stay here, you'll stay.'

'Then we'll have to get a housekeeper.'

'I won't let her in.'

'Be reasonable, you —.'

'I am. I just don't want to be treated like a *child* any more.' Standing up, she leaned on the table with her sleeves rolled up and her mother's apron on and appealed to me. 'Did you have to fight to grow up, Emma? Did you?'

'I refused to stay at school.'

'You see? He wants me to stay for ever. In this outfit.' She banged the rounded front of her gym tunic. 'But I've got to start training for a decent job.'

Her father patted the hand that was tensed flat on the table, the nails still bitten and childish, unlike the long silver talons of her contemporaries. 'We'll see.'

'She still gets worked up,' he said later, when she had gone out to a friend's house. 'I have to go easy with her. Jean and I didn't want her to grow up too fast, like these others I see all the time. Poor silly kids trying to pretend they're women. Now I can't stop her. She mustn't think I'm taking care of her. She has to be taking care of me. The other day, she came into the bedroom when I was looking at Jean's picture.' He was talking slowly, dropping the words on to the tablecloth, with his shoulders hunched and his jaw set in wretchedness. 'She rushed at me and sort of – sort of beat on me, and said, "Don't cry. I forbid you to cry". I've got to be careful, you see, not to let her think she's not enough, so I can't let go with her.'

'You could with me,' I said, 'if you want to.'

'No thanks,' he said politely, as if I had offered him a sandwich.

He was silent for a minute and then he said, 'I wish you'd been here though.'

'So do I.' I didn't know what to say. His grief and loss are so massive. The disaster that has happened to him is so crushing that I don't see how he can crawl back into life again, and yet I know that day after day he is still walking imperturbably into the homes of dirt and stench and ignorance to try and sort out other people's disasters of their own making.

The telephone rang several times while I was there. A mother who had forgotten the day of her son's court hearing. A father reporting a new address. A mother who was worried about her baby. Why don't they call a doctor? A woman who wanted to know how to get to Birkenhead.

'Are you running a new service?'

'It's always been like this. They get to know you, and then they're after you for everything, long after you've put Case Closed on their folder.'

It was time for me to go. I didn't know whether to tell him about Joel. One has this stupid egotism that one's own happiness might sharpen the loss. But when I lost Tom, I didn't mind other people having love affairs or getting married. Their puny lusts and plans had no relation to me.

It would be the same for him. So I told him about Joel, and I was right: it didn't make him feel any better or worse. Why should it? The women with boys in trouble and sick babies and journeys to make to Birkenhead could help him more than I could by needing him.

GEORGE, BOB said. If it's a boy, you've to call him George, God knows why, but I did. You can call a child anything, like naming a dog or a canary, and change it the next week if it doesn't seem to look like that.

Poor little George doesn't look like anything much except those maggots that get into the garbage. He's very pale. I never had a baby so pale, but it's the cold, I expect. We're all pale, those of us that aren't blue, and the kids' legs are mottled all colours, like bruises.

If Susannah goes out, her cheeks get red and sore, like the meat we had to scrape in the nursing home for that old gammer who had to have beef tea, so I keep her indoors, though some days it seems as cold in as out. Her poor nose is raw, where she keeps picking at the crusts that come from it running all the time. I got some cream for her, but Sammy took it and put it all over his face to play shaving. Sometimes you can't help laughing at him.

Soon after I got back here with Georgie, the pipes burst. They have burst all down one corner of the house and it has frozen there like stalactites. Like a picture I saw of Niagara frozen up. Why travel when you can see the marvels of nature right on your doorstep?

The Martins had already moved out because their windows didn't fit. Some people want jam on it. The Sullivans got out too, after the pipes, because that is it for water, and the plumbers have all dropped down dead from overwork. Ruth and Smiler have gone to her sister's a few streets away, and the Martins have gone to a flat the Post Office helped them to find. The people next door, who had the fire when the kid knocked over the paraffin heater, they've gone too, so we are all alone here at the top of the hill, because we have nowhere else to go.

I wouldn't have the energy to move out anyway. I felt bad enough after Emily and Susannah, but this time with George, I feel I have been put through a mangle. Perhaps they did, while I was under the anaesthetic, having that dream again about finding the reason for it all, that explodes as soon as you try to grab it. There's a jigaboo doctor there who'd do anything. Trained in secret Mau Mau tortures.

My chest hurts off and on, so sometimes I just lay down on the mattress and pile all the coats and blankets on top of me, and let the kids take care of each other. I have to lock up the food, because Sammy takes it. He is a thief, on top of everything else. When Ruth came to see me, she said, 'What's that child done to his leg?'

'He fell down,' I said. 'He's always falling down.' Which was the truth. Mrs Martin used to say he had rickets, which was a lie. But Ruth was busy clucking round, cleaning up, swearing at me religiously in the way she does for letting things go.

For the love of sweet Jesus, she'll say. In the name of all the blessed martyrs of Holy Mother Church, and make it sound like filthy language.

She came two or three times. In a way, I'd rather she didn't, for it means I have to pick up a bit before she comes, to escape her tongue, but now two of her lot are ill, and they've got a bit of a water crisis at her sister's house too, so she hasn't come again.

Everybody's got their problems this winter, though I daresay the Queen gets a bath every now and again, and a bit of a warm. Till they get the pipes fixed, I've just got to carry water, like a lot of other people. I fetched some coal in the pram, because they wouldn't deliver although I was entitled to extra, with the baby. He's all right. Never makes a fuss. Just lays there and looks at the ceiling with his empty blue eyes going back and forth as if there was a book written up there. The grate's too small for this big room, but when she left, Ruth gave me an electric heater like a mushroom that blows hot air, and I stand it by his cot. That meter outside eats money, but I have a funny feeling I'm going to like George better than any of the others. Why? Because he's little and white? Because Bob's not here to make an ass of himself and the baby both by hanging over it with that big loose grin and going azoo, azoo?

But when Bob gets home, everything will be all right. I don't really mean that, and I don't know why I say it. There are times when I wish he would never come back, when I wish they would put him inside for life. They should have put him inside before I ever met him. Don't you dare go off, my mother said. I'm going out, and you've got to take care of the little ones. So I met Sonia and those girls she went with at the bus stop, as planned, and we walked up and down near the cinema and these boys did too, like a dance, it was, and we finally came together, and no one wanted Bob, but no one wanted me either, so there it was.

Smiler comes round to see me quite a bit. The last time he came, he said he would make a meal for all of us, but there wasn't much to make it of, because I hadn't felt like going to the shops. Going down the hill is all right. It's coming up with the pram that makes you wonder why you ever embarked on it. I could go the other way, but Grove Lodge is there and it's haunted. One of Em's uncle's shops is at the bottom of the steeper hill, and it makes me remember the day I found her there with that great brown plait hanging over her shoulder like a rope, and she'd pinned on a name she'd made up, just like I would have done. Their sausages are good too.

Smiler said he would go out and get some bread and tinned stuff. I had the chair bed pulled out and was lying in it with Georgie, so I told him to take money out of my purse.

He laughed. 'That's more than Ruth would let me do.'

'What's that?'

'Go to her bag. It's sacred.'

'What the hell does she keep in it?'

While he was getting the purse out of my old pigskin that Em passed on to me when she went away, the piece of paper with the address of her mother's flat fell out.

'You want this?' Smiler picked it up. It was dirty and crumpled from being in the bottom of the bag so long.

'I don't know. Em was my best friend once. Now I've got too far away from her. I don't suppose I'll ever see her again.'

Smiler got out the money and went off to get us something to eat. I didn't see whether he put the paper back into the bag or chucked it away. I didn't care really.

I AM still staying with my mother when I'm in London. Although Connie is beginning to get on my nerves, padding about like a starved wolf in a pair of loose fur slippers, it doesn't seem worth getting a place of my own, since I am in Yorkshire a lot of the time and Joel still doesn't know how long he'll stay, or whether he'll get permission to marry over here.

I have the small back room because Connie has my bedroom. My mother gave it to her in pique when I said I wouldn't be living at home, and old Con moved in with her knit-and-crochet bedspread and her woven mats that shoot your legs from under you if you hurry in heels. That's why she pads. She's always lived with slippery rugs. Her husband died of pneumonia and other complications of a fractured femur, and we now see why.

Husbandless and childless, Connie has begun to mother me a bit, in an eager staring way. When I tumble into the kitchen for coffee, I often find her already up with a breakfast made for me which I have to eat, whether I'm late or not.

She picks up the letters and sorts through them, but there is seldom anything for her except catalogues from shops in Caernarvon and the occasional blue airmail from her cousin in Johannesburg in that kind of stultified handwriting which infects everybody in South Africa.

There is usually a letter from Joel, because he writes every

223

day when he's not on long flights, and Connie watches me read that before she gives me the rest of mine, although I would rather skim through them first and keep Joel's letter for the bus. But then she wouldn't be able to say: Everything all right? and hear me say: Just wonderful, in my American accent which makes her smile and shake her threadbare head, because it is supposed to remind her of Joel.

So it was that I didn't read the letter from Yours faithfully Ronald E. Sullivan until I got to the office, because there were no seats on the bus, and I sat at my desk in a sort of daze of Kate, suddenly insulated from the dragging activity of the place trying to get into gear all round me.

I had not seen her for almost two years, and I had stopped writing because I had given up hope of ever finding her again. We have always been able to come together like quicksilver after being apart. Even reading about her in the short, apologetic letter from this man who had befriended her brought her suddenly close, and I saw her in that horrible room, rank with sour milk and sour baby, leaning forward with the poor punishing birthmark showing above the twist of chiffon scarf.

But where was Bob? There was nothing about him, but no sign that Sullivan had moved in. *I think she could do with some help*, he said, *if you are able*.

Kate.

I left work early and took the old familiar line to the joyless, echoing station, half Underground, half main line, where I used to get off for Molly's house. Londoners tend to drift back to their old neighbourhoods, however ungenial. I had always thought Kate might, and if only Mollyarthur were still here, she would have drifted back to Grove Lodge eventually.

The Common was swept by the same polar wind as on that evening when I first crossed it, going apprehensively to Kate's birthday party, and now there is the snow as well, piled alongside the paths in primeval glacier chunks that will never melt in our day. The path was like stone. When a child running ahead of me fell down, I could feel the agony of the graze to skin already on fire from cold. The mother, bundled up like a Russian collective farmer, dabbed once at his face with her glove, then beat her hands together and hurried him crossly on, because she could care about nothing but her aching fingers.

If Molly were at Grove Lodge, there would be fires in the downstairs rooms and plenty of light to challenge the creeping February dusk. But Grove Lodge was cold and dark and empty. A board by the gate told that it had been taken over by one of the Council departments, and the clerks and typists and reliable women in sheepskin boots had all gone home.

I walked up along the edge of the housing estate to the top of the hill where a road of big dying houses drops down on the other side to a street of lights and shops and traffic. The house at the top was Kate's, a square grey lump that someone had once been proud of, a sick elephant squatting in the dirty snow behind the remains of a hedge worn down to stumps like rotting teeth.

The top part of the house was dark, but there was some light below. I went round to the side door, half basement, half ground floor because of the slope. There was no knocker or bell, so I banged on it with the flat of my hand since my knuckles were too cold to use a fist.

The drain spout beside me had a wide skirt of ice at the bottom between the end of the pipe and the drain. Next to it was a low boarded-up window, scribbled over with chalk as a reminder of the days when children were able to play out of doors.

I didn't hear Sammy coming to the door because he wasn't wearing shoes. There was some scratching and fumbling and rattling of the handle on the other side, and when he finally got it open I pushed it to help him, and he sprang back as if I were the winter storming in.

He stood with his back to the patchy plaster wall and looked at me, and I went down on my knees, because his spindle small-ness made me feel a giant. He is four, I know, but he looks a year younger, although he still has that ancient gnome face with the dark unblinking eyes.

His long hair was spikily on end, as if he had run his fingers through it when it was wet and it had frozen that way. He wore a big boy's grey jersey with the shoulders half-way down his arms and the slack ribbing almost to his knees. On his feet were an old pair of slippers poked into holes by his growing toes, no socks, and a handkerchief tied round a bad leg.

Staring at me, he let me take his hands. They were warm, with an odd dryness to them, but it was when I noticed that the unbandaged leg looked like a tomb effigy that I realized that I felt almost as cold in here as I had outside.

'Where's Mummy?' I took his hand to go along the dark stone passage past shut doors which must once have been larders and pantries and little boot holes where disgruntled maids cleaned knives with pink powder, and I heard Kate's voice call out, 'Who's that? Who is it, Sammy?' Her voice was rough, as if it hurt, and then she coughed, single hard coughs, like a horse.

'It's me!'

Sammy had begun to cry, but I left him and ran over the last uneven flagstones and into the big vault of a room where Kate sat by a smoking fire holding a child with a tangle of filthy blond curls, naked below the waist.

'Hullo, Em,' Kate said, as if I'd just been away for the weekend. 'I like your coat.'

She looks awful. She looked wretched enough two years ago, a slovenly child defeated by being a woman, but now she looks drained, used up, exhausted. She looks, I thought of it at once, like that Irish mother I saw years ago with Johnny Jordan, whose child I crazily wanted to take away. That shell of a woman who had once been pretty, before life got at her. Kate looks, I suppose, like a lot of Johnny's mothers look. I've seen a few of them. He has seen too many to be shocked by it.

When she smiles and laughs, it is my same Kate, and we picked up instantly on the old illusions and esoteric jokes, but her childish eyes, that glance quickly sideways when she is unsure, or wants to tease, are dull, and her skin is waxen, like the children's.

Emily and Susannah are plump, in an unhealthy mottled way, although they both have sore faces from colds, and I've got a full day's work washing them and getting their hair clean (bossy Miss Bullock with her sleeves rolled up), but George, who is only a few weeks old, looks like a baby's ghost, although

Kate assures me that they are all fine and will be as good as new when the spring comes and Bob gets home.

'Where is Bob?'

When she told me, I was really staggered. I had thought all kinds of things about Bob in my time, but not prison. I wouldn't have credited him with the enterprise to try to outwit the Gas Board.

I hated to think of poor tired Kate having to go through this alone. 'Why didn't you tell me? I would have come from anywhere. It must have been a nightmare.'

Kate said, 'Yeah.' Then she said, 'I don't know. I sometimes think I'm better off without him.'

'He's like another child to take care of.'

'I didn't mind that. I could make him do what I wanted then, when he was babyish and silly. He still is, in a way, but in a different way. He's got violent, you know. He used to be such a gentle boy, but that's how getting to be a man has taken him.'

'You mean he – he hits you?'

'Oh sure.' She laughed. 'The things we used to think about marriage, they're not true, you know. Ask Sammy about his dad.'

'My dad's comin ome.' Sammy hardly speaks, just sits and watches, but when he does, his voice is the husky garble of the streets.

'He keeps on like that,' Kate complained, 'like a broken record. It drives you up the wall. I don't know why he should care. He used to go under the bed when the yelling started. Remember that time, Sam, when your dad picked up that piece of wood and swung it at me?'

'Bloody cow!'

I said, 'Sammy, no!' but Kate only laughed and said, 'That's what he heard Bob call me. He don't forget. Not this one.'

Kate has to pay three pounds ten a week for this tomb where she is living with the four children. They stay in the one big room, which used to be the kitchen, because there is only enough coal for one fireplace. But the room is so big and high and damp that the small fire and the electric heater can't warm it. I kept my coat on while I was there, but I was still cold. I don't know how the children survive, unless it is because they

227

never have the contrast of being warm, like Eskimo sled dogs sleeping out through a blizzard.

They haven't got enough clothes. When Kate put something on the bottom half of Susannah, it was a pair of ragged pants and a flannel skirt worn to the texture of cotton, a pair of sandals and no socks. The baby is not dressed, but bundled. That's all you can say for him.

Kate's kitchen, which used to be the scullery, has a stone sink like a horse trough and a small evil stove that would electrocute you if it got the chance. The table in the big room is covered with broken toys and newspapers and old magazines and piles of jumbled clothes which Kate has either washed or is going to wash, there's not much difference. There is a table in the kitchen, but only two chairs, and you can see the marks on the old khaki paint where the cupboards and counters were ripped out. Now there is only a kind of meat-safe high up, which Kate keeps locked because she says Sammy steals food, and a few shelves with china on them and plastic mugs, and some tinned food, some of it incongruously expensive, like tongue and asparagus and chicken breasts, and much of it with the new Bee Bee label that I helped to design, with the bees at the holly-hocks instead of at each other.

'Never go anywhere else,' Kate said, and for some reason, she blushed. The flush spread round from the back of her neck and crept upwards, fiercer because she was so pale.

'Because of me?' I took a chance. I wasn't sure if she hated me for having gone up on the seesaw while she went down.

'Yeah,' she said (Molly used to force her to say Yes), and there is nothing I wouldn't do now to help her. Joel is going to wonder what has happened to my bank balance. It can't be helped. Thank God I've got something.

There isn't even a proper bed. Emily and Susannah sleep on a mattress on the floor, and it is one of those that Jean would have taken out into the frozen junk heap that is the garden and burned, if she had got her hands on it. Our Miss B. will too, when she gets a bed in. Can't do everything at once. Kate sleeps on a chair that pulls out at the bottom. Sammy sleeps on a violated red sofa, sagging and sprung and blackened with dirt and grease.

There is no time to feel sad, or compare Kate with the girl she used to be. There is too much to do. The coalman, a doctor, a plumber, although Kate says that you can whistle for people like that this winter. She has to carry buckets of water from the corner of the road. I put on her dog-eared fur gloves and made enough journeys to fill the tub and everything else in the kitchen that would hold water, and I felt like a pioneer woman, rugged and heroic. But Kate and some of the neighbours have been doing it for two weeks, and they find it neither rugged nor heroic, but just something you do. Something must be done about that dog with the complacent grin. No wonder it looks complacent. There is a stack of Bee Bee brand dog-food tins in the kitchen, and it lies in a chair by the fire on a blanket, and looks much sleeker and healthier than the children. There is a corner of the passage which it has obviously pegged out for lifting its leg.

'What about getting rid of the dog?' I suggested. 'He must cost a lot to feed.'

'Bob's dog?' Kate sounded shocked. 'With him in gaol? He'd murder me if he came out and found him gone. Besides, he helps keep Sammy warm. They sleep together. Touching, it is.'

I asked her if I could change the bandage on the boy's leg, because the handkerchief was dirty, with a moist sticky patch at the back.

Kate told me irritably to leave it alone, but when I came back the next day after work, with my arms full of packages like some ghastly lady of the Manor bringing soup to the peasants, I brought some lint and bandages and antiseptic cream, and when I insisted, Kate shrugged and said, 'OK, if you can make him hold still.'

The handkerchief was stuck to the wound, and the child fought and screamed while I was trying to soak it off. Once he hit out at me, and I slapped him back without thinking, because he had hurt my eye and made me angry with pain. I was instantly ashamed, but it quieted him, and Kate said, 'You're learning fast.'

'How did he do it?' The wound was on the calf of the leg, raw and wet and red round the edges.

'He fell. He's always falling down.'

'It looks like a burn.'

'That's what I said. He fell against the fire.'

'Don't you keep the guard on?'

'Shut up lecturing,' Kate said, 'and open that bottle of wine.'

I had brought red wine, some chops and a chicken, fresh fruit, thick sweaters for everybody, and some diapers, for I had seen from the dump on the table that Kate was using rags.

I had brought another electric fire. 'Take it back,' said Kate, who was reacting bluntly to the presents, because I was clumsily trying to give too much at once. 'They don't give the stuff away, you know.'

'I brought shillings for the meter.'

The last time I had offered her money, she had refused and I thought I'd hurt her in the stubborn knot of pride she has always held within herself whatever happened. But now she slid her eyes round to the pile of new shillings I had got at the bank, and said, 'Good old Em. Now we can cook the chicken.'

The meter was outside in a shed under the front steps of the house, so that if you froze half to death when your electricity went off, you could freeze the whole way going out in the middle of the night to recharge it.

The wine was a great help. When the chicken was cooking, we drank it while Kate bathed the baby in a plastic bowl and I washed the two little girls in the sink and dressed them in the new pyjamas. They capered, clowning with delight, and Sammy joined in, mimicking their bows and the stamping turns and strange stiff pointing gestures which were their dancing.

Although Kate says he is always looking for trouble, he doesn't seem to lead, he follows, taking his cue from the girls for what to do. While they were prancing round the table, he pulled a cord and sent a lamp crashing, breaking the bulb, and sat on the floor and yelled because the lamp had hit his bad leg.

Kate came to the doorless doorway of the kitchen holding the baby and its bottle, and yelled back at him. The dog jumped down from the chair barking, and made a pass at Emily, who shrieked like a train whistle. Kate stopped shouting when she began to cough, and Sammy went under the table.

'Who's your doctor?' I asked, letting Emily into the bulging pocket of my slacks where the sweets were, and putting my fur boot into the dog to get it back to its chair – I was, as Kate said, learning fast how to keep order round here. 'I'm going to call him.'

'He won't come. They're so busy now, they'll only come to sign your death certificate.'

'Then I'll take you to see him.'

'There's nothing wrong with me. It's over, what I had. It doesn't hurt now. Just a cigarette cough.'

She still smokes all the time, leaving cigarettes casually burning in saucers and tin lids, lighting another, putting that down and taking a drag on the first one as she passes it.

When I say, 'You'll start a fire one day,' Kate says, 'The people next door who had the fire from the paraffin heater, they got rehoused in a Council flat.'

'I'm taking you to the doctor. He can see the baby too. And Sammy's leg.' The boy crawled out from under the table when I said his name, and pulled himself upright by the edge of the thick sweater I was wearing today so as not to insult Kate by keeping my coat on.

'No, Em.'

Kate had drunk two plastic mugs of wine. She was a little flushed, much prettier. Her hair was longer now, and she had washed it before I came, and brushed it neatly, soft and flaxen. Straightening up from the baby's cot, looking me in the face with her lip stuck out, for a moment she was almost the old Kate, headed for an argument.

'No, Em.'

'It should be seen. It's not healing. Even I can see it's not a new burn. When did he do it?'

'Oh —' She looked away. 'I forget. Some time ago.'

'It's infected. You must take him.'

Kate looked at me again, dead in the eye, and said, 'I can't.'

'Why not?'

'I can't trust him not to tell the doctor.'

'Go on.'

'All right. I can't lie to you, Em. Why should I? It doesn't matter now. You've been here. If you don't come back, it's all one to me.'

I said nothing, waiting for her to stop acting.

'I burned him with the poker.' She looked down at the baby, and then flicked her eyes up at me, but I kept my face still. 'It was when we last had the power cuts. The stove was right off, and I'd got the poker in the fire to heat a pan of water. He'd been a devil all day. It was when I was sick, I should have been in bed. I felt awful, but there was the baby, and Susannah was bilious, throwing up everywhere, and I was dragging about, and I couldn't stand no more. He messed his trousers – a child of four – and before I knew what I was doing, I'd caught him one across the back of the leg. All right. Now you know.'

'The doctor needn't.' I was surprised how calm I felt now that I actually knew. I had been afraid before, when I wasn't sure. Now I wasn't afraid. I was filled with hopeless love for the child standing by me, his thin shoulders under my arm, listening unconcernedly to what we said, as if it had happened to someone else. My poor Sammy. But it wasn't that alone. Poor Kate, I was thinking. Oh my poor, poor Kate.

'He'll know. The kid will tell him.'

'He didn't tell me.'

'That's because I'm here. They'd get him in a room alone, and he'd tell. My mumma done that! Charming. They'd report me. That's what they do, you know. I heard Mrs Elia say that to my mother once when I'd been shut out in the yard all day. I'll report you, she said, but she didn't dare, with my dad the way he was. Don't tell anyone, Em, please. You treat the burn. Get the proper stuff, you know what to do. It'll be all right if it's taken care of. I've just been feeling so rotten, I've let everything go. Now that you've come, it's going to be different. Don't spoil it, Em. Don't let me down. You swore, remember?'

'I won't tell anyone,' I said, God help me. 'I'll get some burn dressing tomorrow, but if it gets worse —'

'Oh yes, of course, of course, if it gets worse.' Kate began to gabble in relief. She was very flushed, and her shadowed eyes glistened with approaching tears. 'I didn't mean it, Em. I'm not cruel, you know me. I did it in temper. I didn't know what I was doing.'

'You'll have to watch yourself, Kate.' If anything else happens, it will be my fault now. 'You'll have to be more careful.'

'Don't preach at me. You don't know what it's like.'

'It isn't the end of the world to have four children. Lots of women do. On purpose.'

'I don't care. It's different when you're poor all the time and having no one to talk to – even when Bob's home. I can't help it if that kid gets on my nerves.'

'There's nothing wrong with him. He's a darling boy.'

'He's got a devil in him.'

'Don't talk like that. He's only a little child.'

'No one ever said I was only a little child when they —'

'When what?'

'Nothing.'

'If you were unhappy, all the more reason to see your children aren't.'

She was looking at me very intensely, leaning on the side of the cot over the sleeping, snuffling baby, and I thought that she really understood. But she said to me, 'You don't understand. You only have to be with kids once in a while – mine or anyone else's. You don't have to have them *all* the time. Every day. Every night. You feel lousy and you want to stay in bed, and the baby cries and you get up to him half-drugged with sleep, and then you sneak back for another half-hour because you're so tired, so bloody tired. And just as you're going away into the only place where no one can get at you – Waa-aa! It's another one starting up, and you've to begin all over again, and he hits her and she bites him, and they're all wet or hungry or sick or miserable and they all need you, so you may as well get up, and there's another day started.'

'But if you lose your temper,' said our good Miss Bullock, 'they get worse, so what's it do?'

'Look, you don't plan to lose your temper. You just – you just – well, it's just being so tired and fed up and there being no end to it. You've seen a fretsaw snap. Michael, Molly's oldest, he used to have one for his models, remember, with the pedals and that. One minute buzzing along, eating the wood, spitting out the sawdust in a little cone on the rug. The next – ping! Up it flies in the air like a jack-knife – and I – and I can't help it, Em. It's just I'm so bloody tired.'

She began to cry, and then suddenly changed it to a laugh,

with a grimace that was like a convulsion. 'Welcome back, Em dear,' she said bitterly. 'I'll bet you're glad you came.'

She is very near the breaking-point. When I took her to the doctor a few days later, he said that she had obviously had some pleurisy on one lung, which was clearing up now. She would be all right with rest, he said, smiling wearily as if he knew that was a joke word, and he wished that he could send her away.

'But what can you do? I've got a dozen patients waiting for a bed in a convalescent home. By the time I got Mrs Thomas in, she's be better.'

'Or dead.'

'And the baby —' he pretended not to hear Kate — 'nothing really wrong. He's a little feeble. Try the new feeding I've given you. Keep him warm. He'll pick up.'

'He'd better,' Kate said. 'He's my pet, you know. The best I've got.'

I hoped the doctor would tell her not to say that in front of the other children, but he just nodded for us to go and said, 'Try and get more rest.'

He was immensely tired too. I felt sorry for him. There was a power cut on, and he wore boots and a woollen scarf in his consulting-room, and the waiting-room was lined all round with miserable, hollow-eyed women and bronchial old men.

I tackled the plumber next, and after trying three, one rude, one amused and one tottering, I got one to come and fix the pipes and turn the water on again – for a sum.

Darling Joel,

I can't come up next week after all. I'm sorry, but I can't help it. Such an amazing thing has happened. I found Kate, and things are pretty bad for her. There's a lot I must do. She needs me. Please do understand.

I tried to picture his face reading the letter with an understanding smile. But I couldn't.

I went to the coal merchants. The man in the office was large and bland, like an American funeral director, with that fobbing-off note in his voice so well known to the British in times of shortage. Yes, she might be entitled to more coal than she had

had so far. Stocks are chancy, mind you, with the talk of a strike, but we have *some*.

'Well, no, we can't promise *delivery*,' he said, as if I'd asked for the moon. 'People who really want it come and fetch it.'

'But this girl's been ill!'

'So have a lot of people, madam,' he said, 'including yours truly. We're all in the same boat, you know.'

'We're not.' If I thought I was in his boat, I'd jump into the sea and take my chance on a life raft.

I put some sacks in the car the next day, and got them filled at the coal yard, and took them round to Kate. When my mother and Connie went off to Buckingham to look at possible cottages, Connie put her new rawhide suitcase in the coal dust in the boot of the car, and they both said that I had become very selfish and inconsiderate since being abroad.

'Like an American teenager,' said Connie, who has never met one.

Sammy has lost his original suspicion of me and, to my joy, comes running down the dank, doggy passage shrieking; Emmy, Emmy! and hurls himself into my laden arms. His leg is better, thank God. I found a chemist who knew what he was talking about, and the burn is beginning to heal. He says: Ullo Emmy, about sixteen times a day, and sings for me, cracked and cockney, 'A Gordon for Me,' because it was the first thing that came into my head to teach him.

I love that child. 'You can have him,' Kate says. 'Take him home to your mum's. She'd love that.'

'So would Connie.' I made a face, and the thought crossed my mind that Benita wouldn't mind.

I did take him home for one night, after I took him to see a children's Christmas show which had made up its mind to run till Easter. Clean, and with his hair cut and a grey pullover and shorts like a hobgoblin masquerading as a schoolboy, he looked all right, and he behaved well, but my mother and Connie, glad to find something wrong, were horrified at the way he talked.

'What do you expect – newsreel English?'

'Don't be silly, Emma,' said my mother, who in some curious way is gaining a little stature and confidence from having

Connie around to back her up in prejudices. 'Just see that you have him in bed before the people come for bridge.'

In the night, he woke in my bed and cried, and screamed to go home. I comforted him down into quiet sobbing and went to warm some milk, and met Connie in her shaggy camelhair, prowling in a purple hairnet.

'He's all right. Just homesick,' I assured her. 'It's quite natural.'

But it isn't. People say they 'understand children', but you can't. Sammy is rather afraid of Kate, and she nags him all the time and favours the others, so that he tries desperately to make her laugh, because that is when she likes him best. Take him away, and he cries frantically for her. In the morning, he refused to sing 'A Gordon for Me' to my mother, which she took as a personal insult, and when I offered him a treat, he said, 'When we goin ome?'

This is what children do. It's very humiliating. This is the crushing blow to one's pride. You work hard to make a big hit with them, and then they want to go to someone who hasn't even been very nice to them.

I went to Kate as often as I could, and I was happy at that time, because she was letting me help her at last. I was supposed to be in Leeds but, in the excitement of being needed, I kept making excuses to put it off, because there was so much to do for Kate and the children. Finally, I had to go, and Kate grumbled a bit, and said, 'I wish you wouldn't.'

'Everything will be all right now,' I said, as much to reassure myself as her. We had the place cleaned up a bit, and the children were cleaner, warmer, better fed. So was Kate, but she was still on edge, tipping easily over into hysteria, still without energy for anything except losing her temper.

I begged her to be good to Sammy. 'If you ever do anything like that again —'

'You said we wouldn't talk about it.'

'If I had told anyone about his leg, they might have taken him away.'

'Why didn't you?'

'You know why. It won't be me who gets you into trouble. But be careful. For God's sake be careful.'

236

'Oh, I will, Em.'

'Be kind to him. He loves you.'

'Don't worry,' she said, and I said, 'Don't worry' at the same time, and we laughed and hugged, and I thought she would be all right.

'Back in two weeks,' I said, but the architect we had hired got headstrong and I had to find another, and there was drainage trouble, and difficulty in getting the freezer units we had planned for – the problems of building a supermarket in England are insuperable compared with the States – and it was almost a month before I got back to London and hurried down to Kate's with the presents I had brought.

Sammy opened the door to me, childishly without surprise, as if I had only been gone since yesterday.

'Miler's ere,' he said conversationally as he led me along the chill passage to present me, as he always did, in the doorway of the big room like an impresario – 'Ere's Emmy come!'

Kate wasn't there. Emily and Susannah, filthy as when I first found them, were sitting on their new bed, stewing gently in its acrid vapours. Leaning on the fireguard, trying to get warm, was a tall man of about fifty, with a long sad face like an abandoned Army mule.

He pushed himself away from the guard and came forward uncertainly. 'You're Miss Bullock?' He kept the high littered table between us, like a counter to keep civil service employees away from the suppliant mob.

'It's Emmy,' Sammy said, holding my hand in his chicken's claw. 'I told yer.'

'I'm Mr Sullivan,' the man said, 'that wrote about Kate. I hope you didn't think —'

'Oh no, I was terribly pleased. Where's Kate?'

'I'm afraid I've got bad news for you,' Mr Sullivan said. Why did they call him Miler? He couldn't run a hundred yards with those feet. He looked down and twiddled his fingers on the table edge. 'The baby's dead.'

'George?'

He nodded. 'She's very upset,' he added after a moment.

I found to my surprise that I was angry. Not sad. Not shocked. Just angry. I started to rant at Mr Sullivan unreasonably, but he hung his long face down and accepted it as if he had it coming to him.

'It's impossible! The baby was better. He was beginning to gain weight. Didn't she feed him what she was told? Why didn't she take him back to the doctor? What happened? Oh – it's unbearable!'

'Yes, she couldn't bear it,' Miler said.

'I mean, it's unbearable that anyone could be so – so hopeless. You leave her alone for a minute, and —'

'George is dead.' Sammy's bright, newsy voice, as if it were the first we'd heard of it, took the wind of canting rage out of my sails.

'Yes, he's gone away.' That was what Alice would say to her children.

'No, e's dead. I saw im. E was laid there in a box on the table. We washed is face, me and the girls.'

'She kept him here?' I asked Mr Sullivan.

'Two days, I think. I just chanced to look in today in my dinner hour to see how she was getting on, and that's how it was. So I fetched the doctor to take him away and said I'd stay while she went to the undertaker. She didn't want to, poor girl. She thought so much of that baby, you know, she didn't really want to face up to him being dead.'

'How did he die?' I was almost afraid to ask it.

'Pneumonia, the doctor said. Kate told me it was from the cold.'

'What happened to the electric fires?' I had been too angry to notice at first that there was no heat in the big damp room except the small coal fire.

'Someone got into the meter out there and took the money,' he said. 'They cut her off.'

'The baby died from cold.'

'That's about the sum of it.'

'Where's the electricity office?' They would be people against whom you could not win, so I must go now in anger, like Kamikaze.

'They'll be shut now. It's their half-day.' When Mr Sullivan smiled, as he was moved to do at this type of grisly joke, a curious process took place among the deep folds and furrows

238

of his face. From drooping, they all turned upwards, like one of those reversible pictures which is a sad man one way up and a happy man the other.

'I'll go tomorrow.'

He was still smiling. 'Don't expect them to be sorry,' he said. 'All they've said so far about the power cuts is: It's your own fault if you will be so selfish and use all that electricity. Cook a Sunday dinner these days, you feel like a traitor. You'd be too young to remember, but it's like after the war when they used to lower the gas pressure to take us down a peg in case we thought we was somebody for winning. If you're going to stay and see Kate, Miss Em, I'll get back to the job then.'

'Thank you so very much, Mr Sullivan.'

'Smiler, they call me. Everyone does.'

'So long, Miler,' Sammy said.

GOOD OLD Em, she went down to the electric people and paid what was owing, so now at least we've got some light again, and can fry a bit of bacon.

It won't bring back my little baby, but at least he had a sending off fit for a prince. When Em gave me the cheque for fifty quid, I went straight back to that nice man at the funeral parlour and said, 'All right, give me the thirty-pound funeral, with everything of the best.'

I thought they might let Bob come, but he's in bad favour it seems for not working. I wore a piece of black lace for a veil, like Italian women, and I was very brave. Very pale, but very brave. It was only when we got back and George wasn't there that I had to howl.

And somehow then, it didn't help, the lovely funeral.

Em said I was extravagant, getting the nice blazer suit for Sammy and then laying it away in paper, since it's much too good for him to mess about in. We had a bit of a row then. What does she want? I dressed him up for the funeral to please her. She thinks I am too hard on the boy, although she won't say anything more to me about it, because she wants to keep on coming here.

For what? To spy? I have to be careful now, to keep my hands off the child, though it's the only thing he understands. When I took hold of him to get him undressed, he screamed like a pig-killing and ran to Em. 'What's the matter with him, Kate?' she said, upset, and I said, 'Mind your own bloody business,' because I have to say things that hurt her, to take away the hurt in myself.

She would never tell anything against me though. I know she wouldn't. That's about the only thing I do know, these days. And that child cries and carries on, I don't know how anyone is expected to stand it.

'Why wasn't it you that died?' I ask him, 'instead of poor little George that never had a chance?' And he cries then and goes to hide in one of the rooms off the passage, where it's dark.

NANCY HAD stayed late at school to rehearse a play, and I found Johnny Jordan in a white pullover like a gym instructor, making his own supper, very serious, very thorough, with mashed potatoes and gravy and the table meticulously laid for one, which people don't usually bother with when they are alone.

There were only two chops, and I have seen him eat four, so I said I had had my dinner early. I waited until he'd finished eating, because he is a man who thinks better when not engaged with a knife and fork, and then said, 'Do you remember that woman who kept the nasty little shop in Butt Street?'

'Mm-hm.' He was eating cake now.

'She wouldn't let you do anything for her at first, and then, you said, she suddenly cracked, and let you help.'

'I saw her not long ago, as a matter of fact, in the High Street. She's much happier, and the two boys looked quite different. What happened to the daughter, your friend? You lost touch with her, didn't you?'

'I found her again. Don't tell her mother. Kate would hate that.'

'She's different though. More stable.'

'All the more reason. Kate isn't. It's happened to her too. The cracking. The letting go. Johnny, she's been through – she's only twenty-two, and she's been through more than any-one should in a lifetime. Her husband is in prison now, and she's just lost her baby. It died from cold. It died from cold, I tell you!' I raised my voice to beat the horror of it against his imperturbable listening face. 'How can any woman stand that?'

'It wasn't the only one, I'm afraid,' he said, 'this winter.'

'For her it was.' Usually I like him to talk about his work. Now I wasn't interested in his cases. The hell with them. 'She was on the edge before, ill, tired, she'd had about all she could take. Now she's cracked. Something's given way. I don't even know if she's entirely sane.'

'You want a doctor then.'

'Perhaps. But there's something else. I hate this. I swore I'd never let her down, but I've got to tell you. I wouldn't tell it to anyone else in the world, I don't think. It sounds too bad. They'd condemn her, but you wouldn't.'

He is easy to talk to once you get going, because he sits and listens properly without interrupting. He's the only person I've found who can do that, except Bess when she listened so patiently on the boat to my story about Rocky and the kid-napping.

'She's all right with the girls, and she was mad about the baby, but the oldest child – a boy – she's ill-treating him. She did before, when she was ill and lost her temper, but I thought I'd managed to change her so she would be better with him. But she's started again, I'm certain of it.'

'Why?'

'I don't know. She had to marry because of him. Could that have anything to do with it?'

'Perhaps. I'll have to go and see her, won't I?'

'Oh no, you can't. Did you think I came to – to report her? It's not that. I came for advice. Tell me what to do.'

'I want to see her.'

'No.'

'I must, don't you see? You haven't got to worry, Emma. I won't go tramping and shouting Where's this child Emma says you're cruel to? I want to help her, not punish her. It's not only for the child. I can help her too.'

'She'll know I told.'

'She needn't. Go and suggest I could help. Don't say anything about the way she treats the child. Then you and I could go in like a friendly visit, and I could see what can be done.'

'Thanks,' I said. 'I knew you'd have an answer. You always do.'

'It was Jean used to have most of them,' he said, 'but I've learned there's a way round everything.'

'Did that come with this job, or did you learn that in the Army?'

'I only learned one thing in the Army,' he said, 'that was any use to me outside, and it took me twenty years to learn that.'

He stopped and smiled, and I asked him what.

'That I was in the wrong job.' He laughed, the quiet snort with which he used to punctuate Jean's easy, noisy laugh, always a little behind her on a joke. 'All they that take the sword, Christ said, shall perish with the sword. The service, they call it, but who are you serving? For twenty years, I was trained to destroy people. I thought it was about time I trained myself to try and save them.'

I WAS lying down when Em came, on the divan bed she got me. I've had my lot of sleeping in the same room as the kids. Smiler helped me move the bed into the dark front room. It's colder, but it's quieter there. You can't hear anything.

The door was ajar because the milkman hadn't been yet and I wanted to call out to him for eggs, and so Em walked in and went on through to the big room, and then came in to me and said, 'What's the matter, Kate – are you ill again?'

'The doctor said to get more rest, didn't he? I'm resting.'

'The place looks like hell.'

'That's why I'm resting.'

'I'll clean up for you, if you like,' Em said wearily. She never gives up, doesn't that girl. It's amazing.

'I'm going to get up in a bit,' I said, 'and get some dinner started for me and the girls.'

'Where's Sammy? Is he out in this rain?'

'Oh no,' I said. 'He's gone.'

For a moment, she thought I meant that he was dead too, like my little George, and her face was a study. 'Gone where?'

'Away for a visit. To Molly's. She came to see me, didn't you know? And took him back with her for a holiday.'

'Where?'

'Where she lives.' I'd forgotten for a moment, but luckily Em said, 'York?' and I said, 'Yes, that's right. In York.'

She got her sleeves rolled up then, and got to work. Emily can't really talk much yet, big though she is for two and a half, and all she could say to Em was: Sammy gone, and Em carried on that kind of Sammy-back-soon-to-see-Emily conversation like she can do by the hour having more stamina than me, and went off quite happy.

I couldn't tell her about Sammy, because she'd make a fuss, but it's the best thing all round to stop his crying and his tricks. We've got a bit of peace round here now.

WITH SAMMY away, there was no hurry about taking Johnny to see Kate. She seemed calmer, and I thought I would wait and see how she was when the child came back.

I was in Leeds for about two weeks, and then I went on to York to stay with Molly and see what she thought about keeping Sammy. It might be a good thing to get him away from Kate for a while.

Joel has asked permission to marry over here, so I shall be in Scotland soon. I had to drop the fight about giving up the job, because he said, 'If marriage isn't worth that, it's worth nothing,' and I saw his point.

When I told Uncle Mark, he said, 'That's why I never employ women in jobs that matter,' and I said, 'You did me,' and he said, 'I had to. You're my niece.'

I know I have done well for him, so I asked him if it would kill him to say I had been useful, and he admitted, Yes, that was why he was angry with me for getting married.

Once I am with Joel, I won't be able to keep dashing back to London to see how Kate is, which was one reason why I wanted Molly to keep Sammy for a while, at least until Bob gets home again and gets a job and we see how things are.

There is to be a big squadron party at the Base next week, so after Molly's I was going on up to Scotland. At the party, Joel is going to tell everybody that we are going to be married. That is the way he likes to do things, with a splash, so I have bought a gold dress like a skin, very sensational, because everyone will look at me.

Molly is still on the fostering bit. I can't imagine her ever living with just her own children, and her eldest is now thirteen and the youngest seven, so she says she needs to have a few babies about the place. She now has children who can't get themselves adopted, half-caste, or crippled or retarded, and she has bought herself an old van converted into a kind of bus, because she is always taking them to clinics and special schools.

I got a taxi from the station to their house on the outskirts of the town, a kind of north-country Grove Lodge, a Victorian encumbrance that families can never unload except on to people like Molly who don't care what it looks like as long as there is plenty of room.

Molly arrived in the bus just as I did, rocketing round the curved drive and stopping just short of the rhododendrons to disgorge a babel of children of all colours, one spastic boy in a small wheelchair, and a stray goat she had found in the road.

She has two young girls to help her, Care and Prots like Kate was. One of them came out in a pair of black tights and a long angora sweater to bump the wheelchair backwards up the steps, and the other herded the children inside from the chilly afternoon. It is colder up here than it is in London, with eternal snows still in deep solidified drifts, and sugaring the gables and inconsistent planes of the roof. Molly looks wonderful, radiating health like a toothpaste advertisement. When I kissed her as she got out of the draughty old bus, her cheek was cold, but she felt warm from inside, like a stove.

'Where's Sammy?' I asked.

'Sammy?' She frowned. 'You mean Kate's Sammy?'

'Yes. I was so glad when she told me he was with you.'

'But he isn't.'

We stood stock-still on the iron-hard gravel of the drive and stared at each other, with the Yorkshire wind blowing our hair and skirts.

'Didn't you go to London and get him?'

'I haven't been down for months.'

'Oh God. Take me back to the station, Moll. I've got to get back.'

'Come in and have something to eat first.'

'I can get the fast train if we go now.'

Molly never argues or asks for explanations until you have time to give them. She climbed back into the bus and was off before I had got the door shut on my side, but I hung on and pulled it in as we turned left on to the road. On the way to the station, I told her about Kate and Sammy, not everything, but enough, and she bit her lip and pounded on the wheel with her big fur glove, railing at Bob and me and herself and life for our part in the tragedy of Kate.

'What did we do wrong?' I asked miserably, hunched with my collar up on the springless, rattling seat.

'I don't know, Emma. That's the rotten, shaming thing. Even the best we knew to do was a wretched failure.'

On the train going down to London, I tried to read, suspended in a maddening vacuum of time between knowing what I had to do and being able to do it, but the shadowy chamber behind my eyes, where pictures only materialize clearly when you are not looking for them, was full of shapes and nightmare visions. Cold watery afternoon deepened into dusk and then to darkness on the frozen mud and blackthorn of the midland fields, and by the time I got to London, I knew with a kind of sick despair that I was too late.

Too late for what? Whatever Kate had done, she had done weeks ago, before I last saw her. It had been too late for too long.

It was after nine when I got to Johnny's house. Nancy opened the door in a dressing-gown, and her usual doorstep smile dropped when she saw me.

'What's the matter, Emma?'

'Where's your father?'

'In bed. He's tired.'

'Please get him down.'

'He said not to —'

'Get him down, Nancy!'

My hair was still untidy from Yorkshire, strands of it hanging down by my ear like a demented vagrant's. She took two quick steps backwards and then turned and ran up the stairs.

Johnny in a dressing-gown. Heavy wool, tied low with a cord where men think their waists are, a thick brown pillar looking down at me from the top of the stairs.

'It's Kate,' I said. 'Please help me. I have to go to her. I think something terrible has happened.'

'I thought you were in Yorkshire.' He came down the stairs with animal feet in huge warm slippers.

'I should be. I had to come back. Sammy isn't up there with Molly. I don't know where he is. Johnny, I – I —' He came down the last step and put his hands on my arms, and gripped them when he felt that I was shaking.

'I have a terrible feeling she's killed the child.'

Driving to Kate's house in the little blunt blue car, we hardly spoke. Johnny had his jaw set square as if he were riding in a steeplechase. I sat in a ball, holding myself with my arms, for the tension of the journey had left me all bones, freezing cold. I wasn't shivering any more. Johnny had given me a shot of brandy and told me, quite harshly, to get a grip on myself and pin up my hair, or he would go to Kate's without me.

'What shall we say?' I asked him, as we came up the hill from the housing estate and saw the humped silhouette of the lightless house, racing with the moon away from the shredded clouds.

'We'll ask her where the child is. See what she says. Don't rush it, Emma. We may have to talk to her all night before we find the truth.'

'What about Nancy?'

'She's all right. I often get called out at night.'

'Here.' We stopped by the rotted hedge. Most of the snow was gone from the trampled waste of garden, but it was white with frost, like concrete. The house was dark, but we must wake Kate. We couldn't wait till morning. I beat on the door with my usual three flat-handed bangs. 'Kate!' I shouted. 'It's Emma – let me in!' It was like beating on a tomb.

'They've gone,' Johnny said. 'We'll look for her in the morning.'

Almost I went with him, but I had to say, 'Let's try a window.'

The window of the big room was too high to reach because of the slope of the ground, but we went round to the stone trench under the wide front steps where the electric meter was, and knocked on the window of the underground room where Kate sleeps.

There were no curtains. Johnny shone his torch into the room, and I thought she would wake in a panic at the beam of light. The bed was empty. Unmade, filthy, the pillow on the floor without a cover, clothes and wads of paper thrown about, a grotesque long-legged doll hanging from a hook in the wall like a suicide, but the room was empty.

'She's gone.'

'Where to? She had nowhere to go. No one to go to. Smiler perhaps – he might know. Her friend, Mr Sullivan. He told me where he lived.' As we went back round the side of the house, we heard a scratching and whimpering like an animal on the other side of the back door, which was Kate's front door.

'The dog,' I said, 'she's left the dog behind.' With visions of a starving skeleton hurling itself on me, all rabid fangs, I called, 'Bruce? Here, Bruce boy!'

The voice of Emily answered me, an incoherent babble of words with only a few consonants shared between them.

'Where's Mum?'

'Gaw a picya.'

'Pictures?'

'Yiss.' She can say that all right.

'Open the door, Emily. We'll have to go in and wait for her,' I said to Johnny, who stood quietly behind me, letting me take over. 'How could she leave those tiny girls alone? Oh, how could she?'

'You'd be surprised how many —' he began, but I told him not to be so damned imperturbable, and he shut up.

There were some scuffling sounds from the other side of the door, as if Emily was jumping up and down. 'Can't you reach the handle?'

'Naoo,' she whined. She can say that too.

'Get a chair,' I said. 'Get a box. Get something to stand on.'

She began to babble again in vowels, and the babble went away down the passage and didn't come back, although I beat on the door and called again and again.

'Smiler has the upstairs flat,' I said. 'Kate told me they were coming back when it's warmer, so they must have the key to the front door. Let's go and get it.'

I had started away, but he said, 'I'll stay here in case Kate comes home.' He never gets excited. He never dashes off somewhere without thinking. It slows down the tempo, but it avoids mistakes.

Murray Road, Smiler had said. My wife's sister has a big house with two rooms over the garage, so we've been lucky. I found it without difficulty. The other garages were single storey, with pointed roofs. There was plenty of light here and everyone was awake, including all the children. They were scuttling about in droves, like clockwork toys, and there were enough grown-ups stamping about to man a regiment. But no Smiler.

'He's not well,' I was told by a young man in a vest and very tight black trousers.

'Bronchitis,' said an older man, stepping over and round the children to look at me, and hacked out a cough or two to illustrate.

'What is it, Ned? What's all the noise?' A woman in a dressing-gown and green quilted slippers, large but firm, as if she still had her corsets on, came into the hall with her eyebrows at the ready, although there had been plenty of noise before I came in, and I wasn't making any.

'Wants to see Smiler? Well, she can't.' She gave an akimbo impression without actually having her hands on her hips.

'I'm a friend of Kate's,' I said, and her face relaxed as if that had been corseted too, and was now unhooked.

'Poor Kate. Really let herself go, that girl has. It's tragic,' she said.

'We've been out together, and Kate's locked out. She's lost her key. Could I borrow yours and go in from upstairs?'

'Why didn't she come herself?' The corset began to go on again.

'She's waiting with the children.' Lying is easy, to self-important women who are listening to themselves.

'I daresay.'

'Take her up to Smiler,' said the young man in the desperately tight trousers. 'Check her out.'

I was taken upstairs, with an escort of children on all fours, to where Smiler lay wheezing in a vast bed that filled a small room.

'Hullo, Miss Emma,' he said, to everyone's relief. They didn't want to be suspicious. It was their duty. They wanted to help. They wanted to be nice to me.

Too nice. Mrs Sullivan said she would get dressed and come with me. 'It's a tricky lock.'

'No, please. I couldn't bother you.'

'But I insist.'

'I'll manage.' I rush from York in torment, letting nothing stand in my way, and then this, in a flowered rayon dressing-gown and quilted slippers.

A girl with a lot of hanging hair and a hanging lower lip to match had come to a doorway with a television set roaring applause behind her to watch me, treading over the sides of her shoes.

'I'm good with keys,' I said desperately.

'I'll bet.' It didn't mean anything, but the girl made it sound as if it did.

'I'm going to get dressed.'

'I can't wait. It's too cold for Kate and the children.'

'As you wish then.' She was a woman who took defeat ill. I was turning to go, when she said, 'Linda can go with you.'

Ruin. But the girl in the turned-over shoes said, 'Me go out in that cold? What do you think I am?' So I got away alone with the key.

When I ran down the back stairs of Kate's house and let Johnny in, his face was bright red from cold, and his ears on fire. He stood in the big room, stamping his feet and beating his gloved hands. From the filthy, hair-smothered chair in the corner, the sleek dog matched eyes with him, and decided to thump its tail.

Susannah was lying in the baby's cot, and Emily was staggering about rather drunkenly in a pair of Sammy's shorts and a jersey like a sieve, with the sleeves flapping down over her hands. I picked her up and found her smelly. The room smelled worse than the last time I was there.

'This is where Kate lives,' I said. 'Isn't it awful?'

I thought he would be professionally shocked, but he was professionally unshocked. 'I've seen worse,' he said.

Susannah was sleeping heavily, and she didn't wake when Johnny turned her over to see her face. Emily did not seem properly awake. She yawned continually, and when I was holding her, she put her tangled yellow curls against my shoulder and dozed off, even while I was walking about. I found a large aspirin bottle on the mantelpiece, half-full.

'Could be for Kate,' Johnny said.

'Or to keep the children sleeping while she goes out. Mum give you these?' I rattled the bottle in front of Emily's closed eyes and she grunted and nestled into me like a nursing puppy.

'Where's Sammy?' I asked her loudly.

'Where's Sammy?' I shook her, and then put her on the floor so that she had to stay awake or fall over. I crouched in front of her, and she put her hand on my knee to steady herself.

'Where's Sammy?'

'Gone.' She rocked backwards, and I clutched her.

'Yes. He's gone away. Where did he go?'

'Ow air.'

'Where?'

'Ow air.' She jabbed a fat finger towards the window, squaring her bottom-lip to yell with exasperation at the same stupid question. 'In a garn.'

'We'd better get the police,' Johnny said quietly.

'Let's look by ourselves first.'

I put Emily on the bed and Johnny and I went into the garden. We didn't need the torch. The moon was clear of the clouds now, making deep shadows. The piles of refuse and old iron were etched in black and white. Here and there a tin-can, not yet rusted, shone like a cat's eye. For weeks the ground had been too hard for digging. We began to look among the frozen junk, picking it over with aching fingers, turning over a rusted water tank, shining the torch into a scrambled pile of old bicycle wheels with spokes sticking out like broken umbrellas.

I knew what I was looking for, and yet I didn't know. I am nearly twenty-four and I have never seen a dead body. Imagination terrified me and held me back behind Johnny as he calmly searched, a large, slow, matter-of-fact figure in the moonlight. If he saw it first, the pile of rags, rotting flesh, bones – whatever it would look like, I wouldn't be so afraid of it.

Sammy dead. . . . Johnny was working methodically down the slope missing nothing. I made myself think of Sammy alive, with the round black eyes and pointed shaggy head, and suddenly I could step in front of Johnny over a little cracked concrete basin full of sodden filth, where someone had once made an ornamental pool, down to where the chicken house sagged against the iron fence. The door was bolted, dropped on the hinges. I pulled back the bolt, lifted, and tugged it open, I didn't call to Johnny but as I went inside, he was behind me with the torch.

I didn't think Sammy was dead, not even at first when I saw him lying on the floor, with a piece of grey blanket over his legs, stiff as canvas.

He was asleep, curled up on the stinking mattress of old chicken dirt and his own filth, one hand under the sharp bone of his cheek, his hair a caked and sticky mass, his delicate eyebrows raised in sleep as if his dreams surprised him.

A rope was tied round his waist with a knot too tight for his fingers to undo. It was fastened to the wall, long enough to give him a few yards of movement, not to reach the door. There was no window. On the floor were a dented pan, and an empty jam-jar and a darkened lump of bread so hard that he had been sucking on it before he dropped it in the dirt.

Johnny stood very still, bent over under the sloping roof, with his torch shining on the sleeping boy. 'Bear witness to this,' he said to me. 'Bear witness to what you see.'

He had to use his knife to get the rope loose. When he cut it, and pulled it free from underneath the child, Sammy woke and cried, and I saw as he turned him over that a small stain had spread through the many layers of clothes from a sore where the rope had rubbed him.

His gnome face was like a skull, the eyes sunk into the shadows of the sockets, his lips drawn back in a death's-head grin when he tried to smile.

'Ullo Emmy,' he said, as I picked him up.

'Why isn't he dead?'

Johnny didn't tell me about the other children he had known who had lived for more than three weeks tied up in a chicken shed. He didn't tell me anything.

I wouldn't let him carry Sammy back to the house. He was so light, only a bundle of clothes. I clutched him tightly to me. I would never get the stink and filth of him off my coat, my hair, my skin, and I didn't want to.

We put him on Kate's sour, tumbled bed and covered him with all the blankets we could find, and I stayed with him, feeding him warm milk with a spoon while Johnny went to get a doctor. There was no time to think about Kate and what I would say to her if she came home now. When Johnny came back with the doctor, there was no time to think what we would say if she came blinking in from the dark passage and said: What's going on? We would probably push her out of the way and get on with what had to be done.

The doctor did not spend long looking at Sammy. He stood up and nodded at Johnny. 'Get him out of here.'

I wrapped him in the cleanest of the blankets and Johnny and the doctor went off to the nearest magistrate to get a Place of Safety Order which would give them the right to put Sammy into the hospital.

I stayed behind to tell Kate what we had done. Waiting for her, alone in the tomb of the flat with the sleeping babies, I knew that it was going to take more courage than I have ever needed.

If I had stayed with Molly, instead of coming back to London, I would have been in Scotland on Sunday. When I telephoned Joel on Saturday night to tell him not to meet the train, I told him briefly what had happened, and he was suitably shocked. Well, I was shocked too. Sick with shock. So why should his reaction sound wrong? Why shouldn't he say, 'If there's one thing I can't stand it's cruelty to a kid'? Everybody says it.

That's what was wrong.

'I'll have to stay here for a bit, Joel.'

'But the dance is on Friday. Our dance.'

'I'll be there.'

'I want you now.'

'I can't leave Kate just now.'

'Does she need you?'

'She needs someone.' No reason to tell him that she had thrown a milk bottle at me and called me a double-crossing bitch.

'Not you. Come tomorrow.'

'I've got to stay. I must go to the hospital too.'

'I said come tomorrow.'

'All right.'

Johnny said, 'Of course you must, Emma. After last night, you're better away. It won't do her any good to see you till she calms down. Was she drunk, do you think?'

'I thought so, a little. I don't know where she'd been. I don't know – she wasn't like Kate at all. She screamed at me as if I was someone else. I've never heard her like that. Yes . . . Yes, I have though. Once years ago at Mollyarthur's, when something set her off about her mother and she shouted and raved with her eyes shut and then fell down.'

'I was round this morning,' Johnny said, 'to tell her where

the boy was, and see what I should do about the other children. She's all right. And the little girls seemed quite happy. She was making them a breakfast of eggs cooked in butter. And there was cream for the cornflakes. Plenty of cream. But no milk. No bread. No chairs round the table.'

'That's Kate.' I looked at him. His face doesn't often give away what he thinks. 'Don't be disgusted with her, Johnny. I'm trying not to be. But what she did – I'll never forget it, when I opened the door and you shone the torch. When I think of it and see it and smell it, I want to kill her, trample her out like a filthy crawling thing.'

'You're about all she's got,' Johnny said. 'If you give her up now, it's the end of her.'

'I know.'

With Joel, I could forget a little. It is a very gay Base, with parties somewhere almost every night, and the grey stone villages in the valley transformed, a little nostalgically for me, by the Air Force families who live there.

Bright ski pants in the tiny store, where the post-mistress guards her stamps and postal orders behind a fire screen stapled to the counter. Absurd powerful cars crawling in the lanes behind Mrs McKenzie's little green van with the bread and the evening papers. A yellow school bus, shipped from the States, flashing red lights as the girls in thick white socks and saddle shoes jump down with their arms showily full of books they have no intention of opening. The Base cinema, where airmen in parkas with big fur collars throw popcorn undiscriminatingly at the officers while they wait for the first show to let out. Joel in his uniform and his short furry haircut, looking like Joel on Cape Cod. Proud of me. Sure of me. Talking about our children.

When I marry him, it will be escape. I shall start again, in America or wherever they send him, and there will be no more tormented loves or loyalties to tear me apart.

On Thursday, I was in the little hotel by the water, dressing to go with Joel to a cocktail party, when the girl from the bar, who is everything else besides, put her head round the door and asked me to take a call from London.

I went down with my hair loose, and heard Johnny's voice.

'What's happened?' Instantly it was all a dream, the parties, the yellow school bus, the escape. I was caught in the painful pincers of reality. 'What's wrong?' He wouldn't call me unless something had gone wrong. He was always frugally surprised by the nonchalance with which Joel and I made telephone calls up and down the length of the British Isles.

'Nothing. I just thought you'd like to know. Sammy came out of the hospital today.'

'How is he?' I should have been there. Walking down the shining corridor with a parcel of new clothes for him. Through the swing doors and into the ward full of railed cots and nursery-rhyme screens to where he waited, avidly, to see a face he knew.

'A bit weak, of course, and nervous. But there's nothing really wrong with him that feeding and care won't put right. He's in the Home out by the reservoir. I took him there. They like him.'

'They'd better.'

'Yes. Well —' Johnny was never any good at the telephone, and worse at this distance. 'Got much snow up there?' I was reminded of Tom calling me across the Atlantic, when we talked about the weather.

'I just thought I'd tell you. I have to get him into Care, you know. His case is coming up in the juvenile court tomorrow.'

'I thought it would be next week.'

'Not now he's out of hospital. Tomorrow.'

'Friday,' I said. 'My father's court.'

'Yes. Your father's court.' There was a pause. 'Perhaps,' Johnny said, 'it's as well you can't be there.'

We said our goodbyes, and I went back to my room and plaited my hair listlessly, not yet knowing how I was going to wear it. I felt left out. Useless. Superfluous. It was all going on without me, the important things. There was nothing I could do, but God knows I hated the idea of Kate in court again, and this time not the victim.

The faces would condemn her. They shouldn't be surprised. They'd seen everything, and worse than this, but still the faces would condemn, and my father would be too hard.

So often, the cases are on the border – parent, child, whose fault is it? – so that when he gets a clear-cut case with facts like this, he tries to make an example. I've seen him do it: This kind of thing absolutely will not be tolerated. People have got to learn that they can't, etc., etc.

Pointless. There are no public seats. The people connected with the other cases are outside. His audience in the small room are only afficionados who are already on the side of the law.

Sammy would be all right. He would be brought in and looked at with a sympathy not shocked enough to be unprofessional, and the students at the back would make notes.

But Kate would be there alone on the hard chair in the middle of the room, defiant and graceless and probably rude, and no one would be on her side.

She would sit on one of the benches outside in the draughty tiled hall, with the mothers' work-swollen hands turning red-purple on the way to blue, if the list moved slowly, and some of them would know each other, and so would the string of unrepentant boys who had defrauded London Transport of ninepence and the red-haired girls who truanted, coming back and back. But Kate would not know anybody.

They would know about her, because they know everything, the women to whom my father's court is no more intimidating than the headmaster's room at the secondary school. They would know that she was the reason why the Cruelty Man was there. They had seen him. Hullo, Mr Jordan, how's business? And they would treat her like prisoners treat a man convicted of raping a child – with a righteous unloading of guilt on to someone whose guilt is so much greater.

When Joel came up to my room, I was packing. He didn't notice that at first. He said, 'You can't go to the Weidners' like that. You look like an ad for the Shawmut Bank.' He pulled the thick braid tight round my neck like a rope, and kissed me.

'I'm not going,' I said.

I don't often see Joel angry. He is the kind of man to whom enraging things don't usually happen. Cars run constantly for him, and tyres keep their air. His parents give no trouble. His senior officers don't oppress him, and the men in his crew don't make ghastly mistakes. I have never infuriated him. But when I told him why I had to go to London, he was white with fury, and his relaxed and happy mouth was tight and brutal.

'If you go,' he said, 'you can't get back for the dance.'

'I know.'

'I planned this for ages. Our big moment.'

'I know you did. I'm so sorry. I know how you wanted it to be. But it doesn't make any difference in the end. To us, I mean.'

'The hell it doesn't. You're running out on me. That's what it comes to.'

'But I can't run out on Kate. You must see that.'

'I see one thing. You put that vicious little tramp before me.'

'I put her before the dance, that's all. Whatever she'd done, if she'd done murder, I'd still go to her. She's alone. She's got no one, and she's got to go through this in court. Of course that's more important than a party. With balloons and drunken colonels.' I shouldn't have said that. I wasn't supposed to mind the squadron commander letting go at week-ends.

'Everything I've ever wanted, everything I've ever planned for us, you wreck it.' He began to rage like a spoiled child, kicking up the corner of the carpet and kicking it again when it rolled back at him. 'Your father. Your job. Your uncle. Your God damn cheap little gaolbird girl friend —'

'Shut up.'

'I hope they put her in gaol. I hope they lock her up and throw away the key and you can never see her again.'

He was shaking with anger, and I was shaking too, and didn't want to speak, so I began to finish my packing.

'What the hell are you doing?'

'I have to go, Joel. I told you. I'm getting the night train. Will you take me to the station?'

'No.'

'Then I'll get a taxi. What will you do?'

'I shall go to the Weidners' and get drunk.'

He can be so like a child that I sat down on the bed and laughed and held out my arms to him. But it wasn't the childish Joel who turned away from me and said, 'Go on then, but don't bother ever coming back.'

I wore the red coat that Em gave me when she came back from Canada. It's about the only decent thing I've got left. I had to sell some of the other stuff when they came at me with the moment of truth about the rent.

I was glad I wore it, when I saw her waiting on the bench as I came pushing in among the crowd, afraid I was late, for she said, 'Oh good, you're wearing the coat. It looks wonderful.'

To tell the truth, I hadn't expected to see her any more. I thought she was through with me, like everyone else. I am an outcast, a pariah dog kicked into the stinking gutter. The looks I get. No one has smiled at me for days. Except Mr Jordan, and I don't count him. He's a reincarnation of Saint Francis, come back a different shape.

Em was sitting on the bench among all those terrible mothers and things they get in that court, and she got up and kissed me and said, 'The coat looks wonderful,' which was just what I wanted to hear, since everyone was going to be looking at me.

Dear Em. She came. I never thought she would, but she came. She's like a dog that doesn't know when it's licked. She's like those burrs that used to get into my hair when we lived down the lane. You can't shake her off. She came, with that long hank of hair over her shoulder like the first time I saw her in the market. It makes her look like a teenager, though her face really looked tired and white and much older.

But she came. She and I are together again, and I'm not afraid any more. She'll stick up for me. Mr Jordan, he can say what he has to, but Em won't let me down.

I needn't be afraid of her father. He was all right to me last time. And the woman in the fur hat – I swear it's the same one she had five years ago, that kind of curled lamb is very durable – she's not a bad old sow either, though they don't let her say much. It was her suggested me going to Mollyarthur's, so I've a lot to thank her for.

I wish old Moll was here.

It feels funny sitting in the chair, right where my dad sat that day, and they had to tell him to stand up when he answered Mr Bullock. Mr Jordan came in right behind me, carrying Sammy. Some funny clothes they put on him at the Home, I must say. Green was never his colour. I'd been told to sit, but Mr Jordan just stood there, looking too big, holding my child as if it was his own.

A man who had been darting about having confidential words with people as if he owned the place, put some papers on what they call the bench, although it's really only a table, with billiard cloth tacked over.

'Oh yes,' said Emma's father. 'Application for a permanent Place of Safety Order. Yes, Mr Jordan?' He has this lovely liquid sort of voice in his throat, like an actor. Not a bit like Em's, which is rather deep, and loud – you can hear it a mile off. 'That is the child?'

Who else? Did they think he was carrying that great big boy for fun?

Mr Jordan put his hand on the Bible to swear by Almighty God. Why didn't they ask me to swear? I was going to get a chance to tell my side of it, wasn't I? Then he looked round sort of helplessly, and a policewoman got up at the back of the court, rather a pretty one. I turned round to check, for they are sometimes iron maidens.

She was going to take Sammy, but Em's father said, 'Give him to the mother. You take him, Mother,' he said to me, in a voice that had nothing in it, not kindness, but not hate either. Mother. It makes you laugh. Last time I was in here, he called me Katherine and asked me if I was happy at home.

Well, of course when I held out my arms for Sam, he cried, the little bastard, and clung on to Mr Jordan. People nodded oh ho, I could see them doing it, and the woman in the Cossack hat leaned over to say something to Mr Bullock which he ignored, as if it was too obvious.

'All right, Officer. Thank you,' he said to the pretty police-woman, and she took Sammy and he sat with her at the back of

259

the room and beat on the table with a ruler. So Emma's father said, 'Perhaps you had better take him outside. He's a bit too old anyway.'

Too old to hear what was going to be said? Listen, that kid knew it all the day he was born.

Things settled down, and Mr Bullock told Mr Jordan to go ahead, and I crossed my legs the other way, and hitched a bit to pull the edges of my coat over them. I am Mother. Very honest and respectable. Working hard to keep the family going while my man is in stir. I felt terribly alone, sitting out there. I wished I could have held Sammy on my knee. Little bugger. He would go and screw everything up.

Mr Jordan had been talking for about two minutes before I began to extract words from the sound of his voice, and realized I should be listening.

It was about Bob, and the flat and everything, and Mr Bullock listened for a little bit, tapping a pen on the table with his long clean fingers, before he said, a bit too sharply for Mr Jordan, who was doing his best, 'My colleague and I have copies of your case notes here. There's no need to repeat all the background details.'

'Very well, sir.' You could see he was a bit scared, though I don't know why. He must have stood up in this court often enough to tell about people mistreating their kids.

But I didn't mistreat Sammy. I just did what I thought was best, and that's what I'll say, if they do me the courtesy to ask me. If you'd had my lot, I'll say, you'd know that there's just so much a person can take. All right, what I did was wrong, I see that now, but at the time there was nothing else I could do. You can't condemn a person for doing their best.

'We'll take it from the night you came on the scene then, shall we?' and Mr Jordan got his feet planted firmly on the floor and started off again, talking right past the front of me, as if I wasn't there at all, and they were all in a play someone had made up.

It would make a play too. The big man talking, slow and steady, and the people all round the walls of the square room listening and looking at me. The small lonely figure sat alone in the spotlight, in the red coat with the collar so bravely turned up, and the courageous tilt to her head. If only I didn't have this cold heavy feeling inside me as if something awful was going to happen, I might be able to enjoy the drama of it.

'It was on the twenty-second of this month, sir, last Friday. A lady came to my house to tell me that she was anxious about a four-year-old boy.'

'To make a complaint against Mrs —' he looked down — 'Mrs Thomas?'

'Oh no. This lady is the mother's friend. A very good friend. She has known her a long time, and understands the problems, but it wasn't until this day —'

'Just a minute. You know this lady, is that right?'

'I know her, sir, yes.'

'Did she tell you anything about the child at any other time before last Friday?'

No. I could have answered that one. Not Emma. She's nagged at me. Kept on to me about Sammy, although it was easy for her to talk. But it was between us. She's never told about the poker, and she never will.

Mr Jordan looked carefully at the magistrates, and then said, 'Yes. She had spoken of it.'

The poker. Oh my God, he knows about the poker. She's sold me, Emma has. Now I know there's no one in the whole world you can trust. Now he's going to tell them I took the poker to the boy, and how am I going to get out of that?

'She came to me one day to ask my advice. About a month ago, that would be.'

'Is it in the notes?'

'No, sir.'

'Why not?'

'It didn't seem relevant to the case.'

'It does to me, if it was about this particular child. Was it?'

'Yes, it was. She told me that she was afraid her friend wasn't treating the boy properly, and asked for my help.'

'She gave you details?'

'Just a general impression of the mother's behaviour to the child.'

She hadn't told. I let my breath out again.

'And so you made a call, of course.'

'Perhaps I should have, but at the time, because of the state the mother was in, it seemed better for her friend to go back first and ask if she would like me to help her, since she had been through such a bad time, with her husband in prison, and she had been ill, and her baby dying.'

'If you had gone to see her then, this appalling thing that was done to this child would not have happened.'

'I'm afraid that's so, but at the time I did what I thought was right. We can all be wise after the event, sir.'

Good for you, Jordan. I almost got up and cheered. Then the cold lead hit me again, as if the middle part of me had died, and just my legs and shoulders working, and I remembered that they were talking about me.

The woman magistrate didn't smile. I don't think she can. The Nazis cut the muscles when they experimented on her in the concentration camp. But Mr Bullock did, and everybody relaxed a bit.

He tightens wires in the court, more like a prosecutor than a magistrate, and then he snaps them with a smile or a joke, to show he's really just one of the boys. Or is it to show his power?

One up to Jordan though. Why do they seem as if they were on opposite sides? They are supposed to be working for the same thing. To take children away from their mothers. They should try having a baby some time. I reckon if you can go through that for a kid, you've a right to keep it.

'The mother was then seen again by this lady —'

'This lady. The friend. It would be easier if we had her name.'

Like hell it would. That would make you sit up. But no one said anything, so he let Mr Jordan go on. 'And she found that the boy had gone. He had gone to visit a mutual friend of theirs in York, the mother said. Everything seemed satisfactory, so of course there was no reason for me to visit the mother, with the child not there. I would have had to see the child. The friend went away herself about that time and, while she was up north, she went to York to see the child, where she had been told he was visiting. The boy was not there. He had never been there.'

Bloody liar, Kate. But Em had believed it, hadn't she? It would have been a good lie, if only she'd not taken the fancy to go to Moll's, and there'd have been no trouble. I was going to bring Sammy back in again, everyone knows that. I just had to get some rest, and then I was going to bring him back in quite soon, before Bob came home.

'She came straight back to London, and to see me.'

'And this was —' Mr Bullock put on glasses to look at the notes, and then took them off again to talk. They all do that. 'This was on the twenty-second. The same day you found the boy?'

'We went straight round there. The mother was out, but we got a key to get in through the house upstairs from a neighbour.'

So that's how they got in. Anyone who could milk a key out of Ruth Sullivan – good luck to them.

'I found the two little girls in the basement flat. They had apparently been given some aspirin to keep them quiet.'

'They were quite alone?'

'Yes, sir.'

Mr Bullock looked at me thoughtfully for a long moment, and I kept my face inscrutable. The squaw mask. Emma taught me how. I wonder if he recognized it from home.

'We then went out into the garden to look for the boy. We thought she might . . . something might have happened to him.'

Go on. Come right out and say you thought I killed him while you're at it. Then I'll sue you.

'And after about ten minutes, we found the little boy, Sammy, in the old chicken shed at the bottom of the garden.'

You could feel the room stiffening. People who hadn't heard about me before were glad they came.

'Describe what you saw.'

They were all looking at me while Mr Jordan talked. Under the coat collar, my neck burned like a thousand fires. I felt as if all the eyes in the world were on me. I thought I was sitting naked on the chair, exposed in the middle of the room. I squirmed, and hung on to the sides of the seat. I felt that sickening, restless feeling you get when you're going to faint.

263

I couldn't. Not now, and let them think I couldn't take it. I dropped my head down to my knees and let the blood sing back.

'Are you all right, Mrs Thomas?' I wasn't Mother now.

'In a moment.' I looked up, and shook my head to clear the ringing. 'Yes, I'm all right.' I should have told them I was pregnant and made them feel bad, but they knew how long Bob had been in prison. That wouldn't do.

'Get her a glass of water.'

'No. No, thank you. I'm quite all right.'

'Would you rather wait outside?'

And not know what was said against me? 'No, thank you. I'd rather stay,' I said with simple dignity. I would have liked to draw myself up like Edith Cavell before the firing squad, but I had to sit bent over a bit, so I wouldn't feel queer again.

'The child was lying on the floor of the shed, on a pile of filth and excreta. He was warmly dressed, but emaciated and suffering from some degree of malnutrition. There was a tin dish near him and a stale piece of bread, and a jam-jar half-full of water, although the mother told me afterwards that she had been feeding him regularly. He was tied to the wall with a rope round his waist, and it was apparent from the stain on his clothing that it had made a sore. When we found him, the child was asleep and apparently also slightly under the effects of aspirin.'

First thing a mother finds out, that it's safe to give a kid aspirin, up to a point.

Then there was a bit about getting the doctor and taking Sammy to the hospital. Bloody sauce. I'd said to him that morning: You all right, Sam? I said, and he said: Yes, Mumma.

'You saw the mother that night after she came home?'

'I saw her the following morning. Saturday the twenty-third. I told her where the boy was.'

'No one stayed with the other children?'

'The friend, sir. She stayed with them until the mother returned.'

When I got back and saw the lights, I thought Emily had

put them on. It gave me a terrible fright when I went into the room and saw Em standing there like the Statue of Liberty with that cold, accusing face. I think she thought I'd been drinking, but it was just that something flared up in my head at the sheer bloody nerve of it. To break into my house and take my kid away as if I was a common criminal. End of a beautiful friendship, I thought when she'd gone, but you don't get rid of Em so easily, not just by heaving a milk bottle at her.

Mr Jordan was finished. He'd said what he came to say and was ready to go home to his lunch. He shifted on his feet, and Mr Bullock said, 'Thank you, Mr Jordan. Not a very pretty story, is it?'

The woman in the lambskin bonnet said something to him, muttering with her eyes sharp on me as if she thought I'd break and run for it, and Emma's father nodded and said, 'Just one thing we'd like to establish, and that is the exact time the child was shut up in the chicken shed.'

Why don't you ask me? I could tell you. But they don't do things that way.

'The mother's friend last saw him on the day she came to me for advice. It was just before she went away that she saw the mother again and was told the child had gone away. So it would be about three weeks, I would say.'

'About . . . about. This is a court of law, Mr Jordan,' he said, rather unfairly, considering he hadn't even thought of the question himself. He is getting a bit difficult. I remember Em telling me that he'd gone off with another woman younger than him. She doesn't seem to have rejuvenated him too much. Sometimes they can't take it so well, after fifty.

'We should have had the mother's friend here. The exact time of the child's imprisonment should be in the record of the case.'

No wonder the women waiting outside were saying: We're here for the day. He's the slowest beak they've got, they say, and I see why. Bit of an old woman really, on detail.

'The friend is here today, sir. I wasn't going to call her, since I didn't think you —'

'Of course I do. I am anxious to get the facts, Mr Jordan, not guesses, for the mother's sake, as well as the child's.'

Thanks for nothing.

'Yes, I appreciate that, sir.' Poor man, he was sweating a bit, and I must say it was stuffy in the courtroom. I'm not used to so much heat after living in the catacombs. I opened my coat.

The Warrant Officer had gone to call Emma. I got my smile ready so that everyone would know that she was on my side as soon as she came in. She hadn't told about the poker, had she? She would tell them what a good mother I was, and how hard I'd tried, and how my head ached. Who did they think the aspirin bottle was for? Facts, Mr Jordan, not guesses.

I HAVE always gone in through the door behind the bench from the magistrates' room. Now I went into the court by the door I had never used, and my father looked up from the notes and said, 'Emma.' And all the lines of his face were deep and sad.

It must have been a shock to him, but he never appears to be taken by surprise. He reacts very quickly to sudden events, and his face adjusts immediately, with his thoughts.

Why did he look at me so sorrowfully? What have I done? He looked as if I had hurt him very badly.

I had been told to stand by Johnny, but now he stepped back and sat down, and I was left there, with Kate smiling hopefully at me, sickly pale, and my father leaning on his arms waiting, a strange triangle to form in this place.

A little stir had spread round the room when he said my name. People who didn't know who I was were told by those who did. Eyes followed the lines of the triangle with slow curiosity from my father to me to Kate, and back to the bench again to see how he was taking it. Uncertain whether to greet me or not, Miss Draper was trying to look as if this sort of thing happened every day.

When I had said my name and sworn the oath, my father

said, very politely, 'I'm sorry about this, Emma, but there is a point that I think only you can clarify.'

Thank God he wasn't going to call me Miss Bullock. I had been afraid of that, and of having to call him Sir, and the situation skidding too close to farce.

'Yes?' I gave him a non-committal face and voice to show him I was on my guard. If I had been brought in to denounce Kate, they had come to the wrong supermarket.

'We need to fix the exact time that the little Thomas boy was shut up in the shed. Mr Jordan has said that you saw the boy about a month ago – the day you went to him for advice. When you next saw the mother, she told you that the child had gone away. Can you remember when that was?'

'I think so. It was about two days before I went to Leeds. No, three, because I went to Leeds on Monday and I think it was Friday when I saw Kate. Yes, it was.' I remembered now. 'It was Friday. February the first.'

'You're sure?'

'Quite sure.' When I got back to the office after seeing Kate, there was a message on my desk asking me to call Mrs Bullock at a Kingston number. What was my mother up to? Then I saw that it was Benita's number. Odd. I still don't think of anything to do with that house as my father's. It is Benita's address. Benita's telephone number. Benita's taste in pictures. He lives there, till death, I suppose, but I still see him as a visiting lover.

It was Benita's birthday. She wanted me to come for dinner. I almost said Yes. Then I made a rather thin excuse and said No. The excuse was so thin that Benita, who is very honest, said, 'I'm too soon then. Damn. I suddenly thought this might be the moment. It isn't is it?'

'No.' I could be honest too.

'You're very miserly,' she said, 'with your forgiveness,' and I said, 'Yes, I am.' I wonder if she told my father. I wonder if he even knew that she had telephoned.

If the date meant anything to him, he didn't show it. He said to Miss Draper, 'That sets the time then at twenty-two days at the least, even if the child was only shut outside the day before Emma's visit on the first of February,' and they both wrote it down.

To answer my father, I was talking diagonally across the empty space in front of Kate, but it was hard not to look at her, although I tried not to. She was small and thin and horribly young, and she had put on a lot of lipstick that didn't match the red coat, and she had the collar turned up to hide the birthmark. As if that were all that was needed to protect her from the stares! She sat alone in the middle of the room, bowed over a little and shrunk into herself, like a woman who was going to be stoned. From outside, I had seen her go into the courtroom with as much bravado as she could muster, but I guessed that it hadn't lasted very long when her story was told and the eyes of the virtuous began to look at her.

'Thank you, Emma.' I thought he meant that I could go. I looked over my shoulder at Johnny, who nodded, and I was turning away when my father said, 'Just one more thing.'

I waited, looking at him, and he considered me. All right, I look like hell. But he didn't know that I had travelled all night to be here, and that I had left behind the wreck of my future.

'This is a very distressing case,' he said, as much to the court as to me, because he would never forget the larger audience, even with his daughter on the stand, 'and there is one particular aspect of it which disturbs me.'

And me, nodded Miss Draper, although I doubt if she knew what he was going to say.

'It appears that this mother had been ill-treating the child for some time. Now it's possible that there may be some criticism of Mr Jordan for not taking any steps to avert the tragedy.'

'How could he? He didn't know.'

'But you went to him almost a week before the boy disappeared, and told what you knew about the mother's behaviour.'

'Well, I – no, not exactly.' I couldn't look at either Kate or my father. I felt the colour flare up. I had nothing to hide. I was only going to tell the truth, and yet I felt like a trapped criminal. I knew now how it must feel to be on trial for your life, and know you can't prove your innocence.

'Mr Jordan has told the court that you asked him for help.'

'Yes, I did, but – at the same time, I asked him not to help, if you see what I mean.'

My father raised the eyebrow that operates on its own, but he didn't say anything sarcastic. He said, rather kindly, 'Please explain, Emma.'

Explain. Explain. How can anyone explain the mystery of Kate and me and the stubborn force which holds us? How can anyone explain these few years of our youth together, which have made treachery so impossible that I would not even have run to Johnny at the end if I had been brave enough to seek a dead Sammy by myself?

There were three of us in it now. Me, Kate and Johnny. Whatever I said would make it worse for one of us. I could see no help in my father's waiting face. No help in Kate's blank eyes, which had gone too far away in misery. Opposite me sat the clerk of the court, two probation officers and an indifferent young barrister waiting to defend some delinquent whose parents had never thought of fighting for him until it was too late. At the end of the room, a scattering of police, and some downy students with notebooks. On my right beyond the door, the people from the Children's department. Behind me, Johnny and an old-timer from one of the other societies. Any one of them, even the youngest student with the fresh face and the soft clean hair, could have put up a better show than our Miss Bullock, case worker, who was now about to be shown up for the bungler she was.

'I didn't want to make things worse.'

'Go on,' my father said, as he had said so many, many times in my childhood when I had started a roundabout story to try to deflect attention from a breakage, or trouble at school.

'Kate's my friend,' I flung at him. 'I was trying to save her, not sell her. And I knew her very well. I've known her for years.'

You know I have, Daddy. I told you once that she and I were going to live together and you said: I like you, Emma. I like the way you set your heart on things.

'She hates interference. I knew that she'd resent it bitterly if anyone – Mr Jordan or anyone – come uninvited. That's why I said I'd go back and ask her if she'd like him to help.

Then it would be her idea, you see, and she'd co-operate.'

'Had it been going on for a long time, the ill-treatment of the boy?'

I didn't answer. How could I answer, with Kate sitting there in front of me, hunched over and rocking a little, like a child trying to ride out a scolding?

I saw my father's mouth twitch. He could force me, I suppose, but instead, he changed the question.

'Tell me exactly what it was that finally sent you to Mr Jordan.'

'Sammy was missing. You must know that.'

'I mean the time before that. Tell me.'

From somewhere, God knows where, I dredged up the courage to say, 'I know I am on oath, but I don't believe you can make me say things I don't want to.'

After I had said that, I felt very calm. It was like being cruelly teased at school, and you finally plucked up the courage to say: I don't give a damn what you say about me, and you felt you could go away and sleep for a week. The court was on tiptoe to see my father and me at strife, but I felt suddenly at ease, and warmed by something like the old love for him, because we were enemies who understood each other.

'You're hiding something?'

'Not exactly.' You can kill me before I'll tell you that Kate put that scar on Sammy's leg.

'I'm sorry, Emma, to keep on about this, but for Mr Jordan's sake, as well as my own peace of mind, I feel we must get this straight. His reputation is involved, you know.'

'I don't see why. He's been wonderful, over everything.' Thank God Johnny was sitting behind me. My father was gunning for him, and I didn't want to see his face.

'You've known Mr Jordan for a few years, haven't you?'

'Yes.'

'And you've known for some time that this mother was treating her children badly.'

'Not the other children. She's always been good to the girls.'

'The boy then.' He brushed the correction aside. 'If you knew that the boy was being abused, why did you never say anything about it to Mr Jordan?'

It's easy not to answer. I found that out.

'Let's simplify it then,' he said, more legally. 'Did you ever tell Mr Jordan what you knew?'

I should have taken time to put up my hair. I caught sight of the damn plait hanging over my shoulder like a dead snake, and I thought I looked like a rude schoolgirl defying the head-mistress.

'Why didn't you tell him?'

I have always been able to look at him without blinking. As a child, I would do it to try to disconcert him, while I struggled behind the look for an answer that he would find pleasing.

'Did you know that the boy was being abused?'

Alone in the small crowded courtroom, we matched eyes, and then he said, 'Answer me, Emma.'

I pulled my eyes away to the childish huddle that was Kate. Was I supposed to take up a stone too? She suddenly shrugged one shoulder up and pulled a crazy face at me, so like my old incorrigible Kate that I was able to say, 'Whatever I knew, I wouldn't have told him.'

Before my father could say anything, I said it for him. 'I know, I was wrong, but it was what I wanted to do. I wanted to make things right for her myself. All right, I failed. What happened with Sammy – it was my fault. I know that. I knew that as soon as I opened the door and the torch shone in and showed me what was in the shed.'

Bear witness. Bear witness to what you see.

'I'd say it was more the mother's fault than yours,' my father said, and then I did a terrible thing.

A magistrate's daughter, I made a scene, like some of the grievance-maddened mothers do, storming at the unruffled bench, who have them quietly removed, no rough stuff.

'It's not her fault!' I cried out to him. 'Don't you know the kind of life she's had? Don't you *know*? Don't you remember what she was like, here in this court, when she was sixteen? She never had anything, and she's got nothing now. Nothing but debts and dirt and children and despair. No wonder she's half out of her mind at times. Don't let them prosecute her. It isn't her fault. None of it. Don't let them punish her!'

'Take it easy, Emmie,' he said gently. 'Prosecution has nothing to do with me. That's for the police, or Mr Jordan's people.'

'But you can help.'

'It's not my business. This court is only concerned with the child.'

He wouldn't help. Someone opened the door for me, and I went out, hating him. Or was it the law I hated – or was it myself – for making him my enemy?

A T T H E end, when they had all finished talking about me, I was asked whether I had any questions, or anything to say. I had come into the court with a whole lot of things in my mind to tell them, but when I got the chance, for some reason I said No. Nothing to say.

'You agree with everything that has been said?'

'I suppose so.'

Em had done her best for me. What more could I do? I was too bloody tired to care. Em's father had a mumble, mumble with the mutton in the lamb hat, and then he raised his voice as if I was deaf.

'Mrs Thomas.'

'Stand up,' someone said, so I stood up.

'We are going to make an order for your son to go into the care of the local authority. We think that's the best thing for the time being. Do you agree?'

Fat lot of use saying No. I said, 'Yes.' They can slit my throat before I'll call him Sir. My best friend's father. If life had turned out different, I'd have been calling him David.

Emma told me once about a woman she'd seen, who when they told her they were going to take her child, yelled bloody murder and had to be hauled out with her heels drumming the floor. I went quietly. Case over. That's that one out, let's have the next poor idiot in.

I couldn't see Emma, and I felt a bit lost. Ruth had the girls, and there was no one at home. For a moment, I didn't know which way to go, and then someone came up to me, and it was the blunt-spoken woman with the smile who had come from the prison when Bob went inside. She took my hand as if I was a child, so I went with her, and we had some tea and something to eat, and I thought perhaps not quite the whole world was against me after all.

'I HATE HIM. Don't look so moral, Johnny. I hate him.'

'Hush, Emma. It was easier for you than for him. You won't get away with that kind of dumb insolence in a magistrates' court.'

'You're not going to prosecute her!'

'Possibly.'

'I won't give evidence.'

'You'd have to, if you were summonsed.'

'You could get me out of it.'

'No.'

'You're worse than my father. He tried to make me sell Kate.'

'He tried to make you tell the truth. That's no crime, in a courtroom.'

'He tried to make me sell you too. He was hateful.'

'I thought he was pretty decent, considering how badly you behaved.'

'It was for you! It wasn't only for Kate. I was trying to stop him persecuting you.'

'You don't understand. He —'

'Don't treat me like a child, Johnny. I've been in that court before. I understand all right.'

'He wasn't persecuting me. He was trying to protect me. People are quick to criticize, he knows that. They say: Isn't it wonderful, the work they do? But if we make any mistakes, they jump on us.'

'Why?'

'They're suspicious. We work with people who've been pretty much rejected. They've got to find a flaw in that somewhere.'

'My father isn't all that omniscient,' I said, rejecting the celestial choirs. 'I don't think he likes you any better than he likes me.'

'His loss then,' Johnny said cheerfully. Since I got to know him so well, through crisis, he speaks of my father with less deference. 'If it was true. Why don't you give him a chance, Emma? How long are you going to carry on the war?'

'He broke a vow.'

'Everyone can't be as tough as you are,' he said, but not admiringly; too indulgently, as if honour were only a childish obsession. Sometimes he talks to me like my father would if I were still seeing my father. I can't stand it.

'Don't treat me like a *child*,' I said again. 'I can't stand it. Especially now, when everything is wrecked.'

But the wreck, it seemed, might be salvaged. Joel sent me a telegram to say that he was coming to London at the week-end. It would have been all right. We could have rescued it. We would both have said that we were wrong, which was going to be part of our recipe for peaceful marriage. If you say: I was wrong, it makes the other person say generously: 'No, no, you were right,' so that makes you both right. We would have started again, and it would have worked out all right.

What threw everything out was meeting Tom.

I saw the back of his head going into a hotel, and many things became clear to me in that instant.

'Tom.' There was a small crowd going into the hotel, and he turned and saw me across people, and his face, like mine, was stricken, not smiling. He grabbed me and pushed me through the crowd and out of the hotel.

'Where are we going?'

'Anywhere but here. It's a lunch.' We went into a taxi and, like fools, into each other's arms, and all the good of the years of strength and honour was undone.

WHEN MOLLY ARTHUR heard what the court had done about Sammy, she asked if she could have him up in York, and they let her.

Lucky for him. If I'd been sent to someone like Moll at four years old, I could have told a different story.

Mrs Evans from the prison says that they will bring Bob to the magistrates' court. I wish they wouldn't. I'm not ready to face him yet. He loved that kid, Bob did, and when he hears I've let them take him away from me, there's no telling what he'll do.

However, perhaps it's just as well to see him first in a public place like that. He'll be handcuffed, perhaps, like he was when the copper brought him up out of the Tunnel with the big drop on the end of his nose.

See him safely like that, in the court, and then when he comes home next month, it won't be so bad. Mrs Evans says they have a job lined up for him. In the coke yard out at the gas works. He's going to love that. I wonder if he knows.

Em came to the flat the day after I got the summons, and we read it together and laughed at some of the jokes. If you didn't already know what you'd done, it wouldn't make you any wiser.

'Don't worry,' Em said, and I said I wasn't, which is true. I feel sort of shut away inside, like a nun walled up inside Kate. Whatever they do to me, I don't think they can hurt me, but if they want to send me to the birdcage, which Ruth Sullivan says with relish they could do, they'll have to keep the girls for me, which is not going to help bring down taxes this year.

'Don't worry,' Em said. 'I'll be there.'

'I don't want you there.' She almost told lies in front of her father. I'd be afraid of her doing that with a stranger.

'I've got to be.'

'You don't have to speak for me, if you don't want.'

'It isn't that. It's to —'

'Speak against me?'

She nodded, watching me. 'To confirm what Johnny says.'

That hurt, but she took hold of me and said, 'You don't think it was my idea?'

'I don't know. Let go of me.'

'I said I wouldn't go, but they can make me. I got a summons too.'

'Show me.'

'Oh God, Kate, it's not the kind of thing you carry about in your handbag. What's the matter with you? Don't you believe me?'

'Yeah.' Em wouldn't let me down. I know that now. The more I lose – what little there is to lose – the more I trust in her.

Everyone else is against me now. They all know. When I fetched the girls back from Ruth's, I asked her if she'd take them again if I go with Mrs Evans to see Bob, and she said, 'I'd rather not have anything to do with it. There's been too much talk already.' Ruth Sullivan, she's so wonderful, everybody's friend. She'd not have said that if Smiler had been home, but she's pushed him back to work, rattling chest and all. She's after his pension. Em says when she went there, he had a cup of tea by his bed with all weedkiller scum on the top.

I decided not to go and see Bob anyway. If the sight of me makes him angry, it's not fair to give it him when he's where he can't get at me. They've got enough frustrations in gaol already, without frustrated rage as well.

The man in the tobacconist's asked me, 'How's your little boy?' and laughed, and called over his shoulder, 'Here she is,' to his wife at the back of the shop. Filthy witch hunter. The milkman made his little girl stay in the van Saturday, instead of coming for the empties.

Everyone is against me. When I asked Em why she didn't think I was a monster too, she said, 'That's what I ask myself. May as well look human though.' She had come with scissors and rollers and a bottle of shampoo to fix my hair so I'll be all right in court.

'We'll keep it in a long bob,' she said, shaping away at the top layer, while I sat on the chair that hasn't got a back, in front of the fire. 'It's always looked better like that.'

'To hide the mark of Cain.'

'Well, that too. One of these days, I'm going to take you by force to a plastic surgeon.'

'I couldn't stand the pain.'

'You could. It would be worth it, like having a baby.'

'That wasn't.'

She was snipping and clicking away, standing behind me, and I was staring into the fire at nothing, liking the feel and friendliness of it. When I was a child my mother used to cut my hair once in a great while when it began to get into the food. Her hand was shaky, and I always thought she was going to cut my ear off.

'Do you remember,' Em said, 'when I saved fifty pounds towards an operation for you, and you took the money? What was it for?'

'Didn't I tell you it was for a friend?'

'I didn't believe that.'

'Oh. I thought you did. Why didn't you ever ask for it back?'

'It was for you anyway. Pity though.' She put her hand for a moment on the dark red stain that disfigures the back of my neck. She's never done that before. It was cold in the room, but her hand felt warm with life.

'I'm not sure I'd want to be without it now,' I said. 'It's one way to make sure I'll never forget her.'

'Who?'

'My mother.'

'I thought you hated her.'

'I do. That's what I must never forget.'

She had finished cutting now, and was running the comb through my hair, lifting strands of it and letting it fall through the comb softly against the side of my face.

'She put it there, you know,' I said. 'The mark.'

'That's silly, Kate. Things like that happen before birth.'

'That's what I mean. She tried to get rid of me, because she didn't want to marry him. Whatever she did, it didn't work. Typical – she never did anything right. All she did was mark me.'

'Oh no, Kate, that's not possible.'

'Yes it is. She told me.'

'She told you she tried to get rid of you?'

I nodded. 'That's why I never went back there.'

'Why didn't you tell me?' She was standing sort of paralysed, with the comb in one hand and the scissors in the other, looking at me as if I had two heads.

'And tell you that she said to me: I wish to God I had killed you? No thanks. Although there's been times all the same. . . . You ever wish you'd never been born? There's been times when I wished she hadn't bungled it.'

IT MADE quite a nice little story for the newspapers. There was a picture of Kate in some of them, leaving the court with me, and one paper had a picture of Sammy, taken at Molly's when she was out and one of the Care and Prot. girls who had seen no man for weeks, except Jim, let the photographer in.

My mother and Connie were very distressed. They knew the story, of course. I had told them the substance of it straight through, and then gone quickly out of the room and left them to react on each other. They knew about my part in it, but they thought it could be kept a muffled family secret, like a werewolf in the attic. They didn't even think that Uncle Mark knew, although I had told him about Kate when I asked him if I could go on working for him, since I wasn't going to be married. They knew that I had to go to the magistrates' court, and Connie made me a special breakfast, with potato cakes fried in gammon fat, for strength, and they thought that would be the end of it.

But when they saw my picture in the evening paper, walking along with Kate in the pouring rain, both looking grim and at least forty, it was too much. I knew it would be. That was one reason why I didn't go home right away. I stayed with Kate. I was stiff for days after two nights on that chair bed, but she'd slept on it for weeks.

I took the dog to the RSPCA, and I went with Johnny to take Emily and Susannah to the Home, and then I took Kate to the hospital, and stayed with her until she went to sleep, small and lost in the spotless anonymity of the bare room with the window high up, like a cell.

No, not like a cell. Don't be melodramatic, Emma. This is where she belongs, for a while.

When Johnny told me they were going to prosecute, I was angry at first. All for the children and nothing for the parents, and what good will it do Sammy to have his mother in prison as well as his father?

'She's sick, not wicked. I know it was wicked, what she did, but she didn't realize. She was in a queer sort of fantasy state. She didn't know what she was doing half the time. This is cruel, Johnny. They used to put schizophrenics in the stocks and throw rotten pumpkins at them. We're supposed to have come a long way since then.'

He let me storm for a bit. That's one of the maddening things about him. He lets you go on throwing things at the impenetrable wall of his calm, and only tells you at the end that your aim is wrong.

He was taking Kate to court not to punish her, but to make sure that she got the treatment she needs. 'She'd not agree otherwise. We need the court's authority.'

'Suppose they don't give it?'

'They will. She's seeing two doctors, though she doesn't know why. I'll have either them or their written evidence to speak for her.'

'Very subtle. Running the prosecution and the defence at the same time.'

'Well, it's nice,' he said mildly, 'if you can help someone without them knowing it.'

They told me at the hospital that Kate would have no visitors for three weeks, to free her from associations. It felt like abandoning her to the lions.

I still didn't feel equal to facing my mother and Connie. It had been bad enough on the telephone. They had gone out for the other evening paper and then bought all the morning papers and burned the pictures in the fireplace, like a Boston bishop symbolically burning one pornographic book that had already sold a million copies.

I went to two more agents to ask about flats, and then, for some reason, I went out to Ham Common to see my father. I don't know why. Perhaps it was because I didn't want to see my mother.

'He's not back yet,' Benita said. 'Take off your coat and I'll light the fire. I've been making a dress upstairs all day.' She brought it down to show me, a cocktail dress in the kind of brocade you would expect to see on sofas, very gorgeous.

'I wish I could do that,' I said.

'I could teach you.'

I let it go. I don't think she was trying to seduce me, but I have to be careful. 'My father never used to stay at the office as late as this.'

'He had that train journey home. And they're very busy just now. Some kind of merger with a Belgian firm. They're working out the percentage of stock transfer.' Benita knew exactly what went on both in the juvenile court and the firm. My mother never had. But then she hadn't often been told.

'I saw your picture,' Benita said, sitting with the shimmering dress in her lap, picking out threads. 'Not very flattering, was it?'

'Did you mind?'

'Mind – why? I was proud that you had stuck with that wretched girl.'

'Did my father —'

'He was upset. Not because of the publicity. He wanted to go to court, but I thought you'd rather he didn't. He told me you fought him in the children's court.'

'He put me in a spot.'

'You put him in a spot, you know, suddenly appearing like Dracula's ghost.'

'I didn't know they'd call me. It wasn't so bad at the other court. I'd rehearsed what I was going to say. And the magistrate didn't try to make me tell him other things about Kate. Those two bitches who used to live in her house had already done enough of that.'

'The woman who said, "I used to hear screams like the torture chamber"? The papers loved that.'

'Mrs Martin. She looks like a drunk parrot. I could kill her. And the other one, Mrs Sullivan, with her armoured hat. They lived in the flats above Kate before the pipes burst. They were supposed to be her friends. But when they heard about the case, they went and asked if they could give evidence. Can you imagine that? As if it wasn't bad enough, they actually wanted to make it worse. Did you know people could be so vindictive?'

Benita nodded. 'You can't get to my age without finding that out.'

'I'll bet they were furious when they didn't get their pictures in the papers too.' Smiler's wife had frankly been there to show off. She let off so much high-powered logorrhoea about all the things she had done for Kate that the magistrate shook his head like a dog trying to get water out of its ears.

When Mrs Martin told about the screams, and he asked her why she had done nothing about it, she held the top of her handbag like a perch and said, 'It wasn't my business.'

'It seems to me we've heard that before in this court,' he said to no one in particular, and Mrs Martin nodded, with folded lips, taking it to mean that she had said the right thing.

They had brought Bob from the prison. He looked well, a bit fatter, with his hair cut so that it didn't fall into his eyes. He sat with his big limp hands between his knees, looking at Kate in a sort of agony. I don't think he understood much, except that everything had gone wrong, and that when he came home in a few weeks' time, there would be nothing to come home to.

Kate looked at him as if she hardly knew him, scornfully when he was standing up to be questioned. I don't see how that marriage can ever get going again. Johnny says it will in time. I don't even think it should, but that's because Miss Bullock, social worker, is dead.

At first Bob said that Kate had always been a good mother, and treated all the children well. 'Never did no wrong. No, sir. I can vouch for that.' But when he was asked, 'Isn't it true that the little boy was afraid of her because she was too rough with him?' he hung his wet lip and said, 'Yes, that's right. He was.' Poor Bob. You could make him admit he'd shot the Queen if you asked him the right way.

When my father came home, I had to go through the details of the hearing again for him.

'Jack was right to suspend the sentence,' he said. 'The girl is obviously slightly off her rocker. I saw that when she was before me.'

'Why wouldn't you help her?'

'I told you. The children are my job. Whether the parents are sick or sadistic – that's someone else's job to find out.'

He got up suddenly. 'I'm glad you came.' He bent and kissed me. 'I wanted to do that as soon as I saw the car and knew you were here. I stood on the step outside pretending I couldn't find my key, trying to get up the nerve to kiss you. Then I didn't dare, because you looked cool and beautiful.'

'Would you rather I looked the way I did in your court? I'd sat up all night on the train from Scotland.'

'How is Joel?'

'I don't know. It's off.'

He glanced at Benita, but she didn't indicate that I had already told her. 'I'm sorry, Emma.'

'That's why I looked such a wreck that day. You were ashamed of me.'

'No.'

'Why did you look at me like that when I came in? What had I done wrong? You looked as if you were terribly hurt.'

'I was. I was expecting to see a stranger involved in this nightmare thing. When I saw you, it hit me hard that you'd been going through all that, perhaps the worst experience of your life. And I didn't know.'

'You thought I should have come and told you?'

My father shook his head. 'I had lost the right to that. That's what hurt.'

So Miss E. Bullock, case worker, wasn't quite dead after all. There was something I knew I had to do.

Kate hated her mother. The mother had rejected her utterly, from the moment of conception right up to the final moment when she drove Kate away for ever with the truth.

And the wicked fallacy about the birthmark. Part of her treatment will be plastic surgery, I think. If she ever tells the doctors what she told me, that would be the first thing they would do for her. That's what I'd do, anyway. Dr Bullock, psychiatric counsellor.

They might cut out the ugly dark red stain from the back of

Kate's neck, but how could they cut out the dark hatred from her heart? Only one person could do that.

I went to Butt Street one dingy afternoon, when the wind was playing cyclones with waste papers and old drifts of grit, and the dustcart was whining and clanking down the middle of the street, exhaling a sharply active smell in the street of old quiescent odours.

When I went into the shop, Kate's mother was talking to a pinched woman who had soapflakes and scouring powder and ammonia and bleach ranged on the counter as if she were going to fight all the dirt of London. They were only discussing prices when I went in, but they both stopped and looked at me as if they had been plotting against the Government.

I waited by the scarred ice-cream freezer until the customer had paid and gone.

'Yes?' Kate's mother said. 'Is there something you want?'

'Can I talk to you?' I had not rehearsed what I would say. I knew that wouldn't work, because what I said would depend on what she said, and there was no way of guessing that, even though Johnny had told me she was better and happier. He had also told me that I was wasting my time, trying to get her interested in Kate, but he doesn't always have to be right.

She did look slightly better. Well, slightly different. She had cut off the sad, inadequate swatch of faded hair in favour of a basic bob and bangs, too young for her. The overall she wore was pink instead of blue, but equally shapeless and badly laundered. There was no new vanity in what she had done to her face, because she had done nothing. Her thick, slack skin was an airless indoor casualty, and her pale eyes so lacked expectancy that it was almost worth crying out: I'll give you five thousand pounds for the whole shop! to see if you could spark them.

Johnny's improvement must be in the soul, or else she has slipped back.

'Can I talk to you?'

'You're talking, aren't you? You selling something?'

Sal-va-shun! I should have brought my horn.

'I've seen you before, haven't I?'

'I don't think so.' With my hair in a good thick doughnut,

283

and the tent of my blanket coat, I didn't think she could recognize the raw young Emma who had tagged in here with the Cruelty Man, almost five years ago.

'I'm a good friend of Kate's,' I began, and instantly her face shut up. As if I had said: I'm a homicidal maniac, she moved sideways to the door at the back of the shop, opened it a crack and called, 'Dick!' still keeping her eyes on me.

He came out, Kate's father, short and greasy and belligerent, with that punched-up nose spread half over his face. You can see Kate in her mother, not in her father.

'It's about Kate,' his wife said grimly.

'What about her?' He kept his hand on the knob of the curtained glass door, to show that his attendance at this conversation was ephemeral.

'She's had a very bad time,' I began. 'She —'

But her mother cut in with, 'You think we don't see the papers? I've been ill ever since last week, just thinking about it.'

'That's right,' Kate's father said, nodding his battered head – he has what looks like ringworm scars on his greying scalp. 'Very ill, she's been, with her nerves.'

'If the people round here ever got to know that was her,' his wife said, 'I'd kill myself.'

What I had come to say was getting more hopeless every minute, but I blundered ahead and said it. 'I thought perhaps you would see Kate, after she comes out of the hospital.'

'See her!' the father said. 'I'd better not.'

'I mean, perhaps you could help her. Perhaps you could —' Had I expected them to sob gratefully and beg to be taken to Kate?

'I thought you might want to take the little girls for a bit,' I went on and the mother leaned forward on the old lozenge linoleum of the counter and said, 'Leave us alone, do you hear? We're all right. We've got our own kids. We've got our business and my husband is in work. If she told you to come here, you can go right back and tell her I wouldn't stoop to help her if she raised her hand from the stinking pit of hell.'

'A devil,' her father said. 'A devil, that's what she is. We read about it.'

284

'To think of her doing that to that poor innocent little child,' her mother droned. 'Can you wonder we don't want nothing more to do with her?'

'No,' I said dismally, and I went back to Johnny's to tell him that he was right again, rot and blast him, and E. Bullock was wrong.

It is almost a year since Jean was killed, but he and Nancy still aren't able to fill the emptiness of the house. It even looks empty from the outside. The same curtains are there, and the green window-boxes waiting for spring, but it's not the same. Jean's bicycle always used to lean in the side passage. Nancy's generation doesn't bicycle in London.

I had been to see Kate, and when I went to tell Johnny about her, he was still out, although it was late enough for him to be home.

'He works too hard,' Nancy said, more like a wife or a mother than a daughter. 'Since Mum died, he's been driving himself. He makes calls till all hours. He's hardly ever at home.'

'Do you mind?'

'Well, I do. It's rather lonely.' She is enough like her mother to make it very painful to see her bright-skinned face not rounded with secure pleasure, but getting a little heavy and serious.

'You're a good girl, Nancy.'

'I'm not. I'm bitter and horrible. When I hear about these kids my age rejecting their mothers – they talk about it at school, "I saw through her when I was thirteen" – I could do murder. That's one reason I have to get out. They're so babyish. They pile up their hair and stuff their bosoms, but they're still kicking and screaming like two-year-olds in a playpen. I'm not going back after the exams, whether we move or not.'

'Are you going to move?'

'I suppose. The man who will take over here is recovering from an operation. I hope he has a relapse. I don't want to go and live with the Grants.'

'It won't be so lonely for you.'

'I'd rather be lonely here. I don't think Mrs Grant and I are going to like each other. She'll be big and domineering and try to teach me how to do things I already know.'

When I asked her if she had seen Mrs Grant, she said No rather miserably, and didn't want to talk about it any more, so we played cards until Johnny came home.

He was tired and depressed. One of the schools had reported bruises on a kindergarten child, but the family had skipped yesterday, owing rent, and Johnny had been following up false leads, trying to find them for hours.

We talked about Kate. Bob is out and working, and Mrs Evans is getting them a flat, but that's not the end of it. That's just the beginning. Kate is one of the reasons why Johnny doesn't want to leave. Kate and her children and all the other bedraggled families who have become a part of his life. It won't be easy for the new man to go into house after house, flat after foetid flat, and hear, 'Where's Mr Jordan then?' and see the faces drop.

'But Kate will have you,' Johnny said, 'unless you change your mind about your American.'

'No.' I have not told him the whole reason about that. I have not told anyone, and I haven't yet seen Tom again since we rode in the taxi, hanging on like desperate rock climbers. I can't. I'm afraid of what he's going to say.

'I think it – it's pretty good, how you've stuck by her,' Johnny said diffidently. He has almost as hard a time throwing out a compliment as an insult.

'We took a blood oath,' I said, and Nancy asked, 'What's that?' coming in with soapy wet arms from the room at the back. 'Is it cutting wrists? A girl did that at school to someone and then wouldn't do it to herself. There was blood all over the cloakroom.'

I told her about the hairbrush ritual that Kate had taught me. 'You do it with people you make a promise to. People you'll always stick by.'

'Let's do it now. You promise that you'll always stick with us, even if we get swallowed up by big domineering Mrs Grant. Here, I'm washing brushes with the socks.' She brought in a stiff hairbrush and gave it to me. 'Not me, my hands are wet. Do it with Daddy. I want to see you do it.'

Johnny and I looked at each other, then smiled and shrugged, because we were only doing it to please Nancy. We stood up, and I banged on my hand and started whirling my arm, and then he banged on his, very hard, so that the beads of blood began to spring out at once, even before he whirled it. When we put the backs of our hands together, he suddenly grabbed my hand with his other one, and pressed it very hard against his as the blood mingled.

'Blood comrades.'

'Blood comrades,' he said, and neither of us was smiling.

'Once,' I said, 'when I was in London, I telephoned you. It was a time when nothing seemed to matter very much, and I didn't care what happened. You were out.'

'Once when I was in America,' Tom said, 'I telephoned you. Twice. There was no answer. I was going to try again, after the week-end, but I had a cable from London. Sheila was in the hospital and I had to came back.'

'Is she all right now?'

'Yes, thank you,' he said, as if I were an acquaintance inquiring politely about his wife. 'She was very ill. She's – well, she'll never be as strong as she was.'

'I'm sorry,' I began, but he said, 'For God's sake, Emma, drop this. I'm offering you everything. I should have said this long ago. I should have married you long ago. I was too afraid of hurting her. So I hurt you instead. But I know now that nothing matters except you.'

'It's too late.'

'It's not.'

'She'll still be hurt. More so, if she's not well.'

'I don't care. I've had my purgatory. If I die tomorrow, they'll have to let me straight into heaven. Why have you stayed away so long?'

'We promised.'

'You did. A promise to your father – what does that mean? He broke his promise to you, didn't he? And got away with it. Why can't you?'

Why can't I? Oh God, why can't I?

THERE IS one of the nurses here, name of Diller, a great huge woman like a Russian discus thrower, and she's one of those men who get themselves turned into women. I'm sure of that. When they chopped her, they forgot to chop off the moustache.

She is cruel to me, because she is a sadist. That's why she took this job. But everyone else is all right. So is the food and having time to sleep, so I may pretend I'm not cured of whatever it was I'm supposed to have. I've forgotten now exactly what it was.

There's this doctor, he gives me cigarettes and we talk for hours. He doesn't seem to have much to do, so we talk about my mother and the old days, which he says is all right to do, although I've always thought those dark things were better left to rot in secret.

Emma was in yesterday, and I sent her down the corridor with a made-up question to have a look at the faggot. She agrees. It is a man, but we shall say nothing. Some of the poor old girls they've got in here haven't seen a man for years except the doctors, who are all black or eunuchs, so even just the moustache is better than nothing.

Emma told me about a little girl of five whose mother beat her with a strap. They had been looking for the mother for days. She'd gone to ground. But the kid turned up on Mr Jordan's doorstep one evening. All by herself, no one knows who took her or told her to go there, and Emma says her back was all up in welts, and bleeding. She had to cut the vest away when the doctor came, and he found she had two ribs broken as well, and some teeth knocked out.

Can you imagine a woman doing that to a kid? She's a sadist. So is Nurse Diller. She makes lampshades out of human skin.